Storm the Earth

The Shatter the Sky Duology

REBECCA KIM WELLS

SIMON & SCHUSTER BFYR

NEW YORK · LONDON · TORONTO · SYDNEY · NEW DELHI

SIMON & SCHUSTER BFYR

An imprint of Simon & Schuster Children's Publishing Division
1230 Avenue of the Americas, New York, New York 10020

Text © 2020 by Rebecca Kim Wells

Cover illustration © 2020 by Olivier Ponsonnet

Cover design by Chloë Foglia © 2020 by Simon & Schuster, Inc.

SIMON & SCHUSTER BFYR is a trademark of Simon & Schuster, Inc.

For information about special discounts for bulk purchases, please contact Simon & Schuster Special Sales at 1-866-506-1949 or business@simonandschuster.com.

The Simon & Schuster Speakers Bureau can bring authors to your live event. For more information or to book an event, contact the Simon & Schuster Speakers Bureau at 1-866-248-3049 or visit our website at www.simonspeakers.com.

Also available in a SIMON & SCHUSTER BFYR hardcover edition

Interior design by Hilary Zarycky

The text for this book was set in Adobe Jenson Pro.

Manufactured in the United States of America

First SIMON & SCHUSTER BFYR paperback edition November 2021

2 4 6 8 10 9 7 5 3 1

The Library of Congress has cataloged the hardcover edition as follows:
Names: Wells, Rebecca Kim, author.
Title: Storm the earth / Rebecca Kim Wells.
Description: First edition. | New York : Simon & Schuster Books for Young Readers, [2020] | Sequel to: Shatter the sky. | Audience: Ages 14 up. | Audience: Grades 10–12. | Summary: "Maren and her girlfriend Kaia set out to rescue Sev and free the dragons from the corrupt emperor"—Provided by publisher.
Identifiers: LCCN 2020002268 | ISBN 9781534454507 (hardcover) | ISBN 9781534454484 (pbk) | ISBN 9781534454514 (eBook)
Subjects: CYAC: Dragons—Fiction. | Bisexuality—Fiction. | Fantasy.
Classification: LCC PZ7.1.W43557 Sto 2020 | DDC [Fic]—dc23
LC record available at https://lccn.loc.gov/2020002268

For all the people who, like me, have stood at
the bottom of an abyss and doubted their ability to climb it.
You can. We can.

CHAPTER ONE

Maren

Naava roared, her cry reverberating through my entire body. I turned my head just enough to see the sky we'd left behind. The Talons were gaining on us.

"Can you outfly them?" I called to Naava. I'd hoped they would land to investigate the wreckage of Lumina burning—instead the Talons had bypassed the ruins entirely once they had seen us flying in the distance. And for all my bravado, I did not know how to confront a battle-ready Talon or their dragon. It had been mostly luck that I'd escaped those I *had* encountered.

Naava extended her wings to their full span, taking in an enormous breath. *You must hold on. I haven't carried your kind in some time.*

Hold on? I wrapped my arms as far around her neck as I could, hunching forward to keep the dragon kit tucked between our bodies. She squeaked in protest, digging her claws into my shirt. I called to Kaia. "She says to hold on!"

Whatever reply Kaia might have given was lost to the wind, but her arms tightened around me—just in time, as Naava swooped low, and my stomach lurched. The height that had seemed glorious only minutes before turned terrifying. If I lost my grip—I didn't even want to think about it.

Glancing back, I saw that the two Talons had halted their approach, their dragons' wings beating just enough to keep them aloft. The wind shifted, and I caught a whiff of fire root ... and saltwater pearl. The Talons had instructed the dragons to wait. Why?

But instead of taking the opportunity to flee, Naava made a sharp turn—and shot directly toward them.

Kaia gasped, and I grabbed the kit just as she started to slide off Naava's neck. *What are you doing?* I cried.

Naava ignored me, and I tried to control my growing panic as we drew closer to the Talons. The only thing steadying me was that despite our approach, the dragons made no move to attack.

It suddenly occurred to me—the Talons were accustomed to hunting creatures on land. There were few things that could threaten a dragon, and none that could take to the air. And with all dragons in Zefed under the emperor's control, these Talons had never fought against one of their own before. They didn't know what to do any more than I did.

Naava pulled up just outside the dragons' reach, her great wings flapping. The Talons were dressed in identical black uniforms with leather armor and helmets, bandoliers strapped diagonally across their torsos. We were close enough that I could see the confusion on their faces. These Talons must have been told to investigate the disturbance at Lumina, but it was clear no one had warned them about an enormous dragon wreaking havoc upon the land.

I looked at the dragons. They both had dark green scales, though one had a longer tail than the other. On the ground, they would have been at least twice my height. But compared to

Naava, they seemed small. Neither of them carried cargo large enough to be human. My heart plummeted. *Sev must be long gone, then.*

One of the Talons shouted across the sky in Zefedi. "You have stolen the property of His Beloved Grace, the Flame of the West. Surrender the dragon!"

Naava roared in anger, and I almost laughed. How could they possibly think that *I* was the one in control? Of course, a Talon would have no other way to understand what they saw—the concept of a free dragon was entirely foreign to them.

"Dragons are not property!" I shouted back in the language of the empire. "And they have been held in captivity for long enough!"

I nudged Naava with a thought. *They don't have Sev. We should leave while we still can.*

No, she replied. *They smell wrong. They are all—wrong.*

She roared again, letting out a furious jet of fire. The other dragons finally retaliated, their flames cutting so close that I felt heat against my neck as Naava flapped her wings, taking us high and out of their reach. I barely had time to flatten myself against Naava's back before she folded her wings and entered a steep dive toward the Talons. The scent of fire root was strong around us, but as Naava spun through the air, I saw the dragons hesitate.

Kaia screamed as we cut through the space between the Talons, and then we were behind them. Naava banked in a tight turn as the dragons wheeled to face us. She was faster than them, and nimbler, too. The Talons fumbled with their bandoliers, reaching for new vials of oil.

My children! Naava roared.

The dragons' heads snapped toward us. And then Naava sang.

The kits at the fortress had sung in quiet, burbling tones that could be explained away as an uncanny wind by those who worked at the fortress. The yearlings had sung in their sleep as well, their soft voices ringing only in my ears. But Naava's song was furious, an elemental shriek that crashed through the air. To most humans, I imagined that her song must have sounded like a ferocious battle cry. But I could hear the melody, and the sorrow and urgency layered within. There was no Verran equivalent of this song, but I understood what she was doing. She was pleading with the other dragons.

Their gazes followed Naava as she dipped in the air and brought us nearer. I was close enough to see the Talons' shocked faces below their helmets—and then I watched as the dragons' heads tipped curiously to one side. The Talons reared back, yanking at their reins. The dragons bucked in midair and refocused, baring their fangs and spitting fire. Naava snapped her wings closed and dove as a plume of fire rushed into the piece of sky we had just occupied. She pulled out of the dive so quickly that my breath caught in my chest. My arms were burning with the strain of holding on as Naava burst upward again, arrowing straight back toward the Talons.

They split in opposite directions this time, and Naava tore after the dragon with the shorter tail. The dragon kit was pressed rigidly against my chest. Kaia's arms squeezed viselike around my waist, forcing my breath higher and shallower.

We pulled up next to the dragon. The Talon's eyes widened in fear as Naava whipped her tail to the side, striking the Talon across the chest.

The Talon tumbled from the saddle, but her arm tangled in the dragon's reins as she fell, yanking her body to a halt. She cried out in pain as she dangled. The dragon roared and swerved, its head dragged down by the weight. Naava beat her wings, and we rose higher in the air. She was preparing for another dive.

A movement caught my eye, and I turned my head just as the second dragon slammed into us, striking at Naava with its claws.

The sky went sideways. For a moment we hung in the air, weightless—and then we were falling.

I clung to Naava as my head filled with the dizzying image of the ground rising up to meet us. Kaia screamed, and I closed my eyes. For one—two—three breaths we tumbled. Then Naava's wings spread, catching a gust of wind and sending us into a glide.

My hands were shaking with cold and adrenaline, but my relief was cut short by the warm, metallic scent of blood. I looked down—the dragon kit was all right. Her blue scales had grayed around the edges, but she wasn't crying. Kaia's arms remained locked around my waist. I turned, trying to see her face.

"Are you hurt?" I asked.

"No," she said, pressing her cheek into my shoulder.

That was good. But Naava was flying unevenly, her left wing less than fully extended. It was difficult to see against her black scales, but there was a gash above her elbow joint, and blood welling up from the wound.

We had to get to the ground. I looked around. The Talon was busy attempting to help her comrade back into her saddle, which bought us some time. But soon they would recover, and I did not want to contemplate our chances against them now that Naava was hurt.

Naava seemed to disagree. Despite her unsteady wings, she circled us back toward the Talons. She drew in a deep breath, and I could feel her body expanding. Then she opened her mouth and let out a column of flame so large that it engulfed both the dragons and their Talons.

Human screams and the scent of burning flesh filled the air. The dragons dove down, taking the Talons with them. I expected Naava to follow, but it seemed that she had used most of her strength with this attack. Her breathing was hitched and shallow, the flap of her wings increasingly erratic. Instead of swooping after the Talons to finish what she had started, she turned carefully in the air and kept us at a good distance. The Talons were badly burned, but the dragons' injuries looked minor—it seemed that dragons weren't so sensitive to fire.

You have been held by human hands too long, she called to the dragons. *Come with me!*

The dragons startled. It was as though they had never heard one of their own speak before. Perhaps they hadn't. Before Naava, I'd only ever heard a dragon sing.

Despite her exhaustion, Naava was entreating them to join her. There was nothing holding them back now—the wounded Talons were too weak to control them. All the dragons had to do was throw off their riders and follow. But when Naava turned in wobbly circles, looking over her shoulder, the dragons did not come. They simply watched her, as if entranced.

The dragon kit shivered. I suddenly realized that the air around us had cooled, and clouds were rolling in. We were losing height, despite Naava's determination. She would not be able to fly for much longer, no matter what else came our way.

"We have to go!" I shouted aloud.

No! Naava snapped. *I will not leave them.*

But she was done—I knew it as she let out another flame that was more spark than fire. She gave a long, mournful cry.

You're losing strength. We have to get to safety! I pleaded with her.

At first I thought she would refuse to leave. But at last she turned away, leaving the Talons injured and the dragons in a haze as we fled.

Clouds quickly obscured the sky behind us as Naava flew low over Belat Forest. Landing in the forest would be ideal, as the trees would provide shelter and disguise our presence. I cast my gaze to the ground, searching for a safe spot. Naava was listing lower and lower.

"There!" I pointed to a small clearing carved out of the trees. Man-made or natural, I saw no other option. Naava took my direction without hesitation.

We swooped down, narrowly avoiding the trees that hemmed in the clearing. Naava landed heavily, the impact jarring me to my bones. The dragon kit leaped to the ground. I followed, folding into a graceless heap as my legs collapsed. Kaia slid down last. She staggered toward us and dropped down next to me, resting her head on my shoulder. Relieved of her passengers, Naava folded her wings and settled into a mountainous coil, closing her eyes and letting out a gusty sigh.

The dragon kit nestled into my free side, and I looked up. My view of the sky was ringed by the towering pine trees that surrounded us. There was not a sound in the forest besides our labored breathing. We had survived. My arms were too heavy to lift and my legs were shaking and my back ached with the strain of having lain across Naava's body, but we had survived.

My vision blurred and I closed my eyes, giving in to my exhaustion and the waiting darkness.

I woke suddenly, surfacing from a pool of murky, dreamless sleep into—darkness.

I was lying on a cold stone floor. What little light there was fell in through a sliver of a window high up the wall and gave no hint as to the time of day. It was deadly quiet. I tried to remain calm as I took stock of the situation, but my heart was racing. I was alive and mostly uninjured, though there was a sharp pain in the back of my head as I shifted. I reached up gingerly to touch the area, and my fingers came away sticky.

What—? Memory flooded through me. Maren. Lumina. The Aurati handing me over to the soldiers, who had called down Talons to transport me to—

Gedarin. The heart of the empire.

This dungeon had no identifying features, but the emperor would not chance losing me now that he had me in his grasp. And the emperor almost never left his court in Irrad these days. Which meant that he must be there now, and, therefore, so was I.

I forced my breathing into a controlled rhythm. Irrad, the capital of Gedarin. I'd been here once, a long time ago—before my father's death, my brother's treason, my mother—I shook off those thoughts. I'd been a child, but there were details still stamped into my memories. The way footsteps echoed on the floor of the receiving chamber. The endless hallways of burnt black stone, the eerily white walls. The smell of the Flame's coffee in the morning, dark and bitter. I'd hated the place even then. And it would likely be the last city I ever set foot in.

I pushed myself to a sitting position and then slowly got to my feet, grimacing as aches and bruises made themselves known. I stretched, trying to ignore the pounding in my head. There was a mat against the wall that stank of decay, and a bucket in the corner for relieving myself. I should have counted myself lucky. Prisoners enjoying the emperor's hospitality weren't even guaranteed a room free of carnivorous beasts, and at least I had that luxury.

The front of the cell was a wall of iron bars, through which I could see the hallway and into the cells opposite mine. Every last one was empty.

It couldn't be a coincidence that there was no one else here. The emperor of Zefed was a vengeful tyrant. There was no world in which his dungeons were unpopulated—unless he had moved his prisoners to keep me solitary . . . or executed them.

It was disheartening that both scenarios seemed equally likely.

So there was no one here, and nothing to do but wait.

I sat down on the mat and quickly concluded that the floor was the better option, despite the damp. So I lay on my back and began to count the stones in the ceiling. Somewhere above me was the sky, the sun, the world. I thought of Maren. Had she succeeded in her quest to save Kaia? She'd looked so frightened the last time I'd seen her, following the Aurati Prophet, but so resolute. And me? I had fallen directly into the trap that had been set for me. I shouldn't have—

Shouldn't have what? Trusted Maren? Following her lead was what had brought me here, but what else could I have done? What other path could I possibly have taken, from the moment I had grasped her hand and run with her through the streets of Deletev? What other choice could I have made from the moment I had seen her with the dragon kit, from the moment she had smiled at me for the first time, sunlight filtering through her hair?

My breath hitched, and I tried to think of something—anything—else. Dwelling on my past actions would accomplish nothing. Besides, my head was starting to throb with pain, and despite my best efforts, my eyes drifted closed.

When I woke again, I found that a bowl had been pushed through the bars while I'd slept. Though it was disappointing not to have seen the guard, my stomach rumbled at the prospect of food. I picked up the bowl—watery rice, a scoop of unseasoned vegetables floating on top of the broth. The thought of poison flickered through my mind, but I dismissed it quickly. The Flame of the West wouldn't kill me quietly, poisoning me somewhere deep in the bowels of his empire. He had captured the shadow prince of Ruzi, the bane of his existence. He would put my execution on display. The only question was *when*.

So I ate, and then I slept some more, on and off. I saw the guard who delivered my next meal, a tall man who had doubtless been chosen for his uncanny impersonation of a stone statue. I didn't even attempt to talk to him.

My legs cramped if I sat too long in one position, so I stretched them out one at a time. I traced the grooves between the stones with my fingertips. A strange, numbing calmness settled over me like a mantle, shielding me from the fear I knew was waiting. Now what I felt most was regret. I was beyond the reach of anyone who could possibly help me. I would never avenge my mother. I would never tell Maren the depth of my feelings for her, or see the dragon kit grow. The Flame of the West had me now, and I could see nothing in my future but death.

What a pathetic waste.

The next time I woke, the emperor was standing on the other side of the bars.

There was nothing to be gained by feigning sleep—he'd only kick me awake. I sat up. For a moment we stared at each other, the torchlight from the hall illuminating our faces. He was about my height but more solidly built, his black hair hanging in a straight curtain down his back. He was a few years older than my brother, Callum, which put him in his midthirties. Rafael, emperor of Zefed, Flame of the West. The last time I'd seen him, he had newly inherited the throne, and my family had been just one of the other four royal families of Zefed.

He wasn't dressed in court attire—the only signs of his position were the circlet of gold he wore and the three guards that flanked him. I longed to rip that circlet from his head, to squeeze his throat until his face mottled purple and his legs gave out. To take the sword from his belt and—

"Vesper Severin Avidal. The shadow prince of Ruzi, before

me at last." His voice was rich and melodious. A deception, like the rest of him.

I flinched at the sound of my full royal name. I hadn't used it since leaving Ruzi, and hearing the emperor speak it was almost unbearable.

I rose to my feet, my limbs shaking as I approached the bars. For the last ten years this day had haunted me, no matter the lengths I'd gone to escape it. I had dreamed of every scenario, imagined the weight of the sword in my hand, the dragon I would ride, the look on his face as I cut him down—but now the day was here, and I was no avenger, alight with fury. It was over.

Still, I would not give him the satisfaction of seeing me cower.

"Come to kill me?" I said.

"You've been a thorn in my side for too long," he said, his gaze cold. "The little prince of Ruzi. The rest of your family was so easy to dispose of, but you've managed to elude me for years. So you can imagine my surprise when I learned that you'd gone to Lumina. Were you *trying* to get yourself captured?"

When I didn't answer, he continued. "I should kill you, but I find myself curious. I know you've been running around my empire with the Dragons—such a grandiose name for such a pitiful band of traitors. So now that you're finally enjoying my hospitality, it's time you and I had a chat about your ... friends."

The emperor nodded to the guards, who unlocked the bars and entered the cell. Two of them grabbed me by the arms, pinning me between them as the emperor came to stand over me.

"What makes you think I'll tell you anything?" I spat.

Rafael grinned, his teeth glinting in the dim light. "You may be the shadow prince of Ruzi, but within these walls you are *nothing.*"

He raised his hand, beckoning to someone behind him in the hall. I hadn't noticed her before—a woman wearing healer's robes.

Oh no.

"I'll make this easy for you," Rafael said. "If you lie to me, I will break your fingers, one by one. After that, we'll start cutting them off. If you tell the truth, you get to keep them. Do we have an understanding?"

What an enticing offer. I managed to shrug under the weight of the guards' hands on my shoulders. "Seems like I don't have much of a choice."

The healer handed an open vial to the emperor, who passed it to the third guard. I smelled the metallic slick of Brika's kiss, the truth serum used for interrogation back at the dragon fortress. My pulse quickened. I had practiced counteracting the serum, but that had been droplets in water, not an entire vial of it.

The guard pinched my nostrils shut with one gloved hand and pressed the vial against my lips with the other. I considered resisting, but to what end? They would break my fingers and drug me anyway. Resigned, I opened my mouth and drank. The viscous liquid slid slowly down my throat, and I shuddered as I swallowed, my vision starting to swim.

My head lolled back, and I sank to my knees. With my eyes closed, the world sounded like I was listening to it from underwater. The healer's voice drifted by, out of focus.

Fingers snapped in front of my face. "Open your eyes."

I slowly complied. The light was glaring at first, but it dimmed as I blinked. They were still here, around me. I could feel the guards' hands holding me down. My fingers were tingling, my breath echoing in my head.

"Vesper. Who is the girl who traveled with you to Lumina?"

Maren. So easy to let the name slip, but something held me back—fear. Why did the emperor care more about Maren than about the Dragons? How much did he know? If he was asking her name, perhaps he wasn't aware of the kit, or Maren's abilities. I had to keep her safe.

"No one," I said, the words muffled to my ears. "Picked her up on the road in Eronne." I ground out the lie, every word so heavy, it required extraordinary effort to push past my lips.

The emperor snorted and looked to one of the guards. There was a snapping sound and my hand was on fire—I cried out, my vision blurring as I fell forward. The guards pulled me back upright.

I didn't want to look but couldn't stop my head from turning. My finger was still attached, but it was bent back at an unnatural angle. Tera's bones, the guard had *broken my finger.* I swallowed hard, trying to focus. "Is that all?" I taunted, hoping to sound braver than I felt.

Rafael just laughed. "Don't test me again, Vesper. Now tell me, what's the girl's name?"

I breathed out slowly, pretended to weigh the punishment in my head. Sweat beaded on my forehead as I opened my mouth, preparing to lie. "Senna," I said, managing not to choke on the name.

"What do you know of her?"

Sweat was dripping into my eyes now, trickling down my chest, despite the damp, cold air of the cell. "Barely anything." My heart was beating faster, faster, faster—how much longer could I withstand the serum?

"You're lying," he said. "You two were spotted together outside of Deletev. I know all about the girl Maren—how she arrived at the dragon fortress *and* how she left."

No. The pain in my hand intensified, and my ears started ringing. If he knew that, he must know where she came from. Ilvera wasn't safe—did Maren know?

I swallowed down the bile coming up in my throat. "I don't understand. Why are you asking me questions to which you know the answers?"

Rafael brushed the question aside. "Was she working with you from the beginning?"

He knew I had lied already, so what answer would be safest?

"She was my partner." The words flowed without hesitation—technically, it wasn't a lie. We had indeed been partners . . . after escaping the dragon fortress. And if he thought that Maren had only been my accomplice, then perhaps he wouldn't look further into what she had undertaken by herself.

Maren. Her hands on my skin. The fierceness of her expression as she faced down the Talons. The tenderness she had shown when she spoke about Kaia. The way she laughed when she gave herself permission to.

Rafael loomed over me. "Is she an Aurat?"

"No. I don't think so," I said.

"Then who told you about the dragon?"

My eyebrows furrowed in unfeigned confusion. "What dragon?"

He couldn't be asking about the kit. The source of the dragon egg was obvious.

Another lance of fire—another broken finger. I shouted in pain. Rafael grabbed my face in one hand and forced my head up. "Look at me," he snapped. "How did you know about the dragon?"

"I don't know what dragon you're talking about," I said wearily.

It was the unvarnished truth, and the words came so easily that he must have believed me. He stepped back and nodded to the guards. They dropped me to the floor, and I hissed in pain as I fell forward onto my injured hand.

The emperor crouched before me and yanked me up by my shirt so that I could see nothing but his face, twisted with rage. "You are only as valuable to me as the information you provide. If you expect to stay alive, you'll cooperate the next time we meet."

Then he was gone. Two guards followed in his wake—the third remained standing above me. The healer knelt by my side. "This will hurt. Here—bite down." She handed me a leather strap.

I wanted to joke but couldn't catch my breath. Instead I put the strap between my teeth and bit as she took my injured hand and did something that sent white pain searing across my brain—

The healer was the only other person left in the cell when I came to my senses again. She had set my fingers and splinted them against the others while I was insensible. She must have done something else, too—given me medicine, or performed an incantation—because the pain had lessened somewhat, though

I expected it would soon return in full force. Now she was occupied with packing away her supplies.

"What dragon is he talking about?" I asked, my voice sounding hoarse. I pushed myself into a seated position with some difficulty.

She barely looked at me. "Try to get some rest."

"But—"

"Take care of those fingers," she said firmly, cutting me off. "You'll need your strength."

How ridiculous, that she was advising me on best healing practices *here*, in the emperor's dungeon. I laughed mirthlessly as she left the cell, then leaned back against the wall, reviewing the interrogation in my mind. Something had happened with a dragon, or *to* a dragon—that much was clear. And there had been a strange, desperate undertone to his questions. *Fear*, I realized. The Flame of the West was afraid.

I smiled. Perhaps there was something to hope for after all.

The sky is crowded with dragons, more than I have ever seen or dreamed, but they fly with their heads low, the scent of mirth wood oil rich in the air. Naava and I fly among them, and when she roars, her flames flare out toward the horizon. We dart between the cracks of open sky, and at every turn Naava nudges the dragons around her, singing to them too softly for me to make out the melody.

At first the dragons brush off her attentions with ease. But even after my arms begin to tire and the wind bites at the corners of my eyes, Naava stays her course. The sun sets, awash in orange and deep pink. And one by one, the dragons lift their heads and begin to sing.

I started awake, my heart racing. There was only one day until midsummer, one day to break into Lumina, to save Kaia—

No. No, that had already happened. We had escaped. We were . . . not safe, not really. But we'd left the Talons in complete disarray, and we'd slept peacefully well into the night. The forest was painted in cool shades of blue and gray, and Kaia lay still with her head against my shoulder. The dragon kit nestled against my other side. Naava must have moved while we slept—

now she lay curled around us, her mountainous body a shelter from the elements.

I eased my arm out from under Kaia's head and got carefully to my feet. The air was cold outside of Naava's reach, and I rubbed my hands together to warm them. Next to me the dragon kit stirred, then sat up and yawned. Her eyes glowed faintly in the darkness.

"Go back to sleep," I whispered, but it was of no use. She jumped into my arms before settling herself on my shoulder, tail twining behind my neck for balance.

"Well, if you insist." I couldn't help but smile as the kit nuzzled her snout against my cheek.

My entire body protested as I moved. The trauma of the last few days had seeped beneath my skin, and it felt as though my very bones were rebelling. I stretched my arms, feeling the strain of the muscles where I had held on to Naava for dear life during our encounter with the Talons. The skin on my left arm pulled and stung—I'd forgotten about the cut I'd sustained from the Prophet's attack. The wound was shallow and had already scabbed over, but I knew that if I shifted in particular ways, it would reopen. But I still felt the need to *move*.

The dragon kit and I ventured into the trees. The silence here was weighty, and I had a feeling that the forest was full of its own stories, if only I knew how to listen. It reminded me a little of Vir's Passage, and I could only hope there were no vengeful spirits here.

Something rustled in the underbrush, and I pressed myself against one of the trees, reaching for my knife. The kit's claws dug into my shoulders, and then she leaped, gliding clumsily down to the ground and darting off in pursuit of whatever was out there.

"Wait!" I called hoarsely, but it was too late. The kit was gone.

I shuffled forward in the dark, but it was impossible to move quickly without snapping twigs or disturbing branches, and I didn't want to advertise my position to anyone who might be out there. I stopped. The dragon kit had good instincts. She wouldn't have gone off to get caught in a trap . . . would she?

Either way, the forest had gone quiet again. I closed my eyes, listening. After a few moments, I caught the sound of another rustle, something small, coming closer . . .

The kit pranced out of the underbrush, the limp body of a mouse dangling from her mouth. I let out a sigh of relief and scratched the top of her head and she settled down to eat.

That was one problem solved, at least. As long as the dragon could hunt, we would only need to worry about how to feed ourselves.

As if on cue, my own empty stomach rumbled. I sheathed my knife. The thought of food led unavoidably to the question of what we should do next.

"What are we going to do?" I wondered aloud. We had gotten away this time, but Naava was injured and Sev was still missing. We would make a sorry army storming the emperor's palace in this state.

Having finished eating, the kit chirped and darted in a circle around my legs. I sighed. "Well, I'm glad to see that one of us has retained a streak of optimism." I picked her up, and she cuddled against my chest. "Will you speak to me?" Perhaps that was a selfish hope. It was possible that Naava spoke to humans only because she'd been forced to for so long.

"Maren?"

I jumped, almost dropping the kit as I whirled around to see Kaia step out of the shadows. "Tera's bones, you frightened me!" I said.

"I frightened *you?* I woke up and you were gone! I thought you'd been taken, or—"

She cut her sentence short, hugging her arms across her stomach. My heart cracked. Had she truly thought I would leave her?

I put the dragon kit down and went to her, wrapping her in my arms. "I'm sorry. I didn't think you would wake up. I just needed to think."

She muttered something that I didn't quite hear and pulled me closer. "Don't leave like that. I was so worried."

"I won't." An intense wave of relief washed through me, and I leaned into her embrace. "I was so afraid I would never see you again," I said softly.

Her arms tightened around me. "It's all right. We're together now."

Our escape from Lumina had been so panicked—and the confrontation with the Talons terrifying—but those things were behind us now, and the forest around us was calm, and the longer we stood together the more my body remembered that it was more than a vessel for exhaustion.

I buried my face in her hair, inhaling the scent of salt and honey and *home.* My chest warmed, and I felt a familiar ache growing within me.

"Kaia," I whispered. She turned her head and sighed against my lips, our bodies pressing together. We kissed, and it was as though no time had passed at all. We were simply Maren and Kaia, as we had always been.

My heart raced as she stripped off my jacket and pulled my shirt over my head, her movements possessed by a sense of urgency that quickly overtook me, too. I fumbled with her robes—too slow, too slow—she helped with the cords, stepping on the hem and laughing a little as she wriggled free of it. The rest of our clothes dropped to the forest floor, and we followed feverishly quick, her name on my lips, her mouth on my skin, her hands confident. She took me and I let her, let the world wash away from me until all I could think was *Kaia, Kaia, Kaia.*

The forest began to lighten, and I could hear the dragon kit snoring softly a ways from us. I sighed. For the first time in a very long time, I'd been able to rest without being consumed by thoughts of what was to come. Still, I knew we shouldn't linger any longer. I traced one finger across Kaia's arm, then nudged her gently.

She woke with a cry, looking around frantically. I caught her hand in mine, and she curled toward me, shaking. Her eyes flooded with tears, and my throat tightened. "It's all right— you're all right," I said. "But it's time to go."

She nodded, her shoulders hunched. I held her for a moment longer—then, regretfully, I let her go.

We brushed ourselves off and dressed. But as Kaia turned to pull the Aurati robe over her head, I caught sight of large, fading bruises on her back that had been invisible in the dark.

"Kaia—"

"You're *bleeding*," she interrupted.

What? I looked down to find that the wound on my arm had reopened, though I barely felt the pain. "The Prophet cut me when we were fighting. It's nothing, just needs a wash and a bandage. I don't even feel it. But what did they do to you? How did you get those bruises?"

I reached for her, but she flinched, turning away and pulling her robe tighter around herself. "It doesn't matter. It's done. Don't we have to go?"

And just like that, the door that had opened between us in the night slammed shut.

I wanted to plant my feet and refuse to move until she told me exactly what she had endured while she had been held in Lumina. I wanted to hold her and tell her that nothing like that would ever happen to her again. I wanted to grind the Aurati order to dust beneath my boots.

But she was right. We couldn't stay here.

"All right," I said. I whistled to the dragon kit, who woke with a happy chirp, and we started back toward the clearing where we had left Naava. Kaia walked in troubled silence, but I was loath to break it—at least not until I knew what I wanted to say, and exactly how to say it. Instead my thoughts turned to our next problem. The road to Gedarin was long, and we needed food and a change of clothing, not to mention a plan of attack. I would have to consult with Naava.

The great dragon opened one eye as we approached, but she didn't bother raising her head. Her black scales shimmered in the morning light, and her left wing was partially extended, revealing the severity of her wound. I put a hand to my mouth. The gash was long and deep, and still weeping blood. Seeing it clearly, I was shocked that she had remained aloft as long as she had.

I walked closer. "Naava—will it heal?"

In time. Her voice was slow, ponderous. She was even more exhausted than I was. *All of my children . . . none of them are safe. I thought the damage was to my own self only, but they took them all. Chained them. Changed them.*

Her focus was wandering, and the depth of her grief was plain in her words. "I'm so sorry," I said quietly. "But . . . we can free them now, can't we? In your dream last night, you sang—"

Dragonsong requires strength, more than I have now. If I am to free my children, I must rest. Her wing flexed, then lay still. *I cannot heal here. I must return to Ilvera.* Her nostrils twitched, and a thin stream of smoke rose into the air.

"For how long?" I had expected to intercept Sev as he was still being transported. Now he was long gone, and without Naava, there was no way we could snatch him from the emperor's clutches.

As long as it takes.

"But you promised you would help me rescue Sev. There isn't much time."

At this Naava raised her head, leveling me with her stare. *Do you mean to say that the life of one human is worth the lives of all dragons? Because if I undertake this task before I have the strength, I will fail. Would you then put the fate of all Verran dragons in the claws of the kit in your care?*

"I—"

Being a daughter of the mountain does not absolve you of the potential to do harm. I smelled the oils on you before. Now I smell the fear, the desperation. *You say you would never exploit the dragons. But you would value your heartmate's life above the life of a dragon, if forced to choose. You are merely a human, after all.*

"I would not!" I said reflexively. But perhaps she was right. The thought stopped me cold. Perhaps I was more like a Zefedi than I wanted to admit, even now, after everything I had seen and done. I had vowed to free the dragons—and yet I was pressing Naava for her help while she was injured.

Naava shook her head. *I am tired. Soon I must take my leave.*

"What will we do?" I asked, my spirits sinking.

She snorted. *That is easy, child. You do the best you can.*

She closed her eyes and turned away, settling back into sleep.

Kaia took my hand. "What did she say?"

"She's leaving us," I said.

"But where is she going?" Kaia's voice cracked. "Will she be back?"

"She's going to recuperate. To Ilvera."

"*Ilvera?*" Kaia drew me away from the dragon, toward the edge of the clearing. "Maren, what are we going to do?"

The best I can do. Even if I was merely a human. I tried to shake off the sting of Naava's words. Yesterday I had sworn not to rest until the dragons and those I loved were free of the tyrant. I *would* free the dragons, and I would save Sev. I could still fulfill my vow. I had to believe that.

"We'll go to Gedarin," I said, more firmly than I felt. "The tyrant will have brought Sev there—he'll want him close. And that's where the Talons are based. We will free the dragons, too."

Kaia stared at me. "Free the dragons? Maren, what you're talking about doing . . . it's *dangerous*. Really dangerous."

I pressed Kaia's hands between my own. "I know. But so much of what we've been told about the dragons is a lie. The emperor drugs them to keep them compliant. They're captives, and they must be freed. The Verran dragons are our birthright, and even if they weren't, no creature deserves to be used like this. What monsters are we if we don't do our utmost to help them? It's dangerous, but what other choice do we have?"

"We could return to Ilvera. Tell the council. They might be able to help."

I shook my head. "The council refused to act when you were taken. I wouldn't trust them with this." Besides, going all the way back to Ilvera? Much as the idea tugged at my heart, Naava couldn't carry us with her injuries, and we didn't have the time to go by foot.

"The Aurati, then," Kaia countered. "They could be convinced to join your cause."

I recoiled. "The Aurati *abducted* you. They kept Naava prisoner for generations. They are the emperor's sworn servants, and I just tore down their stronghold. What on earth makes you think they would take our side?"

"You don't know them like I do. They aren't all—"

"Torturers? Manipulators? The entire Aurati order is built upon lies and exploitation, especially of Verran girls and Verran dragons."

"You're wrong," Kaia said heatedly. "Some of the Aurati are like that. But most are just people who want more out of the world than what's been given to them. The Aurati's arms are open to anyone."

"Anyone who can stay alive through the trials," I retorted.

She threw up her hands. "Fine! So if the Verran council is too inept, and the Aurati are so evil, they aren't even worth your consideration, then we should wait until Naava is healed."

"No, we can't afford to wait. We have to go now."

"Why, because the dragons can't wait a moment longer? They've been in captivity for a hundred years. What's another few weeks?"

I took a deep breath, tried to keep my voice even. "You're right, the dragons could wait. But Sev can't."

Kaia's eyebrows furrowed. "Sev?" There was a trace of something in her voice that I couldn't identify.

"Sev helped me get to Lumina, but he's been captured. He's the missing prince of Ruzi—we have to get him back."

Kaia blinked slowly. "Maren . . . he's an enemy of the empire."

"Kaia, *I'm* an enemy of the empire. And I could not have gotten to you without him. Sev is . . ." *Heartmate.* The Prophet's word ghosted through my mind—the same word Naava had used—and I thrust it aside. "Sev has allies who would have hidden him. He would be safe now if it hadn't been for me. We owe him. I have to go after him."

"You would risk everything to save him." Kaia looked down. "You can't keep everyone safe, Maren. You cannot swear to that."

"I swore to come for you, and I did," I said.

"And so you did." She hesitated. "Tell me, then. How will we get to him without Naava's assistance?"

My eyes fell on the dragon kit. "I'm not sure yet," I admitted. "But if we can free the dragons from the Talons and turn some of them to our side, we might have a chance."

"This kit hardly measures up to Naava," Kaia said doubtfully.

The dragon kit, completely unaware of our discussion, was engrossed in stalking a butterfly. "You're right. I'm not sure what will happen. But I don't know what else to do but try."

"*Anything*, Maren. We should do *anything* else. Waking a grown dragon, that was one thing. But you're speaking of walking into Gedarin and somehow besting not just one or two, but the entire fleet of Talons! Armed with nothing more than a baby! The emperor will eat you alive."

She was right, of course, but I couldn't think of a better plan of action. Every moment I wasted was a moment that brought Sev closer to death. I couldn't wait for Naava to recover—and that was assuming that she would still be willing to help me when she was well again. "Nevertheless," I said. "This is what I must do."

At this, Kaia bit her lip, looking away. "You—you've changed, Maren."

So had she, but I thought of the bruises on her back and held my tongue. Sadness welled inside me, and I buried the feeling. Nothing that had happened was her fault, and I could not afford to fall apart right now.

"I'm still me," I said. "When all of this is over, I'll ask you to come back to Ilvera with me, to build our house by the lake."

"But not until then."

I shook my head. "No."

She nodded. Then she knelt down slowly next to the dragon kit, holding out her hand. The kit sniffed it before butting her head up against it until Kaia petted her tentatively. After what seemed an eternity, she spoke. "All right. I'll go with you."

CHAPTER FOUR

Sev

It seemed that the emperor had forgotten about me, for which I was grateful. The light in the dungeon never changed, so the only way I marked time was by the meager bowls of food pushed into the cell. I was reasonably confident it hadn't been more than a day or two, but there was no way to be certain. The sharp pain in my fingers had dulled into a persistent ache—I hoped that meant they were healing as expected. After a while, I began to think I'd prefer a quick execution to withering away over the course of weeks, so when I heard a door slam open and the emperor appeared once more, I was strangely relieved.

I stood up, setting my shoulders back. "Back so soon?"

Rafael sneered at me. "Much as you deserve a long and painful death, I've decided to offer you a chance at an alternative future."

Magnanimous of him. "Being alive is generally preferable to being dead," I said slowly.

"Quite so. My offer is this. I will restore your title to you . . . in exchange for your service to me."

I stared hard at him in surprise, though my heart twisted. *Ruzi.* I hadn't seen it in years.

Of course this was a trap. What else could it be? I'd lived for so long with the knowledge that to be caught by the Flame of the West meant death. I'd prepared for that eventuality, though I'd planned and hoped that when we did meet, I would not be the one to lose my life. I had never foreseen a future where we both survived. So what was he playing at now?

"Ruzi has a king."

Rafael waved a hand dismissively. "I put him there. I can easily dispose of him. Swear your loyalty to me, and you could be king."

Loyalty? Had the emperor forgotten who I was? His Aurati had been warning him about me for years. *By the shadow prince's hand the flame will fall.* And now he offered me not only my life, but the rule of a kingdom? All I had to do was kiss his ring. The thought was sickening.

"A generous offer," I said. "What's the catch?"

He spread his arms. "You malign me. Can I not believe in the power of second chances?"

"No," I said flatly. "I know you. I know what you have done to my family. I know what you have done to your empire."

The smile dropped from his face like a stone. "Then know this, boy. My Aurati have told me all about the girl Maren, and her dragon. She is a traitor to Zefed, and soon she will be brought to me. If you wish to ensure their safety, you will think hard before you turn me down." His voice softened. "Haven't you lost enough? Are they not worth your fealty?"

Maren. If what the emperor said was true, she was still free—at least for now.

The emperor wanted my loyalty enough to threaten my friends—to offer me a kingdom, as if that could make up for the last five years I had spent on the run. But why? There was more to this proposition than I understood, but I had no illusions about the price I would pay if I didn't acquiesce. What I wanted was my blade through his chest, which was impossible as long as I was in this cell. I had to bide my time, and in order to do that, I had to stay alive.

Teeth gritted, I said, "All right. I accept."

"Excellent." Rafael snapped his fingers, and an Aurat wearing scribe's cords stepped out of the shadows, flanked by the same three guards from my last encounter with the emperor. "Take our prince to his new quarters and see that he is made presentable."

The woman nodded. Satisfied, Rafael turned and left, leaving me alone with his servants.

The woman unlocked the cell door. For a moment I contemplated pushing past her, grabbing one of the guard's swords, darting up the stairs, and running the emperor through. I could do it, I thought, though the tremble in my legs betrayed me as I left the cell. Days without adequate food had left me weaker than I wanted to admit.

I reluctantly tore my attention from the weapons and followed the woman up the stairs.

It was a long ascent, and I felt every single step. My joints had stiffened from the cold and injuries I'd sustained, and I could feel the ache where the bruises hadn't yet faded completely. So I moved at a snail's pace, and every so often the woman stopped on the stairs ahead of me and waited with what appeared to be aggrieved patience until I caught up.

I had to rest multiple times before we got to the top of the stairs, and the woman sniffed at me when I finally stood beside her on the landing.

"Spend a few days enjoying the emperor's hospitality yourself," I said.

She arched an eyebrow. "This way," she said. Then she opened the door.

I was not prepared for the light. I shut my eyes at once, but the brightness still came through. The guards pushed me forward, and I put my hands over my face, stumbling into the hallway.

When at last I lowered my hands, I saw we were in an empty, unadorned hallway—one of the least trafficked areas of the emperor's palace, I surmised. It wouldn't do for the dungeons to be directly below the throne room.

"Are you quite done with the theatrics?" the woman asked. Now that we were out of the dungeon's gloom, I saw that she was of Celet heritage and not so much older than me.

I resisted the urge to snap at her again. Best not to antagonize people unnecessarily, at least not until I knew how much power they held.

Instead I nodded. We continued down the hallway and through the palace, the Aurat leading a route that seemed designed to confuse me. But soon enough we made a familiar turn, and I was thrust back in time.

The Hall of Watchers. I'd spent more time here as a child than I cared to remember. It was the place where the emperor kept visitors waiting, those he wanted to intimidate. Thousands of glass eyes of varying sizes and colors lined the walls, staring down at us. As a child I had thought these eyes were those plucked from the heads of the emperor's enemies, and I'd had nightmares about them coming to life. Even after I had learned the truth of them, I still took pains to avoid this hall.

Part of me wondered whether this was all an elaborate ruse to give me a false sense of security before delivering me to a public execution. Anything was plausible where the emperor was involved. He was sadistic enough to take pleasure from such a trick.

But if I went down that route, I would never come back from it. Everything was in shadow, every player a potential enemy. I could drive myself to madness, expecting my end at every turn.

I reined in my thoughts and realized that we had made our way to the east wing of the palace. According to the Dragons, this area was filled with executive offices and the like, though our information was sketchy at best. The first emperor of Zefed had commissioned the palace and promised generous sums to the architects who designed it—only to slaughter all involved when the work was done.

The Aurat opened a door and ushered me through into a chamber that clearly had been an office until quite recently, though some care had been taken during the conversion. There was a bed, a wooden wardrobe, and a desk, chairs and a table for receiving guests, and a bathing area in the corner, the bath already filled with steaming-hot water. Hanging curtains separated the room into sections, and I could see how one might partition off the bathing area and the bed from the receiving area to mimic a more fashionable chamber. And there were windows, though again, too small and high to be of any use to me. The youngest child of a poor noble would have a grander room than this, but it was still a far cry better than my dungeon cell.

"This is your chamber," the Aurat said. "Clean yourself up—you're to appear in court tonight. I'll return later."

They were gone before I could reply, but I didn't even spare a thought for the lock turning in the door. I ripped off my clothing, hindered only by my injured hand, and practically leaped into the bath.

I should have been more cautious, but I couldn't help it. A proper bath. I hadn't had one since Belat, and there was a sort of peace that came upon me as I submerged myself in the water. The worst had already happened. I had spent so long avoiding the emperor's clutches, and now I'd fallen into them. I'd lost. And it was a relief not to have to keep looking over my shoulder.

I took my time soaking away the grime of the dungeon and didn't leave the bath until the water had cooled considerably. Then I stood and grabbed the towel that hung over the back of a nearby chair to dry myself off as I looked more closely around the room.

The walls were bare and unadorned, but the carpet beneath my feet was lush. I dug my toes between the fibers. There was a tray with bowls of rice and pickled vegetables on the desk, and I paused only fractionally before shoving a cucumber into my mouth. While the ingredients weren't too different from a meal at any peasant's table, the quality and delicacy of the seasoning made it obvious that this was proper court food, the sort I remembered eating as a child. The thought made my mouth water. I settled into the chair and ate, trying my best to pace myself.

Once I had finished, I turned my thoughts to what was coming tonight. I wasn't sure what to expect, but it doubtless would involve some exaggerated show of loyalty, which meant looking the part of a courtier. I walked over to the wardrobe that stood against the wall near the bed. I opened the doors to reveal rows of well-tailored clothing, but as I drew out one shirt after another, anger rose within me. Every single piece bore the emperor's colors. The embroidered crests, the thin bands that circled the sleeves—all of it in red and silver.

My first instinct was to tear off the adornments. Instead I gritted my teeth and sorted through the pile. I settled on an outfit that was neither the most ostentatious nor the dullest. Red splashed across the front of the gray shirt like blood, but the silver embroidery was muted and easily missed. The deerskin boots at the bottom of the bureau were a hair too small, so I set them by the door for later, then lay down on the bed to rest.

I must have slept deeply, for I woke to the sound of the door slamming. I sat upright, my hand going to my waist before I remembered that I had no weapons. I got up and peered around the curtain to find that the Aurat had returned—alone. She was sitting with her back to the door, at ease.

I could try to overpower her, but to what end? There were probably guards posted outside the door, and I doubted Rafael would allow anyone into close contact with me who was not adequately trained.

"I don't believe we've been formally introduced," I said, entering the receiving area. I sat down across from her.

She smiled. She had pulled some of her dark hair back from her face, but otherwise wore it loose. "I'm Faris," she said. "Your attendant."

I snorted.

"Something funny?" she said innocently.

"Let's not pretend that I wasn't until quite recently staying in the emperor's dungeon," I said. "I'm the disgraced prince of Ruzi; you're an Aurat and a spy sent to report on me. Can we be honest about that much?"

"All right." She tilted her head and touched the Aurati cords that hung from her shoulders, almost as an afterthought. "Let's be honest, then. From now on I *am* your attendant. One you cannot dismiss."

"Ah." I was surprised, both by her directness and by how easily she'd agreed to my request. Perhaps those were her orders—to get close, to trick me into trusting her. Perhaps that was something I could use to my advantage, if I could convince her that I did trust her and then let something slip. . . . "Then I do have a question for you, as my attendant."

"Of course, my prince."

I leaned forward. "What happened in Lumina?"

Whatever Faris had been expecting me to ask, it wasn't this. She leaned back in her chair, considering me. Finally she nodded. "Doubtless you'll hear about it in court tonight. The day you were captured and handed over to the Talons, Lumina collapsed. A great dragon was seen rising from the wreckage with the girl Maren on its back, but they have since eluded the emperor."

That must have been the dragon that Rafael had questioned me about. So it was true—Maren *was* still free. Faris had not mentioned Kaia or the dragon kit, but I had to believe they were safe too. I sat back, in awe of what Maren had accomplished.

Destroying the Aurati stronghold? The casualties must have been catastrophic, among both the Aurati leadership and the initiates. I wondered whether Faris had known anyone who had been there. Her face gave nothing away.

"If Lumina is destroyed, who leads the Aurati?" I asked.

Faris shook her head. "That's not your concern. You'd do better to concentrate on tonight. You will have to apologize quite well to convince the court of your fealty. The emperor will not accept anything less than complete conviction."

"Very well," I said, letting the subject drop for the moment. "So as my attendant, do you have any suggestions for how I can win them over?"

"What makes you think that I have any advice to offer?"

I leaned back, crossing my arms. "I'm an extremely valuable prisoner. You wouldn't have been picked for this assignment if you weren't exceptional in some way."

She leaned forward, resting her chin on her hand as she studied me. "And why should I help you?"

Good question. Most likely she would go along with whatever I said next, if her assignment was to keep a close eye on me. But I still chose my words carefully. "If I'm to make it through the night, I need a speech. And it's been a long time since I've had to give one to courtiers. Scribe's work is boring, isn't it? Wouldn't keeping me alive be much more interesting than watching me get myself executed?"

Faris's face was as still as a portrait. For a moment I thought I'd misjudged the situation completely. And then she laughed. "All right, little prince. I'll help you."

CHAPTER FIVE

Maren

Kaia and I spent most of the day foraging for food. The dragon kit bounded between us as we collected nuts and midsummer fruit, the kind that flourished in wild places. Despite the morning's fraught conversation, our bodies remembered how to walk side by side, shoulders almost touching.

If we had been in Ilvera now, we would have been in the fields together picking the late brambleberries, or the earliest of the sour apples for preserves that would last through the winter. But Ilvera was so far away—my chest hurt at the thought, sharp and unexpected—and I could not reconcile our easy familiarity with the way Kaia had defended the Aurati.

I glanced over at Kaia. She had taken off her Aurati cape and was using the yellow fabric as a sling to carry the peaches we had found. As I watched, she paused to stretch her neck, dropping her head toward one shoulder, then the other. Then she looked up and saw me watching her. I wasn't sure what expression was on my face, but whatever she saw made her reconsider what she was going to say.

"We're going to need more food than this," she said. "And supplies, too."

"Naava shouldn't be left alone," I replied without thinking.

She frowned. "I think she'd be able to handle whatever this forest has to offer. And didn't you say our time is short? If you're so certain of that, we should have left already."

Her tone irked me—so certain, laced with the slightest hint of condescension—as though I was going about this all wrong. And maybe I was, but she wasn't the one who had survived in the heart of Zefed for so long. I had. Though I hadn't done it alone.

I took a deep breath. "You're right. But it's late in the day to be starting out. Tomorrow morning?"

A concession on my part, but she simply nodded and turned back to the peach trees, even humming a little as she did so.

I shook my head. I was imagining things—she hadn't needled me on purpose. Kaia wouldn't do that. But speaking as though she knew best, assuming that I would go along with her? She'd always been like that. The difference was that today it bothered me.

The thought jabbed at me, but I kept quiet. So much had changed. It was foolish to expect that our relationship would settle into its old rhythms right away. The best thing I could do was to let this go and concentrate on how lucky we were to be together again. After all, what did one disagreement matter compared to everything else we had?

The dragon kit nudged my leg. She was holding a peach in her mouth, and when she saw me looking, she released it at my feet. It was bruised on one side—it must have fallen from the tree—but the kit had carried it so gently, I could barely feel the teeth marks when I picked it up. Now she sat back on her haunches, clearly proud of herself, and I couldn't help but smile.

"Thank you," I said, scratching her neck behind the ears.

She preened a moment longer, then bounded away. I returned to the task at hand, and for the rest of the afternoon we worked in silence. Finally we had gathered as much as we could carry, and we returned to the clearing just as the sun dipped below the horizon.

Naava stirred as we approached, raising her head.

I set the food down under a tree and went to her. "How are you feeling?" I asked.

Instead of responding, she opened her mouth, letting loose a small lick of flame. Then she rose slowly to her feet. She stretched her wings above us, and I was struck again by just how large she was. The dragon kit ran to her side, flapping her own wings in imitation.

It is time, Naava replied. *I will go to Ilvera.*

My chest felt tight. I wanted to beg her to stay, but I knew she would not change her mind.

Naava breathed out another plume of fire. The dragon kit chirped and sneezed out sparks, and suddenly something else occurred to me.

"Will you take her with you?"

She looked down at the kit and dipped her head. The kit looked up at her, then at me. For a moment, I stopped breathing.

Then Naava shook her head. *The little one will stay with you.*

"Thank you," I said, exhaling in relief.

It is her choice, not mine.

The kit came to me and nuzzled her head against my hand. She'd become part of me so easily—I couldn't imagine parting from her. She was family.

Family. A wave of homesickness washed over me. I'd tried hard not to think about my parents over the last few weeks, for fear of being incapacitated by my longing for a meal that my father had cooked, or my mother's counsel. For the most part I'd been successful, but knowing Naava would soon be there, and that there was a good chance she would see my parents before tomorrow night . . .

I wanted that for myself, so much. To feel completely safe again, even just for a day.

But I could not have it. And I could not drag them into this. Verrans were no warriors, not any longer.

So instead, I squared my shoulders. "My parents are in Ilvera. Will you give them a message from me?"

What would you have me say? Naava said. She furled her injured wing against her body, and I could see how the movement taxed her. I bit my lip. I didn't have time to compose the perfect letter.

"Just—tell them that I'm with Kaia. That we've escaped the Aurati. That we're well."

"My mothers are there too," Kaia said suddenly from behind me. It was the first time she had addressed Naava directly. "Please tell them I am alive, and—unharmed."

I shot her a glance. That wasn't quite true, but what business had I to moderate what she told her mothers? I had told enough lies to my own parents before I left.

Naava nodded. *I will do that, daughter of the mountain.*

"She will," I said to Kaia.

Naava looked up at the darkening sky and flapped her wings again, more strongly this time. I stepped back, clearing the way for her to fly.

Maren.

I started. Naava had never called me by name before. "Yes?"

I have dreamed of you these long hours.

My palms tingled. She was speaking of dragon dreams. "What did you see?" I asked.

Your path is clouded. You must be careful how you step. Who you trust. But there is hope. If you prove yourself by the time I return, you will have the aid you seek. You may yet prevail.

Naava's prophecies were clearer than those given by the Aurati seers, but that wasn't enough to curb my frustration at the message. "I don't understand—what should I do? When will you return?"

Prove yourself beyond the reach of my wings. I will know when the time is right.

And then she launched herself into the sky, lifting up and out of the trees. A gust of wind swept through the clearing in her wake.

I had known it was coming, but this parting still tore at me. And knowing that there was a possibility she would not return at all . . . I closed my eyes, my jaw tightening.

A hand came down tentatively on my shoulder. "Are you all right?" Kaia said.

"No. I shouldn't—never mind."

"Shouldn't what?"

I took a deep breath before answering her, let it out slowly. "I shouldn't be angry. But I am."

Kaia shook her head. "What does that accomplish? You knew she was going to leave, and she has. We should be deciding what comes next."

I shrugged off her hand and walked a few steps away. I'd intended to share the prophecy that Naava had given me. Now I wanted nothing more than to tuck it away within me, where it would be safe from Kaia's judgment—at least until I could puzzle out what it meant. "Right," I said, the word coming out sharper than I'd intended. "We'll leave tomorrow."

"And go where? You said we'd go to Gedarin, but, Maren, what do you think is going to happen when we get there? If the emperor is holding your friend, we'll need more on our side than a theory that you'll be able to free dragons by yourself. Tell me you have something else planned. *Anything.*"

I didn't—but then an idea struck me. "The Dragons." How could I have forgotten? I'd promised to send word to Rowena once we'd found Sev.

"Something *other* than the dragons," Kaia said.

"No, the army we left outside of Lumina. They call themselves the Dragons. They're Sev's allies—they're devoted to the downfall of the emperor. We can meet up with them."

Kaia crossed her arms. "And you trust them?"

Not really. "Our interests are aligned," I said.

"That's not what I asked."

"I trust them *enough.*" At Kaia's dubious expression I added, "And we don't have any better options."

"You're right," Kaia conceded. "Then we'll have to go back through Oskiath."

"We'll need supplies—and disguises, if we're going back that way." I closed my eyes, trying to picture what we had passed over as we had flown yesterday. "I think we're close to the southern edge of the forest. We'll have the best shot at getting what we need if we get out of the forest. Then we can turn north." There seemed no better way to go about it. I only hoped that we had enough time.

Hallway of white. Girls in yellow running—running from me, as fire blankets the ceiling and crawls down the walls. I can smell their hair as it burns, see the blisters rising on their skin. We're burning together, and there is nothing I can do but scream.

"Maren!"

I woke to Kaia shaking me roughly by the shoulder. "What?" I gasped. My heart was pounding out of my chest, but there was no fire here, nothing but the forest, quiet around us.

"You were having a nightmare. What did you see?"

The dream rushed back to me—the girls, all those girls who had died as Lumina had fallen. *Aurati,* I reminded myself. Each and every one of them complicit in Naava's captivity, in propping up the tyranny of the emperor.

But did that mean they'd deserved to die?

"It's nothing." *Nothing,* I repeated to myself. Not even a dragon dream. Just a wisp of a heightened memory brought forth from the recesses of my mind.

In the gray morning light, I saw that Kaia looked little better than I felt. Her hair had fallen out of her braids and was tangled and matted from lying on the ground. There were dark circles under her eyes, and her Aurati robes badly needed a wash. We'd been too exhausted last night to do more than curl toward each other once we'd lain down, and it still seemed like we hadn't slept at all.

I squeezed her hand. "I'm fine. Let's go."

We brushed away the signs of our presence in the clearing. Then we judged our direction as best we could by the position of the rising sun and set off.

I'd had a vision of what the world would be like, once Kaia and I had been reunited. Even when we were on the run from the emperor's Talons, it would be perfect, because she would have her hand in mine and she would smile like sunrise, and together, our future would be one of endless possibility.

I hadn't imagined that we would be tired, stiff, and dirty, or that I would be preoccupied not with whether I could hold her close to me at all times, but instead by the fact that my tongue was beginning to stick to the top of my dry mouth. The peaches helped, and we each ate several over the course of the morning. But there wasn't much I wouldn't have given for a long drink of water.

Nothing had disturbed us for the few days we'd been in Belat Forest. It was difficult to be certain whether that was by chance or design, though I suspected it had something to do with how Naava had dispatched the Talons. The tyrant would think carefully before he launched another attack. But when we left the forest, we would be without protection. And we needed more than a sack full of fruit to sustain us—and soon.

The last time I had wandered throughout Zefed, it had been with Sev leading the way. I wasn't sure if I could do it myself.

Sev. He'd left the Dragons for me. He'd followed me into Lumina, and I had left him to his doom. If not for me, he would have been safe right now, not waiting for the Flame of the West to decide how to kill him, most likely. If he wasn't already—

A lump formed at the back of my throat, and I took a shaky

breath, holding back tears. I refused to believe that Sev was dead. The Prophet had told me that I had *heartmates* to worry over. More than one. If that was true, then surely I'd know in my heart if something had happened to him.

And yet ... the Prophet had not been all-seeing. Otherwise, why would she have put in motion the events that led to her death? I glanced at Kaia. Surely the Prophet had misspoken. Kaia was my everything. I'd told Sev as much. And a person couldn't have two heartmates ... could they?

The sound of something cracking interrupted my thoughts. The dragon kit had tripped over a fallen tree branch, tumbling forward and landing in a heap. She shook herself off, then ran to me and jumped into my arms. I cuddled her close, trying not to giggle. Kaia and I looked at each other, and I could see the laughter glimmering in her eyes.

"Does she have a name yet?" Kaia asked.

"Not that she's shared."

"Well then," Kaia said, addressing the kit. "How will we know what to call you if you don't tell us?"

The kit chirped. Kaia raised an eyebrow at me, and I shrugged. "We communicate. But it's not quite the same as talking."

"I'm sure she'll get there eventually. How old is she, anyway?"

I had to count back the days in my head as we started walking again. "Only about two weeks," I said, marveling at how independent she already was. I wasn't sure how much of this was to do with a dragon's innate nature rather than the fact that she was growing up without dragon elders around her, but at least she seemed happy. *Two weeks.* My entire understanding of the world had been upended in that time.

"She's very impressive," Kaia said, stroking the kit's back.

"I think so too," I said.

We lapsed back into silence. I hadn't forgotten about the bruises that marked Kaia's body, but I'd been at a loss for how to broach the subject again. Now that we were on our own, I wanted to at least try to cross that distance between us. I cleared my throat. "I didn't want to press you on this. But I wish you would tell me what happened while you were at Lumina."

She stopped abruptly. "I told you, I don't want to talk about it. Bruises fade. It's fine."

"But it's not," I insisted, stopping to face her. "It's not just the bruises. I can't even count how many I have right now. But I wasn't held against my will for over a month and—" I couldn't even form the word "tortured," because the thought alone made me incandescent with rage, even if most of the people responsible were dead now. "Naava sent me dreams about you. I know you tried to escape. I felt it when they—" My fingers crossed my palm, right where the Aurati had struck her, and Kaia looked down at the ground. "They hurt you. Badly."

When she met my gaze again, I knew I'd made a mistake. "But they're gone," Kaia said angrily, fire flaring in her eyes. "It's over. If you saw what happened, why do you feel the need to talk about it? And while we're on the subject, why don't you *talk* about what you dreamed last night? Or what happened before you got to Lumina? If you're so insistent on sharing, why don't *you* go first?"

"Kaia—"

She turned her back and walked away without another word ... and I let her go, my apology caught in my throat.

I looked down at the dragon kit, who sneezed and rested her head on my shoulder. I didn't know how to do this. I didn't know how to be Maren in the relationship of Maren-and-Kaia, not when Kaia didn't want to talk to me. So instead of running to meet her, I trailed behind. I had been the quiet one, back in Ilvera. I could be that again.

We found a stream a few hours later and took the opportunity to drink and wash our faces in silence. I rinsed the dirt out of the wound in my arm and improvised a bandage from a strip of fabric torn from my shirt. It needed attention, but at least it wasn't showing signs of infection.

Soon after that, we came across a path. It was small but clear, suggesting that it was often in use. We paused within sight of it, but no one appeared after several minutes of waiting.

Kaia looked to me. "What do you think?"

It was the first thing she'd said since our argument, and I wasn't about to squander the peace she was offering, tenuous though it might be. "We should follow it. But it's probably best if we stay out of sight." Bedraggled travelers, even Aurati, weren't cause for too much concern. But the dragon kit would draw anyone's attention, and without a pack, I had no way to conceal her.

There was no warning when the forest ended, though. One moment there were thick trees and a shaded path, the scent of greenery and the quiet hum of insects and occasional movements of larger creatures out of sight—and the next there were neatly cut fields almost as far as we could see. I tried to hide my dismay as I looked around. These fields had been harvested too early, just like those Sev and I had come across on our journey to Oskiath. And it was clear they were actively maintained. I called to the dragon kit and held her at my side.

"Which way?"

Kaia shaded her eyes, looking around. "There's a house in that direction. We can get supplies there."

My stomach clenched. We had agreed we needed supplies—I just hadn't thought through what we would have to do to obtain them. *You must be careful how you step. Who you trust.* Naava's words had been a warning, and it seemed wise to assume that anyone we came across was a threat.

"And what do you suggest we say to whoever is in that farmhouse?"

Kaia looked down, her brown curls shimmering in the sunlight. "By now word will have spread about Lumina's fall. It is not such a stretch that an apprentice might have been dismissed in the chaos to make her own way home, without supplies."

"Apprentices aren't dismissed. They're initiated or killed," I pointed out.

She stilled. "True," she said slowly. "But nothing like this has ever happened to Lumina."

"And you think they'll just help you?"

"People help Aurati. We are servants of Zefed, and the people of Zefed by extension."

Her words made me queasy. "But you're not an Aurat."

For a long, awful moment, I thought she would contradict me. Finally she said, "But they won't know that, will they? I'll go in. You stay behind. You're not dressed for the part, and we can't leave the dragon on her own, anyway."

As we approached the farmhouse, Kaia's posture changed—she stood up taller, her shoulders rolled back as she brushed dust from her robes. She slipped easily into the role of an Aurati initiate, and I hated it.

The farmhouse was a large, freestanding structure, with a barn behind it. Wisps of smoke escaped the chimney, and we slowed as we came to the edge of the field.

I held the dragon kit back. "We'll stay here," I said, for the plants were high enough to conceal us.

"Good," Kaia said. "This won't take long." She embraced me quickly, and then turned around.

As she knocked on the door, I found myself wishing that no one was home. There had to be a safer way, even if that meant stealing what we needed. As it was, I was too far away to hear clearly or intervene if anything went awry. But then the door opened, and I held my breath as I watched Kaia through the grass.

The woman who had opened the door looked friendly enough, exclaiming over Kaia's disheveled state before taking her hand and leading her inside. The door closed, and I started upright before letting myself sit back down. Of course they would invite her inside if they believed her story. Why wouldn't they? Everything was fine. Everything was going according to plan. All I had to do was wait.

The plants around me were verdant and alive. At least the fields hadn't been razed after the harvest. Maybe there was a chance for another crop before the winter came. The dragon kit sniffed at one of the plants, then nipped off a leaf and began to chew.

"And how are you?" I whispered.

The dragon kit chirped back, but softly, as though she understood the need for stealth. In the sunlight I could see her color had settled into a deep, rich blue. She looked at me, green eyes large, and for a moment I felt as though I were falling—

A dark room with a bed, and a body on it—Sev—he sits up, opening his eyes—

I blinked, rocking back. I'd been privy to enough of these to recognize what it was. A dragon dream. But I'd never had one while I was awake before. And Naava had left, and the dragon sitting right in front of me was only two weeks old. Yet the scene she'd shown me . . . "What was that, little one?" I asked softly. "How did you do that?"

She sang, and an image flashed across my mind—Sev, laughing. So she'd been thinking of Sev.

"Was that real?" I said, hope surging in my chest. "Can you do it again?"

She closed her eyes and opened them. I met her gaze again, and—

Sev sitting across from a woman—an Aurat. Talking, but he looks pale—and ill at ease. He rubs his neck, looks up, and our eyes meet—

I let out a gasp as the field came back into focus once more. The only being I'd ever interacted with directly in a dragon dream had been Naava—and only then because it had been her dream. In all other instances I had been but a witness, a shadow on the wall or looking out from within someone else's body. But Sev—it looked like Sev had *seen* me.

"Again," I said—but just then the farmhouse door opened, distracting me.

I crouched lower in the field, keeping one hand on the kit's back. Kaia came through the door, holding a large sack and smiling back at the woman inside. Relief flooded through me as I watched her walk confidently down the road, away from us.

I waited until I thought the woman must have turned to another task inside. Then the kit and I ran to catch up.

CHAPTER SIX

Sev

T he first thing that Faris presented to me was a thin book she'd somehow kept hidden in her robes. "This is a list of the current nobles and royals in residence at court. You'll need to have it memorized by tonight."

"This is your idea of helping me? I thought you were going to tell me what to say in order to avoid a messy public death."

"Beggars can't be choosers, Prince Vesper," she said.

"Severin," I corrected. I hadn't been Vesper in years—first out of necessity, then out of comfort. Vesper had been an innocent, and a child. Time had killed both.

Faris nodded. "Very well. If you expect to be taken seriously at this court, Severin, you will have to be able to recognize your peers, both friends and enemies. And I hope you remember the etiquette lessons you were taught growing up, because I cannot help you there."

I picked up the book and grudgingly flipped it open. *Antuan, Camden, Donovan, Annick . . .* A long list of names stared back at me, most of which I didn't know. At least there were markings denoting which houses each of the lords belonged to.

"Fine, I'll look at it," I said, closing the book. "Now, about the speech."

Faris arched an eyebrow and looked pointedly at the book.

"It can't be particularly entertaining for you to watch me read a list," I pointed out.

"If I don't watch you do it, then how do I know you did it at all?" Faris countered.

I rolled my eyes. "Consider the idea that I value my life at least as much as you value yours. I'll look at the list. Later."

"Very well," she said. "The speech. What do you want to know?"

I leaned forward. "I haven't been to Irrad since I was a child. I know *of* the emperor more than I know the emperor himself. What do I say to him?"

"Truthfully?"

I nodded.

"It matters very little whether the emperor believes your words, because he won't. You both know the bargain you made to stay alive. He knows that however well you play your loyalty, it is not freely given or sincere. Even the nobility will suspect you of putting on a show—it's no more than most of them do, after all. I doubt there's a person in court who truly loves the Flame."

Her candor continued to surprise me, though I'd suspected as much. But if I wasn't meant to convince the emperor or the nobility, then who? Suddenly I realized, and I was embarrassed that it hadn't been obvious to me. "The act is for the commoners."

"Yes. You're the shadow prince, the symbol of rebellion. Your words must be believable enough to spread outside these walls—to convince those who listen that you have been properly cowed."

I sat back. What could I say that would be believed? Despite the fact that I had just slept, my head felt extraordinarily heavy.

Sunlight, greenery, blue sky—I'm in a field, an insect buzzing lazily by my ear. In the distance a farmhouse—I turn my head and see Maren, her face intent—her eyes widen as she looks at me—she jerks away, then—

"Are you listening?"

I started upright, blinking my eyes as the light dissipated and I was left once again in this dim office. What was *that*?

"Severin," Faris said, impatient.

"Sorry, I was distracted," I said hastily.

"Then pay attention. Think. Is there anyone in court who will remember you from before? Those will be the hardest to win over."

"Maybe," I said slowly, though my mind was racing. Had that been a dream? A hallucination? It had felt so *real*.

"So keep your story simple. You've been at large for many years, and now you've returned as a loyal subject to oversee Ruzi on the emperor's behalf. They will see through a half-hearted act, so throw in some theatrics. Make a flowery speech. There are more stories about your exploits than I can keep track of—make some up that don't involve acting against the Flame. Fall to your knees. Consider crying, some hand wringing. Kissing the emperor's robes usually goes over well."

I had never thought I would have difficulty selling a lie. But it seemed such a foreign thing, to swallow my hatred when I looked at the emperor's face. To keep the white-hot rage that burned inside me at bay.

"I'm not sure I can."

Faris crossed her arms. "If you aren't equal to this task, you may as well present your neck to the swordsman now. Come on. You were young and impressionable. You're a prince. What were you doing, allying yourself with rebels? Was it the lure of fortune elsewhere? Were you confused by their propaganda? Make me believe that you were led astray . . . *and* that you found your way back to the embrace of our great empire."

I frowned. Once I *had* believed that Zefed was a great empire. I'd been a child of privilege. Before my family had been killed, I'd had no reason to think otherwise.

I shook off the thought, turning back to the task at hand. "When I was young, I strayed from the guidance of the empire," I said slowly. "I was lost. I was . . . under influences that led me down a dark path."

"That's a start," Faris said approvingly. "I'll leave you to it." She set down a piece of paper and pen on the table between us. "You can use that to organize your thoughts. And don't think of spiriting those away—I will be collecting them when I return. You have one hour."

And then I was alone again.

Time was short, and my survival—and Maren's—depended on the performance I was to give this evening. I should have been using my time to compose, to structure and restructure every sentence until it rang with sincerity. But I couldn't stop thinking about the way Maren's face had flashed before me, how she'd seemed to look right at me. The vision had lasted only a few seconds, but it was like a window had somehow opened to wherever she was.

I waited a few moments to see if another vision would come to me. When it didn't, I sighed. Whatever it was, I had to set it aside. I opened the book that Faris had given me and skimmed over it. My eyes snagged on a familiar name—Idai, ruler of

Eronne. They were the only one of the small kings currently in residence, and the one I was least prepared to see. I cursed under my breath, but there wasn't anything I could do about it now. I read on.

Out of all the nobility, there were only two lords representing Oskiath in residence. I took note of their names. Perhaps I could get a message through one of them to the Dragons. If they knew I had survived, knew where I was, they would come for me. I hoped.

Of course, that necessitated having something with which to pass a message, and Faris had told me she would collect the pen and paper when she returned. Given her attention to detail, it seemed unlikely I would get away with ripping off part of the paper. Any plan for escape first depended on surviving this court appearance. So I took up the pen, giving thanks that my dominant hand hadn't been the one injured, and began to write.

When the trumpets called us to supper, Faris and I were escorted to the great hall by no fewer than five guards. I might have laughed if the situation hadn't seemed so bleak. I could forget passing secret messages—right now, it seemed impossible that I would be able to do so much as sneeze without being observed.

The guards fell back as we reached the hall, leaving only Faris at my side. She nodded to the pages, who stopped staring upon her instruction and pulled open the heavy doors. I took a deep breath and walked into a world that was startlingly familiar.

There had been music and loud, bright chatter as the doors opened. But now, as I entered, the music abruptly cut off. The doors closed behind me, and then the only sound was my footsteps.

The floor of the hall was made of inky black stones polished to a glassy shine—easy to slip, if you weren't paying attention. The chamber was crowded with representatives from the four other kingdoms of Zefed, members of each royal family, Talons, Aurati, servants, all with their eyes on me.

My father had walked this floor before me, as had my brother. The thought gave me strength as I looked straight ahead, avoiding eye contact with those who fell out of my path, leaving a clear line between me and the silver throne. The emperor sat there, arrayed in robes of shimmering gems that caught the light and reflected it, making it difficult to look at him head-on.

I climbed the stairs to the throne. I stood before the emperor of Zefed, my head high.

Our eyes met, and he raised his eyebrows. My stomach clenched, sending a wave of nausea through my body, but I had to see this through.

Kneel. You must kneel.

My legs bent. I knelt.

"Emperor of Zefed," I ground out, every word a curse against my family. "I am Severin Avidal, prince of Ruzi. I come to pledge my fealty." I could feel the eyes on me, though I kept my head bowed, staring at the floor.

"When you last saw me, I was Prince Vesper—in my youthful ignorance I was swayed when rebels filled my ears with lies. I strayed from the guidance of the empire, and became lost." I took a deep breath. "I have seen the error of my ways, and beg for mercy. If I am allowed, I would redeem myself in your eyes a thousandfold before I die."

I could hear the nobles behind me murmuring, their fans undoubtedly masking their words. That the emperor had brought the shadow prince of Ruzi, his greatest enemy, to kneel before him . . .

I was a spectacle. I closed my eyes. My father had been poisoned for the reforms he had tried to enact. My brother had led an army against the Flame and been burned to death by Talons. I hadn't seen either of them die, but my mother . . . How they all would have despised what I was doing now.

This would not last, I reminded myself. One day he would be dead at my hand.

Part of me waited for a blade to fall, waited for my life to reach the end of its short tether. But instead, Rafael's voice pitched loudly enough to echo through the hall. "Rise."

I got to my feet, and the emperor stood, opening his arms wide. He continued. "Let no one say that the emperor of Zefed is without mercy. All the children of Zefed are my children, as I am the father of the empire. *Severin* has returned after so many years away, and because he has pledged his loyalty, I have pardoned him. For pardon is possible for anyone who repents in earnest."

He was a monster in the shape of a man. He had destroyed my family, and so many others. He had made me a liar. And yet he spoke of repentance, and when he let his hand fall, the applause that followed was crushing.

"Thank you, my lord." Expressing gratitude to the tyrant felt like vomiting molten glass, but I did it, and I bowed until he bade me rise and raised his hand, allowing me to leave.

I kept my head down and backed slowly away from him, not

turning until I had reached the bottom of the stairs. The music started up again.

"That was well done," Faris murmured in my ear.

"According to whom?" I said.

"You did what you had to do. You confirmed the emperor's story. What more needs to be said?"

I shrugged. There was nothing else I *could* say. Those minutes spent kneeling at the emperor's feet had been the longest of my life. I didn't know what I had expected, but the aftermath was anticlimactic in comparison. One of the servants poured me a glass of wine, which I held mostly to give my good hand something to do.

Now that I was past my own performance, I could spare some attention for my surroundings. The walls were hung with intricate tapestries, each featuring the emperor's colors. Peacocks roamed the floor, unsupervised. The tables were spread with more food than a gathering five times this size could hope to consume. I thought of the people I'd seen on the road in Zefed, the fields stripped to feed the growing armies of the empire. How much of that food had come here instead? And the clothes the courtiers were wearing! I was no expert on fabric, but these dresses and tunics were clearly custom designed and very expensive. Some of the embroidered silks would have taken weeks, if not months, to perfect. And jewels were everywhere—in earrings and nose rings, sewn into coats and dresses, winking on fingers and in headdresses.

I was suddenly aware of how dark my own clothing was in comparison, its austerity marking me as an outsider and captive as obviously as chains around my wrists would have.

The emperor would never give me jewels—I could too easily use them for bribes. I had never been one for show, anyway. As a child I'd been quiet, more attached to books and animals than the latest court intrigue. Being a second son I should have been sent to train as a Talon. But my father had defied the emperor in keeping me in Ruzi.

I still couldn't imagine the excuses he'd made or the leverage he'd used to keep me safe at home. Rafael's father had been the emperor back then. He'd been old at the time, and ailing. Perhaps he'd been thinking more about his own family, his own legacy. Perhaps that's why my family had been able to hide their treason for so long.

I took a sip of my wine and turned my attention back to the food. I needed to eat, no matter what I thought of this wretched excess. Faris stayed at my elbow as I set down my glass and picked my way down the table, nibbling on bread and cheese and pocketing some fruit. I picked up a fork and speared a slice of seasoned meat that had been cut from a large roast, and was searching for a plate to put it on when I looked up into a pair of familiar eyes.

Neve stood on the other side of the table. I schooled my body into indifference and looked away, mindful of the shadow standing just behind me.

I hadn't seen the emperor's Aromatory since before fleeing the dragon fortress with Maren and the dragon egg. Despite the fact that Neve's abilities had been key to my original plan, we had never exchanged more than a few words. It had been pure chance that I had gained Maren's trust instead. But now Neve was here, in Irrad, and her presence was as strange and confusing to me as my own.

The emperor's dragon trainer remained with the dragons. And there were more than a few hatchlings that needed supervision at the moment, and more oils to be distilled—so what was she doing here?

I dared another glance at Neve, and our eyes met again. Her lips thinned, and she looked as though she wanted to say something. But then her eyes flicked to Faris behind me, and she inclined her head ever so slightly in my direction before turning away and continuing down the table, away from us.

The corner of my mouth turned up as I found a plate for my food. The encounter, despite its brevity, gave me more than a small amount of comfort. Neve remembered me. Neve *wanted* to talk to me—I was sure of it—just not in front of one of Rafael's spies.

"Prince Severin."

I turned to see a slight young woman standing before me, a predatory gleam in her eyes. I bowed, trying to buy myself time. I'd done my best with the book Faris had given me, but I could not name this woman. Her coloring was of Old Zefed, and her clothing was fashionable but lacked any indication of familial ties. Who was she?

"You must allow me to congratulate you. Your speech—I must say, it brought tears to my eyes to hear you speak your loyalty to the Flame."

I straightened and cut a desperate glance to Faris. *Help.*

"Erris," Faris jumped in. "How nice to see you looking so well after your indisposition."

Erris! She was of Eronne—not noble, but her family was extremely wealthy. The lady in question flushed slightly. "Thank you—it was nothing." She laid a proprietary hand on my sleeve.

"I want you to know that I would never *dream* of spurning a loyal servant of the empire over a youthful indiscretion. The Flame of the West has pardoned you, and that is the highest commendation one can receive."

It was difficult to believe she wasn't joking, and yet she stood before me, eager and intent. "Thank you," I said after a moment. "I appreciate your support."

"I hope you aren't thinking of returning to Ruzi too soon. Irrad has become so *boring* recently."

Hang me now—she's a leech. It had been so long since I'd been in court—there was so much I'd forgotten. I'd been young enough to avoid such attentions, but Callum had complained long and loud about individuals like Erris. I smiled at her, trying to look genuine. "I'm in Irrad for the foreseeable future. And you? How long have you been at court?"

"Practically my whole life," Erris said. "My father was good friends with the emperor's father, may he live on in everlasting flame. But enough about that! You'll pardon me for asking, but we've all been dying to know—were you at Lumina? Did you see the dragon?"

What should I say? I glanced at Faris, but she only frowned. "I—"

"That's hardly an appropriate topic for tonight's festivities," a young man cut in smoothly. He was dressed in Kyseal colors, his long hair tied stylishly back. "Prince Severin. Welcome back," he said, bowing perfunctorily to me.

I flipped through my mental notes on those in residence from Kyseal. "Lord Annick," I replied, inclining my head.

He turned to Erris. "You promised me a game of alabac."

Erris pouted but didn't argue. "Join us?" she asked me.

"Perhaps next time," I said, holding up my food as an excuse. "Very nice to meet you both."

Lord Annick put a hand on Erris's elbow, steering her away, and Faris and I were alone again.

"You didn't need my help after all," Faris remarked.

"On the contrary. I would have had to grovel indeed if I slighted the richest family in Eronne," I muttered. "You saved me."

Faris let out a bark of laughter.

"Why was Annick so quick to interfere when Erris asked about Lumina?" I said.

She sobered instantly. "Most of what's reached Irrad is rumor, not fact. All the city is curious, but no one dares draw the emperor's attention by speaking of it too loudly. Erris forgot her place." She turned to face the center of the hall. "Enough of that, now. Who else do you not recognize? Let's see if we can refresh your memory before you actually have to speak with any of them."

We hung back from the crowd, and I ate slowly, trying to match the people I saw to the names from Faris's book. She offered corrections from time to time, but as the evening passed, it became easier to sort those around us into their families and positions. I didn't see Idai, and was thankful for the reprieve.

There were a few diversions that seemed to be regular features of entertainment at the court. A fleet of trained dogs was brought to perform, followed by human dancers—all this while the emperor watched from his throne. Something happened with the peacocks that I couldn't quite see, as I kept to the side of the room. My gaze wandered, and then settled on a large man standing near the emperor's throne. I'd never seen him before, and I was almost certain his name hadn't appeared in Faris's booklet.

"Who is that?" I asked Faris, nodding in his direction.

"Milek, the Alchemist," she murmured in my ear. "He is developing a new method for training the dragons."

"Different from the oils?" I blurted, surprised. There was no other way of training dragons that I knew of. Even Maren didn't *train* them—her way with the dragon kit was more like communing.

Faris hesitated. "The particulars remain secret."

A shiver ran down my spine. So Neve had displeased the emperor, and he was replacing her. It was likely she was still alive only because the new techniques weren't yet effective. Which meant that Neve and I had an enemy in common—and that her days were numbered. Maybe that was something I could use to my advantage.

Eventually the music shifted from pleasant background ambience into a driving beat that I recognized as one of the current dances in Oskiath.

The emperor finally rose, and I craned my neck to watch. If he was going to lead the dance, I needed to know who his partner was. I knew there was an empress—had been for several years—but she had been kept behind the scenes, and I had been too preoccupied with my own plans to make inquiries.

He held out his hand, and a woman wearing a deep red gown emerged from the audience. An ornate crown sat atop her dark hair, which was held back from her face in a silver net. She took the emperor's outstretched hand, and there was something familiar about the way she curtsied to him. The emperor bowed back.

As they turned to face the assembly, my heart stopped.

Piera.

CHAPTER SEVEN

Maren

Kaia had done well. She'd secured two packs, one of them large enough for the dragon kit to fit into. Within the other pack were two knives, blankets, a small pot, two water skins—and a few loaves of traveler's bread. It was all I could do not to fall on it immediately. Kaia and I redistributed our bounty between the packs, and then shared one loaf of bread, passing it back and forth as we walked. We took smaller and smaller bites as the loaf shrank, neither wanting to be the one to finish it off.

"I still can't believe she gave you all this," I said.

"I told you, Aurati are looked on kindly in the empire," Kaia said. "I explained what happened at Lumina and told them I was trying to get home, that I didn't know what else to do, and she helped."

"But . . . I still don't understand why. I've spent time traveling throughout Zefed. Aurati are not so benevolent as these people seem to believe. They are the emperor's eyes and ears."

Kaia passed a piece of bread to the dragon kit. "That's true, but the Aurati also assist. In emergencies, we are the ones who keep communications open between villages. Aurati coordinate supplies and help with rebuilding. They are the glue that connects the empire."

She sounded like a recruitment speech, and I grimaced at how she'd used the word "we" to describe them.

Kaia continued. "You have to remember, Zefed isn't governed the same way that Ilvera is. It can be difficult for people to move up in the world. The Aurati provide one such way, especially for those who might otherwise feel out of place."

"But you keep overlooking that they *kill* initiates who can't pass their trials," I pointed out.

"They have secrets that need to be kept," Kaia parried. "Things more important than neighborhood gossip."

I laughed. "You can't possibly use that as a defense. Kaia, they stole a dragon—a *Verran dragon*—and kept her chained for generations. And they would have killed you, once they had the next Prophet secured."

I expected her to fire back at me, as she'd done when I'd asked about her injuries. Instead her shoulders sagged, and she looked away. "I don't know that you could understand."

I bit my lip. "I suppose you're right. I don't."

When disagreeing with Kaia, I was accustomed to giving in. In the past I had thought it was because she usually had the better argument. But maybe it was because she had always been more sure of herself, and spoke more stridently. Now I, too, was unwilling to back down, and I could not bring myself to agree with her position—no matter what she had seen while she had been one of them.

An image of the initiates buried by the collapsing stronghold flashed through my head, and I flinched. Was this what they had thought of the order they had joined? That the Aurati did right by them? That the empire was worthy of their service?

I swallowed hard and changed the subject. "Did you ask that woman where we are?"

She nodded. "There's a village ahead of us with an inn. We should arrive before nightfall. And this road eventually meets the highway that goes from Oskiath to Gedarin."

"Good." At least we were on course. While I was nervous about staying in highly trafficked areas, I knew I couldn't navigate the forest all the way back to Oskiath without a road. And we could not afford to waste time by getting lost. I thought back to the vision I'd had of Sev. He hadn't been lying in a dungeon, but I didn't think he was out of danger either.

It was getting close to evening, and the sky was clear. The haze of summer was heavy in the air, and the scent of sunwarmed earth rose up from the ground as we walked. We hadn't yet seen another traveler, but I warned the kit that she must stay close by and would have to go into the pack if we saw anyone. I let her roam freely otherwise. Soon she would be cooped up again, hiding from curious eyes. Better that she be allowed to run while she had the chance.

For a while we walked in silence, so I was taken by surprise when Kaia spoke.

"Look," she said, pointing to the sky. "What's that?"

It first appeared as a speck on the horizon, and for one instant I hoped against hope that Naava had returned to us. But the blurry dot quickly grew into a dragon bearing a rider—a Talon.

I whistled for the dragon kit, who ran to my side without hesitation.

"What do we do?" Kaia said.

I looked around frantically. We were alone on a dusty road with nowhere to hide. "I don't know."

Naava had broken the Talons' hold on their dragons by singing. She'd told me afterward that dragonsong required more strength than she had remaining, but she'd said nothing of whether other dragons might also have this ability—or what was required to unlock it.

We had a dragon. But was she strong enough? And did I dare put her in harm's way?

"*Maren*," Kaia said, her voice strained.

"I know, I know!"

We had minutes, if that. I crouched down beside the dragon kit, trying to keep my voice from trembling. "All right, little one," I said, taking one of her claws between my hands. "I should have talked to you earlier about this. But there's a dragon coming at us, and we don't have much time."

The dragon kit chirped curiously. She knew dragons to be friends, not adversaries.

"This dragon is . . . being held. Against its will. It may try to attack us, like the dragons we saw a few days ago. Do you think that you could help me free it?"

An expression crossed the kit's face that I would have described as wry amusement if I had seen it on a human. She sang her answer without hesitation. But did she really understand?

"You'll need to sing when the dragon lands, as loudly as you can." I hummed a few notes to demonstrate. The dragon kit echoed me, the song piercing through the air. I smiled. "Yes, just like that." I patted her head.

Kaia stepped closer. "Maren, have you completely lost your

senses? Your plan is to have the kit *sing* to them?" she asked incredulously.

"Naava did it. And the kit will be able to as well."

"But she's so *small*. Naava was enormous—she overpowered those other dragons. That's what you need, not just *any* dragon. This can't be your plan."

I shrugged helplessly. "I don't have another one. Do you?"

"I—I could act the Aurat again. I could tell the Talon that I've captured you, and then—"

"Then we'd be seized and dragged to Gedarin as captives," I said, cutting her off. "I can't risk that."

She grimaced but didn't push back. "Then you'd better be right about this."

I nodded. It would work.

At least, I was pretty sure it *could* work, under the correct circumstances. Naava may have had special power over the other dragons, but *dragonsong*, she'd said, was the way they communicated, in the purest sense. And both the kit and I remembered the way she had sung.

Of course, we would have to get close enough for the dragon kit to reach out to the other dragon before being roasted alive. I hoped the emperor had said that we were to be captured, not killed on sight.

Despite everything I knew about the way dragons were treated by Zefed, I would never be indifferent to the sight of a majestic, full-grown dragon soaring through the sky. The dragon circled us twice, in wide swoops, before landing a cautious distance away. Its scales were a deep red-brown, gleaming in the sun. Its rider raised their helmet, revealing the face of an older woman, her dark hair cut short. "By the decree of the emperor, lay down your weapons!" she called in Zefedi.

We had little by way of weapons—even the blade I'd taken from the Prophet was more ceremonial than functional—but she didn't know that. Kaia glanced at me.

"Put down your pack," I whispered in Verran, lowering mine to the ground. Nothing we had would be a help against dragon fire, anyway.

The dragon kit pressed up against my legs.

I laid one hand on her head. *Are you ready?*

A determined-sounding chirp came back to me.

You'll need to be quick, little one.

It was the most difficult thing, letting go of her. But the moment I lifted my hand, she jumped, surprising everyone with her motion. The other dragon reared up as the kit bounded forward. But just before the two collided, the kit screeched to a stop.

Something was wrong. The kit wasn't singing. In fact, she had frozen in her tracks, as if paralyzed by the dragon towering over her.

The Talon dismounted, and I started to run. If the Talon got the kit, I didn't know what I would do. I barreled into the rider before she could draw her sword, knocking us both to the ground.

We rolled, and I yanked her helmet back down over her face, blocking her vision. I grabbed her arm and wrenched it away from her side, breaking her grip on the hilt of the sword. The Talon punched me in the stomach with her other arm, and I fell back, gasping. I put my arms up, expecting another blow—but none came.

I lowered my arms to find that Kaia had gotten hold of the Talon's sword, and was holding it steadily over the woman on the ground.

"Get the kit," Kaia said, her gaze intent on the Talon. "Hurry."

I scrambled to my feet. The kit was cowering under the attentions of the Talon's dragon. It didn't seem to have made up its mind about what to do about the small creature standing before it, though I wasn't counting on that indecision lasting very long. I had only seconds to act, and only one thing I could think of to try. I stepped between the kit and the dragon.

The last time I had stood against a hostile dragon was when I'd faced down the Talons outside of Vir's Passage, but I had no oils now to tip the scales in my favor. Desperate, I took a deep breath. And then I sang.

The melody that Naava had sung to free the other dragons had been unlike any Verran song I knew, but still, it had sunk into my mind and stuck there. I could not sing in quite the same way as a dragon, but I did my best, weaving together nonsense phrases and snatches of other songs from my childhood to create a human pattern to bring order to the dragon melody.

The air between us stilled, like the calm before a storm. The dragon tilted its head, listening. I couldn't tell if the song was working, but at least the dragon had not yet attacked us. I could hear the Talon yelling as though from a great distance—I shut the sound out of my mind. Whatever I did, I could not stop singing. The dragon's head bowed, and I took a tentative step forward, then another. I was so close that I could feel the heat coming off the dragon's body in waves. Thin wisps of smoke rose from the dragon's nostrils. I put a hand out. Took another step. Raised my hand and tentatively brought it to rest on the bridge of the dragon's nose.

Confused consciousness sparked through me, and my vision fractured. I saw the dragon before me—but overlaid on that, an image of myself, small and bedraggled. My singing faltered, and the dragon tossed its—his—head, throwing me back.

I flew a few feet and landed hard on the road, losing my breath. Whatever connection I'd forged had been broken when my song stopped. The dragon opened his mouth, and I could smell smoke, could feel the impending flames—

The dragon kit sprang in front of me. She was singing now—a melody that was the twin of Naava's song—and the sound spilled over me, coating my senses like snow. She charged at the dragon as her song got higher, shriller, angrier. The dragon fell back onto all fours and stiffened, his spine arching. He bellowed, engulfing the kit in flame. I screamed—but the flames cut out, and the kit stood there unharmed.

The dragon shuddered and sat back on his hind legs. Slowly, he shook his head. And then he began to sing, his voice rising in a rusty crackle that mingled with the kit's song.

Kaia shrieked, and I looked over to see that the Talon had wrestled her sword back from Kaia. But instead of attacking either of us, the Talon ran for the dragon. She pulled up a sleeve and shoved her arm below the dragon's nose. I could smell the lavender oil on her skin. The dragon dutifully dipped his head down, and for a moment I thought all was lost. And then he bared his fangs and bit down on the Talon's arm.

The Talon screamed, falling to her knees. The dragon staggered back, as though surprised by what he had done. He thrashed, spilling his saddle to the ground, and then pushed off into the air. The dragon circled us once, bellowing fire. Then he shot like an arrow across the sky and away.

CHAPTER EIGHT

Sev

P iera Sil'Danne. I hadn't seen her in years, but I knew her in an instant.

She had almost married my brother, in another life. And in that life I had also been in love with her.

We'd grown up together in Ruzi. Her family was one of a small noble court that my father had kept, and despite the gap in our ages—she was five years my senior—she was my best friend, and she was kind, patient, and fiercely intelligent. As I grew older, I began to notice other things: the grace of her neck, the scent of the soap she used to wash her face, the way her voice brushed over my skin. But I was gawky and clumsy and still so young, and she was promised to Callum. Still I flirted, and she tolerated me tripping over my own feet when I asked her to dance. I could make her laugh, and when I did, it felt as though I could do anything.

After the emperor killed my father and brother, I thought I would never see her again. And I was right—save for one night.

I was fourteen. My mother and I had been in hiding for years by then, smuggled between friendly households every few months. But we'd been seen and reported, and had fled without a plan. The Sil'Dannes—a family known to be sympathetic to us, and under the Flame's surveillance because of it—were a last resort, a bed to sleep in for one night before flying once more into the storm.

We arrived under cover of darkness and were bundled quickly through the servants' corridor from one room to the next. The door to a hallway opened, and there she was, ringed in light. I hung back, reluctant to let Piera see me reduced to an outcast dressed in rags and covered in travel grime. But she ran toward us, and I was startled to see that she was crying. I was taller than she was now, and I ducked my head as she approached. Before anyone could protest, she raised herself up on her toes and kissed me on the cheek. I turned into a dumbfounded, sweating statue, my skin tingling long after she had been escorted away.

That was the last time I saw her. Two weeks later my mother was murdered. Not long after that I was found by the Dragons.

And sometime between then and now, she had become the empress of Zefed.

I watched her sweep across the floor with the emperor in a graceful dance. To an outside observer, they made an excellent pair. Both objectively attractive, their dark heads in perfect alignment as they turned. He was older than her, but not extremely so. And as she came from one of the disgraced noble families of Ruzi, it was an exceptional match for her.

How could I have been so careless to not have learned more about the empress? I grimaced. I had dug this hole for myself.

I picked up a glass of wine and downed its contents in one swig. Too late I remembered that Faris was watching me. My reaction to the empress would certainly be noted. Ah well, it couldn't be helped now.

Piera had a son, I knew that much. The emperor's heir was two years old. I wondered how the match had come to be. She hadn't needed to marry at all, and indeed, marriage was falling out of fashion among some of the younger nobles. But she had come close to marrying Callum. The emperor must have known that when he'd decided to propose. So why had he done it? And *how* could she have married him?

A servant refilled my glass, and I drained it again.

I needed to stop. *Now. Stop now.*

I needed to leave this place, but I could not. I needed to be seen enjoying myself. I was supposed to be a loyal citizen of the empire, loyal servant of Rafael, the Flame of the West.

I left my food at the table, swerved around a peacock, and set foot on the dance floor. The music had changed again, this time to a dance from Kyseal meant to be performed without partners. Lucky for me. I didn't think I could keep up my mask at close range. Besides, my broken fingers still ached badly enough that I'd rather not have put them in someone else's hand.

I joined the dance without too much trouble, although a wine-induced haze had fallen between me and the rest of the room. Still, I kept pace well enough, plastering some semblance of a smile onto my face and taking just enough care with my steps.

The song ended, and the room filled with applause. The clapping was loud and jarring, but just as I was turning to go, I felt something press against my side. I turned my head, but there was no one there—just shifting bodies leaving the dance behind.

I kept my expression even as I returned to stand by Faris

and discreetly touched my pocket. There was a telltale wrinkle. Someone had slipped me a note, and done so most expertly. I could not read it here—that would have to wait until I was back in my quarters.

The evening wore on, and I danced twice more before the pounding in my head threatened to incapacitate me. Was it possible that the music was getting louder as it grew later? The chamber was still full, but I hadn't seen the emperor or Piera in some time. I assumed they had retired. I leaned toward Faris. "Can we go now?"

"It's your decision," Faris said. "You are a prince, after all."

I couldn't bring myself to do anything other than scowl at her, consequences be hanged. "I'm beginning to think you've been employed to annoy me to death," I said.

The woman had the gall to laugh at me. "Fear not, shadow prince. You've stayed long enough."

The hallway outside was blessedly quiet, the lamps turned down to give the impression of intimacy. I wondered how many assignations had taken place in the alcoves that bordered the hall. And how many people had done so without realizing how exposed they were to observant eyes?

"What next?" I asked as we reached my door. Half-drunk as I might be, I had managed to memorize the way to my own chamber and was fairly confident I could navigate there on my own in the future, not that I would ever be allowed to walk through this palace unaccompanied.

Faris nodded to the two guards stationed outside the door. It was strange that the chamber was guarded even when I wasn't in it, but perhaps that was to prevent unplanned visits from anyone who might feel too sympathetic to my cause.

One guard opened the door, and I walked inside to find Rafael sitting in the receiving area.

I blinked slowly. This couldn't be a good sign. "What do you want?" I couldn't muster the energy—or control, really—to be properly deferential. Besides, he knew exactly how much loyalty I felt toward him.

"Feeling emboldened after the festivities, are you?" the emperor said. He had changed out of his court attire into a simple black tunic and trousers, his crown replaced by the more informal circlet. Here, in reasonable lighting, I could see the dark circles under his eyes and strands of gray hair threaded through the black. He looked tired . . . or worried. I suppressed a smile at the thought as he leaned back in his chair. "Faris, if you would be so kind," he said, waving a hand.

Faris placed a hand on my shoulder. A sudden, burning pain ignited in my hand, and I flinched, a short, surprised cry escaping my lips. It felt as though someone had taken hold of my fingers and wrenched them in exactly the same way they had been broken only days earlier. But my hand, when I held it up, appeared unchanged. Somehow, that made it even worse.

Bile rose up in my throat and I sank to my knees—and the pain dissipated abruptly. I fell over onto the floor, my ears ringing. Faris had barely even *touched* me, but somehow she'd done this?

Rafael rose from his chair and stood over me, resting one boot on top of my injured hand. "You would do well to remember that your continued existence depends entirely on my good will," he said softly. "You will give me the respect I am due as your emperor. Do you understand?"

He pressed down on my hand, and I clenched my jaw, trying not to cry out again.

The weight increased, and I whimpered. Fire ran up my arm. "Yes, Your Majesty," I said, forcing the words out past the pain.

"I didn't hear that," he said silkily.

Gods, was he going to crush my entire hand? Spots were hovering in my vision, I was sure I was about to vomit, Tera's bones, the pain—*Please*," I hissed, "please, Your Illustrious Excellence, benevolent-Flame-of-the-West-father-of-Zefed-please—"

"That's better," he said, lifting his foot just enough to free my hand.

I rolled away from him, gasping in relief as I curled around my arm.

"For reasons that escape me, the peasantry have adopted you as the figurehead for their ridiculous demands. Your performance tonight was adequate, but you will have to do more to convince the citizens of Zefed of your loyalty. Tomorrow there will be a parade through Irrad. You will smile and wave to the people. You will make them believe that you've renounced your unfortunate upstart ways completely. You will show them unequivocally where your loyalties lie."

I got slowly to my feet. I was afraid of speaking, but I had to know something. "What about my friends?" I asked quietly. "I agreed to this deal because you promised to keep them out of harm's way. To pardon them."

"Did I?" Rafael brushed invisible dirt from his sleeve and looked around the room with distaste, as though he had not specifically chosen this chamber for me. "Well, we'll see how well you perform tomorrow."

He swept from the room without another word, leaving me alone with Faris. I let myself fall into the nearest chair. "So you're a walking torture device," I said.

She spread her hands but made no apology. "Do you think the emperor would have handed you over to just any Aurat?"

Maren feared the Aurati like no other. She'd been more frightened to walk into Lumina than to thumb her nose at the emperor himself, but she'd done it anyway. My feelings had always been more complicated. The Aurati were an institution of the empire, but they were not necessarily *evil*. Of course, that had been before I knew that at least some of the terrifying powers they were rumored to have were real.

"You could have been honest about it."

"And ruin such a good surprise?" She nodded toward the bed. "You'd better get some sleep. Tomorrow's a big day."

I had a feeling that all of my days from now on would be *big days*. Because every single one would involve walking a tightrope and hoping that I did nothing to offend the emperor. The emperor of Zefed, who was famously erratic and might change his mind at any time, for any reason.

Faris left the room, and I heard the door lock behind her. I waited a few moments, just in case there were to be any more surprises tonight. But after I heard her footsteps retreat from the room, I bent over at the waist, a sob wrenching through my entire body.

I had trained with Brika's kiss. I had prepared myself for the possibility of torture. I had withstood years of hiding, days of darkness in that dank cell, the guards breaking my fingers, swearing false fealty, the emperor laughing at me like I was an amusing child. But something had snapped when he'd touched me, his boot grinding my hand into the floor. In that instant, I was viscerally reminded that I was no longer living in the dream of revenge. This was reality, my endgame, and I was losing. My adversary no longer existed only in theory—and at any given moment I was one word away from dead.

I had crumbled so easily. I wasn't worthy of my parents' name. I certainly wasn't worthy of the adulation that had been heaped onto the legend of the shadow prince of Ruzi—I was a joke, a pathetic, shaking, crying human body just like the countless others broken before me. Now I was afraid I might give in to anything, anything at all, under enough pressure. I was defeated and utterly alone.

No. I still had Maren and the dragon kit. *If they even choose to come for me at all,* I thought bitterly. I could not pretend that Maren cared for me in the same way that she loved her heartmate.

After a while my body stopped shaking. Exhausted, I stood up, kicking off my shoes and loosening my clothing before collapsing backward onto the bed.

Something crinkled as I moved—the note in my pocket. The evening's performance already felt so distant, I'd forgotten all about it. I started to reach for the paper before wondering whether I had actually been correct in my assessment that there were no spy holes in this room.

As a precaution, I got up and staggered into the bathing area. It was an enclosed space—the best I could do, outside of climbing into my wardrobe with a candle. I tried to be nonchalant as I took off my jacket and hunched over, palming the paper out of the pocket. My heart skipped a beat as I studied it.

As children, Piera and I had delighted in making up codes and passwords to keep our correspondence secret, one of which was a particular way of folding paper to form a self-enclosed envelope. Like the one I now held in my hand. The only other person who had ever learned how to do it was Callum.

So Piera *had* seen me in court. I wanted to tear open the note but restrained myself. If I were to write back, I would need to reuse the paper.

I unfolded it gently and smoothed it out in the candlelight.

Tomorrow. Garden of Hearts, after supper. —P

What did she want? Could this be a trap?

Anything could be a trap . . . but the emperor already had me, I reasoned. Besides, Piera was the only potential ally I had. Despite the fact that the Dragons supposedly had a presence here at court, none of them had made an attempt to reach out to me today.

Perhaps I was making excuses, but I couldn't deny that the note had lifted my spirits. I wanted to see her. The only question was how.

CHAPTER NINE

Maren

We had done it. We had *freed a dragon!*

My excitement dimmed only as I watched the dragon kit chirping in frustration as she ran after the dragon, her wings flapping. Would she try to fly away from me one day? I had to admit that this was a possibility, especially as she grew older. And that frightened me so much more than I could say. In the short time we'd known each other, she'd twined her way irrevocably around my heart. I couldn't pretend that we would be together for always. But I wasn't ready to let go of her yet.

I called for her before turning my attention to the fallen Talon, who lay on the side of the road, cradling her bleeding arm. She scrambled away from me as I approached, her expression terrified.

"Wait—" I said, but she got to her feet and ran.

My hand strayed to my belt, to the knife that hung there. If we let her get away, everyone in the empire would know exactly where we were, and what we had done. I took a step to follow her, but stopped as Kaia's hand fell heavy on my arm. "Don't," she said. "Look at what she left."

There on the ground was the dragon's saddle. Tied to it was

an oilskin, so large, its contents would have overflowed the pot my father used to make family stew.

I frowned and went to inspect it. The stopper came out easily, and I sniffed tentatively.

Lavender and mirth wood oil. But there was something off about its scent. It reminded me of my own crude attempts at creating the oils. I doubted Neve had had anything to do with manufacturing this oil. But who else in the empire knew anything about the making of the oils? And why did they need so much of it?

The answer suddenly came to me. *Naava*. The Talon must have been sent to subdue her. And if there was one Talon, there would soon be more. If they found Naava they would try to capture her again, to subject her to another hundred years of servitude.

Everything I had done would be a waste.

My jaw clenched. I wasn't certain I could stop that from happening, but at the very least, I could ensure they would not be able to use this oil for their schemes. "Keep the dragon kit back," I said to Kaia. I drew my knife and cut through the oilskin, stepping back as the oil seeped out and sank into the earth, useless. Then I cast my vision skyward. I had to hope that Naava had reached Ilvera and found a safe place to recuperate. *Don't come back*, I thought.

There was a flap of wings above us, and Kaia and I looked up to see that the freed dragon had returned. We watched as he passed overhead, flying toward Gedarin and the village that we could see in the far distance. The dragon swooped low and sent forth a billow of flame, engulfing the fields.

The dry, sunburned grass lit quickly, and my breath caught in my chest. A dragon on the loose was one thing, but an enraged beast bent on destruction at all costs?

Kaia and I sprinted toward the village without speaking, the kit running ahead of us.

Soon we could smell the smoke and hear the panicked cries of people fleeing from the flames. This was a farming village. These people were equipped to deal with deer or rabbits getting into their fields, not a rogue dragon of the realm. They would have no idea how to counter such force—or even that it was acceptable to do so.

In all honesty, I wasn't sure what to do either. We slowed to a halt once we got near. The heat was blistering, the earth cracking under our feet, and the flames were higher than our heads, painting a hopeless picture against the darkening sky. Kaia squeezed my hand. "I'm going to help the villagers," she shouted over the noise, pointing to the house closest to us.

I nodded and looked down at the dragon kit. Any paralysis she had suffered when first dealing with the dragon seemed to have dissipated. She snorted and let out a piercing whistle that cut through the air without effort. The dragon, who had landed on the other side of the field, looked up. He was bellowing flame in every direction, but the kit had gotten his attention.

"You! Over here!" I waved my arms, trying to draw him in our direction. There was a river nearby—we had crossed it this morning. If we could lure the dragon there, that would be a safer environment in which to confront him.

The dragon hesitated, then came our way, cutting through the flames. In his wake ran villagers, flinging buckets of water at the growing fire. At least they had a trench dug between the fields and their houses—but all of their fields were going to be trampled or burned.

I hope you know what you're doing, I told myself as I sprinted toward the river.

I could feel heat against my neck, an all too familiar sensation for me these days. The dragon was gaining on us. I scrambled down the riverbank, skidding to a halt. Then I turned to face the dragon.

"Stop!" I shouted, throwing up a hand—as though that would deter him in the least.

Miracle of miracles, the dragon slowed. But that might have had more to do with the river than me.

I had only seconds to calm him. I planted my feet in the riverbed and reached for one of the oldest songs I knew—a Verran lullaby about climbing a mountain. My mother had sung it to me when I was growing up. My voice was hoarse from smoke and overuse, but I sang anyway. *Listen. Listen to me.*

The dragon stared at me from across the river. The dragon kit climbed up my legs and settled on my shoulder, staring back. Still, I sang.

He wasn't flaming anymore, which I took to be a good sign, but I didn't dare stop the song. When we had first freed the dragon from the Talon's influence, I had connected with his mind without meaning to. All I had done was sing—and touch him.

Did I dare leave the river? The dragon could annihilate me with one well-placed blast of fire or swipe of his claws. And he did seem wary of me, his eyes narrowed. We were at an impasse, and I could not continue singing forever.

The kit was a comforting presence on my shoulder as I kept my eyes locked on the dragon's. I reached the end of the lullaby, and as I circled back to the beginning, I heard the kit join in with me, matching my pitch.

I took one slow step toward the dragon. The river stones shifted below my feet, and I staggered, then paused. I waited, still singing. The dragon watched me, his wings spread menacingly. Then I moved again, until I was out of the river and climbing the bank, each step bringing me closer to the dragon.

When I was finally close enough to touch him, I hesitated—then I raised my hand.

No. The word was cracked and hoarse and angry.

I froze. Had the dragon *spoken?*

Hello? I cast out the question like a net into the sea between us.

His reply was instant. *Do not. Touch. Me.*

A chill swept through me. The only other dragon who had spoken directly to me was Naava. To be honest, I hadn't been sure that the other dragons could speak with humans at all. I had to be very careful. I wanted to converse with the dragon, but it was difficult to do so while I was singing. And if I wasn't singing, I wasn't sure that he would remain peaceful.

I won't, I said, lowering my hand. *I only want to talk to you. Will you speak with me?*

The dragon did not answer, but after a moment he folded his wings and backed up a few paces, giving me more room on the riverbank. I took this to be tacit agreement. So I braced myself and stopped singing. The dragon kit leaped to the ground, taking a protective stance in front of me. The older dragon snorted, as if amused.

What are you? the dragon asked, surprising me. *Humans do not sing in dragon tongue, but you do. And you travel with a dragon who has not been—* The dragon made a sound that I did not understand. At the confusion on my face, he rephrased. *Your dragon is not bound to a human. Your dragon is free.*

"I am human," I said, speaking aloud. "But our bond is not forced by the oils. I'm from Ilvera. I was . . . given a gift." A very incomplete answer, but it seemed simpler than trying to explain everything that had happened to me since Naava had slipped into my consciousness and I had left Ilvera.

And what have you done to me? I do not feel the— He made the same indecipherable sound, something I now took by context to signify the bond forged by mirth wood oil between the dragons and Talons.

"We tried to break it," I replied. "Did it work? Are you free from the Talon's control?"

The dragon huffed, and I realized too late that, though it was important to know, I might have phrased the question more tactfully.

It must be true, he said slowly. *The Talon would never allow me to burn a human village without her direction.* As if remembering that he had until quite recently been doing exactly that, smoke began to rise from his nostrils once more.

"Please don't do that," I said quickly. "I realize that I cannot control your actions. But these are innocent people. They did not have a hand in your captivity."

One could argue about whether this statement was absolutely true, but these people did not deserve to have their lives go up in smoke for the crime of being born in an empire that treated dragons this way.

Then what shall I do? the dragon said. There was something strange and plaintive about a large beast, so fearsome and powerful, at a loss for what to do next. But I understood. His actions had been dictated by Talons his entire life. Though he had gained his autonomy, he did not know what to do with it. He needed guidance.

"I traveled here with another dragon," I said. "Naava. She is very old, and very powerful. From before your time, I should think."

Naava. The dragon's voice was hushed, reverent. *The mother. We still sing of her.*

"Yes. She has returned to the mountain above the place where you were hatched. Ilvera. Do you know the way?"

He looked down upon me haughtily. *I was flying these lands before you were born. Of course I know the way.*

"If you go to her, she will welcome you." We had never spoken explicitly of such things, but I was sure Naava would help any dragon who found her.

The dragon kit chirped in agreement. Apparently having decided that this new dragon was to be trusted, she trotted forward and sniffed at his claws. The dragon looked down at the kit, his expression bemused.

"She likes you," I said.

I never spent much time with hatchlings, the dragon replied. He whistled to the kit, who sang a little tune back to him.

Suddenly I wished this dragon would stay by our side. He was more than a match for any threat we might encounter on the road. Naava had admonished me for assuming that I could use the dragons to my own end. But what if one chose freely to travel with us?

"If I may," I said. The dragon looked back at me, and I bit my lip before continuing. "My quest is to free the dragons of Ilvera, as we have done for you. But it is a dangerous path, and we could use assistance. We would welcome your company."

He paused before answering. *A worthy quest, but I tire of humans. I will go to Ilvera.*

I tried not to feel too disappointed by his refusal. "I understand. If that's the case, you had better get going." Once the fire was contained, Kaia would come looking for me—and the villagers wouldn't be far behind. I didn't know what would happen if the dragon were still here when they came. "But before you leave—what name may I know you by?"

The dragon nodded. *I am Glivven. And you?*

"Maren ben Gao Vilna. Of Ilvera."

And your dragon?

The kit looked up at us.

"She hasn't told me her name yet," I said, feeling a twinge of embarrassment.

Glivven leaned down, putting his head at the same level as the kit's. He sang to her softly, and the kit responded in kind. Then he looked back up to me. *She will, when she's ready.*

He shooed the kit gently away with his nose, and then spread his vast wings. *I will see you again, Maren ben Gao Vilna, daughter of Ilvera.*

I raised my hand as he launched into the air, circled twice, then turned to the south. Soon he was a blotch on the surface of the sky, shrinking quickly. Part of me still wished he had chosen to stay with us, but as I watched him fly toward Ilvera, an unexpected burst of elation swelled in my chest. Naava had told me to prove myself, that if I did so, I would have her help. And in this moment, I was certain that this was what she had meant.

I turned back toward the village, whistling to the dragon kit. But as we climbed the riverbank, my legs began to shake. Suddenly there was a roaring in my ears, and I stumbled as I crested the top of the riverbank—and fell.

CHAPTER TEN

Sev

When I open my eyes, I don't immediately understand what I'm seeing.

Maren. Maren, standing in a wide field of light, her long hair flowing out around her face. I reach out a hand, and she steps toward me—out of the light and into my arms. We embrace, and I'm surprised by the way she wraps her arms tightly around me. This cannot be real.

"I'm dreaming." I must be, if she is here, with me.

"A true dream," she says, and then, as if something is dawning on her, "A dragon dream."

"What?"

Her entire demeanor changes. She draws back, speaking quickly. "We don't have much time. Where are you?" She looks around, as though trying to draw a conclusion from what little there is to see in this one room.

"The emperor's palace in Irrad. I'm being forced to play the part of a loyal prince. Where are you? Are you with the dragon?" I say.

"Of course!" Maren says. Then, "Wait—which one?"

"The one that destroyed Lumina," I reply. "They're talking about it here."

The corners of her mouth pull down. "Naava is gone. I'm with

Kaia and the dragon kit. I'm not sure where we are now." She looks around. "Somewhere in Oskiath, south of Belat Forest. A small village. But are you all right?"

Am I all right? I can't answer that question. She must see something in my expression, though.

"Sev, what is it?" she asks, her voice skating across my skin. I want so much to hold her again—but if this is a true dream, then I can't have her. She must notice the splints on my hand because she exclaims, "And what happened to your hand?"

"Don't worry about me," I say, brushing off my longing. "But the emperor is hunting you."

She shakes her head. "We're coming for you. Hold on."

I fell out of dreaming and into the waking world.

The sounds of rattling and running feet came down from the rooms above mine. Who would be running in the palace at this hour, and for what purpose? But that was a minor question compared to the bafflement I felt in the aftermath of my dream.

I'd experienced something similar yesterday, a flash of vision that had disappeared as quickly as it had come. With everything else that had happened, I hadn't given it further thought. But now . . . What had that been? Maren had called it a dragon dream. I wasn't familiar with the term, but it seemed to be some strange bridging of the minds, such that I could see her truly, wherever she was. I was almost breathless as I considered the possibility. Such a power, if real, could be invaluable.

It had been so *good* to see Maren, who was by all appearances well, though there had been a smudge of dirt on her face I would have given much to wipe off with my thumb. *We're coming for you.*

Her promise washed away my despair from the previous night.

I slid out of bed and availed myself of the bathing chamber before I remembered Piera's note. I took the paper out of my pocket and unfolded it once more. I considered my options. It was too dangerous to carry the note with me, but I couldn't leave it here, either.

Did I really need to reply? Either I would appear in the gardens tonight or I would not. The reward of being able to send a message did not outweigh the risk I took to keep the note until I had need of the paper. So I ripped it into small pieces and shoved them into my mouth, and grimaced as I swallowed. Just in time, as the door opened on the other side of the curtain and someone entered the chamber.

I peeked out from behind the curtain to see a servant set a platter of food down on the table. I waited until he had left before sitting down. I wasn't hungry, but today would be full of trials. My body needed fuel.

I had eaten almost a full plate of rice and pickled vegetables when I realized that there was something under one of the serving plates, tucked so neatly out of the way that I had almost missed it. I lifted the edge of the plate carefully and palmed the item, then hid it underneath the surface of the table.

It was a flower petal, large and white—a Rima flower. If I crushed it in my fist, it would release a sweet, tangy scent into the air. The Dragons were finally reaching out to me. The petal was to open communication, a request to the receiver for information. They had not included anything that indicated that a rescue mission was in play. Perhaps that would have been too dangerous a message to send, but my more cynical side wondered if they intended to rescue me at all.

I shouldn't have felt so resentful, but I did nevertheless. Maren's words had stung when she had criticized the Dragons. It had been easy to join them when they had been a convenient vehicle for my desire for revenge. But during the time I'd spent with Maren, I had come to believe in something better than the continuation of the empire and the exploitation of the dragons.

But beggars couldn't be choosers, even if it looked like I was on my own as far as any escape plans went. *Maren.* I inhaled sharply, reminding myself. She was coming for me. If I believed the dream had been true—and if I believed she would make it. Getting into the emperor's palace was not the same as infiltrating Lumina. And she was alone now, except for the kit and Kaia. I could hope, but I could not plan on her. I slipped the petal into my pocket and returned to my wardrobe to select an outfit for the day.

I was surprised when Faris appeared with a jacket over her arm. She unfolded it and held it up. It was bright red and studded with clear jewels that winked in the light—gaudy enough to compete with anything I had seen at the gathering last night. She had also brought a new pair of shoes to match. They were flimsy palace slippers, not made for anything more strenuous than lounging. Together these would be enough to make me out to be just the sort of pandering prince I had always despised. Perhaps the simple act of wearing them would be enough to convince anyone who saw me that I was not the correct candidate to carry their banner against the emperor.

I took the clothing and retreated into the bedroom to change.

Once I was ready, we left my chambers—how quickly I was beginning to think of them as *my* chambers—and proceeded to the front of the palace. An array of armed guards fell in line behind the two who had been guarding my door.

"Don't you think I should be armed?" I said. "I mean, the emperor seems to think that all of this security is necessary."

Faris laughed. "Nice try."

"I'm serious. As a prince, I will be expected to wear a blade in public. Do you want me to look like a prisoner to them?" I hid a smile as I watched her consider. I was right, and she knew it.

She paused, then told one of the guards to give me a small dagger and a belt.

"This is a child's knife," I protested, fumbling to secure the belt around my waist. The healer's ministrations had accelerated the healing process, but my injured hand still made me clumsy.

"And it's all you're going to get," Faris said. "Come along."

The palace doors were heavy and required the full force of four men, two on each side, to push open. I imagined that stepping forth from within them would make me feel lighter, but instead there was only dread as I saw what awaited me.

Rafael stood in an open carriage, an unexpectedly pleasant smile on his face. It took a moment to see why—the courtyard was large, but the gates leading into the city proper were made of iron bars, and there was an audience of commoners outside. They were all silent.

The emperor's was the second carriage in a parade of six, each led by a team of four horses. Foot soldiers stood at attention around each carriage. Acutely aware of the observers, I stopped a safe distance from the emperor and executed an extravagant bow. Rafael inclined his head magnanimously. I watched him notice my knife, then glance at Faris.

He frowned minutely, but raised a hand and bade me approach. One of the guards opened the carriage door and bowed as I passed him and stepped up. Besides the emperor and me, there were four more in the carriage: three guards and an unfamiliar Aurat. The only empty space was next to Rafael himself, and I settled into it reluctantly.

"My emperor," I said through clenched teeth.

Being this close to him after last night made my injured hand tremble, and I hated it, hated the fear that had crept into my body without permission.

I wanted to take my dagger and stab him through the neck, though if I did, I would not leave this place alive. More and more, this seemed like the inescapable ending foretold by the Aurati. *By the shadow prince's hand the flame will fall.* They had said nothing about what would happen afterward.

But instead of reaching for the blade, I thought of Maren— the fierce determination in her eyes as she'd vowed to come for me. So I forced my hand to loose its grip, to wave at the crowd. The foot soldiers marched out in front of us, clearing the road for drummers and dancers waving red and silver ribbons. The carriages crawled forward.

The emperor leaned toward me, keeping his voice low. "Remember, you are a representative of the empire. Smile."

We passed through the gates and into Irrad. The city had been designed in concentric circles around the emperor's palace and grounds, which stood fortified with walls and gates and guards. The streets were populated by Gedarin nobility, many of whom lined the parade route, clapping politely. They looked loyal enough to my untrained eye, if not particularly enthused.

Of course they would support him, if not because of loyalty, then because of their own security. The emperor was seizing food and resources from the poor, not the wealthy. The nobility would have no reason to complain, because they were not the ones under threat.

Rafael raised a hand, and the procession halted. The drummers stopped, and silence fell in their stead. The emperor stood, glancing at me. I did the same. All eyes were on us.

"My people, we have been blessed by the recovery of one of our own, a citizen I long thought was lost," the emperor shouted. He grabbed my hand and held it up. "I give you Vesper Severin Avidal, prince of Ruzi, by my side once more!"

Vesper. I couldn't contradict him in front of an audience, so instead I waved as the carriage trundled forward, plastering a smile on my face. The crowd applauded loudly. There were only a few scattered cheers, something I took as an indication of the general conduct of this district rather than a statement of how excited they were, or weren't, by my appearance.

The sun shone brightly in my eyes, making me squint, but I smiled and waved nonetheless. It didn't seem as though the emperor expected more from me, which was a relief as we moved into the next district, which housed mostly merchants and highly skilled artisans—still wealthy, still complacent. The quality of the roads did not change as we moved farther away from the center of the city. The buildings, on the other hand, did. They grew taller and thinner, the space between them shrinking from elaborate gardens to narrow alleys. Every so often the carriages would halt for the emperor to repeat his speech. And every time I smiled and waved in the same way.

More people crowded the parade route as we reached the poorer districts, waving Zefedi flags without much muster. It seemed likely they had been bribed or threatened to appear. They were quiet, too—sullen and ragged and watchful. These were the peasants who frightened the emperor. The movement rising against him had a presence here, I was certain of it. That soldiers in uniform and several Aurati were dispersed throughout the crowd made it clear that the emperor knew it as well. And I had been tasked with convincing them that their mythical hope did not exist.

We reached the market gates, and the carriages stopped once more. Rafael rose to his feet, and I rose mechanically next to him. By this time I wasn't even listening to the speech—the sound and timing of it had sunk into my consciousness, so I was surprised when I realized the emperor had fallen silent and was looking at me expectantly.

"Um—"

"Address the people," he whispered, barely moving his lips.

So it was as I'd suspected—the wealthier districts we'd passed hadn't mattered. *This* was the real test. My speech from the palace last night wouldn't convince many people here. *Think.* What would a truly loyal subject say?

"People of Irrad," I called. "We face . . . troubling times. But our emperor, the Flame of the West, has guided us in ways no one else could have done. Today is a day for unity!"

I cleared my throat, unsure of what to say next. It was sickening enough that I'd been forced to say that much.

Out of the corner of my eye I saw something fly toward us and I ducked. It fell short, thwacking against the siding of the emperor's carriage. Only then did I see that it was a rotten cabbage. We watched it roll to a stop on the ground in silence.

One man's voice called out, "Down with the tyrant! Down with the pretender prince!"

Almost immediately more voices joined his, resolving into a chant. "Down with the emperor! Down with the tyrant!"

Tyrant. Only Maren had consistently called Rafael a tyrant. I'd rarely heard the word out of the mouth of a Zefedi. But here they were, and they were angry enough to risk the emperor's ire firsthand. The soldiers rattled through the crowd, but it was of no use—the chant spread like wildfire, rising up into a wall of sound assaulting us from every side.

I looked at the emperor. He was still smiling, but his eyes had turned cold and cruel. He raised a hand to his lips and let out a whistle that pierced through the shouts. For a moment there was no response. Then two Talons streaked across the sky overhead. They circled once, then landed atop buildings on either side of the parade route, staring down at us like birds of prey selecting their next targets.

"Silence!" he shouted.

The quiet that followed was absolute.

Rafael's personal guard pushed through the crowd, though I didn't know how they were going to identify the cabbage thrower. Everyone in this district looked the same: angry, underfed, and overworked. In the distance I could hear the sounds of the army training on the beaches, the call of seabirds.

Soon the guards returned, dragging one unlucky person to

stand at the front of the crowd—a young man in a faded and torn army uniform, his face like stone.

The emperor raised his hands. "One of my own has returned to me, the lost prince of Ruzi, Vesper himself. And this is how you show your gratitude, your respect?"

Oh no. I knew what was coming, but there was no way to avoid it.

The Flame of the West dismounted from the carriage and beckoned to me. I moved woodenly after him. Once we stood before the man, the emperor turned to me, and I could see the malice and glee in his eyes. He was *enjoying* this. Cold understanding hit me like a blow. The night at court, the waves and speeches, all meant nothing. What was about to happen—*this* was the price of proving my loyalty.

The emperor took a sword from a nearby soldier and held it out to me. "Prince Vesper, I charge you to dispense justice on my behalf. Execute this man for treason against the crown, immediately."

I sat up, breathless. In my dream, Sev had seen me—we had spoken, we had *touched*. And Sev was *alive*, and at least seemed to be in one piece. That in itself was an enormous relief, but I had heard tension in his voice—seen him hesitate. He'd been holding something back. But what?

The dragon kit chirped beside me, and I looked at her. "How are you doing this, little one?" If she and I were able to maintain this connection, maybe I could have more dreams with Sev. We might be able to coordinate in the future—strategize or—

A door creaked, and I looked around, suddenly aware of the fact that I was sitting on a cot in what appeared to be a barn, and the light outside was bright. Panic flooded my body. I'd lost hours, at the very least—the last thing I remembered was speaking with Glivven, and then collapsing . . .

Kaia peeked her head around the barn door and, seeing that I was awake, ran to my side. "Maren!"

"Kaia! What happened?"

She sat next to me, taking my hand. "I don't know what you said to the dragon, but it left. You collapsed coming back over the hill. Some of the villagers carried you here, and you've been asleep since last night."

So I'd only lost one night—that was a relief. "Where are we now? What time is it?" I said.

She waved away the questions. "We can talk about that later. First, tell me. How are you feeling? Are you ill? Injured?"

I paused, taking stock of my body. I felt tired and bruised, but otherwise relatively normal. "I feel fine," I said. "Hungry."

"Then I don't understand," Kaia said. "Why did you faint? Was it something to do with the dragon?"

I shook my head. "I don't know. But, Kaia, I dreamed something important."

"Dragon dreams?" Kaia grimaced, and I remembered the argument we'd had the last time I'd brought up dragon dreams and what I'd seen in them.

"Yes, but these are different. I saw Sev—he's alive, and we were able to talk to each other. He's in the emperor's palace *right now*."

"I see," Kaia said slowly. She picked at the blanket with one hand, unraveling a loose thread. "And you're certain that these visions are real?"

"I can't explain it, but yes," I said. I glanced away, my cheeks warming as I remembered the way Sev and I had held each other in the dream.

"Then that's good news," she said, a little too brightly. "Didn't you say that you were hungry? Let's get you some breakfast."

My stomach grumbled, as though it had been listening for an opportune break in the conversation. But the prospect of food only reminded me that I still didn't know where we were.

"From where?" I asked. "What happened while I was asleep?"

"We're in the village. Everyone is alive, and the houses survived, thanks to you. They invited us to take shelter with them.

I thought it was prudent, given the circumstances."

I felt as though she had poured ice water over my head. "But, Kaia—they're *Zefedi*."

"You need to stop saying that like it's a bad thing," she retorted. "We saved their village from a rampaging dragon. They wanted to thank us, and what was I supposed to do? Carry you on my back through the wilderness? Not everyone is a spy for the emperor, Maren."

"But the dragon kit—"

"She will be fine," Kaia said firmly. "Please, just come meet them. You'll see there's nothing to worry about."

Too hungry and fatigued to argue further, I allowed Kaia to help me up. The dragon kit jumped up to my shoulder, and we all emerged from the barn together.

The morning air was cool, and I crossed my arms, rubbing warmth into them. Kaia led the way around the houses toward the center of the village. I smelled the fire before I saw the communal fire pit and the people standing around it. They were singing as we approached, a Zefedi folk song that bore some resemblance to a Celet melody I'd learned as a child. But when they saw us coming, they quieted, parting to create a path to the center of the crowd.

The attention made me nervous. For so long my survival had depended on my ability to pass unnoticed, to hide in plain sight. Now these people knew what I looked like and what I had done. Any one of them could identify me to the Talons. But their silence as we passed didn't seem threatening. It felt . . . reverent.

We went to one of the long tables surrounding the fire pit, and I dropped onto the bench in front of it. The dragon kit jumped down from my shoulder and sat beside me. Someone put a bowl of soup in front of me with a crust of slightly stale bread, and I fell upon it ravenously, all other concerns pushed aside.

The soup was peasant fare but well made and hearty, thick with lentils and carrots and rich in flavor. When I finished the bowl, another was set in front of me, and it was only when I was halfway through that one that I reluctantly looked up.

Our table was surrounded by villagers whose expressions ranged from suspicious to curious to slightly awed, their attention split between me and the dragon kit. I set the crust of bread down slowly. I only had the one knife. What would I do if the crowd decided to turn on us? The dragon kit snatched up the bread, and I put an arm protectively around her.

Kaia, standing next to me, didn't seem to share my concerns. She smiled genuinely—even eagerly—at our audience. Compared to her I was suddenly very aware of how ill-mannered I must have appeared, to have eaten without speaking to anyone first.

"This is the village of Lynd," Kaia said in Zefedi. She gestured to a young man standing at her side. "If it's all right, they have some questions." She put a hand on my shoulder, squeezing encouragingly.

"Um, I suppose," I said, most eloquently.

At Kaia's behest, the young man—a boy, really, a year or two younger than us—circled the table and sat down across from me. He had a pleasant, open face and an easy smile. He looked at Kaia again and then at me.

"Are you a Talon?" he asked. "How did you control that dragon?"

I started to snap out a reply, but then stopped. I should have expected this. These people were far removed from Talons. They were mostly of Celet heritage, not Old Zefedi, and they cared about their village and their family and their well-being. Most of them probably had never seen a dragon up close—their only knowledge of the beasts came from the official stories disseminated by the emperor. Why should it even occur to them to consider that a dragon might fly free, of its own accord?

"I'm not a Talon," I said. "And I didn't control the dragon."

"Then what made it stop the attack?"

There was no getting around this. Talon I might not be, but the fact that I could talk to dragons was *special*. Besides, there was no hiding who we were. Any of the emperor's servants would be able to track us just by asking about a girl with a dragon kit. Telling these people who I was—who I really was—would make little difference now.

"I spoke to the dragon, and he agreed to leave the village."

Shocked gasps spread throughout the crowd. "But how? If you're not a Talon?"

I set my hands on the table before me, palms down. The dragon kit nudged her nose up under one of my arms. "In truth, I don't know exactly. But we are from Ilvera. Before the empire of Zefed was founded, we were the dragon riders. I believe that my ability is connected to my heritage."

The boy held up a hand and called for a drink, then turned back to me. "Tell us," he said. The air was still, as though every person in the audience was holding their breath. And for the first time, I began to believe that there was something to be gained here, something more than food and shelter for the night. If I could change their understanding, I could weaken the tyrant's grip on the dragons, and on Zefed.

So I took the wine that was offered to me, and I told them everything. The truth about the dragons' origin. That the Talons did not have mystical bonds with their beasts—that their control was dependent on the dragons being drugged into a stupor. That the dragons were highly intelligent creatures and didn't deserve to be captives of the emperor.

I didn't know if they agreed with me, but they asked questions, here and there. A few of them wanted to touch the dragon kit. The kit humored them easily enough, though she stayed close to my side. And they *listened*.

Kaia retreated from the circle as the conversation progressed, and I saw her sitting by the fire, speaking with some of the villagers. In between questions I watched her. She smiled and laughed easily, with more light than I had seen from her since I had rescued her from Lumina. It was difficult to describe the uncomfortable swirl of emotions this stirred within me. Relief to see her smiling. Concern, that she interacted so easily with people who could be dangerous to us. And a strange pang of envy, that she was so comfortable in an empire I had only experienced as a fugitive.

Sometime later, I found I was barely able to keep my eyes open. Despite the worthy conversation and the fact that I had slept through the night, I still felt exhausted. "I'm sorry," I said, interrupting a question about a dragon's lifespan. "I'm not feeling well—please excuse me."

The boy—Avery—made sure I had enough blankets and pointed me back in the direction of the barn in which I'd woken.

I didn't even have the energy to look for Kaia—I couldn't stand to be upright a moment longer.

There was a bucket of clean water in the corner of the barn, and I used it to wash my face and what parts of my body I could manage without taking off my clothing. The dragon kit snuggled into a loose pile of hay, and I flopped down onto the cot beside her. Though my limbs felt as heavy as lead, my mind was racing.

Up until now, I had approached the problem of freeing dragons as though it were as simple as finding the correct key to a door. I had not considered the fact that each of these dragons was as individual as any human. I had gotten lucky, after all, that Glivven had allowed me to converse with him and had gone along with my suggested course of action. What would happen to the rest of the dragons when we freed them? What if they didn't agree with what I asked of them? I could not seek to assert control over them. That would only lead to disaster. Humans were not meant to control dragons. History had borne that out clearly enough.

And what of the words that Glivven had used to describe the Talons' bond with the dragons? They had not been in any language I understood, which could only mean that dragons could communicate between themselves without human interference. That wasn't surprising, considering how intelligent they were. But when they were under the influence of the mirth wood oil, what did that communication consist of? Did dragons who were drugged understand that they were not free? I wished I'd asked Glivven before he left.

At that moment I heard the barn door open and looked up to see Kaia entering.

I turned to face her as she lay down beside me. "Hello," I whispered.

"Hello to you, too," she said back, a smile glimmering on her face in the light that shone through the cracks in the barn wall. "Are you all right? Avery said you weren't well."

"I'm exhausted—I slept all night, but I still feel as though I could sleep until next week."

Kaia frowned. "Perhaps freeing the dragon took a toll on your body?" she said uncertainly.

"Maybe . . ." I reached for her, running my fingertips down her arm. "You saved me yesterday. If you hadn't gotten the Talon's sword, that might have been the end."

"I should have managed to keep it," she replied. "If she had gained control of the dragon again—"

I shook my head. "Don't dwell on it. We got away, after all."

We lay listening to each other's breathing for a while, and I was grateful to have this moment of stillness.

"What's next?" Kaia said at last, breaking the silence.

"What do you mean?"

"Are we still in search of the Dragons?"

I opened my eyes wide in an effort to stay awake. "Of course. Why wouldn't we be?"

"Because you just did something monumental. These people will be talking about it for years. You've changed their lives in one day."

"I didn't do it so that people would *talk* about it," I said sharply.

"Right," Kaia said. "But they *will* talk about it. Word of what you've done will spread. Don't you think that we should take advantage of it?"

"How?" I couldn't think of what she might mean and I wasn't sure how I felt about the eagerness in her voice.

"After you left, the villagers were calling you *dragon mistress*. There's power in that. Imagine what we could accomplish if we traveled across the empire. People would listen to you."

I was already shaking my head. "We can't do that right now. We need to get to Gedarin as quickly as possible, and that means meeting up with the Dragons." Besides, we couldn't rely on a convenient dragon encounter every time we wanted attention from villagers. We had freed one dragon, yes. But could we replicate yesterday's accomplishment so easily? The dragon kit was very young—it was an enormous responsibility to place on her wings, and I still wasn't certain the dragonsong would work again. We might simply have been lucky.

"Because of Sev," Kaia said. She said his name as though it tasted bitter in her mouth.

I frowned. "I owe him *everything*—I got you back because of his help. I must save him before we do anything else."

Kaia made a noise that sounded suspiciously like a scoff. "So you'd throw this away? I thought you wanted to make a mark on the world."

No, that had always been *her* dream—not mine. And it troubled me that when she thought of freeing the dragons, she thought of making marks. *Dragon mistress.* The title made my skin crawl. But my head was aching, and tomorrow would come sooner than either of us wanted. "I'm just trying to do what is right," I said softly. *The best that I can do.*

Kaia sighed. "Try to sleep. We can't get anywhere if you're felled by exhaustion." The sounds of the day drifted through the air. The fire outside crackled. Slowly my body began to relax. The dragon kit snuffled a little in her sleep. I rolled so that I could put an arm over Kaia's waist, pulling her toward me. She tucked her head underneath my chin, resting against my chest and hooking a leg over mine. I closed my eyes and sank into the familiar feeling of our bodies fitting together like a matched set. Whatever else was happening, holding Kaia still felt like home.

CHAPTER TWELVE

Sev

I could hear my heartbeat rushing through my ears as the world around me slowed—the crowd, the emperor, the man kneeling on the ground, the dragons crouching on the rooftops above.

If I did what the emperor demanded, I would be as monstrous as him.

But I already was, wasn't I? I had killed to keep my secret. I had killed to stay alive. What was this now, but doing the same?

But this wasn't the same.

This was an act designed by the emperor to shatter the legend attached to my name. We were playing a game he controlled, and I had yet to make a move that he hadn't foreseen. If I continued down this path, it would only end in one place. My destruction.

The fear that had consumed me yesterday came roaring back up. I inhaled deeply, letting it rise through me, then dissipate as I exhaled. In the emperor's presence I had become a boy again, frightened and friendless.

But I wasn't a boy any longer. I was a monster, too, and I could play my own game.

I reached out and grasped the hilt of the sword. Then I

circled the prisoner slowly, as though debating the most efficient way to dispatch him. Poor fellow. I wouldn't have been entirely surprised if he'd been hired under false pretenses, to ensure that there would be someone in the crowd to punish.

I came to face the man and set the tip of the sword under his chin, forcing his head up. He looked familiar to me, I realized, though I couldn't say from where, or even if it was simply my imagination playing tricks.

He stared at me angrily. Then he threw his head back, shouting, "Long live the revolution!"

Despite the Talons above us, there were audible cheers from the back of the crowd. I had to act quickly. I grabbed the man by the collar and struck him hard across the temple with the hilt of the sword. He collapsed to the ground, senseless. Then I turned to the emperor. "The peasant wants to be martyred, my lord. To kill him now would play into his hand."

Rafael raised an eyebrow. "Are you suggesting that he should go unpunished for his treason?"

Let this work—please let this work. I gave another extravagant bow, visible to all. "No, almighty Flame. Only that a swift execution is too good for him. We might extract information from him first."

A muscle twitched in the emperor's cheek. I knelt, offering up the sword for him to take. I was relying on the hope that this whole display was meant to demonstrate his control over me, and that my submission would be enough. But I could still have been wrong.

The Flame of the West took the sword back from me and raised his voice for our audience. "I offer this man a clean, merciful death. But Prince Vesper insists on taking him first as a guest of the palace." The sound of indrawn breaths swept through the crowd. They knew what this meant. *Torture*. Rafael turned to me, his expression triumphant. "I entrust his fate to the hands of my *loyal* servant."

Scattered jeers broke out as the soldiers lifted the unconscious man from the ground and tossed him carelessly into the last carriage. My heart sank as I heard my name cursed among them. I'd thought that if I could put off the man's execution, I might find a way to save his life. But the emperor had used it to turn the people against me nevertheless.

Still, it had been a necessary risk. I had to start making moves of my own, or I would never survive.

A page ran to meet our carriage as we arrived back at the palace grounds. He bowed before the emperor. "Your Illustriousness, you must come quickly. A dragon's been spotted flying over Eronne!"

Maren.

"Put the prisoner in the dungeons and escort the prince to his quarters. I'll see to them later," Rafael said to the guards next to him. Then he leaped down from the carriage, and followed the page into the palace.

The guards retrieved the knife Faris had given me, then walked me back to my chambers and locked me in. I set my back against the wall and sank down to the floor, my hands in fists. Think. *Think.* I was going to be punished for what I'd done—I had to plan my next move while I was alone.

But I was distracted. A dragon had been seen flying free!

Whether or not it was the same dragon that had destroyed Lumina, I had no doubt that it was because of Maren. If I escaped, I could find her again. We could free the dragons together—we could dismantle the system that propped up the emperor.

But first I had to make contact with the Dragons. And I had to find a way to meet Piera, too.

The door slammed open as Faris burst into the room. "What happened? You weren't expected back for another hour."

It seemed unnecessary to obfuscate. "A man threw a cabbage at the emperor's carriage. The emperor ordered me to execute him, and I . . . said that perhaps he should be interrogated first."

Faris's eyes widened. "You disobeyed the emperor? In front of all of Irrad?"

"I—" I stopped. "I did."

She groaned.

"Faris, the man threw a cabbage. It was nothing."

She shook her head. "You of all people should know that doesn't matter."

"I thought I could buy him some time. I thought—"

"That you could save him?" Faris laughed coldly. "Prince Vesper, if you're truly that naive, it's incredible you're still alive."

"*Don't* call me that."

The door opened again, and a guard entered. "You've been called before the emperor. Let's go."

I half expected to be led straight back to the dungeons. Instead the guards escorted Faris and me deeper within the palace grounds. The centerpiece of the emperor's palace was the elaborate array of gardens around which the buildings had been constructed. When I was a child, I could lie on my back and look up and see the stars on a clear night. Every garden had been cultivated around a different theme.

The guards delivered us to the Garden of Glass, where plants were interspersed with delicate glass decorations and arrangements. The pathway was sand—a strange choice, but I stopped thinking about it when I saw what awaited me on the other side of the garden.

An enormous red dragon towered over the emperor. Vix, the Ruiner. Rafael's dragon was reputed to be just as cruel as the emperor himself, though I couldn't be certain whether that was due to its innate nature or the way the emperor used it. My steps slowed as I took in the rest of the scene. The emperor stood above a man kneeling on the ground. The man's hands were bound together in front of him—as we approached, I saw that he was the same man I'd tried to save.

Rafael looked up at us. "Faris," he said. Faris left my side and went to stand by him near the prisoner.

I stopped at a safe distance, taking care to stay as far from the dragon as I could manage. I had seen dragons enough at the fortress, but none as large or menacing as Vix.

"Come here, Vesper," the emperor said.

I approached reluctantly.

"Unfortunately, your peasant friend didn't have any useful information to share with us." Rafael grabbed the young man's hair and pulled up his head, then threw him forcefully to the side. "He did, however, remind me of something else."

He leaned back against his dragon's flank, glanced at Faris, and nodded toward the prisoner. She put a hand on the man's shoulder and closed her eyes. Something prickled in the air, like lightning. The man gasped and writhed on the sandy path, his black hair shielding his face. I took one step forward before reminding myself that this was exactly the reaction the emperor wanted from me.

"I neglected to explain Faris's unique skill to you," Rafael said as calmly as if he were discussing the weather. "It's quite remarkable, you see. She can sense your injuries, no matter how old, and with one touch, she can recreate or amplify them. The pain is extraordinary, I'm told—but of course, you've already experienced that yourself."

I couldn't tear my eyes away from the man in the sand. Last night Faris had made me relive the pain of my fingers breaking. What other injuries might she be able to exploit? I had to do something. But what?

"I thought you said that he doesn't have any useful information," I said.

The emperor smiled. "He doesn't. You do."

I felt suddenly queasy. This man's suffering was all my fault. Because I had protected the man in the city, Rafael believed I would protect him again.

"Tell me, Vesper. How does Maren ben Gao communicate with dragons? She was seen riding one out of Lumina, and I have credible reports that she tamed a rogue dragon without the use of Talon techniques."

I wasn't sure how to respond. I was certain Milek's formulas weren't yet functional. It had suddenly occurred to me that the emperor might be interested in what I said beyond as a means to get control over Maren. If there was a way to command the dragons that did not require the oils, the emperor would want to exploit it.

I glanced at the man on the ground. He was moaning now, a continuous, guttural sound. Faris wasn't even looking at him, her expression blank as she held him down. I had to be very careful how I answered—for both of our sakes.

"I don't know," I said.

Rafael's hand curled into a fist. Faris pressed down on the man's chest. He screamed in agony. No head injury, that—Faris must have found something deeper, older.

"I swear to you, I'm not lying," I said quickly. "I've never seen anyone do what she does."

"And what is that, exactly?" His voice was deceptively even.

"She speaks with them. I've only ever seen her do it with one, but it might be the same for all the dragons. They understand her. And they speak back."

Rafael snorted. "Impossible. Dragons do not speak."

"They do," I insisted. "Maybe not so that you or I understand, but she does. She can speak to them. Without oils or tricks."

There, was that enough? Rafael's eyes narrowed. "And what is her aim? What is she working toward?"

We're coming for you, she'd said. *Hold on.*

I blinked. "When we were traveling together, she wanted war against Lumina."

"An anarchist, then," Rafael said, stretching his neck from side to side. "One girl shouldn't be too difficult to take care of."

Of course he had no intention of keeping Maren alive, regardless of the bargain we had made. I refrained from mentioning the way that she had spoken about freeing the dragons. Better to let him believe that she was out to destroy whatever stood in her way than to give away her actual aim. And as long as Rafael sent dragons after her, he would never succeed.

The man's screams grew hoarse. My head began to ache with the sound. But the emperor clasped his hands behind his back and did nothing but stare at me, waiting. I could do this. I could wait Rafael out. But the man's agony was shrill in my ears, and when I looked down, I saw that his face was turning purple.

I turned back to the emperor. "Please. If you have more questions, just ask them."

He finally nodded to Faris, who lifted her hand. She stepped back, breathing hard. The man fell silent, his mouth opening and closing like a fish cast out of the water.

"This peasant has been sentenced to death. Tonight you will receive a sword. If you want to end this man's suffering, you will use it. If not, Faris will torture him until he dies—and your own demise will follow. The choice is up to you."

He raised a hand, and the guards standing at the garden perimeter approached. "Take him away," he said, gesturing at the prisoner. Then he pointed at me. "You—not so fast. You disobeyed me during the parade. Faris?"

Knowing what was coming did nothing to relieve the pain that lanced through me as Faris put her hand on my shoulder. The wound from Vir's Passage flared to life along my side, and I gasped, sinking to the ground.

Somewhere beyond the boundaries of my pain there was movement. Something large and dark moved past my blurred vision, and then was gone.

When it was finally over, I lay with my cheek pressed against the cool sand, shaking.

Faris's face entered my field of vision, and I flinched away. "You make me sick," I whispered.

She pursed her lips together. "We all do what we must," she said shortly. "The emperor has left."

How long would she have tortured me if the emperor had stayed? I flashed back to the way her face had looked as the man screamed—blank, almost bored. How long had it taken for her to burn away her humanity?

I inhaled, careful not to take too deep a breath. "I want to speak to him. The prisoner."

"You know he's going to die, no matter what you say."

I managed to roll onto my back, though I wasn't confident in my ability to stand up yet. "He would not be in this position if it weren't for me. I feel responsible for his fate."

She considered my words before nodding. "If you insist. I'll arrange a visit to the dungeons."

CHAPTER THIRTEEN

Sev

Descending the stairway down into the emperor's dungeons felt uncomfortably familiar. Under other circumstances I would have thought myself out of my wits to come here voluntarily. It remained to be seen whether this too was a mistake.

Since I had left the dungeon, the place had been repopulated, though there were fewer prisoners here than I would have thought, considering the emperor's reputation. Then again, it had been less than a week.

Faris led me over to a cell, and I took a deep breath before looking inside. The man lay curled on the floor and did not stir when Faris cleared her throat, nor when she rapped on the bars.

"Is he dead?" I asked quietly.

Faris shook her head and raised her voice. "Wake up. Someone to see you."

The man shifted in the darkness. He turned his head and opened his eyes, but when he saw who we were, he scrambled backward to the opposite end of the cell. "Leave me alone!" he said hoarsely.

"I just want to help," I said.

He stared at us, eyes dull. "I want no help from either of you vipers."

I had to give the emperor credit. Despite my efforts, his plan had gone off without a hitch. And once this man was dead, my reputation would never be wiped clean.

I glanced up and down the hall. Anyone nearby, guards and prisoners both, would be able to listen in on this conversation.

"Will you speak with me?" I asked.

The man turned away.

"Let me into the cell," I said to Faris. "You can stand right here the whole time."

She shook her head disapprovingly, but called a guard over to unlock the cell. I took a deep breath. I didn't fancy entering one of these cells again. But it was my fault that this man was going to die. What else could I do?

I approached the man carefully and sat down next him. For a while we didn't speak. His breathing was short and labored. I wondered what injuries Faris had pulled out of him.

"Why did you throw the cabbage?" I asked. "Didn't you know this would happen?"

The man laughed, though it was more of a wheeze. "Because of you." He leaned forward, his face catching the dim light, and once again I thought I knew him—but from where? "The people of Zefed believed in the shadow prince. But when we learned that you had returned to the emperor's side, that belief began to die. I threw the cabbage to remind everyone watching that a movement is larger than one person. I am not afraid to die for it—compared to the rebellion, my life is small."

His words cowed me, but I could not tell him so. Whatever I said would certainly get back to the emperor. "The emperor has ordered that you be executed tonight," I said softly.

He grunted. "Feeding me to the dragons, I suppose?"

The emperor's oubliette—I'd forgotten that particularly gruesome way to die. "By my sword," I said. "I'm sorry."

"Are you? Because it seems to me that you're a coward. You're here because you feel badly about what you're about to do, but not badly enough to avoid doing it."

"It's more complicated than that," I snapped.

"Is it? Because I think you're going to follow the emperor's orders exactly, as long as it keeps you alive."

I gritted my teeth but stayed seated. He was right. And because I was going to kill him tonight, it was my responsibility to hear what he said.

"Do you have family here in Irrad? I will see a message delivered, if I'm able."

"Don't bother, *Vesper*. I don't want you calling attention to them." He brushed the hair away from his eyes. It was such a familiar movement. It didn't seem like there was anything left to say, but I couldn't leave—not without knowing.

"I know you, I think," I said. "From where?"

The man seemed surprised. "I didn't think you would remember. I'm from Ruzi. We used to see each other as children, in the market."

A flash of memory and the taste of caramelized sugar on my tongue—"Owain. You worked for the butcher. But you always had candy on you . . . from that girl at the bakery."

"She settled down with someone else after I was recruited into the army," Owain said.

"I'm sorry," I said.

He scoffed and spat on the floor. "Save your apology, you sniveling weasel."

He closed his eyes, and I knew there was nothing else I could do. I got to my feet and signaled to the guard.

"That was an exercise in pointlessness," Faris said as we climbed the stairs back toward the light. "And you'll never survive in Irrad if you give away your weaknesses so easily."

There was something in her voice as she spoke, a careful emotionlessness that made me wonder what she was hiding behind it.

"Speaking from experience?" I said.

"I am a weapon of the empire. I have no weaknesses," came the quick reply. Too quickly, as if the answer had been rehearsed.

"You might bring grown men to their knees with one hand, but you're still *human*," I said.

We exited the staircase into the hallway, and Faris slammed the door shut behind us. "Do not test me, *Prince*. To your chamber, now."

I kept my expression solemn as Faris marched me back to my rooms and locked me inside. I had touched a nerve. Maybe it was something I could exploit.

I crossed the room to the bathing area and splashed water on my face to wash away the scent of the dungeon. My entire body felt cold. Was I a coward, as Owain had claimed? A sniveling weasel? Perhaps I was. Owain was prepared to die before he would beg for mercy. I had crawled at the feet of the emperor to save myself. What was that, if not cowardice?

But I was more than that. I had sworn that I would see the

tyrant dead, and I intended to keep that vow. I pulled the Rima petal out of my pocket and etched a small symbol on its surface with my fingernail. Tonight I was going to kill a man to stay alive—I had no other choice. But after that, I was getting out. No longer could I sit idly by while the emperor forced me to bloody my hands.

My thoughts wandered to Maren. Tera's bones, I missed her. My dream from last night surfaced in my mind—a dragon dream, she'd said. But I'd had a similar vision while waking. Had I done something to cause it? And if so, was it possible that I could learn how to bring them on?

I settled into a comfortable seat on the chair and closed my eyes. *Maren, can you hear me? I need to speak with you.*

The air was still. A fly buzzed in the late afternoon heat.

My nose began to itch, and I resisted the urge to scratch it.

Ah, this was useless. I already felt foolish, casting my thoughts out as though they really could traverse the vast distance between us. Such doings were for dragons—and Maren, perhaps. It was silly to think that I had anything to do with it. I should just be grateful to have this connection at all—and I should be prepared if the opportunity arose to speak to Maren again.

The evening was languorous, sticky, and hot, but I was ready when the trumpets summoned us to supper. Apparently now that I'd sworn my loyalty to the emperor, I was trusted enough to require only one guard. Tonight my escort was Faris, who was glowering so heavily that I made no attempt to speak with her.

It was clear the moment we stepped into the great hall

that something had changed. The dragon Vix loomed behind the emperor's throne, red wings spread. Rafael and Piera sat below it, dressed in royal finery. Rafael was arrayed with so many jewels that he glittered in the torchlight, catching even the most unwilling eye. He was smiling. But everywhere else the mood was watchful and restive. There was no loud chatter, no dancing despite the music that played.

I touched Faris's sleeve as she moved to usher us through the crowd. "Is this because of the execution?" I asked quietly.

She shook her head immediately, and I knew she was worried. "Be careful," she said. "I don't know what's coming tonight."

"Prince Severin!"

The greeting was loud enough to cut across the quiet hall. I turned to see Erris waving from one of the tables closest to the emperor.

My shoulders tensed. I didn't like the woman, but she was sitting with Lord Annick, two lords from Oskiath, and several Aurati, including Neve. So I waved back, not quite as energetically, and went to sit across from her. Faris sat down next to me.

"Good evening," I said to the table at large, and they nodded back in greeting. "Thank you for the invitation."

"Good evening, Prince," Erris replied, smiling. "I confess I had an ulterior motive."

"Oh?" I wondered whether she would ask about Lumina again. Given the atmosphere, such a question didn't seem wise.

She leaned forward. "It's not often that someone of such renown joins us in court. I must know—is it true that you lived as a peasant for several years?"

"Yes," I said.

Exaggerated shock passed over her face. "Was it terribly difficult?"

"In some ways," I replied. I hadn't been among such courtiers in a long time—I'd forgotten how voracious they could be for stories of those born below their station, whom they considered pitiful. I adopted a joking tone. "Imagine having to do your own washing and cooking!"

"No!"

I reached for the pitcher of wine at the center of the table and poured myself a goblet. "Of course, I weathered it as best I could."

"But living as a peasant must give you some insight, doesn't it?" Erris lowered her voice conspiratorially. "I confess, I don't spend much time outside the first district these days—people seem so *sad*. What do you think could be done to improve their situation?"

I took a sip of wine to keep my mouth occupied by something other than swearing. Judging by the diamond bracelet on Erris's wrist, the stories about her family's wealth were not embellished. How many families could that bracelet have fed? Though that was under the assumption that there was enough food for them to buy. By the emperor's decree, more and more food in Zefed was claimed for the army or the emperor's table.

"I'm sure the Flame of the West has plans for how to feed his citizens," I said, once I could trust myself to speak again. "And in the palace we can only be grateful for what the emperor provides."

Erris seemed slightly disappointed with that answer—had she been trying to lead me into disagreeing with the emperor's policies? She nodded to me and turned to Lord Annick, striking up a conversation about the best places in the empire to spend the winter months.

I looked down the table to my left and tried to catch the eyes of the lords wearing Oskiath green—Rowena would only have trusted one of her own to be her agent in Irrad. One ignored me, but the other, a woman about my age, inclined her head minutely. That must have been the Dragon agent who had sent me the flower. The Rima petal was safe in my pocket. I just had to find the opportunity to pass it to her.

The Aurati were on the right side of the table, closest to the throne. There were four of them aside from Neve, who was sitting diagonally from me. Two of the Aurati wore scribe cords. The other two wore the dark green cloaks that marked them as seers. They were not speaking—not among themselves, not to anyone else. I recalled Faris's warning as we entered the hall. What did they know?

"Aromatory," I said, turning to Neve. There was nothing untoward about the prince of Ruzi addressing a senior Aurat.

The rest of the table didn't seem to notice, but Neve looked up quickly. "Prince," she said. "Circumstances have changed for you since we last met."

"For both of us, I think. What brings you to Irrad?"

I was curious about what she would say, given what I knew about the Alchemist. What explanation had the emperor given for calling her away from the dragon fortress?

"The war on the Seda Serat, as always. The Flame requires my personal attention in Irrad to ensure the Talons and their dragons are ready."

She stressed "requires" just slightly—a confirmation that she was not here by choice.

"Are you working with the Alchemist?" I asked innocently.

Her lips pinched together sourly, then smoothed back into a neutral expression. "My last apprentice proved to be a disappointment. The emperor in his endless wisdom has selected a new one. Milek is doing well—soon he will master all the secrets of the Aromatory."

We both knew there was only ever one Aromatory. As soon as Milek had reached a certain proficiency, Neve would be removed.

Dangerous for her—an opportunity for me. Perhaps she might be amenable to joining forces.

Before I could think of what to ask next, the people beside me rose to their feet—the emperor had stood, Piera with him. The heralds standing in the corners of the room sounded their horns for attention, and one of them stepped onto the raised platform next to the throne.

"The Flame of the West requests the honor of a prophecy to bless our meal. Aurat?"

One of the seers pushed back from the table and knelt in front of the throne. She pitched her voice to carry across the crowd. "From ash and darkness the dragon rises pure. A new day has come."

Vix spread his wings behind the throne, and Rafael mirrored his dragon, flinging his arms wide. "A new day has come!" he crowed triumphantly. "Do not mourn the fall of Lumina, for it was my dragon that brought it down. As the prophecy states, the destruction of Lumina was necessary to stamp out *treachery* in the ranks of the Aurati."

What? Maren had destroyed Lumina, *not* the emperor. And the Aurati, traitors? That wasn't possible. I looked around.

Everyone in the great hall was completely silent, waiting to see what would happen next.

The emperor's voice softened. "Be not afraid. Zefed will rise pure from this trial. The Aurati you see around us today are loyal. Come, come to me." He beckoned to the Aurati sitting at my table. All five, including Neve and Faris, rose and knelt in line before the throne.

Rafael set his palm on the forehead of each Aurat in turn. "Lumina fomented rebellion within their walls. For their treason, they have been punished. Henceforth, all remaining Aurati in Zefed are under my direct command."

Who had made this prophecy? The Aurati were no traitors, so why was the emperor making them out to be? And taking credit for a blow made *against* him? It made no sense. Did Faris know what was going on?

Rafael was speaking again. "Let this be a lesson to all— Zefed will not tolerate treason. Come with me now, my people. There is more for you to see."

He strode the length of the great hall and out of it, Vix stalking behind him. After a moment of hesitation, the rest of us followed. Faris was still near the throne, and I put distance between us as I maneuvered through the crowd. Just at the doors, I managed to brush past the lord from Oskiath, slipping the Rima petal into her pocket. There. That was one thing done, at least.

In other kingdoms, an inner courtyard was a respite, a garden, sometimes a sanctuary. But here in Irrad, the emperor's inner courtyard housed the oubliette.

The massive pit was covered by a woven net of metal, smoke rising from its depths. At the bottom of the pit lived the dragons deemed unfit to bond to Talons. Instead of caring for the creatures, the emperor drove them mad by keeping them hungry and confined in the dark. And starving dragons would eat anything.

Rafael and Piera stood at the opposite side of the pit, the Alchemist at their side. As we watched, the emperor took Milek's hand and raised it. "My Alchemist has been hard at work developing new techniques for training my beasts. For your enjoyment, a demonstration."

He clapped his hands, and guards ran to pull the net back from the surface of the oubliette. Milek stepped forward, taking a vial out of his pocket and uncorking it. Out of habit I found myself leaning forward, as though I could smell its contents from here. The Alchemist walked to the edge of the oubliette and turned the vial over, pouring the liquid down upon the dragons who waited at the bottom.

Angry snarls filled the air, followed by dragon cries unlike any I'd ever heard. These dragons sounded like they were in agony. I searched the crowd for Neve, but she had disappeared.

"Vesper! Little prince!" the emperor called.

I snapped to attention.

"Come forward," Rafael said. "Come see what we have accomplished."

If I walked too near the oubliette, would he push me in? He certainly wouldn't fish me out if I fell. I was careful as I walked, feeling the eyes of my audience on my back.

I reached the emperor and sank into a low bow. "I am at your service, my lord."

He nodded to one of the guards, who presented me with a short sword. There was a commotion at the other end of the courtyard. Two more guards appeared, dragging between them a man. Owain.

The guards brought him to us and forced him to his knees. He was gagged but not blindfolded, and I found myself looking anywhere but directly at him. I glanced at the sword in my hand, steeling myself. I'd known this was coming. I had made my decision. Despite what Owain had said, I had no other choice.

"This man is guilty of high treason, of conspiring with our enemies of the Seda Serat. He attacked me and the prince in the city today, and will now have his judgment rendered upon him." Rafael looked at me. "Prince Vesper. A loyal servant is as good as an additional hand."

There was sweat beading on my forehead and a foul stench rising up from the oubliette, where the dragons waited. The court watched me silently, their faces like masks. They had likely seen many such displays over the years—they knew how to act.

I have killed to survive, and I will kill again. For Maren and the rebellion, I must do this. I raised the sword, leveling the blade against Owain's neck. With a sword this blunt, it would be painful. I would have to strike hard, possibly more than once. His body would fall to the ground. My hands would be red with his blood, and the sword . . .

If I did not do this, Faris would. And I'd already seen what she could do.

I met Owain's eyes. I brought the sword down.

The force of the blow reverberated up my arm as bile rose in my throat. I swallowed it as Owain's body spasmed, the blade stuck in his neck. I pulled it free—*quickly, quickly*—and his body fell sideways . . . straight into the oubliette.

There was no scream, only horrible wet crunching sounds rising from the pit. I turned away, my stomach churning. At least he wasn't alive.

He wasn't alive because I had killed him.

"Well done," said the emperor, grinning at me. He turned to Milek, lowering his voice.

But I didn't wait to listen. I bowed jerkily, like the puppet I was, and then pushed my way hastily through the crowd. At the back of the courtyard I stepped behind a pillar and was sick, losing my supper in a potted plant. Thankfully, Faris didn't appear—even she would allow me some dignity. I vomited again, bringing up only bile this time. Finally I was through. I pressed my cheek against the pillar, letting the stone cool my skin.

Everyone else in the courtyard seemed to still be occupied with the spectacle, including the emperor. No one was paying attention to me—not even Faris.

I turned and walked out of the courtyard, my hands numb. Killing Owain would haunt me, but this might be my only chance to meet Piera. I would not waste it.

CHAPTER FOURTEEN

Maren

We left the village late in the afternoon. The village leaders had been generous with what little they had. They'd given us fresh changes of clothing, more food than we had arrived with, and specific directions for the most efficient way to reach Oskiath. Lastly, they'd spared one of their two messenger hawks.

I'd debated who to write to—as there was always a chance that the message would be intercepted. A messenger hawk from a small village addressed to Rowena ben Garret, a princess of Oskiath, would almost certainly attract attention. At last I settled on writing to Melchior, the healer who had treated Sev in Belat. It seemed less likely that their correspondence would be under scrutiny. Still, I hesitated over what to write.

Cousin Melchior, I began. *We've stopped over in a charming village off Belat Forest. Our journey has been as expected, although my sister's friend has decided to travel ahead of us. We hope to catch up with him closer to Gedarin—likely in the next week or so. Would love to meet you there, if your work can spare you! —M.*

PS: Please convey greetings to your sour friend—I regret that I haven't the time to write her separately.

Melchior was smart, and they knew what was at stake—

they would understand what I was trying to say. That was all I could hope for as the hawk was released from its tether and flew into the distance.

On the road the dragon kit wanted to run again, and I was more than happy to let her wander at her own pace as we walked, since the road was deserted. I was also happy to have a change of clothing. We'd kept our soiled outfits just in case they were needed for a disguise, but I was more comfortable now that I wasn't wearing an Oskiath herald's uniform.

"You did well back there," Kaia said after a while. Now that we were alone again, we'd slipped back into Verran.

"What do you mean?" I asked.

"The villagers. We had an opportunity to connect with them, and you did."

"You were right this time," I admitted. "But we still need to be more careful in the future. Not everyone will be friendly to outsiders like us."

Kaia shook her head. "I disagree. We shouldn't be afraid to talk to the people we meet. Would you hesitate to trust a stranger in Ilvera?"

"Zefed is not Ilvera." The words came out more harshly than I'd intended. "I don't know how many times I have to tell you that this is a dangerous place. That most people we meet will be set against us and our mission—"

"*Your* mission, Maren."

I recoiled. "Is that what you think? That this is *my* mission? These are Verran dragons. We are *Verran*. It's our responsibility to help them."

"The dragons, all right. But your friend? Severin? That's not something you gave me a choice about. Talking about Zefedi strangers, Maren—I don't even know this person! It's a lot, to ask me to risk my life for a prince I've never met."

To my horror, I felt tears welling up in my eyes. I balled my hands into fists, squeezed, released. Breathed. "But you know *me*," I said slowly. "Don't you trust me?"

"I—" She turned and walked a few paces ahead of me and paused, her head bowed. "I do," she said softly. "But you need to explain to me why your friend is so important to you. You said that you dreamed about me when we were apart. And now you're dreaming about him—and not only that, you're somehow able to have conversations with him?"

"They're just *dreams*," I said.

"Are they?" she asked.

Somehow I had to cross this divide. "While we were parted, Naava sent dreams about you to me. She wanted me to see you. The dragon kit connects Sev and me now. I don't know why we can interact in these dreams—there's so much I still don't know about dragons. It might be because the dragon kit knows both of us, and Naava knew only me."

"But there might be another reason," Kaia pressed.

"What are you asking me?" I said. "I don't understand what you *want*."

She shook her head, crossing her arms. "I could say the same thing about you. You've changed so much since Ilvera, sometimes I think you're an entirely different person."

I felt as though she had punched me in the stomach. I was the same. I *was*. Just—sharper. Stronger. *Better*. At least, I thought so.

Was I wrong?

At that moment the dragon kit ran out of the tall grasses, chirping insistently.

"What is it?" I turned to see a person on horseback approaching us, riding fast. "Quick, get in!" I crouched down and opened the pack, and the dragon kit jumped in. Her head poked out of the flap, and I had to push her down gently in order to get it closed. This wasn't going to work for much longer—she was growing faster than I had previously thought possible for any being to grow.

Kaia and I looked at each other, our argument instantly set aside. At least we had changed our clothes. Assuming that the person hadn't seen the dragon kit, there was nothing in particular to identify us as two Verran girls. I could easily pass as Zefedi in this outfit, and Kaia looked like any other Lirusan girl.

I put my hand on the hilt of my dagger, then paused. Innocent travelers would not be traveling with blades at the ready.

"It's going to be all right," Kaia said, her eyes on the rider. I wasn't so sure.

The rider reined in their horse, halting at a safe distance. "Are you the dragon tamers?" they called in Zefedi.

I exchanged a glance with Kaia before replying. "We're just heading to Oskiath," I replied.

The person tugged down their hood, revealing a young woman with long dyed hair the color of silken straw. "Please," she said. "We've been attacked. Two dragons, and they've burned their way through three villages. Even the Talons have been unable to stop them. We didn't know what to do, until we heard about the other village." She pointed past us in the direction we'd come from. "They told us what happened. What you did."

So I'd been right—news of what we'd done *had* already spread. These must have been the dragons that Naava had freed, but I wasn't confident we could help now. The kit and I had had such a difficult time freeing even one. Would I even be able to replicate what we'd done yesterday with dragons I'd never connected with? And what had happened to the Talons?

"You said there were Talons, and they couldn't help?" I said.

"Yes. They're gone now—I think they were afraid that they'd lose control of their own dragons." The woman's lip curled with disgust. "Please, we don't know what else to do. We have nowhere else to turn."

I already felt like we had lost too much time. But if there were confused dragons running amok through the empire, we had to help them. On the other hand, what if they were already absolutely free, and had made the decision to take their anger out on the empire? Glivven had agreed to go in peace after I'd had the chance to talk with him. But what if these other dragons disagreed? What if they wanted to keep up the attack?

If I was being honest, I wasn't sure what I would do if that was the case. Was it my right to coerce them if they didn't stop? If I tried, would I be any different from the tyrant?

Kaia leaned toward me and blocked her mouth with a hand as she whispered, "We have to help them."

"But—"

"You have this ability, and the responsibility that comes with it. This is important."

Of course she wanted to help. I looked back at the woman, whose desperation was written clearly across her face.

"I can't promise anything," I said finally.

Her relief was palpable. "Thank you. We're grateful for anything you can do." She looked around as if noting our surroundings for the first time. "I should have prepared better. I didn't bring another horse for you to ride." She dismounted from the horse. "You'll have to take her—you'll travel faster that way."

She waved us closer. "Don't worry, Clem is very gentle. And she knows the way home."

She was being too accommodating, and it made me suspicious. But Kaia didn't hesitate. She took Clem's reins and looked back at me. "Come on."

It seemed the decision had been made. The woman gave me a boost into the saddle, and Kaia swung up behind me.

"Thank you," the woman said. "Just follow the road—you'll see the smoke soon enough. Tell them that Olina sent you."

She patted Clem on the nose and whispered to her, and then we were off at a modest trot.

I waited until we were out of earshot before speaking. "You don't think that was strange?"

"No, why?" Kaia said. "Her village is burning down. What else do you expect her to do?"

"But a stranger just gave us her horse. We could easily steal it. We could easily be *anyone*. Even if they had heard the stories, how would anyone know what we looked like?"

"I suppose there aren't that many young women traveling in pairs by foot on this road," Kaia pointed out. Which I had to agree with. We had been walking for hours and hadn't yet encountered another person. This road wasn't forgiving for travelers on foot—and it would be night soon. Anyone else would have been seeking shelter by now.

Now that we were on the move, neither one of us seemed particularly interested in picking up our previous argument, so we rode in silence. It wasn't long before I caught the scent of smoke on the wind, and soon we saw flickers of fire in the distance. We crested a small hill, and my breath caught in my throat as we looked out upon a landscape of destruction.

My head felt light. I pulled the horse to a halt. I had never seen a war field, but this was what I imagined one must look like. The fields had been completely razed by fire, and the ground scorched in its wake. I could see charred skeletons and the crumbling foundations of a few houses. But by and large, this village had been burned to the ground.

I dismounted. My boots settled softly in a layer of ash. A breeze stirred it up, sending flakes dancing into the air. All was quiet.

Was this what Lumina looked like now? I was hit with a wave of nausea at the thought that I had caused such devastation as this.

The dragon kit poked her head out of the pack and rested it on my shoulder. I let her nuzzle into me, but there was nothing I could say. This amount of destruction would have far-reaching consequences, even for the survivors. Where would they *live?* What would happen when the seasons changed? I was ashamed that I had doubted Olina's story.

"Are you all right?" Kaia asked.

I couldn't speak—only reached out and took her hand in mine, squeezing tightly. I had a task to complete here. I could not turn and run, no matter how much I wanted to.

The temperature rose as we passed through the scorched landscape. Small fires still burned on either side of the road—or what was left of the road. It was hard to distinguish it from the rest of the blackened earth. Sweat beaded on my brow, and the smell of burnt things I didn't want to identify overwhelmed my senses. There were people ahead of us working to stamp out the flames, but it was clear that they were nearly spent. They barely spared us a glance as we passed, though one raised a hand and pointed—there, in the distance, two dark shapes twined together on the ground. The dragons.

CHAPTER FIFTEEN

Maren

The dragons lay side by side on the ground, large enough that they might convincingly pass for two small hills to an unobservant passerby. There was no question that these were the two we had encountered with Naava—I remembered their coloring, a matched dark green pair.

Since we couldn't be sure of how the horse would react to being in close proximity to the dragons, we left Clem tethered to one of the only trees still standing. The dragon kit squirmed, and I let her out onto the ground. I wasn't certain how to proceed. At least the dragons weren't actively attacking, but it seemed that was only because they'd decided to rest—or they had run out of things to burn. They appeared to be sleeping.

The kit darted through the ash, kicking particles into the air. I coughed, my eyes smarting. After I wiped my face, I realized that she was gone.

No, not gone—she was heading straight for the dragons. *Stop! Come back!*

She spared me one glance over her shoulder before trotting off determinedly once again. I chased after her as quietly as I could. She was so small in comparison. What would happen if she woke them? Forget malice—they could just as easily crush her if they rolled over in their sleep.

I lunged and missed—the kit dodged away from me and leaped, bounding until she was close enough to the other dragons to touch them. I stopped in my tracks, throwing out an arm to stop Kaia from passing me. If our motion did not stir them, they could certainly smell us at this point. If they were awake. And I very much wanted them not to be awake.

The kit stretched out her neck and sniffed at one of the dragons' claws. Then she darted back, as if surprised by her own daring. When neither of the dragons stirred, she did it again. And then reached out a claw and poked at a tail.

Kaia let out a small cry. One large yellow eye shot open, and I clapped a hand over my mouth to stifle my own scream. My heart rate soared.

The eye fluttered almost closed—and then opened again.

The kit looked up at the dragon in awe and chirped in greeting.

The dragon lifted its head lazily. I held my breath as it leaned down to sniff the dragon kit. The kit let out another little chirp and bounced on her feet excitedly. Then she turned toward me, her tail flicking.

The older dragon turned as well. Its eyes narrowed as it saw us so close, and it spread its wings, knocking the other dragon into wakefulness. The air stilled and heated, and I knew that if I did not intervene, we were about to burn.

Please listen, I said, holding my hands out, palms up, to show that I had no weapons. *I was there when Naava freed you from the Talons. Do you remember?*

The dragon looked beyond me, her gaze inward. *Yes*, she

said slowly, her voice low and musical. *There was a dragon. Carrying humans.* Her eyes narrowed again, and I realized that a dragon carrying humans was bound to remind her of the Talons.

I'm not a Talon, I said. *I promise. Naava carried me because she chose to. And she wanted you to have that choice as well.* The dragon's wings wavered, then folded in as she considered what I'd said. This was going better than I'd feared. I took a tentative step toward her.

Then where is she? said the dragon that had been silent until now, a male. *If the mother freed us, then where is she now? Why are you here instead? Why do you have a hatchling?*

The dragon kit chirped again, climbing up onto the male's tail. The scene would have been amusing were it not for how close we were to disaster.

Naava has been ill for some time. She has gone to—

There was a thin whistling in the air, and the female dragon's eyes widened before she heaved upright, casting herself into the air.

Run! For the hatchling, RUN!

I was slow to react. Too slow. I turned, feeling as though the world was whirling while I stood still. A hot wind cast ash against my face, and I put up a hand to shield my eyes. Over the distant hill flew four Talons, their dragons screaming battle cries as they ripped toward us, spitting fire—

The male dragon swept Kaia and me backward with his tail. We flew several feet before landing hard, just as a plume of fire obliterated the ground where we had been standing. The dragon kit tumbled against my stomach. Then the dragon launched into the air, against the Talons. Kaia scrambled to her feet and grabbed my hand, pulling me up. We had to get out of here—but what about the dragons?

Go to Ilvera! I shouted to them. *Find Naava.*

I had no time to share anything else with them, for one of the Talons broke formation and veered off to the side, around the freed dragons. I picked up the kit, and Kaia and I ran.

How had they found us here? Had the Talons been hunting the dragons, or us?

No time to consider that now. Clem was still tethered where we had left her. I passed the dragon kit to Kaia, then grabbed the reins and swung up into the saddle. Kaia handed the kit back to me, and hoisted herself up. I wheeled around and urged the horse into a canter. But where could we go?

The village being razed meant that we could see for miles around—but the Talons could see us as well. The sun was already setting—would the coming dark give us cover? I didn't know how well dragons could see at night.

Wait—was that a line of trees on the far side of the burnt fields?

Too late to make any other decision. We didn't stand a chance against four Talons ready for battle. I steered Clem toward the trees and held the dragon kit steady in front of me as the horse lengthened her stride into a gallop.

Heat touched the back of my neck, and a dragon roared somewhere above me. I glanced over my shoulder and saw that one of the freed dragons had managed to block a Talon from following us.

I couldn't look any longer, not without losing my seat. Clem galloped, crossing from the farmed fields into wild grasses, and then the trees.

Immediately the air changed around us. No longer dry summer—the air was damp and cool, the trees forming a canopy that blocked the sky almost completely. I could barely hear the dragons' skirmish from where we were now. It was as though a curtain had come down between us and the battle we had left behind.

Kaia's arms tightened around my waist. "Where are we?" she whispered.

"I'm not sure," I said. Within these trees, it felt as though we had left Zefed altogether. The last place that had felt so separate from the rest of the world had been Vir's Passage. But I wasn't sure I was ready to bargain with ghosts again. Especially when I hadn't yet fulfilled the oath I'd made to the last ones.

Far above us a dragon shrieked, and my body tensed. Regardless of how far removed this forest felt, I couldn't rely on a *feeling* to keep us safe. The trees hid us from view, but if the Talons defeated the freed dragons in battle, they would likely come after us next. We couldn't rely on the cover of night. We had to keep moving. I nudged the horse gently, and we rode farther into the forest.

The longer we rode the more I suspected that this was indeed no ordinary forest. For one thing, it had appeared as just a small copse of trees from the outside. But we had been riding for at least an hour, and the trees showed no signs of ending. If anything, the forest seemed to get even denser the farther we went. There had to be something *otherly* at work here. The dragon kit sniffed the air from her seat in front of me, peering curiously around at our surroundings.

Kaia pressed her face against my back. "I don't like it here," she said.

"I think it will be all right," I said softly.

But there was a chill in the air, and she was shivering against my back. We could not continue as we were going, not for long. We needed to find shelter.

I pulled Clem to a halt.

"What are you doing?" Kaia asked.

I looked around. "When was the last time you heard a dragon cry? I think we've left them behind. And the Talons wouldn't come after us on foot. We should try to find a place to rest."

"Are you sure?" she said doubtfully.

"Yes," I said, making myself sound more confident than I felt. "Besides, Clem needs to rest too. She's traveled a long way today."

We dismounted. I let the dragon kit onto the ground, and Kaia took Clem's reins as we picked our way carefully through the trees. I wished for a clearly marked path. The tree canopy was so thick that it would be impossible to navigate by the stars. What if there was a presence here, and it was malevolent? What if the price for trespassing was being doomed to wander forever, until we died of exhaustion?

Suddenly Kaia raised a hand and pointed. "Look, there's a light!"

I followed her gaze. She was right. There in the distance, a light shone clearly. "I'm not sure," I said.

"What's not to be sure about? If there's a light, there must be people."

Or ghosts, I thought darkly. But it seemed our best option. "All right. Let's investigate."

We crept as quietly as we could through the trees. After a while, the light resolved into a square of light—a window in a small house, snugly built. There didn't seem to be any movement inside.

"Let's wait to see if anyone comes out," Kaia suggested.

But strangely, the house seemed warm and welcoming. I couldn't put it into words, but I felt certain that there was no one here tonight—that somehow, this house was meant for us. "Let's go inside," I said.

Kaia shot me a look of pure horror. "But anyone could be in there!"

"I know," I said. "I can't explain it, but it feels like we were meant to come here."

She looked skeptical but didn't stop me as I approached the house and knocked tentatively on the door. When there was no answer, I pushed the door open and stepped inside.

The house was one large central room, with a fireplace on one side and a bed on the other. A large pot hung over the fire. I walked over and found it was filled with Zefedi porridge, heavy with dried apples and cinnamon. I inhaled and felt instantly ravenous.

"Someone was clearly just here," Kaia said from the doorway. "We should go."

"No," I said. "I think we should eat." The dragon kit chirped in agreement.

"I think we shouldn't," Kaia said. "We already have perfectly good food." She held up her pack, and I frowned. While the villagers had given us fresh supplies, I didn't know how long we would be on the road. It seemed imprudent not to take what had been offered.

"I know this sounds ridiculous, but . . . I don't think we would be stealing. I think this is for us." I looked at the table, where two wooden bowls had been set out with spoons. I wasn't completely convinced that they had been there before I walked into the room.

There was a definite presence here. But unlike the ghosts of Vir's Passage, this presence didn't feel malevolent. Merely . . . watchful. Not for the first time, I was reminded that this land was older than the empire. There was knowledge and memory in this earth that I had no understanding of.

"I think the house wants us to eat. It wants us to feel at ease. Safe."

"Or this could all be a trap," Kaia said, though she still looked longingly at the food.

I took a bowl and spooned porridge into it. "You can eat our rations, if it makes you feel better. But I'm eating the porridge."

Kaia was too hungry, or too exhausted, to hold out any longer. She sighed and took a bowl for herself, and we sat at the table and ate.

Despite Kaia's apprehension over the mysterious porridge, nothing untoward happened while we ate. When our bellies were full and our hunger sated, we sat back against our chairs and stretched out our legs. The dragon kit ate porridge straight from my bowl, and when she was done, she dragged a small blanket off the bed and onto the floor. She patted it into a nest, turned around three times, and immediately fell asleep in front of the fire.

Kaia couldn't help but chuckle at that, and I laughed along with her.

"I feel better," I said, kicking off my shoes.

Indeed, it felt as though my burdens had, if not been lifted from my shoulders, at least somewhat lightened. The troubles that we had already faced and the challenges that remained ahead were somewhere outside these walls. Inside this house, it felt like nothing could touch us.

Kaia stood and took off her jacket, then folded it over the chair. She stretched her arms toward the ceiling, and a smile broke across her face as she tilted her head back. She looked relaxed, even happy. She looked like *herself.*

I wanted to go to her, but I felt suddenly shy. I hadn't forgotten the argument we'd been having before the dragon attack interrupted us. It seemed like we'd circled the same fight over and over the last few days without coming to any new understanding. But she was still Kaia, and she was smiling at me.

I stood up and held out my hand. She came to me, putting her hand in mine. I raised it to my lips and pressed a kiss to the center of her palm.

"It's going to be all right," I said, as much to myself as to her.

She nodded, tucking a strand of hair behind my ear. But when I leaned in to kiss her, she pulled back.

"What's wrong?" I said.

"I feel—I don't even want to ask this. But I have to know. Maren, did anything happen between you and Sev while you were traveling together?"

"What? No!" I said.

Kaia pressed further. "I wouldn't . . . I wouldn't blame you.

I'm sure it was an awful situation. You didn't know if I would still be alive, there were times when you almost died—"

"Nothing ever happened between us, Kaia. I promise. You're my heartmate."

But guilt still flooded through me. The Prophet had said *heartmates*. And I *had* kissed Sev in a dream. Worse than that, I'd wanted to kiss him in reality.

But no. The Prophet had been a liar, and I controlled my actions. I controlled my fate. Kaia was my heartmate. Nothing was going to change that.

"Come here," I said, pulling Kaia into a fierce hug. We stood that way for some long minutes, letting the warmth of the house seep into our bones. "I love you," I whispered into her ear, and I felt her smile against my cheek.

"I love you," she replied.

I ran my fingers through her hair, then untied her robe and let it pool down on the floor. I knelt before her and pulled off her boots, then fumbled with the ties on her pants before getting them free. Then I stripped off my shirt and stagger-hopped out of the rest of my clothes as Kaia giggled. We were both smudged with ash, but she was still the most beautiful girl I had ever seen. The firelight flickered over our skin as I framed her face between my hands, leaned in, and kissed her.

The last time we had been together had been hazy and urgent. Tonight was different. Tonight I took her hand and led her to the bed, and she lay down hesitantly, waiting for me to join her. I tripped as I climbed in, catching a hand on her stomach.

"Ow, Maren!"

"Sorry! Are you all right?" I landed next to her, and we lay side by side.

Kaia held up a hand. "It's fine." But she made no move to pick up where we had left off.

Usually Kaia led when we were intimate. Without her taking charge, I almost didn't know what to do.

The fire crackled, and the dragon kit snuffled in her sleep. I turned onto my side and propped up my head with one hand so that I could see Kaia's face. She was staring at the ceiling, hands over her stomach.

"Do you just want to sleep?" I asked.

She looked at me. "No," she said softly. "Kiss me?"

There was something she wasn't saying, but I was afraid to ask what it was.

So instead of speaking, I did as she asked. I kissed her, and trailed my fingers across her breasts and along the curve of her hip. When I touched her, she pressed herself against me fiercely, biting my shoulder and holding my hand in place until she let out a small choked sigh and lay still, breathing quietly in the dark. She was the most precious thing, and I was inconceivably lucky that she was my own.

She was still Kaia, and I was still Maren. We were going to be all right. I would make it so.

CHAPTER SIXTEEN

Sev

T he Garden of Hearts was the one closest to my chamber. I'd heard that the first Flame of the West buried the hearts of his enemies here, but that story was far from corroborated. Whatever the truth, it was now a traditional garden. Despite the emperor's murderous proclivities, someone was still employed to keep this place a pristine retreat from the court's politics. Well, I supposed being a murderous tyrant didn't mean one couldn't also appreciate plants.

This garden was made up of long walkways bordered by thick shrubs and tall trees, a perfect place to walk and not be seen, or bothered. Piera, if she was here, could be anywhere.

My race to get here unseen had been fueled by adrenaline. Now it was dissipating, leaving me cold and tired. I was still carrying the sword, I realized suddenly. The sword I had used to kill Owain, to chop through his—

I dropped it, and it fell to the earth with a dull thud.

You have to hold yourself together.

The sword. It was just a sword, just a blade on the ground. *Think.*

It was a weapon. I had to hide it.

I looked around. There were several likely spots under

shrubs. I picked one and dug up some dirt, then buried the sword shallowly in the earth. A rotten hiding place, but it was the best I could do right now. I wiped my shaking hands on my trousers—*stop shaking*—and walked to the fountain at the center of the garden. I cupped water in my hands and drank.

It's not your fault. That was Maren's voice in my head. She was loath to think well of any Zefedi, especially the tyrant, but she was forgiving when it came to me. She would tell me there was nothing I could have done. What had happened to Owain was the fault of the emperor and no other. But my own vicious thoughts disagreed. There had to be something I could have done. If I had killed him back in the city, the way Rafael had wanted me to, he wouldn't have been tortured. His body wouldn't have been torn limb from limb and devoured by the dragons. I had tried to keep my hands clean, but I had only succeeded in prolonging his agony. If only I had—

"You came."

I whirled around. Piera stood on the other side of the fountain, looking at me solemnly.

"Piera." My voice was suddenly hoarse.

She came quickly around the fountain, and it was like standing before a ghost, an apparition. I had thought I would never see her again, and here she was. Whole. And an empress. Fury rose within me. How dare she stand here, alive, when my brother was dead? How could she, after everything she had seen, turn her back on Ruzi and marry such a creature?

"You've raised yourself high," I said bitingly.

She took my hands between hers, giving them a squeeze.

Her eyes were shining—were those tears? "Everything comes at a price. You must know that."

"You're a noblewoman of Ruzi. There were so many paths open to you. And you chose *him?*"

She shook her head. "I did what was necessary to survive. But we do not have *time* for such pettiness," she hissed. "We'll be missed soon enough."

"Then tell me why you brought me here, *Your Illustriousness,*" I said mockingly.

"Because—" She threw up her hands, turning away from me. "Because this place is a pit of vipers, and my husband's war against the Seda Serat is wrong. The way he treats his people is wrong. The way he conducts his court . . . it sickens me, and I can do nothing about it. He listened to me, once. But he's losing control, and he's too proud to admit it. He's turning all of his allies into enemies. I need to get out, and I need help to do so."

I felt as though all the air had been sucked from my lungs.

"You want—my help?"

She turned back around, tears streaming down her face. "We were like family, once. Please. I cannot ask this of anyone else."

"I'm a prisoner here. Why do you think I could help you, even if I wanted to?"

"You're the shadow prince of Ruzi. The people outside speak your name like it's a prayer. You spent years in hiding. Surely you must have allies."

"I haven't received word from anyone since I was captured," I said, truthfully. "I can guarantee no assistance."

"But you could try, couldn't you?"

"Piera . . ." I stepped away from her. "I don't even know what you are asking of me."

A light breeze blew through the garden, ruffling her hair. She patted it back into place with a casual hand. "I have friends in Old Zefed. If you can get my son and me safe passage to Ruzi, I can take him out of the empire."

A door slammed nearby, and we both flinched. Our time was running short. I shook my head. "You're talking about the emperor's heir."

"He's a *child*," Piera said, her voice shaking. "My child. He's barely more than a baby." She touched my shoulder gently. "*Please*, Sev," she whispered. I could smell her perfume, a dark, heady scent I couldn't identify.

We were close enough to embrace—to kiss. Once, I had been in love with her. But how could I trust her now?

"What happened in the great hall today?" I said. "I know the emperor did not destroy Lumina himself. And the Aurati are no traitors."

She bit her lip, looking away. I stepped back, and her hand fell to her side.

"You're asking me to risk everything for you. Tell me."

At last she nodded. "You're right. Rafael knows that someone else brought down Lumina, but most others don't. The destruction was so complete—whoever did it must be powerful enough to rival any Talon. Even the emperor. It was a major attack. And he fears that if people know that someone else did it . . ."

"They'll believe he can be brought down," I finished.

"Exactly," Piera replied. "That nonsense about the Aurati was just the lie he told to explain why."

"The Aurati can't be happy about that," I mused.

"Rafael has always been impulsive," she said. "I fear he hasn't thought this through. But, Sev—I have to go. Will you help me?"

I was making a mistake. I knew it even as I nodded. "I'll try," I said.

She smiled brilliantly, and for a moment I saw the girl I had grown up admiring. She pressed a kiss to my cheek and squeezed my hand once more. Then I saw the mask she pulled over her face, the face of the empress of Zefed, as she swept out of the garden and away.

I waited an appropriate amount of time before leaving, but I walked quickly once I did. Better that I be discovered in a hallway than in the gardens—otherwise, they might take it upon themselves to investigate what I had been doing there.

As I approached my rooms, I saw Faris coming toward me from the other end of the hallway. Her face was pinched with worry, though it smoothed as soon as she saw me.

"Where have you been?" she demanded.

"I got lost," I said. "It was chaotic back there. I couldn't find you."

She looked at me for a very long moment. "Well, get back into your chambers. The emperor will want to know that you found your way safely home."

"I will."

There was no reason to linger—it had been a long night already—but something made me pause before entering my chambers. "Faris? Are you . . . all right?"

She just looked at me, perplexed. "What?"

"Before—what he said about the Aurati. You must have lost someone at Lumina. And I know the Aurati are no traitors. It must have hurt to hear them slandered. It would have hurt me."

She swallowed hard, but her eyes flickered toward the guards at my door. "Go to sleep, Sev. I'll see you tomorrow."

She *did* feel something; I was certain of it. But I went without complaint. I sank onto the floor, staring up at the ceiling.

Piera, Piera, Piera.

I'd only had a few confidantes as a child. Most of them were dead now.

I thought of Callum, the day before he'd ridden into battle against the emperor. He'd known he likely would not survive— we all had. My mother had begged him to swallow the story of my father's death, to kiss Rafael's ring, to do whatever was necessary to spare himself. Callum had refused. "Father's death is our sorrow, but make no mistake—the empire is watching," he had told us that day. "They wait to see whether anyone will stand against the Flame. I cannot be the man who betrays his own convictions out of fear."

Mother had wept at that. But then, after Callum had led his army out through the streets of Ruzi, she had distributed the majority of her jewels among our servants and dismissed them. By the time Rafael had landed triumphantly in Ruzi, the castle stood empty. We were long gone.

From Callum I had learned conviction. But from my mother I had learned how to survive. Who would I be betraying now, if I committed to helping the empress of Zefed?

I had to help her, didn't I? She'd been so young when she'd married. She'd claimed she'd done it to survive. How was that worse than what I'd done? And the way she'd looked at me and begged me to save her son, who was innocent in all this . . . She couldn't have lied about that.

And yet, Maren could never do what Piera had done, no matter what price she might pay. I wished so badly to speak to her now, to ask her advice.

I cursed, hating my sympathetic heart. I had given my word to help them both, and I would honor my promises . . . though I had to be careful. Piera and I had been like family. But even family was capable of the cruelest betrayals.

CHAPTER SEVENTEEN

Maren

*S*ev in a garden, head buried in his hands—which are covered in blood.

I approach him cautiously. When he looks up, his face is ashen. "Maren. Is this another one of those . . ."

"Dragon dreams," I finish.

He nods. "Then you have to know the Aurati gave a prophecy today, and the emperor interpreted it to claim credit for the attack on Lumina—he lied and said that the Aurati had turned against him."

"What?" I understand the words he says, but not what they mean.

"He lied because he's frightened of your power," Sev says impatiently.

Not only that—Naava is long gone from Aurati power. So who was making the prophecies? "The prophecies aren't real anymore," I say. "Any prophecy that you hear from the Aurati is made up."

He hears me, but does he understand? I look down and am mesmerized by the blood on his hands. "What happened to your hands?"

"I—" His voice cracks, and he begins to cry. The sight frightens me, not because of the tears alone but because of what they mean. Has he given up? In all the time I've known him, I've never seen him weep.

I wrap my arms around him, and he curls into me, shaking. I hold him for a long time.

"I killed an innocent man today," he whispers, so softly, I can barely hear him. "And now I can't get the blood off my hands. I can't take this place, Maren. I have to get out."

"I'm coming, I promise."

"When?"

"We're on the highway to Irrad. Give me a week."

"I don't know if I'll last that long." He pulls back from me. "I have to get out of here. I'm in contact with the Dragons."

"Will they come?"

He hesitates. "Neve is being held here in Irrad. The emperor doesn't trust her anymore. If she'll leave with me, the Dragons might take us both—and Piera."

The dream slips, wobbles in and out of focus. "Who's Piera?" I say.

"It doesn't matter." A shadow crosses his face. There is a streak of blood on his cheek that I want to wipe away. "Will you hold me?"

My heart wrenches. I don't know what I can say that won't cross a line, so instead I just gather him in my arms and rest my chin on the top of his head, waiting for morning to come.

Sometime in the night I stirred, and for a moment I thought Sev lay wrapped in my arms, his head nestled under my chin. Then I blinked and remembered it was Kaia's body pressed against mine. An ache that was equal parts longing and shame bloomed in my chest. How could I have thought it was Sev beside me, even for an instant?

Kaia shifted, and I feigned sleep as she stretched and got up from the bed, then wrapped a blanket around herself and went to sit by the fire, staring into the flames. My thoughts were racing. Kaia had said to my face that I seemed like a completely different person—but how could that be when we knew each other's bodies almost as well as we knew our own? When we had so much history and shared secrets between us?

I couldn't bring myself to think further than that. So instead I counted my breaths until I fell asleep again, rousing only when Kaia slid back under the covers. I reached out without thought, catching her shoulder with one hand. She turned toward me, her breath warm on my cheek, and held on to me as though I were the only thing in this world keeping her anchored to the earth.

In the morning I woke before Kaia. A patch of early light fell across the bed, and I kissed her hair before easing myself free of her embrace. The fire had gone out, and I shivered as I pulled on a modicum of clothing. When I opened the door, the air was fresh and clean, and there were birds chirping, and everything seemed somehow new. I found a place to relieve myself and, afterward, stood there, taking it all in.

I put my hands in my pockets and felt something jab one of my fingers. Frowning, I pulled out—my silver hair clasp. In the tumult of the last few days I'd forgotten about it, yet somehow it had survived the journey out of the depths of Lumina and across the Zefedi sky. And before that, Kaia had kept it safe. Because I'd given it to her.

I sighed and pocketed the clasp once more. My relationship with Kaia was comfortable, its patterns marked and treaded—Kaia the leader, Maren the follower. But what if I was no longer content within those bounds? Things had changed—I had changed.

And then there was Sev.

I couldn't help but remember how Sev had treated me, the

way he had seen me exactly as I was—and how I aspired to be. And I couldn't lie to myself about how my heart had broken when I'd seen his misery in the dragon dream, and how I would have given anything to ease that pain.

Heartmates.

I shook my head. Whatever feelings I had for Sev were only that—feelings. What mattered were the choices I made and the actions I took. I chose Kaia, the dauntless girl I had chased across an empire to save. But that didn't change the fact that Sev's life was more in danger every day that I wasted on the road. We needed to leave.

The dragon kit yawned and stretched as I opened the door to the house. I scratched her on the head and went to Kaia. "Good morning," I whispered in her ear.

"How long have you been awake?" she said sleepily.

"Not long. But we have a lot of ground to cover today. Let's go."

Sleeping one night in this house seemed to have dissipated Kaia's nerves, because she laughed when I presented her with another bowl of cold porridge topped with the last of our peaches and ate it without hesitation.

"Let's not go," Kaia said as I assessed our supplies and packed them away again.

She was joking, and the words brought an involuntary smile to my lips. "Do you know who you sound like?" I said.

She shook her head, her hair falling loose down her back.

"Me," I said. "Before we left Ilvera."

She frowned, just slightly.

"Don't you remember?" I said quickly. "I wanted to stay so badly, and now you're the one who doesn't want to leave."

She had been lacing up her boots. Now she paused and let her hair fall over her face, masking her expression. "I remember. What's your point, Maren?" There was an edge to her voice.

"I was just making an observation."

"Well, you're right. You've changed. I've changed," she said curtly.

I fiddled with the strap of my pack. "I feel like you're angry with me," I said. "Why?"

"I'm not—" She shook her head, brushing me off. "It's fine. Let's go."

She picked up her pack and left the house without another word. I followed her out, ready to insist that she tell me what was wrong. We were going to talk about this tension, or whatever it was between us, because it had been building for days now. But instead of having to run after her, I was surprised to find her standing stock-still right outside the door.

"Kaia, what . . ." I trailed off as soon as I saw the figures emerging from the trees.

There were ten of them forming a semicircle around us. At first glance I thought we had been ambushed by the emperor's men—but then I looked closer. These people, a mix of Lirusan and Celet, weren't dressed like soldiers or mercenaries. And they were of a variety of ages as well, and genders. A few of them held knives or swords, but the rest hadn't drawn their weapons. I eyed them warily, my own hand poised above my knife.

"Who are you?" Kaia asked in Zefedi. "What do you want?"

"Which one of you is the dragon mistress?" a young woman out front said. Her hood was down, revealing dark hair cropped close to her head.

Kaia and I exchanged a long glance. I didn't want to answer that, not before we knew who they were.

"We asked first," I said.

The woman narrowed her eyes at me and opened her mouth to reply. But the dragon kit chose that moment to appear from behind me, and more than one person in attendance let out a shriek of fear. The kit recoiled, then tried to hide behind my legs again, with very little success. She poked her head out, sniffing curiously.

The woman, who appeared to be the leader, stepped back, her sword raised. "So it's you, then. You're coming with us."

I drew my knife. Ten was more than I wanted to fight, but I was confident that the dragon kit could help hold them off— and all we needed to do was get through them and to Clem— wait, where was the horse?

An arrow buried itself in the earth in front of me, and I jumped back. I looked up and caught the glint of something moving in the trees. So there were archers above us.

"This doesn't have to be difficult. But we only need you," the woman said, pointing at me.

Her tone was threat enough. I sheathed my knife and found Kaia's hand, squeezing hard. We were quickly divested of our packs and weapons. When the dragon kit lashed out, one man approached her with an open vial of lavender oil. Where had they even gotten that?

I thrust her behind me, blocking his way. "I swear I will kill you if you come near her with that."

"Then control her," the man said. "We have a long way to go."

I reassured the dragon kit as best I could, telling her multiple times that all would be well. Not that I knew anything of the sort.

They separated us so that Kaia walked several steps in front of me. I kept my eyes on her as we proceeded through the forest. These people were clearly familiar with it, as they walked on paths I could scarcely make out. Before long I heard the sounds of a village up ahead and was surprised when we entered a clearing to find nothing there.

One of the people let out a whistle, and suddenly camouflaged branches were lowered and shifted to reveal an entire network of shelters and walkways roped between the trees. It was both ingenious and foolhardy, it seemed to me.

"What will you do if the emperor sends a Talon to burn the forest to the ground?"

I shouldn't have said it, but the question was out.

The silence that followed was aggrieved. For a whole minute no one answered me. Then the leader said, "The Talons are occupied in other places. They don't come into the Forest of the Doran."

Convenient for them. "What's the Doran?" I asked.

This question went entirely unanswered. Braided rope ladders dropped from above, and we were instructed to climb into the trees. I whistled to the dragon kit and placed her into my pack for the climb. Once we'd managed our way up onto one of the platforms, our hands were bound. They put us in an empty tree shelter, tying us both to one of the posts supporting the wall. The dragon kit hissed as they reached for her.

"You'd better not," I warned. "She may spark, and you wouldn't want this whole place to go up in flames."

They had a brief whispered argument, and I was relieved that they left the dragon kit in the shelter, though they did loop a loose leash around her neck and tied it to one of the support poles.

"I *knew* we shouldn't have stayed at that house," Kaia whispered furiously in Verran.

"That's very helpful of you," I said. "But things could be worse."

"Captured and tied up isn't your worst-case scenario?" Kaia said drily.

"Compared to being burned alive by dragons or captured by Talons and sent to the emperor?" Even the thought of it made me shudder. "Sev and I were once trapped in a cave with malevolent ghosts after he was wounded by a Talon. *That* was worse than this."

"Fair," Kaia said begrudgingly. She leaned over, trying to look out the open door. "What do you think they want with us?"

"Well, something to do with the dragons, I assume. But I have no idea who they are. Do you?" I asked, realizing that she might have learned something in her time as an Aurat that would be useful.

"Separatists of some kind is my guess. There's been a movement over the last year or so, while the emperor has been ramping up his war with the Seda Serat. But there aren't many of them. It's a difficult life, not pledging loyalty to any kingdom. And the emperor is . . . vindictive."

There was a wooden creak, and I looked up to see the same young woman who had captured us enter the shelter. She crouched in front of us, putting herself at our eye level. "We need your help."

CHAPTER EIGHTEEN

Sev

My head ached something fierce when I woke up. I'd thought I'd made my peace with killing Owain, but I clearly had not—it had only seeped into my dreams, where Maren had seen how low I'd been brought.

Even thinking about it made the pain worse, so I turned my attention to my immediate problem: how to escape.

Convincing the Dragons to rescue not only me but also Piera and the crown prince of Zefed would be a gargantuan task. They would doubtless balk at aiding the emperor's family, and then what would I do?

Neve. I'd mentioned her to Maren last night, but the idea had floated away in the course of the dream. Now I considered it again. The Dragons had lost Maren. They would jump at the opportunity to have the true Aromatory on their side. But would Neve cooperate? I resolved to find out.

The palace today was indolent and drunk on the blood that had been spilled last night. People lingered over their food, drinking too much and laughing too loudly. The distracted atmosphere served me well. Faris had been called away on other business, so two guards accompanied me when I went to the great hall to eat, and they were both more interested in gawking at the nobility than in paying attention to me. Unluckily for me, I didn't see Neve or anyone else worth approaching. At least Erris wasn't here either.

I ate mostly to pass the time while I watched people coming and going—most of them strangers, and all of them useless to me. It wasn't until I was about to leave that I saw Idai, king of Eronne.

They entered the great hall with servants in tow and looked around, their gaze passing over me once before I saw recognition strike them, and they turned back to me. I waited for them to look away. Instead they exchanged a brief word with a servant, then walked over.

Eronne had a close relationship with Gedarin—they were the kingdom that claimed Maren's reluctant mountains, as well as the dragon fortress. So it wasn't surprising that Idai would be called to the emperor's court.

They had been in power much longer than one might have supposed, given their youth. They were only about my brother's age, but had ruled their kingdom since they were thirteen. For once the fault did not lie with the emperor—it had been a bad plague year, and both of their parents and one older sister had passed from it. Though unexpected, Idai had the benefit of a strong regency that kept the kingdom well in hand until they were ready to assume full rule.

They had been friends with Callum once. I remembered long letters written back and forth that my brother had kept close to his chest. I had stolen one once, only to discover that the salacious content I'd expected was in fact arguments over theories of governance and the best ways to increase crop production.

Truly thrilling stuff. I still believed that my brother had been at least a little infatuated—Idai was one of those people who drew eyes wherever they went, and their intellect had left Callum starry-eyed and stammering. But it was against the law of the empire for heirs to marry each other—the kingdoms could not be united. And neither one of them would ever have abdicated their thrones. Idai's consort was a woman of their own court, though I couldn't recall anything else about her.

The film of memory dropped from my eyes as Idai arrived at my table. I scrambled out of my chair and bowed. "King Idai," I said.

"Prince Severin," they said, voice pitched low. I noticed with satisfaction that they said Severin, not Vesper. "I am glad to see you in good health."

So we were going to make small talk. I wondered what Idai was actually after. "And you as well. I haven't seen you in some years—how go your affairs?"

They waved a hand dismissively. "There's always something," they said, but their solemn expression belied their words.

"I was in Eronne not too long ago," I said. "If I may say this, it seemed to me that many of your people have been affected by the crop shortages. And I hope that you've been able to manage the disturbances in Deletev. I know there's been trouble with some people harassing your Seratese citizens."

They frowned, lowering their voice to a murmur. "We've tried, but with the abiding narrative . . . it's difficult to counter a message sent from so high. And we are preoccupied, making sure the emperor's army is well stocked with provisions and young fighters."

Idai's confirmation that the emperor was spreading lies about his own citizens made my blood boil. He was using the Seratese as scapegoats to bleed the empire dry of resources and claim its children to train for an army—and for what, other than his own greed?

"What will you do?" I asked, not taking my eyes off them as I drank from my glass of wine.

"Punish those who attack others. But it's difficult to reach out to the Seratese without inadvertently fanning the flames. There are those who would see such actions as favoritism, or corruption within the government. And, not surprisingly, many Seratese do not trust my government's intentions."

"I'm sorry," I said. Whether Idai was loyal to Rafael or not, I knew them to be honorable and well intentioned when it came to their own people. I didn't doubt that they were trying to do right by their subjects.

I glanced around. No one was paying attention to us. I leaned in closer to Idai. "Some might say that the emperor does not act in the interest of his own people."

Idai nodded, their voice shrinking to a whisper. "Some might. But he is the emperor."

"What if he were not?"

They looked sharply at me. I was taking a great risk, speaking to a small king about the possibility that someone else might come to power in Zefed. "That would depend on the alternative," they said carefully.

"Someone who would not blame their own problems on innocent bystanders. Someone who would listen to the people."

Idai hesitated. Then they said, "If such a person existed, I think they would find they have more support than they realize." My heart leaped. So they supported the removal of the emperor—and they might support me.

A servant signaled to Idai, and they stepped back from me. "You sound like your brother, Severin," they said, smiling. "It heartens me to remember him through you." They nodded to me and swept away from the table before I could respond.

Idai's mention of Callum hit me in the heart, but I could not react, as someone cleared their throat near me, and I smelled the Rima flower. I looked up to see the lord from Oskiath I had marked earlier.

"You're of Oskiath?" I said, indicating the flower she wore on her lapel.

She nodded shortly. "I'm in Lord Benedic's train."

There was no Lord Benedic—that was the Dragons' code word.

"Give him my regards, would you? I haven't seen him in some time."

Her dark eyes flashed toward mine, then back down at her food. "He thought perhaps you did not wish to renew the acquaintance."

A chill swept through me. I could not have the Dragons think that I had thrown them over for the emperor. "Nothing could be further from the truth. I assure you, the delay has been out of my control," I said quickly.

The woman picked up a pear and inspected it, then put it back on the table. "I will tell him that."

"And—I find that the summer in Gedarin has been hot. It makes me miss cooler climates."

"I understand." She looked past me, her expression shuttering. "Aromatory," she said, nodding. "You look well."

I turned to see that Neve had suddenly appeared. She waved off the pleasantries. "Yes, yes, we're all well. Prince Severin, a word?" she said, effectively dismissing the Dragon representative.

"For the exulted Aromatory? Always." I bowed low. She took my arm, and we strolled casually toward the back of the hall.

"I admit, I'm surprised by your attention," I said. That seemed innocuous enough. "We were never good friends at the dragon fortress."

"Ah, but that's because you were just a lowly guard. I didn't know you were the famed shadow prince of Ruzi," she said lightly.

How unlike Neve to say that. Titles meant nothing to her— she looked down upon all equally. I glanced at her, puzzled.

"Play along," she whispered, barely moving her lips.

I glanced around. We had walked the length of the hall, and my guards hadn't even noticed I'd moved. She clearly intended to take me out of the hall—and then what?

"Where are we going?" I said, smiling and nodding to a courtier who bowed to me.

"You'll see," she said, ushering me through the door.

The corridor outside was close to empty, and there were no guards once we turned the first corner. She dropped my arm. "Let's go. Quickly, now!"

I followed as she swept up a staircase to the second floor of the palace, and then through a dizzying set of turns that had me thoroughly lost by the time she arrived at a plain-looking door in a disused hallway. She unlocked the door, and I followed her in.

I was standing inside the Aromatory's laboratory. The countertops were clean and spare, with glass beakers and flasks and other tools I couldn't identify stored on the shelves.

Neve leaned against the counter, looking hard at me. "Only Milek is allowed in this room, so we have some time. Now tell me, what's your plan?"

I hesitated. Should I trust her? She was an Aurat. She'd worked for the emperor longer than I'd been alive.

But the emperor had turned against her. And I suspected that she'd helped Maren more than a little during her time in the dragon fortress.

"Are you on the emperor's side?" I said.

She paused, clearly choosing her words carefully. "I love the dragons, but Rafael does not. I shared the Aromatory's secrets with an outsider because of the ways the emperor mistreats them. And for that, he will see me dead before the year is out. So no, I'm not on his side. The emperor has become my enemy."

I wished Maren were here. She knew Neve better than I did—she would know whether to trust her words the way I wanted to. Either way, I knew that the Dragons would not take the empress unless I made it worth their while. I *needed* Neve's cooperation.

"If you had a way out, would you take it?" I asked.

"My duty is to the dragons," Neve said. "I can't do anything that will jeopardize their care."

"And allowing Milek to poison them with oils that do not work is caring for them properly?"

She looked down her nose at me. "Me being here to tend them *is* caring for them, no matter how short a time that may be. Things are not always so simple, Prince Severin."

I crossed my arms. "What if the dragons were freed?"

"Are you implying that you would give up the chance to claim a dragon for your own?" Neve said skeptically. "I've heard whispers about how you mean to challenge the emperor."

"I'm no dragon rider. There are others more worthy," I said, and found that I meant it.

Neve's eyes gleamed eagerly. "Maren."

I nodded. "Would you leave, if the dragons no longer needed your care?"

"Yes," she said immediately.

Yes. I felt a surge of relief, followed quickly by triumph.

"I have a plan. I can't tell you everything, but if you commit to using your talents as an Aromatory, my allies will get you out of here."

"And what do you get out of it?"

Piera's escape. But her part in this wasn't mine to tell, not yet.

I shook my head. "Trust me, and be ready. I'll tell you more as soon as I'm able."

After a moment she held out her hand. "All right, Prince Severin. We have a deal."

CHAPTER NINETEEN

Maren

I can't believe I'm even saying this, but where I come from, kidnapping people isn't usually part of the process of asking for help," I said to the woman.

"Well, here it's necessary when you can't be sure that the person you need isn't a spy for the emperor," she replied.

I let out a sharp bark of laughter. "Why would you think that *we* are Zefedi spies? It makes much more sense for *you* to be the spies, not us."

"We've heard the stories of the dragon mistress. But from where I stand, only Talons have control over dragons. It's a reasonable conclusion to draw that the dragon mistress might be a Talon in disguise."

"And yet you still took the trouble of hunting us down because you needed our help." I sighed. "We can go around and around like this, or you can tell us who you really are and what you need. Think about it this way—if it turns out we're Zefedi spies, we're already tied up. Very easy to kill."

A grin flashed across the woman's face. "You're not wrong about that." She thought for a moment. "Look, some people on my council won't like that I'm about to tell you this, but we don't have time. We're Ruzian. Our kingdom has been under siege by Talons."

"That doesn't make any sense," I said. "Ruzi is a part of the empire. Why would the tyrant make war on his own kingdom?"

"Because of the protests," the woman responded. "The new ruling family that the emperor installed cares nothing at all about governing the kingdom. And the emperor brought his fist down hard with taxes and army recruiting. We've been protesting for better treatment for a long time, but instead of negotiating in good faith, the emperor cut us off from the rest of Zefed. There are Talons stationed along the border—no supplies in or out. They're trying to starve us into surrender. We have some stores, but they'll run out soon enough. The rest of the empire is hurting—we wouldn't expect much help there. But Ruzi has a trade agreement with Old Zefed. If we could just get the dragons off the mountains for long enough to resupply, we would stand a chance."

She looked again at me. "We heard reports about someone sabotaging Talons. We hoped that you could do the same in Ruzi."

Kaia nodded. "That makes sense. Lumina lost contact with the Ruzian Aurati branch not long ago."

Freeing more dragons—and having the opportunity to scuttle the tyrant's goals—was a worthy endeavor. But Ruzi was southwest of where we were, in the opposite direction from Oskiath. If we went with the Ruzians, we might give up our only chance of meeting up with the Dragons in time to get to Sev.

On the other hand . . . relying on the Dragons had always been a flawed plan. Their about-face after Sev had abandoned them was suspicious. Despite Rowena's assurances to the contrary, I doubted she had any intention of deviating from her original agenda to take over the empire without reforming anything. Allying with them would have meant confronting that reality sooner or later.

But the Ruzians . . .

"Did you ever meet the shadow prince?" I asked.

A flicker of pain passed over her face. "Most everyone who lived in the capital crossed paths with the royal family at some point."

"Were they fair rulers? I only ever heard that they were executed for treason."

The woman sat back on her heels, studying the floor. "They were aware of the emperor's cruelty. They tried to do right, for what good it did them."

She spoke like someone in mourning.

"If you were to see Prince Severin again, what would you want from him?" I asked.

The woman let out a sigh, considering. "The prince didn't deserve what happened to him. If he were to gain power . . . I don't know, but something better than living and dying under the emperor's thumb. We all deserve that."

I nodded, relieved. If she had resented Sev—for a variety of reasons, I recognized that one might—it would have made my idea completely unworkable. I only had one more question for her.

"And the oils you threatened to use on my dragon. Where did you get them? How did you know to use them?"

"Some of the Talons have been careless with their secrets, and we got lucky stealing a shipment. Before we heard of you, we were planning on using the oils to try to sabotage them."

All right. "Then we'll help you—if you agree to two conditions. First, Sev has been captured by the emperor and is being held in Irrad. Before we go to Ruzi, you must send a small force to accompany us to Irrad and help rescue him."

The woman let out a snort of laughter. "No. He may be the shadow prince, but he is one person. The people of Ruzi need help *now*. I cannot leave them for a mission with such a high likelihood of failure and such a small reward."

I wanted to snap back that saving Sev was no small reward. Instead I took a deep breath. I was not in control of this situation. And much as I hated to admit it, she had a point.

"Afterward, then. If we succeed in forcing the Talons out of Ruzi, you will come with us to Irrad."

"That's a more reasonable request. What's the second?"

"You will give all of your dragon oils to me."

The woman looked wary at the idea, so I pressed on. "Part of my mission is to free the dragons from their captivity. I can't allow humans to stockpile oils that have the ability to keep them in bondage."

After a moment of consideration, the woman nodded. "I'll take your proposal to my companions. Excuse me."

She exited the shelter, leaving a heavy silence behind her.

"That's why I'm angry at you." Kaia's voice was flat as she switched back to Verran.

Surprised, I turned to look at her. "What are you talking about?"

She pulled on the rope tying her to the post and shifted her position. "You just negotiated with that woman on both of our behalves without even asking me first about any of it."

"What else was I supposed to do? I thought you wanted me to help more people. *This* is helping people. And if they agree, we'll have what we need to make our way to Irrad as well." I didn't understand how she could be complaining about this.

"But you didn't even *ask* me! What if I wanted to do something different? What if I told you that I was done—done being abducted and running for our lives? That I didn't want to go with you anymore?"

"Is that what you—"

She cut me off. "Whether I want that or not isn't the point—the point is that you didn't ask me. You're so set on what *you* want, you're not thinking about me anymore. When is the last time you truly thought about what I wanted at all?"

Now my temper flared. "That's a bit rich coming from you, don't you think?" I said. "Back in Ilvera, all you ever thought about was leaving the mountain. You never concerned yourself with what I wanted then."

"But I thought that *was* what you wanted!"

"I only said that because I was *in love with you*, and I knew you would leave without me. Because I wanted you more than I wanted anything else. I couldn't stand leaving the mountain, but I couldn't stand losing you more. And while we're on the subject, it would be easier to know what you wanted or how you were feeling if you would actually *talk to me*. I know you went through horrible things in Lumina. Why can't you just talk to me about it?"

Kaia put her head back against the wall and let out a cry that sounded half-exhausted, half-outraged. "Because I don't want to talk about it, any of it. Don't you understand? I hate myself for what happened, and I hate you for seeing it."

My heart broke. "Kaia—"

"I always knew that I would accomplish something extraordinary," she said bitterly. "But instead I ended up a prisoner, and you're the one who became extraordinary. You're the dragon mistress, but it should have been *me*. You're right—I'm the one who wanted adventure. I had to practically drag you into agreeing to go downmountain with me, and *this* is what I'm stuck with now?"

I reeled back. *Stuck* with me? That's what she thought?

Her lip was trembling. "Your abilities strike fear into the emperor's heart. You can talk to dragons, ride dragons, you even have your own dragon companion, and what do I have? *Nothing*. It's a joke, Maren. You wanted to live in one village your whole life, and instead you have everything I ever wanted."

"I would give it to you if I could," I said miserably.

She sniffed, shook her head. "Don't lie, Maren. Not about this, and not about what you feel for Sev."

"This has nothing to do with Sev!" I said.

Kaia took a deep breath and held it before letting it out slowly. "You're right," she said quietly. "Maybe that was unfair of me. The problems between us are ours. But I've watched your face when you speak of him. You *do* have feelings for him, and I won't let you pretend any longer that you don't."

Sev's face flashed through my mind. "I told you, nothing ever happened between us," I said, though even as I spoke, I was aware of how flimsy that sounded.

"That's not the point, and you know it. I know we're in danger now. But you're going to have to decide what you want once we're on the other side of all this." She shifted, stretched out her legs. "I'm tired now. We'll go to Ruzi, like you said. But next time, do me the courtesy of asking for my opinion."

I, too, felt exhausted. Kaia and I had spent days being careful with each other. I'd tried so hard to turn us back into the Kaia and Maren of Ilvera, but now that the truth of our feelings was out in the open, I felt wounded and raw. Tears burned at the corners of my eyes, and I turned away, hoping Kaia wouldn't notice me crying. After a while I felt myself begin to drift off to sleep, and I just hoped not to have another dragon dream—if I saw Sev right now, I knew I would fall apart.

After a while we were woken up and taken out individually to relieve ourselves before being put back exactly as we'd been. The dragon kit was handling captivity well, but I knew that her good behavior was contingent on me acting as though everything was all right.

I didn't know how much longer I could wait. We'd been left alone for so long that I was certain the Ruzians had decided not to accept our bargain. Which meant that we needed to escape, but I was at a loss for ideas, and Kaia still wasn't talking to me.

It had been easy to let things go when we were running for our lives. Now that everything had finally spilled out, I feared we stood on opposite sides of a chasm across which there was no bridge. I was not willing to give up who I had become since leaving Ilvera. Kaia's envy ate at me. When she had been the celebrated one, I had lifted her up. Why couldn't she do the same for me?

At last the woman who had spoken with us returned. She was smiling—I took that as a good sign. "We've agreed to accept your proposal," she said. She cut our restraints, and I got to my feet, rubbing my wrists. "Apologies for the kidnapping. I hope you understand why we felt it was necessary. I'm Efren."

"I'm Maren, and this is Kaia," I said. Kaia nodded but did not speak. I felt bruised just looking at her.

"And the dragon?" Efren asked. She was clearly curious about the kit but remained wary. She waited for me to remove her leash, rather than doing it herself.

"She hasn't told us her name yet," I said.

"I see," Efren replied. "Come and eat. Everyone is very interested in meeting you, officially."

Now that she mentioned it, I *was* hungry. I wasn't sure how long we had been kept tied up, but the bowl of porridge we'd eaten in the morning seemed like a lifetime ago.

"Yes, let's," I said. We followed her out of the shelter and toward the smell of food cooking.

CHAPTER TWENTY

Sev

There was a sharp knock at the door just as Neve and I shook hands.

"Milek?" I asked.

"Milek wouldn't knock," she said. "Are we done here?"

I nodded. Neve went to the door and opened it a crack.

Faris was standing outside. "Aromatory. I'm looking for Prince Severin. Is he here?"

"Here." I bowed to Neve. "Thank you for indulging me, Aromatory."

She shrugged indifferently, and I saw myself out of the laboratory and into the hallway, where Faris was waiting.

"You left your guards," she said.

"They were preoccupied. Is it my fault that they didn't notice me walking *very leisurely* out of the great hall? And I was in the company of a senior Aurat. His Highness can't possibly object to that."

She snorted. "What were you two talking about?"

We began walking down the hall. Faris had to navigate—being on the second floor had completely flummoxed me. "Oh, nothing worth mentioning. The habits of dragon hatchlings. How many scales the average dragon sheds each year."

"And if I asked Neve what you were talking about, she would say the same?"

I laughed. "I'm almost certain that the Aromatory outranks you in the Aurati order, so I wish you luck in interrogating her. Besides, I don't know how long you've been acquainted with Neve, but I've never known her to be anything but an unhelpful, crotchety grump."

"So a casual conversation about dragon scales necessitated her bringing you into her private laboratory."

"I imagine it was out of an abundance of caution, considering how careful the emperor is about the dragons and their secrets. Of course, I am a prince of the realm, but that isn't true of most others at the palace," I said airily. "And anyway, where have you been? I'd almost begun to miss you."

She waggled her fingers weakly in answer. So the emperor had been putting her interrogatory skills to use.

"Doesn't he have others who can handle those tasks?" My fingers that had been broken ached suddenly, and I resisted the urge to touch them.

"Ah, but none with such flair." Faris's voice was light, but she looked exhausted. Did using her powers take a physical toll on her? I hadn't been paying close enough attention before to tell.

We reached the staircase, and Faris paused before taking her first step down. I hesitated. It seemed wrong to offer help to a killing machine who worked for my greatest enemy—who had *tortured* me. And yet it seemed there was something truly wrong with her.

"Are you all right?" I asked after a moment. "You seem ... peaky."

The look on her face was pure poison.

I held up my hands in submission. "I'm serious!"

Faris's only response was to glare at me again and lean heavily on the banister as we made our way downstairs.

My mind was racing. This was an opportunity. I could make a plan to elude the others, but Faris was my most dangerous guard. And if she wasn't feeling well, perhaps she could be overpowered.

As if reading my thoughts, Faris said, "Don't worry. I still have quite enough strength to make you suffer."

I believed her.

The next day, breakfast was interrupted when three palace Aurati entered the great hall. The Aurat in the lead carried an ornate scroll between her outstretched hands, and conversation throughout the hall fell away as the trio approached the throne.

The emperor set down his glass as the Aurati knelt before him. The Aurat held up the scroll, keeping her head bowed. When the emperor nodded, the herald standing at the emperor's left side stepped forward and took the scroll. He unrolled it, and read off the paper.

"The Aurati seers have spoken," the herald said. "They say, 'The hand of our father rests over the sea.'"

Something flashed across my mind—the dragon dream. The last time I'd spoken to Maren, she'd told me that Aurati prophecies couldn't be trusted, that they weren't real.

Rafael had claimed control over what was left of the Aurati. Did that mean that he was writing the prophecies?

The emperor smiled, standing. He rested his hand briefly on the first Aurat's head before raising his voice to address the hall. "This prophecy is a gift. The time to set sail once more is upon us, and our fleet is almost ready."

A cheer rose from the audience, and my jaw tightened. These nobles didn't care about the true cost of war. Why should they? None of their children were going to fight in it, and the emperor had taken care to make sure they'd felt no shortage of any kind while he had obtained the timber and the labor for the ships, and recruited Zefedi peasants to fill them. So they would applaud the Flame of the West because they feared retribution if they did not, then carry on with their lives of excess without another thought.

The emperor raised his hand, and the hall quieted once more.

"Our brave soldiers must have a leader, and our Aurati have graced me with the knowledge of who that person will be. A stalwart servant of the empire, a man bonded to me by sworn loyalty. Prince Vesper Severin Avidal, the shadow prince of Ruzi. By his hand the flame of our enemy will fall."

No.

Faris had her hand under my elbow, forcing me to stand. I did so and faced the applause of the nobility around me, a wooden smile on my lips. Even the emperor was clapping for me.

"In seven days, the fleet will sail," the emperor called.

I forced my smile wider. My mind racing, I took the largest bow I could. Then I stood up, looking the emperor in the eye. "I am eager to carry out your bidding, Your Excellence," I said loudly.

"Then you will go to the docks today to inspect your soldiers. There is an escort waiting for you in the courtyard now. Go with fire, Commander."

Commander. What a laugh. No doubt I'd be knifed in the back by some unknown assailant the moment we set sail. I would be dead, and all the people of Zefed would ever know was that I had died upon strange waters, doing the emperor's bidding. Much better than a public execution that would only galvanize any who opposed the emperor's rule. But I bowed again and pushed myself back from the table.

Faris fell in line with me as I left the hall. "Are you ready?" she said.

"For the surprise inspection of soldiers who weren't under my control until just now? As ready as I'll ever be," I said.

The emperor meant this display to reinforce my image as a loyal servant of Zefed, and I had no doubt that it would serve its purpose. But it was also a trip outside the palace, which meant that it was an opportunity, if only I knew how to take advantage of it. I had only seven days now to escape, or die. Maren had said she'd be here in a week, but I couldn't count on it. Not when her delaying by even a day would mean my death.

The escort waiting for us in the courtyard was a fine military processional. Every soldier wore armor polished to a shine, guaranteed to catch eyes as we passed through the city. No fewer than three Talons circled overhead. The emperor had truly created a spectacle.

I was surprised to see a few others waiting—King Idai was seated in the first carriage, and Erris and Lord Annick stood near it on the ground. Erris waved when she saw Faris and me coming toward them.

"Are you joining us?" I asked as we approached. I was surprised—Erris had mentioned feeling uncomfortable outside the noble districts.

But she nodded eagerly. "I've never been in one of the royal carriages before." She lowered her voice. "To be quite honest, the emperor frightens me a little. I didn't know when I'd ever have the opportunity again."

I couldn't tell if she was being deliberately obtuse, so instead of replying, I simply raised a hand to Idai and Annick. Faris settled into the seat beside me, and the procession began.

As we passed through the palace gates and into Irrad proper, I realized there was another explanation for the Talons' presence. The people.

The last time I had been outside the palace, the streets had been quiet through the noble and merchant districts. The unrest we'd encountered had been in the poorer districts, and even then, they had been easily cowed. Things were different now.

Most windows in the noble districts were shuttered, and the people on the streets were not nobility—at least, they weren't dressed like it. They were commoners, and they were angry. Someone on the side of the road held up a sign as we passed—white, with red lettering: REMEMBER OWAIN. As I watched, a group of Aurati materialized and started toward the sign holder. The sign disappeared from view, and I was left wondering if I had even seen it to begin with. Faris's expression was studiously blank.

The atmosphere was dark and unfriendly as we passed through the outer districts. We were given a wide berth, much larger than our carriages required, and almost everyone turned away from us as we passed. No merchants called us over to their stalls, and no one smiled at us or even waved.

Erris and Annick were occupied in conversation, and Idai

was on the far side of the carriage. I turned to Faris. "This is all because of Owain?" I murmured.

Her jaw clenched. "I can't possibly presume to understand the minds of peasants," she said.

I lowered my voice even further. "Don't you feel any sympathy? I can't imagine you were a noble before you were an Aurat." While the ranks of the Aurati were open to any who passed the trials, most nobles chose not to undertake them.

"I am an Aurat," she said frostily. "And that is all you need to know. Now wave to the people."

I lifted a hand and waved unenthusiastically as we proceeded through the city. The road sloped downward as we approached the ocean, and the breeze was salty and brisk by the time we reached the docks.

The soldiers halted in unison, and we disembarked from our carriages to proceed on foot.

The emperor's palace sat at the highest point of Irrad, the rest of the city set on a slight incline. The story went that if you dropped a ball outside the palace gates and let it roll, it would eventually find its way to the ocean. But the harbor, normally bustling with friendly activity, was crawling with soldiers today. There were only a few workers about. And at the north end of the harbor, the emperor's fleet waited.

There were no oceans bordering Ruzi. We had rivers and sleek, maneuverable riverboats—nothing like the ships now floating in Irrad Harbor. These ships were massive. Entire towns might fit in each of them, provided the towns were small. And it seemed that was exactly the plan, judging by the sea of tents stretching up the beach and out of sight. The magnitude of what I saw stopped me in my tracks.

There had never been an army this big in Zefed. The first failed fleet the emperor had sent to attack the Seda Serat couldn't have been more than half the size of this one. The small kingdoms had ground forces, but the bulk of the peacekeeping—and war making—was done by the emperor's Talons and their dragons. The dragons were an unstoppable force, so there had never been a need to raise a large army. But now the emperor had created a force to conquer nations.

A group of soldiers was busy running supplies to the ships on our right. Ahead of us was a squadron performing drills with mismatched swords—some of them barely long enough to qualify as more than a large knife. The soldiers looked tired and untrained. Enormous this army might be, but its supplies were castoffs—anything that had remained after the first invasion of the Seda Searat. Soon the emperor was going to order them all stuffed into these ships for a weeks-long journey to a distant land. There was a chance none of them would make it back, and for what? And if I boarded one of those ships, I would be signing my own death warrant.

"This is wrong," I said quietly.

"The emperor's will is intractable," Idai said, coming up next to me. They flicked their gaze upward, indicating the circling Talons.

I glanced around to make sure Erris and Lord Annick were out of earshot. They were bustling up and down the docks as though they were the ones on parade. I turned to Idai.

"Have there been ramifications in Eronne?" I said.

"One person from every family has been called. The loss will be incalculable."

Faris materialized at my side, as if out of nowhere. "Well, you've seen the ships. You've seen the soldiers. It's time to return to the palace, *Commander*."

It was exactly as I'd suspected. The emperor did not care about me connecting with the soldiers—no doubt he preferred that I did not. The entire excursion had been an excuse to show me off to the city, once again a loyal prince, surrounded by the military might of Zefed. But I would not play along so easily.

"I'm going to meet the soldiers," I said to Faris. "These are the people risking their lives on behalf of our empire. They deserve that much from their *commander*."

"I'll come with you," said Idai. "Some of the soldiers are from Eronne."

It was exhaustion, more than frustration, that passed over Faris's face. But she didn't refuse in front of Idai. At least in this moment, I held power.

I squared my shoulders and approached the squadron. An older man was barking instructions at them, but the moment he noticed Faris, he called them to a halt and bowed deeply. "Aurat," he said.

"The Flame of the West has appointed a new commander." She gestured to me. "I present Prince Vesper Severin of Ruzi. He will lead the army when it departs. Severin, this is General Garan."

The general's bow was perfunctory but polite. "Commander," he said, his face betraying no emotion. A true military man. Unlike Lord Patak, it seemed that Garan might actually be competent. He was probably the person who would take over command of the campaign once I had been removed from the field. Perhaps the emperor had even assigned him the duty of dispatching me.

"General," I replied. "I'm here to acquaint myself with our current state of readiness. Is there anyone who would be able to show us around the camp? I don't want to interrupt your operations."

He looked at Faris. Whatever expression he saw seemed to reassure him. He pivoted to face the squadron. "Alton." A young man stepped out of formation. Garan waved him over. "Please escort the prince through camp."

Alton saluted the general, and we set off.

"Have you been in service long?" I asked.

"A few months, my lord," Alton replied. "My sister was called, but she runs the family business. So it fell to me."

"Where are you from?"

"Kyseal," he replied shortly, his tone discouraging questions along that line. Perhaps he feared retaliation against his family if he angered me.

Alton led the way through the camp without much further discussion, though he took care to point out the different squadrons and explain their tasks. It seemed that many soldiers had been involved with the building of the fleet. Now that the ships were seaworthy, tasks ranged from packing and loading supplies to training under the command of General Garan and his subordinates.

The army leadership seemed to be doing what they could with insufficient resources. We walked through row after row of tents. Most of them were shabby and makeshift, and the people sitting or standing near them looked much the same. They all looked sleep deprived at best, and ill at worst. This was the army the emperor was sending to war? I felt suddenly exhausted.

Idai split off from our group to approach a squadron flying the flag of Eronne. Faris and I continued on without him, trailing Alton at a short distance.

Faris was faltering. The weakness I had seen yesterday was back. She was deliberate about every step, as though she knew she would not be able to recover if she tripped. I fell back to match her pace.

"Are you ill?" I asked, quietly so Alton wouldn't hear.

She shook her head stubbornly.

"I know something is wrong. Tell me. Is it because of—" I held up my hand, imitating her use of power.

She pressed her lips together. Then, finally, she nodded. "It gets worse. Every time."

Triumph flared within me. The emperor was clearly demanding more than she had to give. *And* she had trusted me enough—or been weak enough—to let that secret slip. Possibilities blossomed in my mind. Could she be turned from the emperor's side? Would she be too weak to stop me when the time came to escape?

For a split second I contemplated running right now. Then I realized—if the army didn't stop me, the emperor's military guard would. They were well trained and well fed. And even on the slim chance that I could get away, I'd made a promise to Piera. Could I leave her?

I should. She was the empress. She was in no danger where she was.

But—she was Piera. And I'd promised.

"I've seen enough," I said to Faris. "Let's go."

We turned around, and then something flew through the air, narrowly missing my head. I watched it fall to the ground—a bowl, with a scant layer of rice and pickled cucumber. I looked up.

A group of soldiers huddled together, their arms crossed,

faces angry. No one claimed responsibility. Faris started forward, and I grabbed her arm. "Don't," I said. She relented. Back at the palace she might punish me for what I did here, but she couldn't undermine me in front of the army.

I wanted to apologize for my role in their circumstances, however small. But with Faris at my side, I could not speak my mind. "The Flame of the West has assigned me to command this army," I said. "I will do my best on your behalf."

I saluted them, then nodded and walked away.

"That was gross insubordination," Faris said as we made our way back to the carriages. "They must be punished." But her voice was weak—it was an empty threat.

I shrugged. "Most of the army would probably do the same, given the chance. If you tortured all of them, there wouldn't be anyone left to sail the ships. Leave them be."

She shook her head. "The emperor won't like it."

I looked around. Alton had left us—there wasn't anyone close enough to eavesdrop. "You just told me that you suffer every time you use your powers on the emperor's behalf. But you're powerful enough to break free. Why are you still loyal to him?"

She glared at me. I stopped walking and crossed my arms. "Well?"

For a moment it seemed she was wavering. Then we were interrupted by shouts coming from the civilian side of the docks. There was some sort of commotion, though we were too far away to see what was going on. I took a step forward.

"Leave it," Faris said.

I looked at her. "No." Then I waded through the crowd, toward the disturbance.

CHAPTER TWENTY-ONE

Maren

Now that we were in agreement, Kaia and I were welcomed with curiosity and open arms. The village in Doran Forest was home to refugees from all over Zefed who had fled the tyrant's reach. There were about fifteen in Efren's group, all of whom had escaped Ruzi a few days earlier to come in search of the dragon mistress. They hadn't tracked us—they'd tracked our dragon encounters. Every new report of a dragon acting strangely had let them closer.

Efren led the group efficiently, and the next morning—after far too little sleep—we were on our way to Ruzi. Despite the way in which our paths had collided, I was happy to be with Efren. I knew less about the geography of Zefed than I should, and having a knowledgeable guide—to Ruzi, and then to Gedarin—made me feel safer. The dragon kit was having fun entertaining the Ruzians with wing flaps and snorts of flame. None of them had ever seen a dragon so young before, and they were mesmerized.

But Kaia still wasn't talking to me—she'd even found someplace else to sleep last night—and that remained the case as we covered ground. I stayed quiet too. I knew that she was expecting me to take the first step toward reconciliation, but I was *angry*. She'd said she was *stuck* with me? I wasn't going to apologize. Not when she'd said that and had the gall to claim I never thought about what she wanted. I was making the decisions because someone had to, not because I relished being the one in control. My dragon-touched abilities didn't make me special—but they did feel like my *own*, like I had discovered a part of myself that had always been there. I would never wish to give them up. And Sev...

It had torn at my heart to watch him cry, even in a dream. And I had been *jealous* when he had mentioned Piera, whoever that was. Sev had seen me. Where Kaia had stifled me—unintentionally, but still—Sev had encouraged me to shine.

I watched Kaia across the distance that she had put between us. Despite our argument, she was still here, because she loved me. She disagreed with parts of what I was doing, she wasn't even speaking to me, but she was still here. But were we still meant for each other?

The question terrified me. I couldn't answer it—could barely even think it. Even the act of asking cracked open the agonizing possibility of another timeline, a future different from any I had ever pictured. What would I do when this was all over, if she wasn't by my side? For the first time in my life, I looked into the future and saw only shadows.

And as the afternoon waned, we reached Ruzi.

At first it was a shimmer in the distance, something that didn't match the rest of our surroundings. But over the course of the next hour, the landscape resolved into a growing line, and then a sweeping ocean of dusty red flowers that took my breath away. I'd never seen anything like it in my life.

"What is this?" I asked.

Efren smiled. "The Red Plains of Ruzi," she replied. "This is the border between Oskiath and Ruzi. The soil underneath is red as well—that's why it looks as it does. Useless for growing crops, but it's something to see." She shaded her eyes with one hand, looking around. "This is also where we need to be careful of Talons. We'll wait under cover until night falls. Then we'll go underground."

Underground? The memory of Vir's Passage was still fresh in my mind, and I wasn't eager to repeat the experience. "For how long?" I said, well aware of the worry in my voice.

Efren looked up at the sky. "An hour before night. Then a few hours more in the tunnel."

"All underground?"

The dragon kit wound herself around my legs and leaned her head against my knee.

Efren shrugged. "I'm sorry. It's the only way in."

The only way. Despite the jump of my stomach, I told myself that this was a minor challenge compared to everything else I had faced—and had yet to face. I should have been laughing about it.

Efren's group had dug foxholes at the edge of the forest that were covered by woven mats painted to look like the Red Plains. Kaia and I ducked into one together, along with the dragon kit. There was enough room for each of us to sit, though it was a tight fit. It was the closest that we'd been since leaving the forest.

Even if Kaia wanted to apologize, she would never say it first. It was up to me to speak.

"We should talk," I said quietly.

Kaia looked straight ahead. "Have you made up your mind?"

The gaping black hole of the future yawned open at me

again. I closed my eyes. "I don't know what to do. I want us to be all right."

"There's distance between us," Kaia said. "Maybe we're both to blame for it, but it's there."

"Then help me close the gap," I said.

In the semidarkness of the foxhole, her hand found mine and squeezed, and my heart contracted around that gesture. I took a deep breath.

"I was a food taster at the dragon fortress," I told her. "That was the only position open when I got there. I tasted such rich food, but every time I thought it might be my last."

"Did you ever get poisoned?" Her voice was hushed.

"Gods, no!" It was easy to laugh about, now that it was in the past. Lord Patak, Lilin, Kellyn—I'd been so frightened then. Now they mattered not at all. "Probably the closest I ever got to dying was when I broke out of the fortress. I thought I could tame a yearling and escape—instead I almost drowned, and that dragon almost ate me alive."

"What happened?"

"Sev saved me," I said, sobering. "I wouldn't be alive if he hadn't been there."

"Oh." Kaia went quiet for a while. "What did you do next?"

I looked at her. It was difficult to read her expression in the dark. "Do you really want to know?"

She nodded. "I do."

I had been reluctant to tell the whole story before. Not because I had kissed Sev—I hadn't—but because I knew that in the telling, I wouldn't be able to conceal the depth of the connection that we had forged. But now I knew I had to be honest—to know who I had become, Kaia had to see what had made me. So I took a deep breath and told her everything.

Once I had finished, she said nothing about Sev. Instead she said only, "You came for me. Through all of that."

"How could I have done anything else?" I turned to her. "Kaia . . . what happened to you in Lumina?"

She shook her head. "I can't."

"Please."

She sighed. "At first they told me that I was special. Gifted. Chosen. But when they put me in front of the dragon, it was clear that something was wrong. That *I* was wrong." Her hand trembled as she held it out in front of her. "I tried to do what they wanted, but—" Her breath caught. "Maren, I can't."

I took her hand and pressed a kiss against her palm. "I'm so sorry," I said, an awful pain in my throat at the thought of what she had gone through.

"I tried so hard to prove myself, but it wasn't enough. *I* wasn't enough," Kaia said, her voice breaking with a sob. Her words reminded me suddenly of Naava's last words to me. I hadn't thought of the prophecy at all since our last dragon encounter—if I didn't prove myself, I would not have Naava's assistance when I most needed it.

"Naava told me I was wrong too," I confessed. "When she left us to return to Ilvera. She needed to heal, but she was angry with me as well. She said that I was using the dragons for selfish purposes. That if I wanted her help again, I had to prove myself beyond the reach of her wings. So . . . I understand. About not being enough. About proving yourself."

Was I doing that? We were going to Ruzi to free dragons.

That counted, didn't it? Even if freeing those dragons was also instrumental in securing other allies?

"I can't believe you," Kaia said, cutting through my thoughts.

"What?" I said.

"Maren, this is *critical* information, and you didn't tell me! If you don't have Naava's support when we reach Irrad, what are we going to do?" She barreled on without waiting for a reply. "Did you think that since you're the only one who can speak to dragons, you're the only one who should know what they say? This is just like before—you're keeping things from me and making decisions without me."

"It's not like that at all! I just—" How could I explain that I had felt ashamed? That I didn't want to talk about the prophecy because it would mean admitting I *hadn't* proven myself yet? That she was right—there *was* a chance that Naava would stay away, but there was nothing else I could do but follow this path to its conclusion?

"Just *nothing*. I can't believe you did that to me, Maren."

She crossed her arms and turned away from me, and I let her.

There was no privacy in this small space, so I pretended that I didn't see her crying—because I knew that she would push me away if I reached out. We didn't talk after that. But later, as I was close to dozing off, I heard her whisper.

"Perhaps I'm a fool, but I still want to be with you. I still want the adventures we talked about. You're my heart."

I didn't trust myself to speak. Instead I shifted so that I leaned against her, resting my head on her shoulder and taking her hand in mine. She made me want to cry. But all of the adventures she'd spoken of in Ilvera were predicated on one thing—the empire.

What *would* happen when the dragons were freed? I had tried to pretend that I didn't care, that everyone who benefited from the system that exploited the dragons was complicit and therefore equally culpable. But that wasn't exactly true. Almost no one in Zefed had known about the captivity of the mother dragon. And the emperor's iron grip on the dragons meant that there was no way to protest their treatment even if one wanted to—other than outright rebellion. Now . . . I had vowed to free the dragons and take down the empire. But what would grow in its place? If I broke this world, was it my responsibility to help put it back together?

Sometime later Efren thumped on the top of the foxhole. "Time to go," she said.

We climbed out to see that darkness had fallen, giving us cover. We crept carefully across the Red Plains until one of the Ruzians held up a hand. He knelt down in the darkness and drew aside another woven mat. Underneath was a large hole that had been dug straight down. One by one the Ruzians lowered themselves into the hole. A light flared to life—the tunnel was shallower than I'd thought. I nodded. Having a light made the whole situation significantly more bearable. Kaia went before me. Then I jumped down, and Efren passed the dragon kit to me before following, pulling the mat back over the hole.

We were in a tunnel that had clearly been designed and built by people who knew what they were doing. It wasn't large, but there was enough room for two people to walk side by side, and there were wooden beams supporting the ceiling. "Who built this?" I asked.

"Best as we can tell, one of the royal families that thought they needed an escape route from the city. But it seems to have been forgotten until recently. The current king certainly doesn't know about it," Efren said. She took a torch from one of the other Ruzians. "Let's go—it's a long walk."

Time passed differently underground. Unlike in Vir's Passage, at least I had the torches to help keep track. We were nearing the end of our third torch when Efren held up her hand, stopping our group.

We stood, silent, and I became aware of a low muffled hum. We were close. Efren doused her torch, and the other torchbearers followed suit. I blinked, my eyes adjusting, and soon I could see a glimmer of light up ahead. We had reached a doorway.

Efren went to the door and pulled gently on a cord that hung there. Then she stepped back, drew her knife, and held it steady. The other Ruzians did as well, so I reached for my knife too. Was this part of the plan? Were we expecting to fight our way out of this? Though, I felt that if that were the case, we would have been told.

The door creaked, and we tensed.

Then it opened fully, revealing a young Ruzian man.

Efren's shoulders relaxed, and she sheathed her knife before hugging the man. "How goes?" she said.

"The streets are quiet. Everyone's exhausted, Ef." The man peered around her. "Did you find her?"

"Yes! Maren, come!" Efren waved at me, and the Ruzians

nudged me forward. The dragon kit jumped up to my shoulder—she was getting too heavy for that—and I stepped out of the tunnel and into what looked like an abandoned basement.

"Maren, this is my brother Jase. Jase, Maren. The *dragon mistress*." Efren said the words with a certain amount of relish, and I found my cheeks heating up at the way Jase looked at me—awed, and perhaps a little frightened.

"I'm happy to help," I said. The rest of the group filed out of the tunnel and closed it off again, then piled furniture in front of it until it was hidden from view. "Where are we?"

"Local tavern," Jase said. "It's become our base of operations."

"And you're not concerned about being discovered?" Kaia said.

"The Talons are starving us out with minimal effort. I don't think they really care what else happens in Ruzi as long as we remain within the perimeter. And the royal family has barricaded themselves in their palace." There was a bit of a sneer in his voice.

"Which should give us the opportunity to pull this off," Efren said. "Let's eat. Then we can plan."

The food was meager—not enough rice, with only a bit of shaved carrot for each bowl—and everyone ate slowly, trying to draw out their meals. When it was over, Efren rose and offered a hand to me. "Come with me."

I hadn't realized that it was an invitation for me only. I looked back at Kaia, whose hurt flashed briefly over her face before she called the dragon kit over to her. "Go," she said. "I'll watch the kit."

I went.

I was surprised to see that it was early morning—our walk in the tunnel had taken longer than I'd thought. The streets were close to empty. Efren led me to the edge of a neighborhood square. "This is the best place to see the Talons."

"Not from the roofs?" I studied our surroundings. The buildings in this district were only two or three stories, but every bit of height would help in getting a view of the Talons' barricade.

Efren shook her head. "They burn people off the roofs. They don't want anyone getting too close. We shouldn't be up there until you're ready to . . ." She waved her hands expressively, and I realized that she was concerned that someone might be listening.

I nodded, and she looked up at the sky. "It's almost time. They do an air maneuver with the sunrise to remind us they're here."

We waited.

So this was Ruzi. I looked around, trying to see Sev anywhere in these streets, these buildings. The city wasn't as open as Belat—the walls were higher, the structures more fortified. I supposed that made sense, considering that Ruzi was a border kingdom that edged up against the mountains separating the empire from Old Zefed, the place from which the first Flame of the West had come. The two empires coexisted peacefully, for the most part—at least, that was what I understood.

"Have you ever been to Old Zefed?" I asked.

Efren looked at me. "No," she said. "Why do you ask?"

I shrugged. "I'm from Ilvera. Before all this, I'd never been anywhere. I never even thought about Old Zefed, not really. But you're so close. I was just curious."

Efren nodded. "Ruzi does some trade with Old Zefed. Of course, to them, we're New Zefed. I've heard that Old Zefed even sent some relief supplies since the riots started, but we've been cut off completely."

Compassion, from another empire? That was hard to fathom.

Suddenly she pointed up. "Look!"

I followed her gaze and watched as the Talons of Zefed flew overhead.

During my travels, I'd seen Talons alone and in pairs. But I had never seen so many at once. I counted six in the first pass, and another five as the Talons wove around one another in a braidlike pattern, dancing across the sky. Eleven Talons total, and the emperor had been able to spare them? Not to mention the ones we had already come across on the road . . . For the first time, I began to reckon with the size of the emperor's force.

How would we free so many dragons at once? It seemed impossible. I needed Naava. But she had said she would not come until I had proven myself. Had I done enough? I was almost certain I had not.

I shook my head. It didn't matter—I had to do this. The dragons were relying on me, as was the kingdom of Ruzi. And so was Sev.

"Have you been able to discern any patterns of movement or behavior?" I said. "They can't be flying like this all the time."

"Aside from the group maneuvers, they patrol in shifts of five—and two in each shift are stationed above the city at all times. And there's one that I think is the leader."

All right. Five at a time, then. Five wasn't so many more

than two. I could handle five—at least, five was a lot fewer than eleven. But this was a city, and freeing dragons came with risks. While we might have been able to free five at a time, it seemed unlikely that we would be able to talk five confused dragons down from their anger.

The ghosts of piercing screams swept across my mind, bringing with them the memory of the stench of burning flesh. I swallowed down bile and thrust the memory away. Five dragons could destroy the entire city.

"If you've been tracking me, then you know what dragons usually do after they are freed," I said slowly.

Efren nodded, frowning.

"There's a good chance that there will be damage. I don't know the city. Is there somewhere that's been deserted—or without buildings? A place with running water would be ideal."

Efren snapped her fingers. "There's a park on the south side of the city, along the river. The royal family—Prince Severin's family, I mean—had a house there. Because of what happened to them, it's been abandoned."

"Perfect. When do the Talons change shifts?"

"Midnight and midday."

"Tomorrow, then. Midday," I said. If we were going to free five dragons at once, I needed to be rested. Tomorrow would come quickly enough.

CHAPTER TWENTY-TWO

Sev

I grabbed a sword from a soldier's scabbard as I passed him, ignoring his cry of outrage. Then I pushed my way toward the center of the crowd.

"What is going on here?" I shouted.

At first there was no response, so I raised the sword in the air and shouted again. "I am Prince Severin of Ruzi, commander of the armies of the Flame of the West. I ask you, *What is going on here?*"

At this they took notice. Though the crowd did not quiet, the scrum broke apart to reveal a Seratese man crumpled on the ground, his arms held protectively over his head. I ran to his side. He didn't appear to be seriously injured, though his cheek was already swelling where they must have hit him.

I looked up into angry faces. "Who did this? Must I conclude that you attacked him for sport?"

"A curse upon the Seratese!" someone shouted, and jeers rose from the back of the crowd.

"You have no reason to believe this man has ill intent!" I cried. "He is a man of Zefed!"

Another shout carried through the air. "A curse upon the traitor prince!"

Something flew through the air at me, and I turned instinctively, catching it with the edge of my sword. The projectile, a glass bottle, broke against the blade and fell, shattering on the ground.

"Curse the traitor prince!" The cry came again, and this time, it was echoed. The cry became a chant, growing in strength as the people raised their voices and their fists. I was abruptly aware that I was one person standing alone against this crowd. Where was Faris? The army?

"Get up!" I said to the Seratese man. "Quickly!"

The man struggled to his knees. I put my free arm under his shoulder, hoisting him to his feet. Then I raised my sword. "Make way!" I roared.

I forced my way back through the crowd, supporting the man at my side. Something slimy hit the back of my collar, but I could not stop moving. These people were lost to reason—if we hesitated, we might not get out at all.

The carriage waited in the distance, with the military guard in front of it, their swords drawn. We stumbled up to the guard, which parted to let us through. I boosted the man into the carriage and climbed up after him. Then I turned to look behind us. The crowd had tripled in size, at least, and I could hear nothing but a sea of shouts as they advanced on us.

Another bottle broke against the side of the carriage, and Lord Annick ducked as something flew near his head. Nothing good would come of this.

"To the palace!" I shouted. The military guard formed ranks around us, and together we fled before the wave of fury coming after us.

Outside the carriage was a cacophony of anger. Inside, we were silent. Erris, Lord Annick, and King Idai sat on the seat opposite us. The Seratese man was sprawled on the seat between Faris and me.

"Are you all right?" I said to the man.

The look he gave me was one of fear, and suddenly it hit me—I might have saved him from the mob, but to him I was still Prince Severin, the hand of the emperor. And we were in the emperor's carriage, heading for the emperor's palace . . .

"I want to help you. Do you need an escort somewhere?"

His gaze darted about the carriage—he was clearly making note of the people he was riding with. "I—"

"Leave him be, Severin," Faris said, her eyes on the road behind us. "You've done enough."

But I could not have left the man to be beaten, or worse. And in this moment it didn't matter to me who heard what I said. "Whether or not the war is just, the emperor's vendetta is not grounds for attacking his own people," I said hotly.

She looked as though she wanted to snap back at me, but then the carriage went over a bump in the road, and she fell forward, out of her seat. I grabbed her arm and pulled her upright. Her skin was feverishly hot to the touch, and her eyes unfocused.

"Faris?"

She didn't respond.

"What's happening to her?" Erris cried.

"She's sick," I said, hailing the driver. She needed a healer, as soon as possible.

Idai's mouth was a thin line as they watched the mob following us. "The emperor's wrath will be vast," they said, too quietly for any to hear but me.

That was what I was afraid of.

We arrived at the palace at a run, pursued by shouts and the sound of breaking glass. When we stopped for the gates to open, the Seratese man unlatched the carriage door and jumped down to the street, then darted away before I could intervene. Then we were through, into the courtyard as the gates slammed shut behind us.

The guards called for healers, who were on the scene almost immediately, whisking Faris away and leaving the rest of us behind. I stared at the gates as Erris and Lord Annick ran for the palace. What would happen if the mob broke through?

Idai grabbed my arm. "You need to go," they said. "You have to be as far from this as possible when the emperor hears."

They were right. I ran.

I had been the match, but the tinder had been ready and waiting. What would Rafael do in response? What should I do?

I found myself in an empty hallway and leaned back against the stone, trying to tame my racing thoughts. Irrad was becoming more unstable, and I was certain the emperor would only escalate the violence. And the further he was pushed, the more likely he was to break. I could not wait for a rescue—I had to get out as soon as possible.

It was just after midday now—an excuse to visit the great hall. I had to find the lord from Oskiath.

I entered the hall and picked up a plate. I was the furthest thing from hungry, but the longer I lingered over food, the likelier it was that I would see her.

There—across the hall. She was several tables away, but the hall was well occupied despite the disturbance outside. I would have to sit near someone—why shouldn't it be her?

I set down my plate and took a seat.

"The emperor's high commander should not sit with a lowly lord," she said so quietly, it was barely audible.

"You know I am no commander," I whispered.

"I have a message for you, then. From a friend in a high place."

"Yes?"

"She says that they will wait no longer. They will visit us soon."

Rowena . . . sending her army to march on Irrad? I was confused, but there was no time to ask about that—we could be interrupted at any time.

"I need them to get me out of here now—before the army leaves," I said urgently. "With two passengers."

"Passengers?" she replied, surprised.

I glanced around. No one appeared to be listening to us. "The wife of our leader, and her son."

The lord's face went almost white. "*Absolutely not.* Your friend cannot risk herself for so little."

It was the response I had expected. "She still needs a beast keeper. If you take us, you will have Neve's services at your disposal."

The lord stood from the table, making a show of gathering up her cloak. "You are certain?"

As certain as I could be. I nodded.

"I will pass this on. You will know the answer."

"Soon," I said.

"Soon," she agreed. She slipped a folded sheet of paper underneath her plate. Then she was gone.

I pushed food around on my plate for a few minutes longer to keep up appearances. Then I palmed the paper from under the plate and hid it in my pocket. Rising, I retreated to my chambers as quickly as I could.

The paper held an encoded message from Rowena. I decoded it quickly and read.

> We ride for Irrad. Expect to meet up with your
> friend and the little one at the border. For the
> future.

I was relieved, and then puzzled. Maren had made no mention of returning to Rowena, so why would Rowena be speaking of Maren? At least the Dragons were coming. And if they had finally committed to riding to war, then they were more likely to accept my proposal. Perhaps this would work after all.

CHAPTER TWENTY-THREE

Maren

We slept long into the day in Efren's tavern. Late-afternoon sun was casting long shadows when I finally woke again. Kaia had left the room. The dragon kit nuzzled against me, and I nudged her back.

"How are you feeling, little one?" I said.

Sev.

I stilled. She'd spoken. The dragon kit had *spoken*. "Sev? What about him?"

He's sad. We miss him.

She climbed into my arms and curled herself into a ball, resting her head on my arm. I scarcely breathed, I was trying so hard not to move, even though she was almost too big for my lap now.

"You're right. We do miss him. But we might be able to get him back if we can free these dragons today. Do you think you can do it?"

The kit sniffed in disdain, which I took as an *of course.*

"Are you certain?" I said. "There will be many of them."

Many is like one.

Many . . . ? I didn't follow.

The door opened, and Kaia came inside, carrying a tray with

a small loaf of bread on it. After splitting it down the middle, our portions were little more than a mouthful each.

"Were you all right after I left?" I said. "I'm sorry—I should have brought you with us, but everything happened so quickly—"

Kaia shrugged. "It's fine," she said in a way that made it clear that it was *not*.

I tried again. "How long have you been up?"

"A few hours. I went out."

"In the city? Really?"

"Oh, are you the only one who's allowed to do dangerous things?" Kaia crossed her arms. "I was fine. I went to find the Aurati."

The dragon kit spilled off my lap as I sprang upright. "*What?*"

"You heard me," she said. "Efren and the others don't trust the Aurati."

"As they shouldn't!"

Kaia held up a hand. "The Aurati in Lumina lost contact with the Ruzian Aurati when the blockade was put into place. You may find this difficult to believe, but the Aurati are still people. I thought I could find out what they think about what's happening here."

"And?" I said through clenched teeth.

"They're *fractured*," Kaia said, practically glowing. "Some of the Aurati are loyal to the emperor and the current ruling family, but others are not. They remember the way it used to be, and disapprove of how the emperor has treated Ruzi since the charge of treason. And there are many of the younger ones who would be protesting on the streets with the rest of the Ruzians, if they could."

If they could. I refrained from rolling my eyes. They *could*, anytime they wanted. But they knew that if they did, they would be cast out or killed. "So?"

"So this proves what I've been thinking all along," she said smugly. "The Aurati order isn't an evil monolith. It's made up of *people*. If I work with the Aurati, I could change their minds. I could lead a revolution within their ranks—especially now that Lumina has fallen. There's no central Aurati authority."

"You're dreaming, Kaia. They won't turn on the emperor, no matter who is leading."

Kaia's expression faltered. "They might."

"They won't. And I'm not going to entertain this fantasy of yours, not with everything else going on." I beckoned the dragon kit. "Come on, little one."

Tasia.

I stilled, shocked. Could that be—? "Is that your name? Tasia?"

The dragon kit—Tasia—nodded firmly.

"Is she *talking* to you?" Kaia said in astonishment. "That's new . . . isn't it?"

All of our discord was forgotten as Kaia knelt next to the dragon kit, looking at her in awe.

"What is she saying?" Kaia asked.

Tasia tilted her nose up. *Hungry.*

"She's hungry," I said, giggling in spite of myself.

Kaia laughed as well, and for one moment, all was well.

Then reality sank back in. Kaia got to her feet, looking away from me. I beckoned Tasia to my side, trying to calm my mind.

Tomorrow would be the biggest test of Tasia's and my power. We could not fail, not with so much at stake.

The Talons' shift would change at midday. We had agreed that the best time to set our plan in motion would be about an hour prior, to take advantage of tired dragons without risking an encounter with all eleven. Which meant that I had only this evening to familiarize myself with the royal house and its workings.

Kaia, Efren, and two other Ruzians from her group accompanied us across the city that evening. Once again, all was quiet, devoid not only of protesters but also of merchants and guards. It was eerie. There should have been people here, but there were none.

Even though there didn't seem to be anyone around to observe us, Efren insisted that we keep to the shadows, hugging the sides of buildings and skirting the edges of open spaces. She seemed almost too cautious, but from time to time a Talon would swoop overhead, and I would remember.

It took less than an hour to get from the tavern to the royal family's house. There were signs that it had once been guarded—a long fence that had been partially torn down and a small structure that had clearly been a guard station—but it was long abandoned now. Most likely no one had wanted to use a house that would bring to mind the treason of its former inhabitants.

The house itself was three stories high, built solidly of wood. The roof was slightly slanted, but it looked all right to stand on. The door didn't open when Efren tried to force it. Instead, after taking a look around, she broke a window and climbed inside. I flinched as the glass shattered.

After a minute Efren came back out through the door. "It's all yours," she said.

I stepped over the threshold and took a deep breath, adjusting to the stillness of the house. Something about this place felt familiar to me, though I couldn't explain why. Perhaps it was because I knew that Sev had spent time here as a child. Tasia sniffed the air—it was stale, with the faint scent of old books. The staircase creaked as I went from the first floor to the second, and then the third. There was a carved wooden ladder standing by the staircase, which meant there had to be an attic or a skylight. I opened every door and found the skylight in the southernmost room, so I brought the ladder in and climbed up. The skylight was unlocked, though the wooden frame had warped slightly, and I had to shove it to get it open.

Tasia and I poked our heads out onto the roof. There was a clear view of the two Talons patrolling the eastern side of the city.

I climbed onto the roof, staying low. I wasn't going to linger, but I wanted to make sure that the roof was still sturdy. There was a section on the eastern side where the roof buckled slightly under my weight, and I quickly backed away. Well, I'd just have to stay away from that side.

Satisfied with my exploration of the house, I went back down through the skylight and closed everything up. We were ready for tomorrow.

Efren and Kaia were waiting outside when Tasia and I came down. "Will it work?" Efren asked.

I nodded. I hadn't explained much about freeing dragons to the Ruzians. They trusted my abilities without further explanation. I trusted them too—but not enough to share everything that I knew.

"Good," said Fefren. "We'll have people hidden in the forest in case something goes wrong."

"Let us help you," Kaia said, once we were back in the tavern and alone in our room.

"Who is 'us'?" I asked.

"The Aurati."

My jaw tightened. "We have enough help," I said, though I was hesitant about whether having the Ruzians along was the right thing to do. Would they be able to contribute when the time came, or would they simply be potential victims in the event that something went wrong?

"The Aurati have more exposure to the Talons than the average Ruzian citizen. They could help distract the dragons while you're busy freeing them."

"*No*," I said sharply. "I cannot trust the Aurati after what they did to you. They cannot be part of this."

"Everything the Aurati did, they did to *me*," Kaia snapped back. "I should be the one making decisions about their involvement."

I shook my head. "I don't understand what you hoped to achieve by seeking them out, but I don't have to. It was your choice to make. But they are not coming with us tomorrow."

Kaia looked at me for a long moment. Then she walked to the door, opened it, and left the room without speaking.

I looked down at Tasia. "She doesn't understand," I said.

Tasia jumped onto the bed next to me and turned in a circle, then curled into a ball at my side, resting her head on my lap. *Maren sad,* she said softly.

Somehow, every conversation I had with Kaia seemed to go wrong. No matter what I did, I ended up feeling bruised. I flopped backward onto the bed and stroked Tasia's back, trying not to think about it. *Go to sleep, little one. Tomorrow will be here before we know it.*

CHAPTER TWENTY-FOUR

Sev

The sound of moving water sends a prickle of awareness down my arms. Then the smell—old books and a hint of pipe smoke. I know where I am without opening my eyes.

My parents designed this house together, and we came here every summer of my childhood. I know that the jar where the cook hid jelly tarts is on the bottom shelf in the pantry. I know if I shift to the left, one of the floorboards will creak under my weight. Callum and I fought battles with wooden swords over every foot of this house while my parents read before the fireplace. And as long as I don't open my eyes, I can pretend they are still here, waiting for me.

"Sev."

I open my eyes. Maren stands in front of me, a somber look on her face. "I miss you. I don't know how—"

"How did you get to Ruzi?" I ask. "What are you doing there?"

She frowns. "There's a Talon blockade around the kingdom— the emperor is starving them out. I'm working with a rebel group to break it. But your house—"

My throat is suddenly tight. "Whatever you need to do, do it. I'm running out of time."

"What do you mean?"

"I've been appointed commander of the army. The fleet leaves *for the Seda Serat in seven days. If I'm with it, I'm as good as dead."*

I look around. There is the table that my mother accidentally scorched by putting down a hot pan. There is the daybed where my father read his letters. Sunlight filters in through the window. There is peace here. Or the memory of it.

"Seven days," Maren repeats. "I can do it."

She reaches out to me, and the house dissolves into fire.

The door slammed, startling me awake.

I sat up, alarmed, as Rafael burst into my room, a lit torch in his hand. "Get up. Now!"

I scrambled out of bed and bowed. "This is an unexpected honor, Your Excellence. I admit I'm surprised by the hour."

"Don't play coy with me, you impudent worm. You know what you did."

Rafael backhanded me casually without missing a beat. My head snapped to the side, my cheek burning. *The mob.*

"I gave you specific instructions to visit the army. There was no provision in those instructions that covered *interfering with civilian activity.*"

I licked my lip and tasted blood. "I was only trying to act as a commander should, Your Highness. As I thought you might. I meant no disrespect—I had no idea it would lead to a riot."

"In the future, you will do exactly as I tell you. Nothing less, and *nothing more,*" Rafael said. "Now follow me."

I had a bad feeling about this but didn't dare argue. Instead I just dressed and pulled on my boots, shivering in the cold. Faris was standing outside as we left the room, but she would not look at me as six guards escorted us down the hall. At least she was upright again.

I was still close to yawning as we reached the front of the palace, but as the doors opened, I became abruptly awake. The mob had not abated—rather, it seemed to have been emboldened by nightfall. The air was filled with furious shouts and the sounds of destruction.

The courtyard was lit and busy with activity. The military guard was standing just inside the gates, and archers lined the walls, their bows drawn and ready. Vix the Ruiner crouched in the center of the courtyard, wings spread menacingly. I looked up and counted six Talons flying overhead.

The emperor strode to his dragon and leaped into the saddle. "Faris—take Prince Vesper to the wall. Let him see what he has wrought." He leaned forward in his saddle, murmuring to Vix.

The dragon launched into the air, its great wings sweeping a gust of wind about the courtyard.

Faris touched my elbow. "Let's go," she said.

We climbed to the top of the palace wall. From here I could see the city laid out before me, a sea of torches marking the protesters. I gripped the wall in front of me, my jaw clenched. What was the emperor about to do?

Rafael and Vix circled above the palace gates. The dragon roared, letting out a burst of flame, and the crowd quieted.

"Citizens of Irrad," the emperor cried. "It appears that some of you have forgotten that we are a city at peace. We do not raise our arms against our fellows! We do not cry out in the streets like children!

"Prince Vesper has suggested to me a solution. It pains me

to consider it, but consider I must. He tells me that the only way to make you understand how fortunate you are is to take something away. Something precious."

Now he truly had the people's attention. The streets were as silent as death.

The emperor raised his arm. "I have no choice but to take his advice. Tonight, and every night until these protests are finished, I will burn one building in Irrad. Vix!"

Vix flapped its wings and rose higher in the air, then burst away from the palace. I watched as it flew over the noble districts and past the merchant houses. Soon I could no longer see it clearly, but everyone saw when it dipped in the air, opened its mouth, and let loose a river of flame onto a building in the southern part of the city.

The wood must have been bone dry—it caught within moments, sending a pillar of fire into the sky. Someone in the crowd shrieked. I looked down. It was a woman, kneeling in the street and sobbing. More cries of anguish joined hers—but there were shouts of anger, too. Not everyone was cowed by this act of cruelty. I saw movement at the back of the crowd. Some of them must have been running to save what they could and stop the fire.

Vix and the emperor hung in the sky a safe distance from the flames. Once he seemed satisfied that the building would fall, the emperor pulled Vix's reins, and the two tore away into the night. Faris leaned heavily against the wall, her shoulders slumped—in exhaustion, or in sadness?

"Is this still the person you want to serve? You are more powerful than him. What holds you?" I said quietly.

She pretended she hadn't heard me and walked quickly

away. I decided to consider that a success—on another day, she would have slapped me down for daring so much.

A small stone broke away from the wall into my hand, and I rolled it between my fingers. The emperor had meant this night as a lesson—to the people about where my loyalties lay, and to me about the consequences of disobeying an order. But the crowd was subdued, not vanquished. Rafael had struck them, and they had risen once more. I had no doubt that in the morning, they would still be there. I could only hope to be so brave.

It was only once I was alone again in my chambers that the dragon dream came flooding back to me.

It had been foolish of me to think that I could put Ruzi behind me. Remembering my family's house caused a pain in my chest, and Maren's words had done worse. I'd thought I'd buried everyone I loved, but I had forgotten about the kingdom itself, and its people. I didn't know all of them. I wouldn't even see all of them over the course of my life. But Owain had indicted me for everything I had done wrong, and I had killed him. Now the emperor was starving Ruzi because of me. I couldn't abandon them.

Even if Maren was able to break the blockade, Ruzi was still *mine*, and they needed help. The Dragons could not be diverted—they were already on their way here and could not split their forces. They only had a small army. But Callum had loved Ruzi the way I did, and I knew there was at least one other person in Irrad who understood that devotion.

CHAPTER TWENTY-FIVE

Maren

S even days.

I burst out of sleep, the urgent refrain pounding through my head. *Seven days.* If I didn't get to Sev before then, he would be dead. One week was not enough time, not when one counted how long it would take to get to Irrad *and* the fact that I didn't have a plan of attack for when we arrived. I couldn't wait for tomorrow—I had to free the dragons *now.* Even half a day was too much to waste.

For once I was pleased that Kaia had slept elsewhere. I got out of bed and dressed, then picked Tasia up and carried her quietly into the hall. I grabbed an unlit torch and went downstairs, out of the tavern, and across the city by night. The bells tolled as we trod through the dewy grass in one of the parks. Ten o'clock.

Sev's house stood dark and still when we arrived. Tasia kept close to me as I pushed the door open and stepped inside. There was nothing but the soft sounds of the house settling around us.

I stroked Tasia's nose. "Are you ready, little one?"

She nodded eagerly.

We climbed to the third floor, then up the ladder. I opened the skylight and peered out.

At night the city was silent and dark. This made seeing the dragons easier, as they spouted fire as they flew, warning the city of their destructive power. There were three far to the west, near the border between Ruzi and Old Zefed—and two close to us at the eastern wall.

Two Talons. We could do this.

I hefted Tasia up onto the roof and climbed up after her, staying low. The plan was simple. First, get the Talons' attention. Then, as they approached, sing to the dragons.

Easier said than done. My heart began to beat faster. All I had to do was stand up and wave my arms. But I felt as though my limbs had been nailed to the roof, that I could not stand even if I wanted to. What was wrong with me?

Then it dawned on me—I was *afraid*.

I stared down at my hands planted firmly on the roof. *Get up. All you have to do is get up.*

Tasia had made her way to the end of the roof and back. Now she was at my side again, looking up at me curiously. *You are frightened. Why?*

I pressed my forehead against my hands, holding in my breath. *Because . . . because of everything.*

What is everything?

I couldn't explain it to her. She was a baby. I was being pressed down by the things I couldn't say, about staying alive and freeing dragons and defeating the emperor, and Sev and Kaia and Ilvera and the future and, and, and—

This roof is very high, I said instead.

She burbled in my mind, a little laugh. *Then we fly.*

I snorted. Simple enough. *Are you ready? We must sing the same way we sang to the dragons before.*

She nodded determinedly.

I stared down at my hands on the roof, feeling my heart beat faster, faster, faster. *You've done this already,* I told myself. *It's just the same as last time.*

It wasn't. But there was no other way. I gritted my teeth and forced myself to stand.

There was a pause. The dragons were in the distance, too far away for me to shout at them. How long would it take for them to notice me, if all I did was wait? Too long. Much as I dreaded drawing attention to myself, it had to be done. I lit the torch, then lifted it over my head, waving it like a beacon.

It didn't take long. The dragons were flying in long loops along one side of the city, but as I watched, they came together and hovered, their Talons likely conversing. Then one dragon broke away and flew toward us.

As soon as I thought they were within earshot, I began to sing. Despite my nerves, the dragonsong was stronger in my mind than ever, and I sang it clearly, without wobbles. Tasia sang with me, and our voices blended and rose together. The Talon paused at a distance, and I caught the distinct scent of fire root. They weren't going to flee—the Talon intended to force their dragon to fight.

The dragon bellowed, shooting fire into the sky, and I redoubled my efforts. Then the dragon dove toward us.

The instinct to flee rose up inside me, but if we ran now, that would mean turning around, breaking the song.

I clenched my fists. *Hold your ground.*

If this was going to work, it would work now. I reached out, trying to sense the dragon's consciousness through the haze of fire root. There was something there, but it was faint, difficult to grasp.

Hello? I called.

The dragon's head jerked to one side, and it dipped in the air before recovering its flight. Tasia sang fiercely by my side, but the air around us was heating. We had seconds before they would be upon us.

The dragon fire reached us first, catching the edge of the roof and setting it aflame. The Talon pulled the dragon out of the dive. Its wings beat heavily, fanning the flames. Smoke stung my eyes. We had to get off the roof, but if we did, the connection would be lost. Tasia beat her wings in anger and lifted slightly off the roof before coming back down. I saw the Talon uncork another vial, the dragon waiting for instruction.

I couldn't let that happen. I had one shot at this—we couldn't sing much longer in this smoke. I inhaled as deeply as I could in the smoky air and planted my feet. Then I *screamed* the dragonsong, putting all my will behind the sound. The dragon recoiled, bucking in the air—and screamed back at me, the force of her mind slamming into mine.

I staggered backward—and felt the shifting of wood collapsing beneath my feet.

When I opened my eyes, there was night sky above me. The roof had caved in, and I was lying on the floor inside the house. But the house hadn't yet burned. How much time had I missed? Where was Tasia? We had to get out!

My first attempt at movement sent excruciating pain through my body, and I stilled at once. *Tasia? Where are you?*

Help!

I could see movement out of the corner of my eye and turned my head to see that one of Tasia's legs was trapped by a fallen beam. She was mewling in pain as she tried to pull it free. My heart wrenched at the sound.

"Stay still!" I shouted. "I'm coming!"

Something creaked above us, and I looked up. The dragon had landed on the crumbling roof. There was no Talon on her back, but the sight still gave me pause. She didn't seem confused, the way some of the other dragons had been upon being freed. She seemed furious, and focused entirely on Tasia.

The dragon ripped at the roof until nearly half of it was gone. Then she climbed down into the wreckage. She went directly to Tasia and lifted the beam that was trapping her leg. But when Tasia started toward me, the dragon blocked her way.

Let her go! I cried, but the dragon ignored me. She wrapped one enormous claw around Tasia's body as easily as she might have carried a parcel. Then she spread her wings, readying herself to fly.

No! She could not take Tasia. I struggled to my feet. The dragon spat fire at me, and I sprang out of the way just in time. I tripped over a beam and fell, barely catching myself, against the wall. Something collapsed from above, knocking me back down to the floor. I sobbed aloud as pain lanced up my leg.

I reached down gingerly, trying not to cry out again. I'd been pinned down by heavy beams, too large for me to lift by myself. I was trapped in a house that had caught fire, and the dragon was getting away.

Should I call for help? I tried to think who might hear. This house was in a remote location—there wasn't supposed to be anyone in the vicinity. The only people who knew I'd be here were the Ruzian rebels, and there was no reason for them to think I was here early. Then, of course, there were the Talons.

Was it worse to be captured by Talons, or lose Tasia?

That choice was easy. I screamed, as loudly as I could. And then I filled my lungs with smoky air and screamed again. Nothing mattered in this moment as much as the dragon kit. And I was losing her.

I was shocked when I heard heavy footsteps on the stairs. That couldn't have been Talons—they would have arrived by air. I sensed movement behind me, and Efren burst into view, followed by Kaia and Jase.

"What happened?" Efren said.

"I don't have time to explain, she's getting away! Help me!" I cried.

Together they were able to lift the beams holding me down. The second I was free, I was up and limping down the stairs and out of the house. *Tasia!* "Tasia!"

There was a body sprawled on the ground not too far from us— the Talon's neck must have broken when the dragon threw them off.

I looked up. There was no chance of catching them now. The dragon was almost out of sight in the night sky, flying east—away from the city. I sank to my knees in the grass. "No," I whispered.

Efren patted my back awkwardly. She said nothing, and I was grateful for it. Kaia had been right. I shouldn't have tried to do this alone. And now I'd lost Tasia. The rest of the Talons would soon be after us. We had to get clear, but I could think of nothing except the dragon kit, helpless and afraid—

"Look!" Jase said, pointing at the sky.

Incredibly, the dragon was returning to us.

As they approached, I saw that Tasia was struggling in the dragon's grasp, thrashing and nipping at her claws. The dragon landed a safe distance away, and let Tasia go. The dragon kit ran to my side and huddled next to me, shaking.

The dragon roared in anger. *You hold this kit captive. You must release her!*

Surprise washed over me, followed by a wave of relief. The dragon had been freed, and she hadn't tried to attack Tasia—she was trying to save her?

You have this wrong. She isn't my captive. She is my . . . I struggled for the right word.

Family! Tasia said firmly.

The dragon shifted uneasily. *Family? You would call a Talon . . . family?*

I am no Talon, I said.

She took a cautious step toward me, inhaling deeply. *You do not smell like them. But you have a kit.*

She is with me by choice.

Is that right? She was clearly addressing Tasia.

Yes, Tasia replied.

Our mission is to free the dragons of Ilvera, I continued.

So, you can break the bond between dragon and Talon, the dragon said, almost to herself. I could feel the pleasure that she took in the thought.

We've broken yours. And we mean to break the bonds of every other dragon here. A thought occurred to me. If her first instinct upon breaking free of her Talon was to come for Tasia . . . would she want to do the same for the rest of the dragons? *Will you help us?*

Tendrils of smoke rose from the dragon's nostrils as she looked down at us. She bared her fangs. *Yes.*

CHAPTER TWENTY-SIX

Maren

The dragon's name was Alora, and she had been Talon-bonded for thirteen years. She was smaller than Naava and angrier than Glivven—I could feel her vindictive glee as I explained what Tasia and I had set out to accomplish.

I'm glad you've come, she said. *I've wanted nothing more than to do exactly this.*

"So . . . we trust the dragon now?" Efren whispered. She wasn't hiding behind me exactly, but she'd taken care to let me stand between her and Alora.

"Yes," I said. "This dragon's name is Alora—she will help us free the other dragons."

"Good," Kaia said, "because I need to talk to you. *Now.*"

"If I may," Efren interrupted. "We don't have much time. The Talons will soon realize that something is wrong."

"You're right," I said. I turned back to Alora. *Do you know a way to keep the Talons away?* I asked.

I will burn the house. It is not so unusual—the Talons often tell us to do such things, Alora said. *But that will not convince them for long.*

She snapped her jaws menacingly. Then she reared back on her hind legs and let out a burst of fire. Flames enveloped the house—Sev's house—cracking greedily. I swallowed down the lump in my throat and took a deep breath, reaching for my resolve.

"All right," I said, turning back to the humans. "Once the Talons realize what's happened, all ten of them will come for us. That's too many to free at once—can you think of a way to keep them separate?"

After a moment, Efren snapped her fingers. "The roofs. If we put people on top of the roofs with torches, the Talons will have to separate to investigate them."

"The dragons won't burn the buildings down?" I said.

Efren and Kaia exchanged a glance. "At this point, we're going to have to take that chance," Kaia said. "The Aurati are standing by. They will spread the word."

"You called on *them?*" I said.

Kaia shot me a murderous look. "They will do what needs to be done," she said icily. "Watch the roofs."

She walked away before I could reply, leaving me fuming.

Efren cleared her throat. "I'm not a fan of the Aurati either, but in this case, I agree with Kaia," she said.

I ignored her and addressed Alora. *My friends will help distract the Talons*, I explained. *But I think Tasia and I will be more effective in the air. With your permission, will you carry me?*

The dragon nodded and bowed down so that Tasia and I could climb into her saddle. Then Alora bent her knees and launched us into the sky.

Alora flew faster and more erratically than Naava, swerving to catch wind pockets and executing an occasional twirl. But the feeling of flight was the same—that this was where I was meant to be. In the air, the world felt far away. Here there was only my hair streaking back with the wind, the beat of Alora's wings, and the task ahead of us.

We circled in the night sky. I watched the city below us, waiting for Efren's group and the Aurati to reach their positions. The Talon and dragon that had stayed behind as Alora attacked were nowhere to be seen. Where had they gone?

I closed my eyes, casting out my consciousness. They were close by.

Do you know where they are? Are they alone? I asked Alora.

Yes, Alora replied. *There is a place Braith likes to go.*

I wasn't sure whether she was referring to the dragon or the Talon. Alora beat her wings and sped through the air, and I turned my attention to Tasia.

Are you ready, little one?

Tasia had managed to negotiate a comfortable position in the saddle, for which I was thankful.

Ready, she said.

One moment we were flying alone through the night—the next, another dragon roared out of the darkness, almost colliding with us. Alora screamed, swiping her claws at the Talon. I could smell spiny pine—for clarity of thought and action. Wind whistled by my ears. The Talon reached for their bandolier, and fumbled in their haste. I reached out for Tasia—we opened our mouths and sang.

Every time I sang, it became easier to shape my mouth around the dragon melody. My consciousness slanted and expanded— now there were auras hovering on the edges of my vision, bright against the night. I closed my eyes, and the shimmering shapes clarified. I gasped. Was I somehow sensing the dragons?

I had to be. I couldn't tuck my chin into my chest without being struck by the glowing mass of light underneath me. And

I could sense Tasia's presence. Ahead of me, the—essence?—of the Talon's dragon glowed, but there was a dullness to it, as though someone had dropped a film over the creature.

But as we sang, a silvery thread spooled out from our bodies, soaring across the sky, toward the Talon's dragon. The thread touched the dragon's chest and dissipated. For a moment there was nothing—and then the dullness dissolved, leaving only light behind.

I opened my eyes to see the dragon snarl and buck in the air, swerving away from us as it attempted to throw the Talon from its back. Alora folded her wings and dove toward the dragon. As we closed in on it, she opened her mouth and spat a plume of fire directly at the Talon. The Talon recoiled, losing their grip on the reins. The dragon twisted in midair, and the Talon fell.

Alora's grim satisfaction reverberated through my mind. She spared no attention for the fallen Talon—instead, she focused entirely on the newly freed dragon. She spoke using the same sounds that Glivven had used when we'd conversed—the language that I had decided to call dragon tongue. Soon enough the dragon's flight evened out, and it fell into line beside us in the air.

What did you say? I asked.

That Braith will never be captive again, Alora said fiercely. *That I will not allow it.*

Alora's words hit me like a blow—I had thought almost exactly the same thing about Kaia. For a brief moment, I wondered whether dragons had an equivalent to human heartmates. There was no time to ponder that now, though.

One by one, lights sparked to life across the city below us.

They were everywhere, more than I could easily count—many more than I had expected. And every one of those lights was held by a person who was willing to give everything for this cause.

In the distance I saw the rest of the Talons speeding across the sky. I closed my eyes, noting the splashes of light that illuminated the darkness behind my eyelids. And for the first time, I had no fear.

We freed the first dragon easily. Perhaps the Talon was untrained, or perhaps they just never expected to face two furious dragons in the air, fighting against them. Either way, it wasn't long before the Talon leaped from the saddle as we flew over the river, abandoning their dragon to us. The dragon's essence brightened as Tasia and I sang. As soon as it was free, it shot like an arrow away from the battle.

Alora snorted. *He was never much of a warrior,* she said dismissively.

But why should a dragon be a warrior? I barely had time for that thought before a plume of fire burst out of the darkness. Five Talons had coordinated their attack—two came at us from each side, and one head-on. Braith roared and dove down, while Alora took Tasia and me higher in the sky, dodging the flames that chased us up. I coughed as heat singed my cheek. The scent of fire root was heavy in the air.

I cleared my throat and began to sing again, though maintaining the melody was becoming difficult. The air was smoky, and my throat was growing hoarse. But Tasia's voice cut through the sky like a knife. When I closed my eyes, I saw the same silvery thread arc out toward the dragon closest to us. It was growing, now more like a rope than a thread. As I sang, it seemed to pass through the dragon's chest and loop across the sky toward the next, and then the next, weaving a silvery net in the air. Tasia's words came back to me—*many is like one*. Was this what she had meant?

The net expanded until it formed a perimeter I could only see when I closed my eyes. Confused consciousnesses flashed through my mind as the dragons woke one by one, yielding to our song, and then struggling against the Talons' attempts to recapture them with oils. Our song swelled. The net turned a brilliant, blinding silver and contracted—then suddenly exploded outward across the sky. Light hit my chest and sent me rocking back in my seat. One by one, the dragons threw their riders from their backs. And one by one, they began to sing.

Alora called out in dragon tongue, soothing the newly freed dragons. I reached out, counting each of them in turn. Eight. Eight dragons freed and flying.

There were still three Talons left, scattered over the city. But they had seen our battle—as we turned toward them, they flew in the opposite direction.

Ready? I asked.

Alora made no reply—only folded her wings and fell into a dive, the rest of the dragons following behind.

We chased the last three Talons beyond Ruzi's borders, until Alora finally admitted that we should turn back. If we went much farther, she explained, we risked running into larger groups of Talons. After a short conversation between the dragons, only Alora and Braith stayed with us—the others elected to fly to Ilvera.

The sun was rising as we finally flew back into Ruzi with the sunrise. With the Talons gone, there was no further need to avoid populated areas. We flew over the city and circled down to the ground near Efren's tavern. I staggered as I set foot on the ground, my legs feeling like jelly. Tasia jumped down beside me.

"Maren!" Kaia came forward, hugging her arms across her body. Tasia ran over and leaned against her legs until Kaia knelt down and scratched her behind the ears.

"We're fine," I said. "Three of them got away, but we were able to free eight." *Eight dragons.* And to think that once I had despaired of ever even *seeing* a dragon.

Efren appeared behind Kaia, wonder on her face. She looked at the dragons, then back at me. "I have to admit it, I thought you were done for. But—" She gestured helplessly at the sky. "What you've done is . . . amazing."

Tasia chirped and nipped at my elbow, demanding attention. I knelt down and stroked her back, right in between her wings. "It's not just me. Tasia is the one who deserves the credit."

"Do you think the emperor will send more Talons?" Efren asked.

"My guess is that he will," I said. "Your people should take the opportunity to leave, if they want, or bring in more supplies."

I was just beginning to feel the aches that came with riding a dragon into battle, and there was a deep bruise on my leg from falling through the roof. Tomorrow would be worse, but there was nothing I could do for it. No matter how much I wished for a hot bath, there was no time to spare.

I took a deep breath and squared my shoulders. "I've held up my side of the bargain," I said. "Who will you send to guide us to Irrad?"

"Me," Efren said instantly. "Jase will come too."

My face fell. "No more?"

She scratched the side of her neck. "You must understand. Ruzi has a chance now, but it may not last. Most of my people have families. I can't tell them that they cannot see to their own, not when the blockade might go up again at any time."

I couldn't argue with that. But there were only six days left. The tyrant's army would soon sail. We didn't have time to walk, and we didn't have any horses. . . .

My eye fell on the dragons.

I had asked Glivven to stay with us, and he had declined. But Alora wasn't Glivven, and something told me that she would enjoy the prospect of annihilating the emperor's fleet of Talons.

I walked over to the dragons and cleared my throat. Alora opened one eye lazily.

Yes, little human?

My name is Maren, I replied. *My quest does not end here. I intend to go to Irrad and free every dragon that is bonded to a Talon.*

Braith yawned. *And?* Her voice was lighter and more musical than Alora's.

You are free dragons, and you may do as you please. Most of the other dragons have chosen to retreat to Ilvera to rest and recover. But I am asking—will you come with us to Irrad?

Alora bared her teeth in a dangerous smile. *Rest does not interest me. I prefer to burn.*

Someone touched my arm, and I turned around to see Kaia, her expression stony. "Come with me," she said.

We walked from the celebratory gathering in silence, dread suffusing my body with every step. She'd been relieved when I landed alive, but she was still furious, and making no effort to hide it.

Once we were well out of earshot, Kaia whirled on me. "After everything we talked about, how could you go off after the dragons by yourself? We had a plan! What happened?"

"We were running out of time," I said helplessly.

"And you thought that a few hours would make such a difference?"

I scrambled to respond. "I had another dragon dream," I said. "The emperor is setting Sev up to be killed. He only has a few days left."

"*Sev.*" She spat the name like it was poison. "So you shut me out *again* because of him?"

"I promised I would come for him!"

"Can't you hear how that sounds? You promised you would come for *me*."

"I am doing my *best*."

"Really? Is your best going off by yourself without any help at all? You could have been hurt. Killed! That dragon almost took Tasia! And the Ruzians—our *only* allies—could have lost their lives for no reason. What you did was reckless!" Kaia shook her head. "You infuriate me."

She turned and walked away without waiting for a reply.

I was furious too—but on the heels of that anger came bleak mortification. I sank to the ground, pulled down by the weight of her words. I'd thought only of Sev and his safety—but that had made me unconscionably reckless. Worse, it had put others' lives at risk. And what she'd said about Sev—I had chosen Kaia, and yet my feelings had still betrayed me. The chasm between us had widened, and I feared I wouldn't be able to bridge it this time.

Again, the terrifying question resurfaced at the edge of my thoughts: Were Kaia and I meant to be with each other? I bowed my head and began to cry, tears of shame for my mistake—and for us, and what we still stood to lose.

CHAPTER TWENTY-SEVEN

Sev

~⌒~

A needle pulls through fabric. Blue thread breaks."

The air in the palace was hazy with smoke. The fire in Irrad had spread overnight, but Rafael had forbidden the Aurati to help put out the blaze. I was stunned that life could carry on normally after what he had done last night, but somehow, it was another morning, another meal, another prophecy. From his throne, the emperor was now declaring the meaning of this prophecy—something about loyalty above all else. Vix loomed over the throne, its presence a warning to anyone who might think of crossing the Flame of the West today.

Faris was back to her usual post at my side, which put a damper on any plans I might have had to make contact with my tentative allies. Despite the warm day, she wore thin gloves that ran over her wrists and up into her robes.

"Cold?" I said.

She shot me a cutting glare. "My power sparks when it's used too often. These are precautions, in case fools like yourself get too close."

An ache ghosted through my hand, and I looked down at my splinted fingers. I tried not to think about who she might have been using her powers on more recently.

A door slammed, interrupting Rafael's speech. One of the palace guards burst into the hall and ran to kneel before the throne. Rafael bade him rise. There was shouting in the distance, I suddenly realized.

"What's happening?" I said, looking around. Had the protesters broken through the palace gates?

Faris ignored me. Her eyes were fixed on the throne, where the guard was whispering into the emperor's ear. After a moment the guard stepped back, and Rafael stormed from the hall without another word. Faris stood up and went after him. I watched her progress from the table to the door that led to the emperor's council chambers. The air filled with curious whispers. The shouting seemed to be growing louder.

I glanced around the hall. The distraction was perfect cover for connecting with Idai, but I didn't see them anywhere, or the lord from Oskiath. So instead of retreating to my chambers, I followed the crowd that was filing out of the great hall and toward the front of the palace.

We walked into the courtyard and slammed into a wall of sound. The palace gates were still shut and locked, and a row of guards stood behind the bars, swords drawn. But beyond the gates stood a mob stretching as far as I could see. Protesters covered their faces with masks, and some of them carried signs painted with names. The only one I recognized was Owain, but it was easy to conclude that the rest had also died at the emperor's hand. It didn't seem like any of them were heavily armed, but their numbers alone would be enough to overwhelm the palace guards . . . if they were able to get through the gates.

This had to be because of last night. They had not been

cowed—they had been emboldened. I swallowed, remembering the way that the building had burned.

"Are you all right?" Someone touched my arm, and I flinched away. I looked up to see Idai next to me.

"I—"

They looked around. We were lost in a crowd of frightened nobles—what guards I saw were occupied with the palace gates.

"Come with me," they said, tugging on my sleeve.

We broke away from the crowd and quickly walked in the opposite direction. They led the way with confidence, slipping into shadowed spaces away from anyone else walking these corridors. Eventually they ducked behind a tapestry hanging on the wall and beckoned me to follow them. I did so with some trepidation, and found that Idai had brought me to a hidden passageway. I had a moment of panic—was this some sort of a trap?—before letting myself continue.

At the other end of the passageway was a garden.

It was overgrown and wild, but there were signs that once it had been regularly tended to. And despite the only light coming in through a dusty skylight far above us, there was something about this place that still felt light and airy. A massive tree formed the centerpiece of the garden, and hanging from one branch was a swing large enough for two adults.

"What is this place?" I said.

"Someplace forgotten," Idai said, putting their hands in their pockets. They settled their gangly frame on a stone bench across from me. "This is where I first met Callum. I still come here, sometimes. To remember."

The memory of my family had hung around my neck like a

stone, a weight driving my quest for vengeance. And somehow along the way, I'd forgotten how to remember them in peace. Maybe that had been necessary for me to survive. But hearing Idai acknowledge Callum's existence caused a lump to form in my throat. And while their tone was sorrowful, I could hear the affection in their voice.

"How old were you?"

They tipped their head back in thought. "Twelve? Rafael's father had called a summit of the small kings to discuss trade between kingdoms, I think."

I pictured Idai and Callum as children sitting together on that swing. They'd likely traded treatises on governance like love letters. The thought brought a wry smile to my lips.

"Why did you bring me here?" I asked. "Not simply to reminisce, I hope."

"Because of my respect for your brother. There are limits to what I can do for you, but I would help, if I can."

This was more than I'd dared hope for. I tried to tamp down the relief that leapt up within me. "I know that the emperor has set a blockade of Talons around Ruzi," I said carefully.

Dismay crossed Idai's face. "Severin—"

I held up a hand. "I'm not asking you to lead an army against the Talons. But my people—Callum's people—will soon starve. Can you send them relief supplies?"

They frowned. "What good will that do? The supplies won't be able to get through the blockade."

I smiled. "I have reason to believe the blockade won't be standing for much longer. Will you at least send something to the border?"

Idai stood up and paced one way, then the other. "You seem remarkably certain of this."

I had to believe that Maren could do it, in part because I had precious little else to believe in. But I also truly believed that she was capable of everything that the emperor feared, and more. "I am," I said.

"All right," they said, after a moment's consideration. "I'll come up with a reason to leave Irrad tomorrow. I'll see that something is sent."

I sighed in relief. "*Thank you.*" For a moment I considered begging them to smuggle me away, but Idai's friendship with Callum was well documented. It seemed impossible that their party would not be inspected on the way out. The moment passed.

"We shouldn't linger here," Idai said. "I've never seen anyone else in this garden, but we may be missed." They held out a hand, and I clasped it firmly. "You remind me of Callum, more than I thought possible."

Then they released my hand and left me in the garden, speechless and alone.

I had never compared myself favorably to Callum. Callum was the strong one, the charismatic leader wholly devoted to governance. I was the younger brother trailing in his shadow. And yet Idai, who had known Callum better than almost anyone else, saw similarities in me.

I hoped that he would be proud of what I was doing now.

"Interesting."

I froze. Faris stood in the doorway, watching me. How long had she been there? Had she heard my conversation with Idai?

She walked into the garden, looking around. "This is a good

hiding place, Prince. I doubt even the emperor knows of its existence. And you've made a friend in King Idai. That *is* something His Excellency should be informed of."

No. She'd heard everything, and if she told the emperor . . . I couldn't allow that to happen. I was reluctant to kill Faris—if I was being honest with myself, I'd actually grown to like her. As much as one could like an Aurat and a servant to the emperor, anyway. But if she was threatening to give everything away, I would have to choose myself. She'd been weakened by the overuse of her power. If I could strike at her without putting myself within arm's reach, I might stand a chance. I looked around discreetly, searching for something I could use as a weapon.

"What's stopping you?" I said, trying to buy time. She was toying with me now, I was certain.

But Faris hesitated. "You asked me why I remain loyal." She held one of her hands in the air, studying it. "My parents called me cursed, when they discovered what I could do. I joined the Aurati because I had nowhere else to go—not because I was made welcome. The emperor is a monster, but he was the first to call my ability a *gift*."

She sighed. "Maybe my parents were right after all. To the Flame of the West, I have no value beyond the terror I inflict upon his enemies. This talent has raised me high in the world, but the price has become too great. I'm . . . fading."

I stopped, stunned. I'd hoped I might be able to persuade her to turn on the emperor, but I hadn't expected this.

"You could kill him," I said softly. Rafael would never even see it coming.

"And then what? Free myself and leave the rest of the world

to burn? I am not such a fool to think that killing one man will fix the destruction that he has wrought."

"Leave that to me," I said.

Faris shook her head. "I like you, Prince Severin. But you have not convinced me that you have what it takes to wrest control from those who would rush in once the emperor is dead."

Her criticism needled me, but I pressed her further. "Then at least help me escape. I have plans for the emperor—for Zefed. If you're not on guard duty when it happens, no one will suspect your involvement."

After a moment she said, "I'll consider it, little prince. And I won't say anything about this to the emperor . . . for now."

CHAPTER TWENTY-EIGHT

Maren

Both Alora and Braith were full-grown dragons and could easily carry three humans each. Kaia, Tasia, and I rode on Alora. Efren and Jase rode together on Braith, though it took them time to become used to each other, and even then Jase sat stiffly, his shoulders hunched up near his ears. After some deliberation, we had packed the Talons' oils into a wooden chest, which Braith carried in her claws. Though I wasn't sure what I would do with them, I didn't want to risk them falling into the wrong hands in Ruzi.

What would Naava think when she saw the other freed dragons arriving in Ilvera? So many of my actions since parting from her had been tied to considerations other than her nebulous entreaty for me to prove myself. We'd freed dragons so that they wouldn't attack us. I'd agreed to go to Ruzi because I needed support going to Gedarin. I worried that I'd muddied everything up—that Naava might look at everything I had done and say that I had done it out of self-ishness. That I had proven nothing and therefore deserved nothing.

The fear ate at me as we flew, as did Kaia's silence. She'd withdrawn from me again, spending our remaining time in Ruzi with the Aurati. Her message was clear. She was waiting for me to apologize—and commit to a decision.

The choice was not so clear. Both Kaia and Sev held parts of my heart.

The distance that had grown between Kaia and me was stark. I loved her—would always love her—but from the moment I'd kissed her for the first time, I had never been alone. I'd adopted her dreams as mine. What little I wanted for myself had been easily subsumed by her certainty. Now I had a new purpose that was solely my own, but what would happen after it was over? Could I change myself to fit her needs when the dust had settled?

At the same time, I could not truthfully say that Sev was my future. Our connection was deepening, but our relationship had been forged under duress. Would there be anything left once our shared goals were achieved? What did he even want, beyond the death of the emperor? And what did *I* want?

When will we see Sev? Tasia asked.

I tucked my chin over her head, holding her steady. Alora had asked whether Tasia wanted to ride in her claws, and she'd immediately scampered backward. Despite our partnership, Tasia was still skittish after our first encounter with the newly freed dragon.

Soon, I hope. I hoped Sev would be able to stay out of trouble until we got to the capital.

Kaia yawned behind me, her head nodding on my shoulder. The Talons who had managed to escape us had headed straight for Gedarin, which meant the emperor had to know what we had done in Ruzi. In order to avoid detection, we were flying by night. The lights of small towns spread out below us, and the air smelled like autumn leaves crackling in fires.

"How much farther?" I asked. After consulting a map, Efren had suggested landing near a small forest a few hours' walk south of Irrad. The forest would provide cover, and we would be able to get into the city by foot to get a feel for the atmosphere.

Soon, Braith replied. She was quieter than Alora, but furious in her own way.

I had been concerned with crossing paths with Talons on patrol, but Alora assured me that this was unlikely. The emperor was accustomed to being in complete control of the skies. Even now that he was not, it seemed unlikely that he had formulated a plan so quickly for how to combat other dragons in the air.

Braith was right—soon enough the lights of Irrad spread out below us. For the middle of the night, it was very bright. The dragons adjusted their path to give the city—and the Talons patrolling above it—a wide berth.

"Is that normal?" Kaia whispered.

Alora inhaled, her nostrils flaring. *The city is burning.*

A moment later the discomforting scent hit me as well. Irrad was the emperor's seat of power. What could it possibly mean that the city was burning? I watched Irrad pass in the distance as we flew. Soon after that the dragons began a slow descent, bringing us down gently on the outskirts of the forest. After we unpacked our supplies, the dragons took Tasia into the trees to hunt, leaving the humans behind to make camp.

"What's your plan for Irrad?" Efren asked as we brushed a circle on the ground clear in preparation for a fire. She gathered a handful of twigs and dry leaves together, then lit a match and dropped it onto the pile, blowing carefully to grow the flame.

"I want to know what the full fleet of Talons looks like. And I want to see the palace. Any ideas for how to accomplish that?"

Jase frowned. "How many Talons do you think have gotten a good look at you? Would the emperor be able to identify you?"

I paused, considering. I'd been seen by Talons, certainly. And both Kaia and I had spoken to any number of people in that village we'd saved from Glivven. But my appearance wasn't remarkable—I could easily pass for someone with Old Zefedi heritage. It was only when traveling with Kaia and the dragon that I was notable.

I looked at Kaia, knowing I was about to anger her. "I don't know if you should come with us tomorrow. You look Verran—you might draw attention."

The look she gave me was murderous. "You need all the help you can get. And I can make contact with the Aurati."

The Aurati, again?

Efren piped up. "The Aurati in Irrad aren't like the Ruzians. Most of them are hand chosen by the emperor. They are extremely loyal. You won't be able to infiltrate them so easily." She eyed me thoughtfully. "Braid your hair before we leave and don't look too many people in the eye, and you should be fine. But we do need someone to stay with the dragons."

Jase volunteered—after his initial caution around the dragons, his curiosity had burgeoned. Alora and Braith tolerated his attention well enough, even though they could not speak directly with him.

Kaia looked at me pointedly. "Maren, a word?" I sighed. This was becoming uncomfortably familiar.

We put some distance between us and the camp before Kaia spoke. "Why don't you want me to come with you into the city?" she said.

"I told you—the guards might be on the lookout for you. The Aurati *certainly* will."

She leaned back against a tree trunk. "So this is just because you're afraid of us being recognized if we're together."

I tried to bury the frustration that flared within me. "What else would it be about? Besides, I can't leave Tasia alone with strangers. She doesn't know them! I need you to look after her," I said.

It was difficult to make out her expression in the darkness. "I don't know, Maren. We've traveled so far together. Why is this city different? Is it perhaps that you think you'll run into Sev, and you want to make sure I'm not there?" she said pointedly.

"Of course not!"

"Then I don't understand what you're thinking, Maren. The last time you went out on your own, you almost got yourself killed. I won't be your assistant any longer. I need to be your *partner*. I made a difference in Ruzi, and yet this is just another decision that you've made without consulting me first."

My frustration boiled into anger. Of all the things to complain about, it wasn't that she was hungry, or tired, or frightened. It was that I wasn't *including* her on a dangerous mission that might get all of us killed if we took one wrong step.

"I would have been *fine* without you in Ruzi, and we're going to be *fine* without you tomorrow," I snapped. Kaia opened her mouth, and I barreled forward. "You heard Efren. The Aurati in Irrad are different from the Ruzians. The risk that you'll be recognized is far greater than the likelihood that you'll be able to make friends with one of the emperor's hand-picked Aurati."

"And why are you the one who gets to make those decisions?"

"Because I'm the dragon mistress!" I shouted.

Kaia sneered at me scornfully. "You're just a girl, Maren! Playing with dragons doesn't give you the right—"

"It does!" I spat back. Why was she being so impossible? Couldn't she see I had to keep her safe? "And I don't care what you think about it! Believe what you want, but you are not coming to Irrad with us tomorrow. I cannot take that chance. I can't—"

"Fine!" Kaia yelled, before I could finish. She turned and ran away, and for the first time, I didn't want to follow her.

"Maren, wake up. We have a problem." I opened my eyes groggily to see Jase standing over me. The fire had long since burned out. Tasia was at my side, but the two other dragons were awake and looming over ... a group of humans that had *not* been there when I went to sleep.

I shook myself awake. "Who are they?" There were five of them seated together on the ground, wearing traveling clothes. They had four horses, which were tolerating the dragons' presence admirably.

"They say they're travelers heading to Eronne," Jase said.

It wasn't an entirely implausible story. We weren't that far off the most trafficked route between Irrad and Deletev, the capital of Eronne. But we had chosen this forest specifically because it was out of the way. Travelers shouldn't come this way unless they too were trying to avoid the emperor's notice.

Efren intercepted me as I approached the group, grabbing me by the arm before I made it too close. "Stay back," she cautioned. "We don't want them seeing your face."

"Who are they?" I said.

She scowled. "One of them says they're the king of Eronne."

Oh, Ciara's blood. A small king. The only higher authority in Zefed was the emperor himself. I pressed my forefingers to either side of my nose, trying to control my breathing. How were we going to get out of this?

"How do we know they're telling the truth?" I said.

"I saw King Idai once in a parade," Jase offered. "They look about the same."

That was hardly conclusive. And why would a small king be traveling with so few companions?

I looked to Efren. "What do you think we should do?"

"We can't trust them, so we can't let them go," she said.

Hold a king captive? How long would it be before someone came looking for them?

"We have to make a decision," Jase said. "If you don't leave soon, we'll have to wait another day to get into Irrad."

"Then talk to them," Kaia said.

I looked at her. "But—"

She rolled her eyes. "You don't want to be recognized? Put a scarf over your face. Easy."

I resisted the urge to glower at her, as despite her sourness it was a reasonable suggestion. I took a scarf and draped it over my face, then stepped forward as Jase held up a torch.

"So one of you claims to be the king of Eronne," I said, trying to sound menacing.

One of them, a person with a lanky frame and wavy brown hair, raised their chin. "I am King Idai," they said.

A small king without uninterrupted Old Zefedi lineage? It seemed impossible—but Jase had seen them once. I crossed my arms. "If you're a king, what are you doing traveling by side roads with only four escorts?"

Their eyes flicked up to the dragons and back at me. "I suspect for a reason similar to yours. Something illegal and seditious."

I snorted. The king of Eronne, fomenting a revolution? Tasia was at my side, her nostrils flaring. As I cast around for something to say, she took a step forward.

Wait! I said, calling her back.

Smells like Sev, she replied, but halted, one claw in the air.

What? I knelt at her side, wondering if I had misunderstood her. *Who smells like Sev?*

She pointed her nose in the king's direction. *Sev's friend.*

King Idai was Sev's friend? Was it possible they were telling the truth after all?

I cleared my throat and stood up. "Very well. King Idai, you are coming from Irrad, are you not?"

They nodded.

"Then you must know Prince Severin."

If they were surprised, their face gave nothing away. "It appears we have that acquaintance in common—assuming I am in the presence of the dragon mistress? He has spoken of you."

Could they be lying? What if Sev had betrayed me to this person? The thought flashed through my mind before I banished it. That was ridiculous. Sev would never. And to what end, exactly? No one could have known that we would be here, so this encounter couldn't have been planned.

I had to end this conversation—I couldn't allow my thoughts to keep spiraling. I leaned over the king, pitching my voice low. "I don't have the time to waste on the niceties I'm sure you're accustomed to. If you're a friend of Sev's, if you claim to be working against the emperor, then tell me what you're doing on this road. Otherwise we have no choice but to hold you here."

"If *you're* a friend of Sev's, then you'll let me go. He's the one who asked me to leave Irrad."

"But you're not going to tell me why."

"Are you going to tell me where you're going, that you don't have time to speak to a king?" Idai countered. "I have no reason to trust you."

This was going terribly, and we were running out of time. I turned around and walked back to the group. "Keep them here. The dragons can guard them until we return."

I ignored the disapproving look that Kaia gave me. Instead I knelt down in front of Tasia. *Wait here, all right? I'll be back soon, I promise.*

She sniffed but settled into a watchful stance that mimicked Braith's, her eyes narrowed as she regarded the humans.

"We'll be back before nightfall," Efren said.

"Fine," Kaia said.

"Really? That's all you're going to say?" I said.

Her lips pinched as she looked away. "I don't think there's anything else *to* say. You're leaving. I'm staying here. We'll see each other when you're done saving the world."

Whatever words were the right ones, they weren't coming. I couldn't wait any longer—I had to walk away.

CHAPTER TWENTY-NINE

Sev

The door to my chambers was slightly ajar when I arrived that night, and my guards were gone. I stopped well short of the door. Had someone searched my chambers? But why would the guards be missing? Escape flitted through my mind, and I discarded the idea—with the protesters outside the gates, I knew of no other way out of the palace. Besides, I was curious about who I might find inside. I suspected that if I had a visitor, they were no friend to the emperor. Still, I wished for a weapon as I leaned cautiously around the door.

The lanterns were lit, and there was someone standing by the window—Piera.

I stepped quickly inside and closed the door behind me. "What are you doing here? It's not safe."

She crossed the room in quick strides, and took my hands in hers. "I had to see you. I haven't heard anything from you, and I'm *frightened*. Sev, do you have a plan?"

Of course she hadn't heard anything from me—she was the empress. It was almost impossible to get near her. "I'm working on it, I promise."

She shook her head. "You saw Rafael burn the building. He's seeing conspiracies in shadows—you never know who he might turn on next. *Please*, Sev. I have to get out."

I squeezed her hands. "Soon, I promise. I'm not sure when exactly, but you have to be ready to go at a moment's notice."

Piera nodded eagerly. Then she bit her lip, looking around the room. "This is where they put you?"

I almost laughed. She truly had grown into her new station, if she could take a moment like this and turn it into a criticism of my living arrangements. "It's a far cry better than the dungeons," I said with a shrug.

"Of course. Of course you're right." She turned back to me and touched my cheek with a gentle finger. "It's been so long. I never got a chance to tell you—I'm so sorry about what happened to your mother."

I swallowed down the lump that had suddenly formed in my throat. "Thank you," I whispered.

"I'm sorry about a lot of things, actually," she said. "Sev, will you hold me?"

She wrapped her arms around me without waiting for an answer. And then, without warning, she turned her head and kissed me on the lips.

I froze, startled. Piera's lips were softer than I'd once imagined in my boyish daydreams, and yet . . . I felt nothing. None of the heated passion that had fueled my boyish daydreams. Time and perspective had changed me.

That, and the fact that I was in love with someone else.

I stepped back, taking her hands in mine. "I'll always care for you, Piera. You know that. But—"

"I understand," she said quickly. She laughed a small,

embarrassed laugh. "I suppose I should just be grateful to have had the chance to see you again."

I smiled at her. "When there's something to know, I'll send word. But you should get back now—you shouldn't be missed."

She nodded, smiling a bright, forced smile. "Good night, Severin."

In the morning Idai was gone.

Their absence was barely noted by anyone except me, though I didn't know how they had made it out of the palace, as the protests had grown into full-fledged riots.

It seemed that the Talons and the emperor's soldiers had been unsuccessful in quelling the uproar. Curfews had been ignored, and more and more people were joining the crowds that stood, jeering, outside the palace gates. Overnight, some-one had blown up a building in the noble district. But the palace walls held, and in the afternoon, the Talons set another building on fire.

Being inside the palace was eerie by contrast. I'd been woken not by the rioting, but by the sound of strings playing through the halls. Vix was a constant presence behind the throne, its very body heating the air. A group of musicians stood to the left of the throne, playing frenetically. And in the center of the hall were the dancers. Instead of addressing the protesters directly, the emperor had called for music and dancing. He was trying—unsuccessfully—to drown them out. And while Rafael's dragon towered over the proceedings, it had the effect of making the emperor himself appear . . . small.

He was still dangerous, but in the way that cornered predators were dangerous. The people of Irrad had succeeded in doing something that I could not have done myself—they had changed my perception of the tyrant. I was no longer terrified of him. For the first time, I looked at him and saw someone who was within my power to defeat.

The floor rumbled under my feet. Something was coming—something big.

A green dragon burst through the door of the great hall, a Talon on its back. The music skittered to a halt, as the Talon slid down to the floor and ran to the throne. She dropped to her knees before the emperor, clearly exhausted.

"My lord," she gasped. "The Ruzian blockade has fallen."

Maren. A wave of relief washed over me, both for her success and for Ruzi. I barely kept the smile from my face.

"*WHAT?*" The emperor's shout echoed through the hall.

"There was a girl and—a baby dragon, I think. They did something to make the dragons turn on us. Only Tove, Seku, and I made it back—the rest are . . . lost."

Three Talons had escaped. I didn't know how many had fallen, but the emperor was almost apoplectic. The hall was silent, the only noise the muffled sounds of the riot outside.

The emperor raised his hand, and the page standing at the side of the hall stepped forward. "Find Milek."

The page took off at a run, and the great hall filled with nervous chatter. I looked around, at a loss for what to do. I should stay, shouldn't I? I needed to look innocent—curious, even.

Someone jostled me from behind, and I spun to face the lord from Oskiath.

She grabbed my arm as if to steady me and leaned close,

whispering in my ear. "The Dragons are close. Midnight tonight. Meet in the stables."

I nodded, my head spinning. I had a way out, finally—for myself, Neve, Piera, and her son.

Within a few minutes the page returned with the Alchemist. The emperor waved him forward. "Alchemist, how fare the dragons under your care?"

The Alchemist bowed his head. "There has been progress, my lord. We are close."

"Then I believe it is time for a test. Take one of your dragons . . . and set them on the streets."

A gasp swept through the hall—the emperor had managed to shock even those most loyal to him. They all knew the same thing I did: Milek's work was untried. And one rogue dragon was enough to burn the city to the ground.

"My lord." Piera stepped forward out of the shadows. She set her hand on Rafael's shoulder—he jerked away from her touch, but she spoke softly. "Such an important task should not be trusted to half-trained beasts. The fires will risk the entire city. The safety of your son could be compromised."

I'd never seen her speak in public before. Was this how they were even behind closed doors? There were so many reasons why the emperor should not send a rabid dragon into the city with no direction. She should not be forced to cite his son to make him see that.

"Fine," said the emperor. He looked across the hall. "Prince Vesper! Faris! To me!"

Now I *was* surprised. Would he order me to stop the riots? Such a request was impossible.

I followed him as he spun and retreated into the council chambers. Faris met me at the door, and I raised an eyebrow. She pressed her lips together but did not speak as she ushered me inside.

The moment the door closed, Rafael whirled on me.

"Tell me what your friend is doing to my dragons," Rafael said softly—dangerously. "I will not ask you again."

"I've never seen her turn a dragon against its Talon," I said truthfully.

He stared at me inscrutably. "Faris?"

Even knowing what was about to happen, there was no preparing for this. Faris's hand fell onto my shoulder, and fire ignited in my leg. I had fallen from a tree and broken it as a child—I'd forgotten about the pain until now.

"Where does this power come from? How can it be stopped?" the emperor said. I could barely hear him over the roar of torment in my head. Faris lifted her hand, and I rolled over, gasping.

"Kill her, that's the only way," I choked out. *Just let this stop.*

But Rafael wasn't satisfied. "I am the Flame of the West, master of dragons. That power should be mine! How did she get it? Where did she steal it from?"

Faris brought her hand down once more, and then I couldn't hear anything as the very air around me buzzed with agony.

"I don't know! I don't know!" I screamed. The pain was endless, undulating in waves through my entire body.

And then Faris cried out, collapsing to the floor next to me. Rafael swore. "Get up!"

But she didn't move, not when Rafael cursed and threatened

her, nor when he picked up a chair and threw it across the room. It slammed against the wall and fell to the floor, the sound echoing across the chamber. The emperor let out a scream of rage, then kicked me hard in the stomach. I flinched, moaning in pain—I didn't even have the strength left to cry. "This isn't over," he said. Then he stalked out of the chamber, slamming the door behind him.

It hurt to breathe, and I was certain that I would vomit if I moved too quickly. I turned my head gingerly to look at Faris.

She lay almost motionless, staring up at the ceiling. I didn't mind not moving, not as long as the floor was cool and quiet. But after some long minutes of silence, she cleared her throat. "You win, little prince. I'll help you."

CHAPTER THIRTY

Maren

D o you . . . want to talk about it?" Efren said after a while. We had been walking in silence for about an hour. We hadn't been able to come up with disguises—in the end, I had finger-combed and rebraided my hair, and put on a light hood that shaded my face. After walking, I smelled more like the road than I did dragons—at least enough to fool any humans we met. There was no perfect substitute for an actual bath, but it was better than nothing. If we came across a stream, I'd have the opportunity to wash my face, too.

"I really don't," I said.

She snickered, just barely.

"*What?*" I snapped.

"I'm sorry. It's nothing." She pulled her expression into a passing semblance of solemnity.

I sighed. The road ahead was long, and if there was joviality to be had, I could use some. Besides, now I was curious. "It clearly isn't nothing, so you might as well tell me."

She pursed her lips as though she was weighing her options. "All right. If you really want to know . . ."

"I do!"

"All right, all right. Well, I know there's a lot at stake here.

And I have the utmost respect for you—and Kaia. But there's just something a little funny about the *dragon mistress* having issues with her girlfriend. I used to think of kings and queens and those sorts of people as being above such common problems." She looked at me, clearly unsure of how I might react.

I was taken aback. Whatever I'd expected, it wasn't that. And yet she was right. When put like that, it was ridiculous. I smiled, and then chuckled. Soon enough tears of mirth were spilling down my face as I laughed helplessly, Efren laughing at my side.

After a while we calmed down again. "You're right," I said. "But I'm hardly as lofty a figure as a *king*."

Efren smirked. "I suspect there are a lot of people in Zefed who would disagree. But . . . are you sure you don't want to talk about it?" When I didn't respond, she cleared her throat. "If I may . . ."

I looked at her and sighed, inclining my head to let her know I was listening.

"You've been together for a long time, I think."

"Years," I said. "How did you know?"

At this Efren smiled. "First love is easy to spot. And first love is precious. But that doesn't mean it's meant to be your only love, or that it's worth your misery. Sometimes people fight because they're looking for a reason to leave. And the truth is, if something isn't right? You don't need another reason."

Tangled emotions roiled through me, and my eyes brimmed with tears. I felt embarrassed that an almost-stranger had seen such things in my relationship. Angry that she'd dare say as much to me. And afraid—that she was right.

Because she'd managed to articulate things that I hadn't dared to voice myself. The future I'd always envisioned with Kaia was still there, but it had turned hazy and difficult to reach. I didn't know what I could possibly reach for instead—but more and more, I wasn't certain that this was the path I wanted.

"Thank you," I said quietly.

Efren cleared her throat and squinted up at the sky. "We'd best move faster."

We'd covered a good amount of ground on our way toward the eastern edge of Gedarin, and the ocean. The air smelled of salt, and it occurred to me that there was a persistent sound in the air—something that lulled rhythmically back and forth. The sound woke something in me—somehow, it felt both foreign and familiar at the same time. Soon the forest thinned, and grassy hills spread before us. The grass was short and flaxen, and the wind blowing through it made little shushing sounds as it moved.

It would have been an idyllic scene, were it not for what awaited us ahead. The land had been completely razed of trees, leaving only stumps behind. The wind changed, and I caught the scent of dead wood drying under the sun.

"What happened here?"

"What else? The emperor needed to build his warships."

"Hasn't he destroyed *enough*?"

It was a rhetorical question, but Efren didn't take it as such. "To some, one can never have enough money or power. He wants the Seda Serat, so he must have it, at any cost."

I didn't want to walk through this graveyard, but there was no other way. I counted hundreds of stumps before I forced myself to focus instead on the horizon, trying not to think about what had stood here—what was gone. It took too long, but eventually we were through and climbing a small hill. And as we reached the top, my breath caught in my chest.

The ocean.

It was more beautiful than I had ever imagined, and more impressive. My brother Tovin had explained it to me in a letter—a body of water so much larger than the lake in Ilvera that you could not see its end. A body of water that was indeed so large that no one in Ilvera even knew if it *had* an end. Perhaps it kept flowing into eternity. Tovin had always dreamed of discovering the answer to that question.

And now the ocean was before me, blue and endless under a cloudless sky.

I knew that we were exposed here. Anyone could see us from overhead. But I didn't care. I stopped and stared.

"You've never been to the ocean before?" Efren said quietly.

I shook my head. "Isn't it magnificent?"

She smiled and nodded. "Let's go. There's so much ocean that soon you'll be sick of it."

I highly doubted that, but we did need to keep moving. I tore my eyes from the horizon and looked down. We were at the top of a cliff. At its base was a set of rocky beaches that spread up and down the coast. To our left, in the distance, was Irrad. *Sev.*

We were so close. I had done more, and given more, than I had ever thought possible, and I was finally almost there.

It was slow going, picking our way down the cliff to the beach. Part of the problem was that there was no actual path—only small hints of trails created by goats or deer. But we managed, slipping and shuffling down the unsteady incline. The wind was in my hair, blowing strands against my lips so that every time I opened my mouth, I tasted salt. Gulls flew above us, and below I saw the glimmers of fish under the surface of the water. I was close enough now that occasionally the salt spray blew up to us. That was what made it seem finally *real*.

At last we reached the rocky beach at the bottom of the cliff. Closer to the water's edge the rocks grew smaller until they were almost gravel, but here the rocks were the size of my palms or larger. I bent and picked one up, turning it over in my hand. The wash of waves had erased any hard edges over the years, leaving the stone completely smooth. I put it into my pocket and looked out across the water.

I had often stood on the Verran mountain and looked out across the horizon and made believe I could see the ocean. On a clear day I could see it in truth, a line across the edge of the world that had always seemed more hypothetical than real, a wish more than a plan.

And now I, Maren ben Gao Vilna, daughter of the Verran mountain, was standing with my feet at the edge of the unending ocean.

Kaia would love this. Maybe I had done the wrong thing by insisting she stay behind. After this all ended, I would make it up to her a thousand times.

Soon enough Efren called to me, and we continued up the beach toward Irrad.

We had prepared for security checks, considered what we would say if someone asked what our business was in Irrad—but instead of facing resistance, we walked until the beach ended, waded until we got to the docks, and climbed up into a scene of chaos.

In the distance were the charred skeletons of what had until recently been buildings. Somewhere ahead of us was an angry crowd—I could hear the shouts in the distance. Efren and I exchanged a glance.

"What do you think?" I said.

"Your guess is as good as mine," she said. "At least it doesn't seem like this is good for the emperor in *any* way."

"Well, let's just keep our heads down and see how far we get." At the very least, it looked like the Talons—of which there were several circling overhead—had their hands full today. We shook the sand off our clothes and left the docks behind, heading directly into the streets of Irrad.

Now that we were here, I had to confess to myself that I had only ever pictured the emperor's palace, not the surrounding city. Irrad was closer in style to Deletev than Belat, which made sense, considering the security requirements. But it was a port city, which meant that the streets connecting the docks to the rest of the city were wide and well trafficked. A few carts rolled by as we passed, but mostly we walked among people on foot, some of whom were wearing masks made of black cloth that obscured their features. The shouting grew louder.

Efren leaned toward me and put a hand over her mouth as she whispered. "I think whatever's happening is taking place near the palace."

"Wouldn't that be good for us? We'll blend in with a crowd."

"Sure, as long as the crowd doesn't get arrested or burned out by the Talons."

Oh. I stopped, considering our surroundings. "Is there somewhere else we might be able to get a good look from?"

We glanced around, but there didn't seem to be many options—most of the buildings in Irrad were equipped with hooks and platforms designed to make it easy for Talons to land their dragons, and we certainly didn't want to use one of those.

My gaze suddenly snagged on a lantern hanging on the other side of the street. The lantern itself was unremarkable, but the intricately woven rope that was hanging from it . . . "That's a Verran knot," I said.

"What does it mean?" Efren said, her hand straying close to her knife.

"They can stand for many things." I looked up and down the street before approaching the lantern. "This one is a herald's knot. Usually this would be a call for a community meeting—because of an incident, or a messenger has arrived in town, something like that."

"A call for a meeting," Efren repeated. "How many Verrans live in Irrad?"

I shrugged. "Not many."

"We should move," Efren said. "We've lingered here too long."

I nodded. "Let's go."

But there was a knot on the next lantern we passed, and the next. They formed a trail on the left side of the street, one that clearly led somewhere. Our time was limited—Aurati and soldiers were patrolling the streets—and we still needed to get to the palace. But I was distracted by the knots. I wanted to know who had gone to the trouble of putting them up, and why.

"I want to follow them," I told Efren.

"We don't have time," she said. It was nearly midday now. If we meant to get out of the city and back to our camp before dark, we couldn't afford a detour.

I grimaced. "I know. I can't explain it, but I think this is the right thing to do."

She pursed her lips. "You know we might not have another chance at this."

"I know."

She nodded slowly. "Well, this is your operation." An agreement, if not a ringing endorsement.

We followed the knots along the outer edge of the city until we arrived at a side street with canopies hanging overhead that blocked us from the view of the Talons. There was a tavern on the right side of the street. Its sign had been eroded by time and weather—the words were unrecognizable. What *was* recognizable, though, was the knot hanging below it. I knew it immediately.

"That's my family's knot," I said. Anyone familiar with Verran customs might have learned a herald's knot. But only those in my immediate family knew this one. Hope and dread mingled in my stomach. I went to the tavern door and pushed it open.

The tavern was empty—in fact, it looked as though it had been abandoned except for two people, a man and a woman, sitting at the far table. They stood as we entered the room, and there was something about the way he moved that reminded me of—

"Maren?" said the man.

My eyes had adjusted to the gloom of the tavern, but I still could not make sense of what I was seeing.

"Tovin?" I said hesitantly.

"It *is* you." He crossed the tavern in a few great strides and wrapped his arms around me, pulling me into a long hug. After a moment of surprise, I hugged him back. My brother was taller, I thought. And a little sturdier, and his skin was definitely sun browned. But it was still him.

Family. Everyone deserved one, whether they were born into one or made it themselves. Despite our years of separation, Tovin was still as familiar to me as the mountain. Did he feel the same? He'd known the person I had been before I had stood atop the Verran mountain and vowed to bring Kaia home. And that person was so different from the person I had become.

Finally, we broke the embrace. "What are you doing here?" I said in Verran. "Did you set out the knots?"

"Mother and Father wrote me. I've heard you've been busy, Little Sister."

Mother and Father. My eyebrows furrowed. "They knew I'd be here? How? I don't understand."

The woman at the table behind us cleared her throat, and Tovin jumped a little. "Come, come," he said. "We have much to discuss."

CHAPTER THIRTY-ONE

Maren

Tovin drew me over to the table and the woman standing there. She was Seratese, with short-cropped curly black hair. She wore a round shield across her back and had two knives strapped to her arms. I liked the look of her immediately.

"Maren, this is Davina. Davina, my sister, Maren." Tovin switched to Zefedi as he made the introductions. He didn't put words to their relationship, but I could tell by the warmth in his voice that they were something other than friends.

We shook hands. "This is Efren of Ruzi," I said, introducing my own companion.

Efren raised a hand in greeting, but Tovin seemed surprised. "Where is Kaia? And the dragon kit?"

I stared at him. "How do you know about the kit?"

"I told you—our parents wrote me."

I shook my head. "You're going to have to start at the beginning."

He ran a hand through his hair, sighing. "We don't have much time, so I'll make this short. I've been traveling with a war fleet out of the Seda Serat. We know that the emperor intends to bring an army against the islands. Davina and I have been sent ahead to figure out the best way to stop them."

I interrupted. "That doesn't seem like the beginning to me. You still haven't told me how you left the mountain to become a sailor and instead defected to a foreign island nation." Not that I had any problem with it. Ilvera always maintained that we were not part of the empire of Zefed so much as an involuntary neighbor.

He and Davina shared a conspiratorial glance. "He was a sailor on a trading ship," she said. "We met at the port on Lavalia—one of the islands."

"And you just ... became friendly?"

Davina snorted with laughter. "Have you met your brother? Can you imagine someone he would *not* be friendly with?"

That did sound like Tovin.

"Besides, he has the curiosity of a puppy. Always asking questions, always hanging around. And with that grin on his face the whole time!"

I couldn't help but laugh. "Yes, that's exactly what he's like."

Davina nodded but sobered as she spoke next. "Anyway, his ship was caught in the crossfire the last time the Zefedi Talons attacked. He was stranded, and he—he listened. He learned."

I was itching to ask exactly what he had learned, but I had the feeling that just because Tovin had been accepted by Davina and the rest of the Seda Serat, that acceptance did not automatically extend to me. There were many things the Zefedi people did not know about Ilvera—I did not want to assume that I understood everything about the Seratese, or that I was welcome to that information without invitation.

Tovin jumped in again. "About a week ago, I received a letter by hawk from Mother. She said that a great dragon had just landed in Ilvera and told them this fantastical story—that she had been held captive by the Aurati, and that a Verran girl had freed her. Imagine my surprise when I read that this mysterious dragon mistress was my little sister. The dragon said that you were coming to Irrad. So we set out the knots and waited. But we thought that you would be traveling with Kaia, and the dragon kit."

"They're waiting outside the city," I said.

Tovin sat back against the table, crossing his arms. "So it's true," he said. He whistled in admiration. "Maren—how?"

Why was I suddenly nervous? Perhaps it was because he was too close to home for me. Sev had only known me for a few months. I had been able to choose the version of myself I presented to him, and he had understood everything I had done through that lens. Even Kaia, who I had known since childhood, hadn't seen me first thing in the morning and last thing at night since I'd been born. Would Tovin see me differently once I told him what I'd done?

So I didn't look at him as I spilled out, as straightforwardly as I could, the entire story. He held still while I spoke, though I could feel his attention sharpening at crucial moments. And when I was done, he sat for a while. "You've grown up, little one," he said.

I punched him gently in the arm, though the nickname brought a smile to my face. "Don't call me that. You said it yourself—I'm grown now."

"My little sister, taking down the empire of Zefed by herself. I almost feel we needn't have bothered with the war fleet."

I laughed, but Tovin's face sobered. "Maren—what we're about to tell you is knowledge that is not shared outside the Seda Serat. But these are . . . unusual circumstances, and you two already have knowledge about the way that dragon bonding works. You know the mirth wood oil?"

I nodded. That oil was the key to training all dragons.

"It's sourced from the Seda Serat. The reason the emperor has been attacking the islands is that they have withheld it from him. They learned that the oil was used to train the very dragons that were threatening them. So they captured some of the Talons and kept their dragons."

My stomach turned. "You have dragons?"

"*Free* dragons," Davina said. She said something in Seratese to Tovin, who frowned but didn't reply. She looked at me. "Every Talon your emperor has sent has been brought down. Their dragons are dead or free. Those with us are here willingly. We do not use mirth wood oil for such purposes." The twist of her lips made it clear what she thought about the emperor's tactics.

"But the emperor can't afford to lose the oil," I said slowly. "That's the true reason for this war." So many things were falling into place. The emperor had painted the Seratese as Zefed's enemies, but he could not tell anyone the reason for this aggression— if he did, the secret of the dragon bonds would be out.

"Yes," Tovin said. "Now tell me. The emperor's fleet of Talons is vast. How will you free all the dragons from their masters?"

"I'd hoped to have Naava's help," I confessed. "But I've run out of time. We have two dragons who have agreed to assist us. But you're right—I can't take on the entire fleet of Talons at once. We need some way to separate them and draw them away from the palace."

"A diversion," Efren said.

"Yes." I turned to Davina. "How far out is the Seratese fleet?"

She looked at Tovin before replying. "Close," she said. "But we are not interested in igniting a war. We are here only to prevent them from sailing against us."

Suddenly something occurred to me. "Then sink the ships. You said already that the emperor has lost the Talons he's sent against you. He cannot risk sending more. If you sink the ships, he won't be able to send any of his forces. Not until he can build new ones, at least. And by then . . ." By then I hoped he would be dead, even if I had to see to it myself.

"Yes," Davina said, her eyes alight.

"Can you do it?"

She snorted. "Of course."

"Then when?" Efren asked.

She leaned back, thinking. "Sunrise tomorrow," she said finally.

Less than a day. I nodded. "We'll be ready. Burn the ships."

"But where will you be?" Tovin said.

It had been so long since I had heard that particular familial worry in someone's voice. It warmed my heart and made me homesick at the same time. "I'll be on the back of a dragon, leading the charge."

I could tell that he wanted to object. I put a hand over his on the table. "I can do extraordinary things," I said. "Don't worry."

Tovin smiled. "I've heard. But you're my little sister. I'm still worrying."

I thought of one more thing. "There is one thing you could do, though. Do you have access to a messenger hawk?"

He nodded.

"Then write to Ilvera. Tell them everything—and ask the dragons to come."

"Will they?" Davina said.

Prove yourself beyond the reach of my wings.

"I don't know," I said. But there seemed no other option but to try.

By the time we had finished, there was no opportunity to linger in Irrad. We had to be clear of the city before curfew, and the streets were in danger of being overrun by Aurati and Talons.

Efren and I traveled hastily, not wanting to be caught on open ground once the sun set. But when we reached our camp in the forest, it was immediately clear that something was wrong.

Tasia ran at me as we walked into the camp, and jumped into my arms even though she was almost too heavy to do so safely. I hugged her close before letting her down—she was in obvious distress.

They left! she cried.

"Who?" The word left my lips in surprise. I looked past Tasia. Alora and Braith were there, but King Idai's party was gone. And so were Jase and Kaia.

CHAPTER THIRTY-TWO

Sev

Smoke hung in the air, stinging my eyes, but what rattled my nerves more was the persistent sound of hammer against stone. Rafael had ordered the servants to dig a path into his oubliette so that the dragons inside could climb out. There was no word on how they would be used, but his purpose was obvious. The riots in Irrad showed no sign of abating. Soon, the emperor might use the dragons to burn protesters at the gates rather than acquiesce to their demands.

Work on the oubliette halted only when the emperor called an audience in the courtyard to demonstrate the Alchemist's progress. It was a smaller crowd than usual. I hadn't realized before, but it seemed that more than one noble party had quietly slipped away from the palace in the midst of the uproar. Hope glimmered in my chest. They were abandoning Irrad, which could only mean they believed there would be no retribution—that the emperor would fall. An unthinkable statement even weeks ago.

I was certain Rafael had noticed, though he made no mention of it. After we were gathered, he called a Talon forward with his dragon, a tall creature with polished gray scales. I recognized the Talon, though we didn't have much of a relationship. Seku had escaped from the attack on the Ruzian blockade.

He was about my age, a younger son from one of the noble families of Kyseal. If I had been sent to join the Talons, we would have been in the same training class.

Milek, the Alchemist, presented him with a fresh Talon case, its leather polished and gleaming in the light. I watched as Seku opened the case and drew out a new bandolier and switched it with the one he was wearing. The expression on his face was apprehensive, and I cast a look around the courtyard.

Neve was standing across from me, her lips pressed together tightly as she watched. If the oils worked, the emperor would have no further reason to keep her alive. On the other hand, we were all on the brink of disaster if the oils failed.

Our eyes met, and I took a pointed step backward. She did the same as Seku adjusted the fit of the bandolier. He then knelt before the emperor. "My wings are yours," he said, putting a fist against his chest in a salute.

Rafael looked down upon him. "Then you will execute the dragon dance."

Most of the audience didn't react, but my heart stuttered at the proclamation. The dragon dance was a ritual performed by a Talon as part of their graduation from their training program. The dance showed that a Talon had mastered their dragon, as dragons did not naturally perform elaborate dances on foot. I understood that it was easy enough for a full Talon to do, but with inferior oils? There was a good chance that this was about to go sideways, and Neve and I were the only people in the audience who were aware of that fact.

Seku opened the first vial and sniffed it, then poured a drop onto his wrist and offered it to his dragon. I held my breath. An eternity passed as the dragon lowered its head obediently, but there was no outburst. Seku's shoulders relaxed minutely. He moved on to the next vial, and when the dragon had partaken, he climbed up onto the dragon's back and settled into the saddle.

Taking up the reins, he whistled to the dragon, which raised its right foot and stepped forward, then back. Clapping his hands, Seku began to hum. The rest of the audience hummed along. This song was well known throughout the empire—though Talons were the emperor's elite force, watching a dragon dance was something that bound all citizens together. And this dragon dance was going well.

I caught Neve's eye and tilted my head. As the people around us moved forward, craning their necks for a better view, Neve and I melted out of the courtyard.

In the hallway we were alone. Neve grabbed my elbow and steered me quickly around a corner. "What do you want?" she said.

I skipped all preamble. "The emperor doesn't need you anymore. But I have a way out. Tonight, midnight. Can you get to the stables?"

"Yes," she said immediately. "What else?"

"You've heard of the Dragons working against the emperor? I told them I could secure your assistance training their own dragon." At Neve's alarmed expression, I kept going. "Don't worry—I don't think you'll have to follow through. But that was the price for taking the empress and prince as well."

Neve grimaced. "If you're taking the empress, I'm not going."

"I—what? Would you rather stay here and be killed?"

She sighed. "Severin, if you're working against the emperor, you cannot trust her. No matter what lies she's fed to you, that girl is a snake."

I shook my head. "She came to me. She begged me to get her out."

"I don't care. If she's in, then I'm out."

And that was it. My entire plan, crumbling. Maybe the Dragons would take us without Neve—after all, they'd already gone through the trouble of organizing the escape. But what if they didn't? What if they took one look at us and turned their backs?

I let my head fall back against the wall. "They won't take us without you," I said.

"I don't care," Neve said simply. "It's your choice, but if you won't make it, I will."

Choice. But there was more than one . . . wasn't there? "Then it's you," I said. "I have to get out. Stables at midnight, all right?"

There was something truly novel about standing in a hidden alcove with the emperor's Aromatory, watching emotions flicker across her face. Once she had seemed so remote, so powerful. Now she was just a human like me, weighing her options, all of them bad.

The faint sound of applause reached us. So the dragon dance had been a success. I watched the realization, and its implications, hit Neve.

"I'll be there," she said finally. "Now, if you'll excuse me."

She brushed off her clothing and left the alcove. I took a deep breath and blew it out. I couldn't leave Piera behind. So I had to hope that once we were all gathered, Neve would decide it was too late to back out. However she felt about the empress, being so close to freedom would have to sway her decision. Now all I needed to do was find a way to get the message to Piera.

"I need your help," I told Faris back in my chambers. The emperor had finally dismissed her—a rare occurrence these days—and she was now lying on the carpet, arms out to her sides. Her skin was sallow, and there were dark hollows under her eyes. She looked—she looked as though she was dying.

"Now?" She opened one eye and peered at me. "You want me to get up and help you *now*?"

"Yes, now," I said. "I need you to find an excuse not to be on guard tonight, and tell me what the guard cycle is. And I need to write a letter to the empress."

She laughed weakly, propping herself up with one elbow. "The guards, easy. But what makes you think that writing a letter to the empress is an appropriate action for you, the disgraced prince of Ruzi, to take?"

I crossed my arms, staring down at her. "Do you have a better idea for how to get a message to her? If she hears a message direct from you, she'll know you're involved. But I'm going to be sent overseas with the army. The empress was a dear friend of mine when we were children. She's one of the only people from my childhood still *alive*. After I leave, there's a good chance I'll never make it back to Zefed. It is right and proper that I might want to say good-bye."

"The emperor will intercept it."

"Not if I leave it unsealed. Then you can say you indulged me because I annoyed you into it—whatever you want—but that you inspected it thoroughly. No secret communications."

She let her head fall back against the carpet. "It's not the worst idea you've had," she admitted.

"Then 'not the worst' will have to do," I said.

"Fine." She rolled her eyes. "Enough of this. I'll get you paper, but I'm going to stand over your shoulder as you write it."

I executed an exaggerated bow. "Your magnanimousness is noted, as usual."

Faris rang a bell, and a guard stepped inside the room. "I require paper and pen," she said, waving a hand dismissively.

I shut my mouth and behaved until the writing implements were delivered, and didn't say a word as she watched over my shoulder, making amused sounds as I considered what to write.

Twenty minutes and countless eye rolls later, I handed Faris the letter. She plucked the paper out of my hand and scanned what I had written. "I suppose no one ever told you that you're a terrible correspondent."

It wasn't my fault that the code we'd come up with as children had been horribly convoluted. Two words for every letter, cross-switched and reversed every other line? We must have been insufferable. But the message was there. Midnight tonight. We were getting out.

CHAPTER THIRTY-THREE

Sev

The last time I had attempted a nighttime escape had been my flight from the dragon fortress, and nothing about that had gone as planned. I was plagued by doubt as I waited—for the sun to set, for the guard to change, for the bells to toll midnight. Was it right to help Piera and her son escape? Would the Dragons keep their word? Would Neve go along once she realized that I had lied to her about Piera?

And what would happen once I was out? I couldn't shake the feeling that I was overlooking a reason to stay. But the army's departure for the Seda Serat was fast approaching. I could not kill the emperor if I set sail. And as I had no good plan to kill the emperor now—he had taken to keeping his dragon at his side at all times—I had to stay alive until I did. Which meant escape. Which meant the Dragons.

When the bells tolled at half an hour to midnight, I got up and rumpled the bedclothes and arranged the pillows so that at first glance it would appear that I was still in bed. Then I reached into the wardrobe and grabbed the ends of the sheet I'd ripped into wide strips earlier in the night. I went to the curtain and stood just to the side, so that someone approaching the bed from the receiving area would not see me. There were only two guards stationed at the door. The emperor had ordered more and more guards put on the palace wall, and since I'd never tried to leave my chambers after curfew, he'd taken one from my detail.

I took a deep breath and let out a shout. I had made an assumption that the guard would investigate strange disturbances, and was gratified when the door slammed open and I heard running footsteps. I readied myself—and when the guard ran into the bedchamber, I leaped at him and wound the sheet tightly around his neck.

The guard struggled. I kicked away his flailing knife and pulled back hard on the sheet, bracing myself as he clawed at the fabric and threw himself against the wall, trying to dislodge me. But the gaurd quickly weakened, sinking to his knees and then to the floor. I took a moment to feel for a pulse. I didn't want to kill any of them, if it was avoidable. Relieved that he was still alive, I tied him up with the bedsheet. Then I got to my feet and grabbed his knife. One down, one to go. The fingers that had been broken were throbbing, but they hadn't kept me from doing what needed to be done. I turned my attention to the next task. I'd depended on protocol keeping one guard outside the chamber, in case of some sort of trap. But he would be suspicious if his companion didn't appear soon.

I took the guard's helmet and put it on, trying to ignore the sweat that ran along the rim. In the darkness, that might be enough to fool a casual observer. Then I ran out of the chamber, throwing myself against the second guard hard enough to knock him to the ground.

We grappled with each other until I managed to wind one

arm around his neck and press the knife against his belly with my other hand. "Be still," I growled.

The guard stopped struggling.

"Give me the keys to the chamber."

Something jangled onto the floor. I didn't turn my head. "I don't want to kill you, but I will if you make me," I said softly. "Don't move."

He didn't protest as I bound his wrists and gagged him with strips of bedsheet. I prodded him into the chamber and struck him on the head with the knife hilt hard enough to knock him unconscious. Then I locked the door behind me and looked up and down the hallway. So far, so good, but I still had the uneasy sense that something wasn't right.

I checked my helmet and fidgeted with the knife I'd taken off the guard. All had goned as planned—I just needed to get to the stables. So I quelled my worry and went on my way.

Faris had given me the patrol schedule. Each route was patrolled by two guards at a time. Routes in the inner circles of the palace were patrolled less frequently than those toward the outside. I had the guard's keys in my pocket, so I could get through the outer door once I got there. I just needed to avoid the guards as I did so.

I made my way through the hallways, keeping to the shadows and pressing myself into alcoves whenever I heard footsteps.

The most direct way to reach the stables was through the main palace door—but that was also the most visible. Instead I cut through the kitchens and down the servants' corridor, snagging a stale bread roll as I went through. Then I was standing before the door that led to the outer courtyard, my instincts at war.

Too easy, they screamed. But what else was I going to do? Turn around and go back to bed, untie the guards and try to pass this off as an elaborate test?

No. I had come too far. I couldn't go back now. I flicked through the keys on the ring and opened the door. And then I stepped through into the night.

I hadn't been outside unescorted since my capture, and despite the urgency and the smoke, there was something intoxicating about being *alone*. I closed the door gently behind me and walked to the stables, listening the whole way.

There was nothing except my heart pounding, my thoughts dogging my steps. *Don't. Don't, don't, don't.*

The stable door was cracked open. I adjusted my grip on the knife and peeked inside.

The Dragon representative was there, just as she had promised. She leaned back against one of the stalls, her leg bouncing against the ground. Nerves? Or did she know something that I didn't?

There was no one else there, and the bells were tolling midnight. Had something happened to Neve, or Piera?

I hesitated. Would the Dragons take me if I was the only one to appear? I *was* wearing a guard's helmet. If the Dragons wouldn't help me, maybe I could get out into the city on my own. If I was lucky.

The bells stopped. The sound echoed and faded into the night. Midnight had come, but I was the only one here.

The air shifted behind me, and I whirled—to see Rafael grinning at me. His dragon loomed above us, its fangs gleaming in the torchlight.

No. How had he known?

"Drop the knife, Prince Vesper," said the emperor.

The knife clattered from my numb fingers. A group of guards converged around us, then ran into the stables in pursuit of the lord from Oskiath.

"Very good. I believe you know my wife?" If I hadn't known better, I might have mistaken his tone for pleasant. He raised his hand, and Piera stepped out of the shadows to stand at his side.

"Piera . . ." I couldn't stop myself.

"You will not address the empress without permission," Rafael said coldly. "Did you really believe you could turn my own wife against me?" His hand landed heavily on her shoulder.

"What?" I stared at Piera, shock befuddling me.

She raised her chin high and waved a piece of paper in front of my face. "Clever of you to encode your message, but I could not let your deceit stand. Of course I showed the emperor."

"I don't understand," I said hollowly. My vision narrowed until all I could see was her face, pale in the night as she looked back at me without a hint of remorse. "I was already your prisoner. What was the point of any of this?"

"To flush out your allies, of course," she said.

"Besides," Rafael interjected, "it amused me."

I couldn't bear to look at her, but I couldn't turn away. Inside of me was a desperate hope that somehow, this wasn't real. "I would have done anything for you. We were family."

She smiled thinly at me. "We are not children anymore, Severin. We cannot all be idealists. Some of us must live in reality."

And this was the reality she had chosen, I realized. She had walked into that marriage with her eyes open. She had made the bargain willingly, and she had been on his side all along. I was the one who'd closed my eyes to what I did not wish to see.

"You've chosen a monster's reality, Piera."

"I have done what I needed to do," she replied. "And you've been quite helpful, for what it's worth."

I couldn't breathe. The Dragons. Their secrets would last only as long as it took the lord to break. They should have abandoned me after all. It had taken only one sad story to make me throw caution to the wind. I was singlehandedly responsible for their downfall. The army that was coming would not find a city sleeping—they would walk into a trap. The only thing I could be grateful for was that Neve hadn't come. "Are you finally going to kill me?"

"Don't worry. You'll live to board your ship," the emperor said.

"Do not pretend that is not a death sentence," I spat.

"All the same," Rafael said. He raised his hand, and the guards closed in around me. "Take the prince away."

And away we went. Not to my rooms, but back to the dungeons, down the endless stairs to the cell where I had spent my first days in Irrad. The door locked behind me and I dropped to the familiar floor. All those things I'd done only to end up exactly where I had started, and what had I accomplished? Nothing. In fact, I'd only ended up ruining my image in the eyes of the people of Irrad and betraying the Dragons.

How could I have taken the emperor's bargain? I should have just pushed him to kill me until he'd had no other choice but to grant my wish. I wished for Maren to stay away, to forget me. To stay safe. There was no hope left for me now.

CHAPTER THIRTY-FOUR

Maren

Kaia!" I shouted. "Kaia!"

Efren grabbed me roughly by the arm. "You have to be quiet," she said. "We don't know who might be out there."

My heart pounding, I knelt down next to Tasia. *Tell me again*, I said. *From the beginning.*

Jase and Kaia said mean things to each other. Kaia untied Sev's friend. She was still agitated, and I could feel her emotions fluttering against my consciousness. She was only truly familiar with me and Sev—Kaia was a substitute, and when even Kaia had left her . . . She shivered and huddled against my side, and I hugged her back.

So according to Tasia, Kaia had willingly freed the king of Eronne, which meant she couldn't have been kidnapped. Unless they had kidnapped her after she had freed them? But why? And why had she freed them in the first place?

Alora and Braith lay curled together some distance away. Some guards they had been. But it seemed likely that they would know more about what had happened than an upset dragon kit.

"I'm going to talk to the dragons and see what they know," I said.

Efren nodded, pulling her knife. "I'll see if I can find any tracks."

She left the camp and ventured into the forest. I approached the dragons. *Alora!*

Alora snorted and stirred, and a wisp of smoke rose from her nostrils into the air. She grumbled something indistinct in the dragon tongue and rolled back over.

"Alora! Wake up!"

She roared a little as she sat upright, and I darted back. *What?* she said, almost growling.

I tried to keep my mind level. *What happened to Kaia and the others? You were meant to be guarding the king and their company.*

She bared her fangs at me. *I am not a human's dog anymore, to be called and ordered without thought. You did not ask me to keep them from leaving.*

I bit back an angry retort as I thought back through the morning's events and realized she was right. I hadn't asked.

You're right, I said. *I'm sorry.*

She seemed surprised that I had acknowledged her point. She inclined her head, accepting my apology.

But tell me, please. What happened?

She yawned. *Your girl left with the leader and the rest of them. I wasn't paying close attention.*

My heart was sinking with every word. *Did Kaia want to go with them? They didn't take her against her will?*

Seemed like. They headed south.

And Jase?

"Here!"

Efren came into view, supporting Jase as he leaned against her. He was limping. I ran over to them. "What happened? Who hurt you?"

Jase lowered himself to the ground, wincing. "Nobody hurt me. The king told Kaia some story about helping your friend Sev—something about sending supplies to Ruzi. Which, don't get me wrong—it's desperately needed. But it didn't make sense to me. Why would a small king risk their own neck to help a kingdom that's fallen under the emperor's wrath? Anyway, she decided to go with them. I went along for a while. I thought maybe I could talk her out of it, but I couldn't. Eventually I decided to turn back. I didn't want to leave the dragons on their own too long, especially not the little one. Stepped into some animal's burrow, though. My ankle's twisted pretty bad."

She'd left. She'd left *me*. "When did they leave?" I said.

"Not more than an hour after you."

So they were ahead of us by the entire day, and they were riding horses. I couldn't catch up on foot. And even if one of the dragons consented to carry me, what could I say once I found her? Kaia knew what we were up against, and she'd chosen to leave me instead.

Efren looked at me. "What do you want to do? The ships—"

"I haven't forgotten about the ships," I snapped. "I—I need to think. I'm going for a walk."

Tasia scampered to catch up with me as I stormed out of the camp, my jaw clenched. My body moved as though it wasn't even mine. My legs screamed to run, but daylight was fading fast, and I could not afford to get lost. And then, suddenly, I started to sob. I shouldn't—how could I ever have left her? I had to go after her. No—how could she have left *me*? Chosen the unknown, to trust a complete stranger over me?

This was a different sort of pain than the agony I had felt when the Aurati had taken her. That had been crushing. It had seemed like my world was ending. I had been wrong. This—*this*—was what it felt like when the world ended. I had always been so sure of one thing in my life: Kaia and me, as constant and unending as the sun in the sky. And to face proof that our bond was breakable—that she had chosen to break it, willingly . . . I wanted nothing more than to stop here, forever. No matter what thoughts I had entertained in my doubting moments, I still didn't know how to go on knowing that she was in the world, and that she had chosen to leave me.

I wanted to put my fists through a wall. I wanted to scream until my voice was gone. I wanted to run until I was as lost as I felt, until my legs collapsed beneath me. Instead I settled for crying until I was completely empty, until there was nothing left inside me except dull resolve. I had to move forward. The emperor's fleet would burn in the morning. We could not miss that opening.

Tasia waited patiently until I was spent, and walked with me without speaking until we made it back to camp. Efren had fashioned a makeshift brace for Jase's ankle while we were away, and they were occupied with roasting some nuts over the fire.

"We can't afford to go after Kaia," I said, my voice hollow. "When the ships explode, we fly."

Efren nodded. "Get some sleep. I'll take first watch."

I didn't believe I would ever sleep again, but as my companions settled into their places, I felt my eyes drifting closed in exhaustion.

I stand in the ocean, surf washing over my ankles. Tasia is at my side, frolicking in the waves, but I am completely and utterly defeated. I do not care what happens now. I want nothing more than to be obliterated.

"Maren." Sev's hand settles on my shoulder, and I turn into him, burying my face against his chest. He's comfortingly warm, and he holds me as I sob, my body shaking. "Maren, what's wrong?"

"She left me," I blurt around the tears.

"Kaia?" He sounds confused. "Why? I thought you were . . . heartmates?"

"I thought so too," I say. "I thought—it doesn't matter." Because this is a dragon dream, and I can't waste it in tears. I wipe at my cheeks with one sleeve. "We're coming tomorrow. You have to be ready."

"I will be," he says, his arms around me. "You're going to be all right. I promise."

The water moves around us, and suddenly he's pulled away from me, out toward the deep. I lunge for him, but it's as if my feet are encased in stone, and instead I fall.

CHAPTER THIRTY-FIVE

Sev

A wall of sound crashed into me, sending me tumbling off the grimy cot onto the floor of the cell. The floor shook under my body, then lay still again. Had the rioters blown up another building? It hadn't been the work of a Talon. A dragon might burn a building, but they could not produce such a cacophony. And they might shake the ground when they landed heavily, but not like that.

I got to my feet and looked up at the window. Bright orange light cast down into the dungeon. That was a fire. But were the two connected? What sort of fire could—

The floor shook again, sending me stumbling against the wall. Maren's words from the dragon dream came back to me. *Tomorrow*, she'd said. Was it tomorrow already? Was this what I needed to be ready for?

Something swooped low across the sliver of sky that I could see, then was gone in a flash.

A dragon, I thought. There was a dragon flying across the sky, and though I couldn't identify it from here, I hoped it was no Talon.

I smiled. Something was happening in Irrad that was outside the emperor's control. Above me came the glorious sound of running feet. *Run*, I thought. *She's coming for you.*

A door slammed, and I heard footsteps on the stairs. I stood up, bracing myself to face Rafael's fury.

But instead, the person who appeared on the other side of the bars was Neve.

"What are you doing here?" I said, dumbfounded.

"Breaking you out." She produced a ring of keys from her pocket and started trying them against the lock. Her hands shook slightly—the only indication that she was nervous in any way. The fourth key turned, and she swung open the door.

"Where are we going?" I said, confusion making me slow.

"Do you want to talk, or do you want to live?" she said.

Point taken. I darted from the cell, and Neve handed me a set of yellow Aurati apprentice robes. "Put these on." I pulled the robes over my head and followed her. The bodies of four guards were slumped at the foot of the staircase that led up to the main floor of the palace. I stepped over them as Neve led the way back up the stairs—I thought they were still breathing, though I couldn't be absolutely certain.

Neve held out a hand to stop me as we reached the top of the staircase, and she peered out into the hallway. I could hear footsteps and raised voices on the other side of the door.

"All right, let's go."

I pulled the Aurati hood up so that it hung low over my face, and we trotted through the palace halls. Our haste wasn't out of the ordinary—most of the people we saw were running.

We made it upstairs to her laboratory without being caught. Neve locked the door and pushed a table against it once we were inside. Then she sank into a chair, breathing hard.

My body was beginning to catch up to this extraordinary turn of events. I paced, full of nervous energy. "Not that I'm not grateful, but do you have a plan for getting out of the palace?" I said.

Neve shook her head, and my heart sank.

"Then why—"

She held up a hand to stop me. "The emperor's fleet has been destroyed."

Maren. Fierce joy rose in my chest. There wasn't even time to wonder how. If the fleet was destroyed, the army could not sail. And Rafael would not send Talons across the ocean.

"I know you lied to me about the empress," Neve said, sending my spirits plummeting. "I thought long and hard about whether to leave you in the dungeon. Perhaps that was just what you deserved. But the emperor will come for you soon. I thought it was only fair to give you a fighting chance."

"And you?" I said. "The guards will identify you as the person who set me free."

Neve squared her shoulders. "I've spent my life trying to balance what was asked of me against what I believed to be right. Until recently, I thought I could do no better than what I've done. But Maren has proven me wrong. She has *freed dragons* from bondage. Bondage that I helped perpetuate." She looked around the laboratory. "The time has come for me to act. It is perhaps too little, too late, but I cannot change the past. I can only change what I do going forward."

She stood up and picked up the chair she had been sitting on. Then she walked over to an open cabinet and swung the chair hard against it, smashing the glass vials on its shelves. Muddled scents flooded the room, overwhelming my senses. I had to put an arm on the table to steady myself.

Neve, the emperor's Aromatory, was destroying her life's work. With this act, she was as good as dead.

As was I, now. With no fleet to set sail, there was no reason to keep me alive. If the emperor caught me, he would kill me.

"Can I help you? Do you want to come with me?" I said.

Neve looked up. There were oil stains on her skirt and scratches on her arm from where glass had shattered and fallen. "I have to stay. I must find a way to destroy Milek's potions. Get out, if you can."

The expression on her face was final and determined. "Tera be with you," I said. Then I ran.

I had the advantages of the disguise I was wearing and the chaos around me, but that was it. I didn't know where Faris was, and I had no further allies in the palace. Given the attack on the fleet, the palace was certain to be locked down—unless there was an assault on the gates.

I could hide somewhere in the palace and hope to avoid detection until all this was over. I could fight and try to catch the emperor distracted.

Maren. I wished desperately I could speak to her. In the dragon dream she had been despondent over the loss of Kaia. She was shaken and clearly heartbroken, but she had still vowed that she was coming.

I walked briskly, keeping my hood up and my eyes lowered as I descended the staircase to the first floor of the palace. From there I bypassed the great hall and made my way toward the gardens. I had to hope that the sword I'd buried in the Garden of Hearts was still there.

I was just approaching the door to the garden when a group of guards rounded the corner. I turned away from them, but it was too late. "There he is!" one of them shouted.

I abandoned the ruse and sprinted, racing for the palace doors. I burst out into the courtyard—

Fire arced through the air in front of me, and I skidded to a halt. Vix the Ruiner stood before me, bearing Rafael, the Flame of the West. The emperor was dressed for battle in full armor, a curved sword in his hand. Vix was similarly armored.

A chill ran across my skin. Rafael motioned to the guards without speaking. They swarmed around me and dragged me forward, then pushed me to my knees in front of the emperor.

"You have failed in every possible way," the emperor said, leaning over me. "But you may serve one more purpose yet." He snapped his fingers and the guards produced shackles. They bound my hands and feet so that I could only shuffle, not run. "You're coming with me."

On his dragon, into battle?

Then it dawned on me. The emperor thought that Maren was out there—and I was to be bait.

"You overestimate my relationship to the dragon mistress," I said quickly.

Rafael only laughed, a frightening gleam in his eyes. "Then it will be just as easy to let you fall."

At his signal, Vix shifted and rose to its feet, shaking its massive head. I held still as the dragon walked to me and wrapped its claws around the chains that held me. For such a large beast, its claws were surprisingly gentle. Then, with two powerful flaps of its wings, it took off, carrying me into the air.

I had been unconscious the last time I had traveled by dragon. Now I lurched back and forth with every wing beat and felt bile rise in my throat. I forced myself to focus on the horizon, trying to find some balance—and saw dragons flying toward us.

That didn't make sense. Did it? We'd taken to the air surrounded by the emperor's full fleet of Talons—thirty strong, at least. Why would there be dragons flying in from the ocean? Dragons that had—I squinted—*Seratese riders?*

The dragons from the ocean flew down to the harbor. They let their riders off onto the ground, then took off again, turning in the air to face the Talons as we approached. I couldn't take my eyes off them.

The emperor whispered something to his dragon, who let out a fierce cry and a billow of angry flame. The Talons shot past us in formation. The sky was quiet for one breath, then two. And then the lines of dragons crashed into each other.

The world went sideways and upside down, and for a moment I clenched my eyes shut, giving up on trying to keep track of what was happening around me. The scent of something harsh filled the air. Then the emperor pulled his dragon up, flying free of the combat. I opened my eyes, and the city spread out before me. A pillar of flame on the docks drew my attention, and I grinned. Neve had told the truth. The emperor's war fleet was burning.

I had never seen anything like this dragon battle. The dragons twisted and twirled in the air, colliding and breaking apart. We were high enough in the sky that I wasn't too concerned that one of them might accidentally torch a structure, but I could still look down and see the dumbfounded faces of people in the city below, looking up. What would happen if one of the dragons was knocked from the sky? At this height, they would probably demolish a building on impact.

These new dragons were better at air combat than the Talons, from what I could see. This made sense, since the Talons weren't trained in air combat. And their method of training, using oil to direct the dragons, did not work well in quick-response situations. But the emperor's fleet still had one advantage: there were simply more Talons than Seratese dragons.

Vix avoided close combat, instead dodging and diving and letting loose plumes of flame. The emperor then pulled his dragon back around and flew down, level with the roofs of the buildings. Logically I knew that I wouldn't collide with one of them, but that didn't stop me from craning my neck as far away from the roofs as possible.

What was Rafael doing? Vix was the largest of the emperor's fleet. They should have been closer to the battle, even if the emperor was focused on keeping himself safe. But instead, they were sweeping across the sky methodically—searching. They were searching for Maren.

"Dragon mistress!" the emperor yelled into the open sky. His dragon mimicked him, shrieking out across the city. "Come out and face me directly! I have your prince!"

Maren was too smart to fall for something like that, if she was here at all. She had to know that one life was nothing against the power that she wielded, to singlehandedly change the course of the empire. She would not give herself up just for me. There was no way.

But still I looked for her as we passed over the streets of Irrad. On the ground, there was another battle raging, though it was less flashy than the one in the air. There appeared to be a force of Seratese fighters—where could they possibly have come from? I had not thought there were so many Seratese people in the entire empire—systematically advancing from the direction of the docks toward the center of the city. Most civilians didn't seem to be giving them trouble—in fact, it looked like most of the protesters had joined forces with them. The army was putting up a half-hearted defense, but they were outmatched—or they had decided to switch sides. The soldiers were soon overwhelmed, and the Seratese advanced. And there—there to the north, another small force converged on Irrad's outskirts. The Dragons had come!

Now I understood why the emperor had panicked. The problem with a military force composed primarily of dragons was that the emperor could not control his own city without burning it to the ground. The dragons were fierce because their power was huge and ferocious—but that meant that they could burn entire town squares, not arrest one person. I didn't know how the Seratese had managed, but they had exploited this weakness by taking the fighting into the city, which Rafael wasn't yet willing to destroy.

Then I saw them.

At first the emperor did not. He was still looking down at the city. But Maren was coming from the south—and she was riding on the back of a dragon. The dragon kit rode with her, a flash of bright blue against the larger dragon's deep green. Maren's hair was loose around her face, she was wearing Ruzian clothing, and she looked unimaginably fierce as she raised her arms and *sang*.

Maren. Here, in Irrad. And the emperor was turning his dragon toward her.

We were in the air before dawn.

Braith carried Efren and Jase, while Tasia and I flew with Alora.

I had thought of this moment often—ever since I had descended into the depths of Lumina and discovered the darkest secret of the empire. I had expected I would feel rage, excitement, readiness. I had never thought that I would fly into this morning feeling empty.

I had told myself to put it behind me, but I still felt Kaia's specter haunting my every step. Sorrow had drowned me in my dream last night, and Sev's presence had done nothing to relieve the pain. Despite every guilty thought or unhappy impulse, I had believed in her—in us. But she had walked away from me without even saying good-bye.

The wind whipped my hair around my face. Alora flew quickly—the idea of ripping the limbs of some Talons from their bodies particularly appealed to her, and while I didn't necessarily condone the idea, I did nothing to deter her from it either.

We flew wide over the ocean and, as we approached the docks, were met by a group of five dragons bearing Seratese riders. One of them raised their hand in greeting. As we approached, I saw that the rider was Davina.

"Ready?" she shouted.

The city spread out before us, rumbling with discontent. And we were about to set it on fire.

"Ready!" I called back. And then we dove as one toward the tyrant's fleet.

The dragons opened their mouths as we came within range, blanketing the ships with fire. The wood caught quickly, and the fire spread greedily. There was a sharp whistling sound, and then one of the ships exploded, sending debris flying through the air. Alora dipped, avoiding a plank of wood.

We pulled out of range to wait. Someone must have been on watch in this city. They would call for the Talons soon enough.

Fires raged below us, but the sky was quiet. I scratched Tasia's head and breathed in the scent of the ocean. Alora flew steadily, her wings catching the wind. The other dragons were equally calm, flying in companionable harmony with their riders. As I watched them, I found myself wondering how they had fared in the Seda Serat, and whether they would choose to return there, once this was all done.

"There!" Efren cried, pointing.

From the distant center of the city, Talons poured into the sky.

I gulped. We needed more than what just Tasia and I could provide if we were to have a chance at winning this battle. We had seven dragons on our side, but there were at least thirty Talons in the air. In Ruzi, there had been only eleven—and I still hadn't managed to free all the dragons.

I assumed the dragons that had come from the Seda Serat

would be better at combat than the Talons, but we were still outnumbered. They would soon be overrun. If I didn't act now, we would lose the advantage. How quickly could Naava come, if I called? Could I even reach her at such a great distance? I didn't know, but I was also out of other options.

So I did it, after warning Alora and Braith what was coming. I steadied myself against Alora's flanks, placed one hand upon Tasia's shoulder, and called, trying to make my voice into a beacon. When Kaia had been taken from me the first time, Naava had felt my heartbreak across three kingdoms. Surely she could hear me now. *Naava! We need you!* I tried to convey the urgency of my request, flashing toward her an image of the dragons filling the sky. Three times I called, and three times there was no response. We were alone.

The Talons flew toward us over the city of Irrad. Alora roared and folded her wings, shooting toward the incoming Talons. I tried to tamp down the doubt that had sprung up within me. Could we do this without Naava?

I didn't know what the answer was, but we were about to find out. I placed my hand between Tasia's shoulder blades, feeling her eagerness. She was completely unafraid, and I tried to absorb her surety. *We must do this ourselves,* I said. *Are you ready to sing?*

She nodded.

The world slowed around me, tapering down to the wind through my hair, the smoke rising toward my face, my heartbeat deep in my chest. This was it. Everything I had been running toward, in this moment. I raised my head, staring into the tangle of dragons ahead of me. I opened my mouth and sang.

Tasia added her voice to mine, and we sang through the sky, our song soaring through the air. Alora beat her wings, rising high above the battle, above the city. At first nothing seemed to be happening. And then, one by one, the dragons turned toward me.

I reached out to their consciousnesses. They noticed my song, and they were tugging against their Talons' reins. They were *waking*. I sang louder, stronger, feeling the way the dragons' thoughts flickered in my direction, interrupted from what the Talons were telling them to do. I closed my eyes, and the battlefield lit up behind my eyelids, dragons shimmering in and out of focus. There were so many of them—I felt like a child trying to stretch my arms around an enormous tree trunk, unable to enclose it. I could not hold them all in my head at once. The lights shone brighter, spreading across my entire field of vision. This was too much—I couldn't hold on for much longer—

A harsh voice cut through the air. "Stop what you are doing, or I will kill him!"

My eyes snapped open.

An enormous blood-red dragon hovered in the sky before me, and riding it—the tyrant, the Flame of the West himself.

He was almost exactly as I had always pictured him to be. Dazzlingly armored, sitting tall in the dragon saddle, a fearsome blade in his hand and a sharp cut to his cheekbones. He must have been imposing on the ground, for he was terrible and glorious to behold in the air. I could imagine how he must have appeared to the people who worshipped him. Even knowing the evil within him, I saw it.

But that was nothing compared to the way I felt when I saw what his dragon was carrying in its claws: a human in shackles. *Sev!*

My song faltered, but I clenched my fists and held myself

together. Was he even alive? The dragon was holding him tightly—but as I watched, he raised his head in midair and met my eyes. *Don't stop*, he mouthed.

Tears brimmed at the corners of my eyes. I knew that any bargain the tyrant offered was false. I knew that both Sev and I would die if I gave in. And I knew that I could not control what happened to Sev—that the only thing I held in my own hands was the song that spilled from my lips, the dragons in the sky who faltered, wheeling in one direction and another. But at the same time, if I had to watch Sev fall, I didn't know what I would do.

"Stop!" the emperor snarled. He gestured to his dragon, and Sev slipped—the dragon had opened one claw.

I cried out, breaking the song—but Sev had wound his shackles around the dragon's ankle, holding tightly. The dragon swerved in the sky, shaking its claws, but Sev held on.

So I faced the tyrant, the emperor of Zefed himself, and sang once more.

I sang directly to his dragon, trying my best to reach through the air, to speak across the distance. *You do not have to serve this master*, I said. *You can fly free.*

For a moment I thought it was working. I thought I saw the flicker of awareness in its eyes, the slight shake of its head. Then the emperor yanked on the dragon's reins and poured oil down his arm, and I smelled the fire root instantly. The dragon roared, and Alora dodged the plume of fire it spewed toward us. The song died on my lips, and in the flicker of an instant, we became the hunted.

Alora dove so close to the ground that I could have reached out and touched brick. Then she veered up and cut through the fury of battling dragons, trying to shake the dragon on our tail. Tasia craned her neck, spitting a thin stream of fire back at the emperor.

The air was heating around us. I licked my lips and tried to sing once more, but smoke filled my lungs and I coughed instead. It wasn't just the emperor's pursuit—the sky was full of fire and smoke. Buildings had caught fire below us, and there were strange pockets of thick, scented haze. Somewhere, Talons' oils were burning. Dragons dipped into and out of my sight line as they chased one another across the sky. Right in front of me, one Talon fell from their saddle, screaming. I looked away before they hit the ground. A gray dragon tangled with an orange dragon above us—the orange dragon fell, its wing clipping my shoulder on the way down. I was half out of the saddle before I was able to wrench myself back in. We had to get out of this frenzy. But Alora wasn't as fast as the emperor's dragon. If we left the battle, they would catch us.

What other option did we have, though? We were losing— how could I have ever thought that I could do this myself? I had done my best, and I had still fallen short. I had proven nothing except that everyone's faith in me had been misplaced. Even if we made it out of this battle, what of those who had followed me here? Not all of them would survive the day. *Sev* would not survive. What had I done?

My eyes streamed with tears. Tasia crouched in front of me, her tail wrapped around my arm like an anchor. All thoughts of strategy fell from my mind as I could only *hold on—*

A roar broke through the air, so loud, it disrupted Alora's flight. I looked around. The emperor's dragon flinched at the sound, its wings contracting. It wobbled in the air before regaining balance. What *was* that?

At first I could see nothing. The haze and noise of the battle obscured my vision, but there was something out there, speeding toward us, and I realized—*Naava.*

She was bearing down upon us, flanked by five dragons, her eyes dark and furious. She roared once more, and every dragon in the air cowered. I had always known that she was enormous, but seeing her among other dragons only made the difference more stark. She was easily three times the size of some of the others—large enough that she might have *carried* them.

Alora banked to the right to avoid a tangle of dragons, and I glanced behind us. The tyrant sat frozen, his gaze fixed on Naava. But his dragon was not distracted by Naava's call. It surged forward, coming level with Alora and swiping through her wing with one claw.

Alora screamed, listing hard to one side—I scrambled for purchase, but found none—I fell—

I reached for something—anything—but there was nothing but my body tumbling, the fractured sky, the ground rushing toward me.

I saw a black blur out of the corner of my eye, and then suddenly I landed hard—but not on the ground. I was on a dragon's back—Naava! My vision swam as I tried to reorient myself. I was all right—Naava had saved me. But where was Tasia? Panic overtook me. I pushed myself upright, fighting through nausea as I searched the sky around us. *Tasia!* She wasn't here with me, nor was she with Alora. We were over the middle of the city, too far up for her to have fallen and come away unscathed. *Tasia!* There was no answer.

"Tasia!" I screamed, my heart pounding. "Tasia!"

A delighted squeal broke through the air, and I looked over Naava's side. Tasia soared throught the air, flying confidently. I gasped, putting a hand to my mouth as the tiny dragon spread her wings and twirled, letting loose a stream of chirps.

Alora regained her balance next to us, flapping her wings weakly. *Maren.* The strain was evdent in her voice.

Go, I said

She wheeled in the sky and retreated to the south. I lay forward, letting my cheek fall against Naava's neck in relief. *You came. You saved me.*

It was time, she rumbled. *You have done well, daughter of Ilvera. You have sent many of my children home.*

She flapped her great wings, gaining height as the emperor screamed at his dragon and doused himself with fire root. The red dragon did an about-face—we had them on the run.

Naava opened her mouth and sang across the sky. This time there was no question that the dragons heard her—all of them. They twisted and bucked against their reins, forcing the Talons to halt their attacks. Then Naava darted across the sky after the emperor.

The dragon was streaking toward the palace, but Naava bore down upon it effortlessly. She breathed a precise stream of flame toward the emperor, who ducked his head and twisted away. Sev remained secure in the dragon's claws, for which I was grateful as Naava flapped hard, gaining height.

Hold on tightly, she said. Then she dove.

The red dragon didn't stand a chance. In one moment we were far above them. In the next, close enough to touch, to speak. I caught the emperor's furious glare as Naava struck the red dragon across the chest with her claws, gouging deeply. The emperor yanked on the reins, but it was no use. Time stood still as they hovered in midair.

And then the dragon fell, plummeting to the ground with Sev still clutched tightly in its claws.

CHAPTER THIRTY-SEVEN

Maren

The red dragon hit the roof of a low building and crashed straight through it, sending dust and debris into the air. My body jolted, as though the impact had passed through me.

"Sev!" I screamed. Fear clawed at my throat. *Take me down!* I cried to Naava.

There is more to do, she replied. *I cannot leave my children now.*

All I could think about was Sev. *I know, but I have to get to him. Take me down. Please!*

Naava nodded. She found an open patch of sky and descended into the city, landing in a small square not far from where the emperor's dragon had fallen. I slid down to the ground, and Tasia landed beside me. *Good luck, daughter of dragons,* Naava said. Then she was away again, her song calling to every dragon in the air. I closed my eyes and saw the dragon lights painted across my vision. No Talon stood a chance.

Then I looked down at Tasia. She had *flown!* My pride at her accomplishment was dimmed only by the direness of our situation. I had only a dragon kit and a knife that I wasn't trained to fight with. I had no mother dragon, no allies. And I was about to confront the emperor of Zefed himself.

But I saw no other way forward, so I started down the street at a trot, Tasia by my side. There were a few skirmishes in the streets, but most of the ground fighting seemed to have ceased. I elbowed my way through a group of Seratese fighters standing side by side with Zefedi soldiers, their mouths agape as they watched the sky.

There was destruction everywhere in Irrad today, but smoke rising a few streets ahead of us called to me like a beacon. I ran toward it, and rounded a corner to find the building into which the emperor's dragon had crashed. One wall had collapsed, and another leaned in precariously . . . and it was on fire. Sev!

I took off my jacket and pressed the cloth against my mouth, trying to block out the smoke as I picked my way through the rubble toward the door. My eyes smarted as I peered inside.

It was difficult to see through the smoke, but there was no dragon here, nor did I see any human bodies. I retreated, coughing, and looked up and down the street. I didn't know the full extent of the dragon's injuries, but I didn't think it would still be able to fly. Then where had they gone?

Tasia brushed up against my leg. *Sev.*

I— I swallowed. *I don't know if he—*

Sev, she repeated, indicating a curiously clean sweep of ground. I followed her nose. That was strange. It looked as though some massive snake had slithered through here . . . or perhaps an injured dragon.

Can you smell him? I asked.

Tasia nodded eagerly and immediately jumped onto the trail, which led away from the building and up the hill. I placed one hand on the hilt of my knife, ready to pull it free.

We followed the scent trail toward the center of the city, and the farther we went, the surer I was that we were heading the right way. While Tasia tracked without hesitation, there was another clear sign of a dragon's presence. Buildings on either side of the street had been set ablaze, creating a foreboding pathway wreathed in smoke and flames. The emperor's dragon was burning the city down. Of its own accord, or the tyrant's?

Some people were fighting the fires—others had simply abandoned their houses and fled. Passing through these panicked streets, I felt as though I had come to the end of the world. I had seen enough of Irrad to know we were heading toward the tyrant's palace. With such destruction behind us, I couldn't fathom what Tasia and I would face when we got there.

I was surprised, then, when we arrived at the palace to find the gate hanging ajar and the outer courtyard empty. But I was certain the dragon had passed through—there were fresh scorch marks on the stone walls.

I looked down at Tasia, whose nose was twitching. She stared at the palace doors, which appeared to have been battered open. *Are you ready to rescue Sev?*

Yes, she said decisively, an angry gleam in her eyes.

I steeled myself, drew my knife, and walked through the palace doors.

It was eerily quiet inside—this hallway was completely deserted. Where had the guards gone, the courtiers? Had they been ordered to evacuate? Or perhaps they had abandoned their posts. I allowed myself a small, vindictive smile at that thought.

We ventured farther into the palace. Beyond the sunlight entering through the door, the hallway was dim, the only light shining from torches fixed to the walls. We walked down the hall, listening intently for a sign that anyone was approaching.

For a while, there was nothing. Then there was a slight trickling noise, as though there was running water nearby. The sound tickled at my ear, insisting on attention. I shrugged it off. This hall was enormous, surely built to accommodate both humans and dragons, and there were more doors leading off it than I could easily count. I didn't have time to explore what was behind every single one.

Light shone through an open door up ahead, and I approached with caution. On the other side was a hall large enough to house hundreds of people. Rich tapestries hung on the walls, and there was a line of tables filled with platters of food. But there was no one here.

The cloying scent of rot hit me as Tasia and I entered the hall, our footsteps echoing across the floor. The food must have been sitting in the summer heat since this morning, at least. I breathed shallowly and tried to shut it all out—the stench, the dead air, the sweat dripping down my back. This was a distraction, nothing more.

I looked down at Tasia. Which way? She turned in one direction, then another, before sitting back hesitantly. My heart sank. She'd lost the trail. Sev could be anywhere.

But we had to keep moving. *Let's go, little one.* I smiled encouragingly at the kit, and we continued on.

At the far side of the hall stood two silver thrones that gleamed in the torchlight—the tyrant's throne, I realized, and that of the empress. The rulers of Zefed had sat here every day surrounded by such decadence, all the while ignoring the troubles outside their gates. I shivered and hurried past—I hated the very sight of them.

Behind the thrones another set of doors stood open, leading to a smaller hall with a floor as black as a starless sky. I stepped out onto it—then stopped.

I knew this place. I had been here before.

Not in reality, but in dreams. Before I'd even truly known Sev, I'd dreamed that we would be here together. I'd *kissed* him here, in this hall, and the memory brought a blush to my cheeks.

I had to find him. I walked down the hall, listening as I passed door after door. This place was labyrinthine. I didn't have time to waste going down the wrong path. Until—

I heard a sound coming from behind one of the doors I'd already passed. I doubled back carefully, making sure that Tasia stayed behind me. I readied my knife. Then I took hold of the doorknob and turned it silently.

For a moment I thought I'd crossed into some alternate realm, so different was this place from where I had just been. I stepped from a palace into a lush garden, its trees and shrubs forming a veritable indoor forest. The air was fresh and cool. From somewhere ahead of me came the sound of a running fountain.

Tasia ventured forward, sniffing the air in front of her. Suddenly she nosed her way to the dirt under one of the bushes and started pawing at the earth.

What are you doing? I hissed.

She ignored me, digging faster. I considered dragging her away, then decided that would create more noise than it was worth. So instead I rolled my eyes, sheathed my knife, and went over to help her. Soon, our efforts uncovered something—a hilt. I reached into the dirt and pulled out a short sword. I looked at Tasia. *How did you know this was here?*

Smells like Sev, she said.

Really? I could only smell the earth it had been buried in. I would have to trust her on this. I took the sword between my hands. Then I stood up and ventured farther into the garden, listening as carefully as I could. As I rounded the last hedge, the fountain at the center of the garden came into view—as did the woman standing in front of it.

She was an Aurat. I recoiled on instinct, then paused. She was young and seemed ... distressed? I ran through my options. Kaia would have tried to befriend her. I could confront her, but what purpose would that serve? I was looking for the emperor and Sev. Unless she knew where they were ... I looked down at my sword and at Tasia. The woman looked unarmed. My odds were probably good, though I hated to walk into anything on the basis of assumptions.

My decision was made for me when the woman whirled, spotting me before I could duck behind a tree. Her eyes widened as she saw Tasia beside me—but instead of speaking, she turned around and ran through a side door.

I ran after her without hesitating. She was the only living person I'd seen in the palace—I almost didn't care if she was leading me into a trap, as long as I found more people there. I then cut through an office and yet another hallway until I ducked through a door and into a large room that smelled of fire root and mirth wood, both of them so thick in the air that I nearly choked.

The Aurat was nowhere to be seen—but there was a man standing next to a small table across the room, and a large, irregularly shaped hole in the middle of the floor. Something that vaguely resembled a stairway had been cut into one of the sides. A chorus of shrill cries echoed off the walls, and I suddenly realized what was at the bottom of that hole. Dragons.

Bile rose in my throat, and I gagged, trying not to vomit. Sev hadn't exaggerated when he'd told me about the emperor's oubliette. It was horrific.

"I am here for the emperor," I said, sounding braver than I felt. "Tell me where he is, and I will not harm you."

The man looked at me. "So you must be the one they call the dragon mistress. You're younger than I expected."

Why had he expected me at all?

"And I've heard nothing about you," I said, though I had a sense about him, based on the way he stood so familiarly near the oubliette, his dress and the belt he wore around his chest. But if I was right, that would mean . . . "Has the Aromatory died?"

He shook his head. "Her days are numbered. Soon I will take her place."

In a flash I realized that this must be the manufacturer of the oils that the Talons had carried to try to subdue Naava. That was why the scents smelled wrong—Neve hadn't had anything to do with it.

The longer I stood here the more I could distinguish the scents in the room. This man must have been completely loyal to the emperor, to have been selected for such a post. But I was certain he had not been chosen for his expertise with scents, or his understanding of dragons.

I circled the oubliette carefully, keeping my back to the wall and Tasia behind me. The worst thing I could do was turn away from the enormous hole in the floor housing vengeful beasts. The man did not move, except to cross his arms as I approached. I stopped at a careful distance.

"Let me pass," I said.

He laughed. "Not a chance, dragon mistress." He took a step forward.

"Don't move," I said, leveling the sword at him.

He looked at the blade, and then at me. An amused expression came over his face. Then he grabbed a shallow bowl from the table and threw it at me. I ducked and the bowl missed me, but its contents splashed over my face and into my eyes. Stinging fire root oil! I staggered back, yelling in pain, and he was upon me.

We tumbled to the floor, and the sword flew from my hands. My face was burning as the man wrenched my arm back. I screamed, then lunged forward and bit down hard on his forearm. He yelled and reared back. I scrabbled for my knife, pulling it out of its sheath, jabbing wildly. The man wrapped his arm around my neck and squeezed. I clawed at his arm, but spots began to appear at the edges of my vision. I was running out of time.

There was a heavy thud, and the man suddenly fell back. I kicked my way free and scrambled to my feet. Neve was standing a few feet away, holding a Talon's case in both hands. She must have hit him with it.

"Neve!"

She ignored me, keeping her gaze fixed on the man. He lurched to his feet and fell back to the table, where he picked up another bowl. "Your master is losing, Milek," Neve said. "Give up now!"

Milek's eyes slid between us. "The emperor should have had you killed a long time ago, Aromatory."

"Put down the bowl," Neve said.

He lowered his arm—and then tossed the bowl up into the air. It flew over our heads and came down behind us, shattering and spilling its contents—pure mirth wood oil, I noted faintly—on the floor right in front of Tasia.

Tasia!

She bent down, inhaling the scent as it enveloped her small body. *No!* I'd worked so hard to keep her free—and that was far too much oil for such a young dragon. I ran to her and pushed her away from the oils, wiping the substance from her scales with my sleeve.

Tasia, are you all right?

She didn't reply.

No. This couldn't be happening. *Tasia, speak to me!*

But she seemed utterly under the influence of the mirth wood. She melted to the floor, where she lay still.

"Tasia! Come back to me!" I shouted aloud.

Her wings fluttered sluggishly.

Tasia! I threw my arms around her, hugging her tightly. Naava had said the only thing that could break an oil bond was a free dragon's song. Every time I had sung before, it had been with Tasia by my side.

I bowed my head and wept. Closing my eyes, I could see that the oil had already dulled her light. Usually so bright, Tasia's consciousness had withdrawn so deeply into her body that I could barely see it. But it was still there. Could I draw it out again?

I swallowed my tears and sang, sinking deeply into my memories of the dragon kit. The day she had hatched in Vir's Passage, and I had been so afraid that she might die. The first time she had seen sunlight. The way her scales had shimmered and deepened into a brilliant blue. Tasia spreading her wings, hunting butterflies, speaking—*flying.*

Tasia, I sang. *Come back, little one.*

I was so absorbed in my task that I didn't hear Milek approach until the sound of a sword being unsheathed broke my concentration, and then it was too late. I turned to see him raise the blade above his head—and then Neve was there, throwing her body between us as she thrust forward with a knife—my knife.

They both fell to the floor, the sword clattering down a few feet away.

I pushed myself up, drawing in my breath in shock. Milek had caught Neve diagonally across her stomach, slashing deeply. Blood poured from beneath her clothing. She had wounded him too, but he was recovering, pushing himself upright. I had to stop him. I charged forward and shoved him hard, putting all of my strength into the blow. He fell back, tripped—and tumbled down into the oubliette.

The dragons attacked. I threw myself away from the pit, trying to block out the man's screams and the wet sounds of flesh separating and bones cracking. Tasia sprang into my arms and huddled there as I cried, tears streaming down my face. What had been done to these dragons was monstrous—and it was all for nothing more than a tyrant's vanity.

After a while there was only silence from the oubliette. I got shakily to my feet and went to Neve. She was lying where she had fallen, her hands pressed over her stomach.

I sank to my knees at her side. "You saved me," I said.

A ghost of a wry expression crossed her face. "You're the dragon mistress. The world needs you." Her body spasmed, and she winced in pain. "There's—no time," she said, her breath coming shallow and fast. "The emperor has Sev. Go to him."

"But what about you?"

Neve shook her head minutely. "Don't—worry about me. It needed doing."

She had saved my life—how could I leave her?

Sev was in danger—how could I leave him?

"Thank you," I whispered.

I got to my feet and ran to the table that Milek had left and picked up the bowls, sniffing until I found the lavender. It was a poor blend, but it would have to do. I took the bowl to the edge of the oubliette, dipped my fingers in, and dripped the oil down upon the dragons. This was nowhere near what they deserved, but it was the best I could do for now—I had to find Sev. I hoped this would soothe them until I returned.

I turned to Tasia. *Are you here with me, little one?*

She shivered in response but ran to me. I closed my eyes briefly in relief. Then I grabbed my sword and ran back to the garden to dunk my head into the fountain, scrubbing until the worst of the fire root oil was washed away. My eyes were still stinging when I was through, but at least I could open them for more than a second at a time. I dunked Tasia into the water too, washing away the essence of the oil from her scales.

Do you want to go to Naava? I asked when I'd finished bathing her. I didn't know what was happening outside the palace, but it couldn't be worse than what she'd just gone through. She was a child—she shouldn't have had to see such things.

I was relieved when she shook her head and spoke. *I will stay with you. We will find Sev.*

I nodded. *All right. Let's go.*

I had been afraid that the confrontation with the inferior Aromatory would bring guards running, but once again, there didn't seem to be anyone here. It almost began to feel more unsettling than fortuitous as Tasia and I moved through the deserted halls.

As we turned down yet another empty corridor, there was a flicker of movement at the end of the hall. I froze. It might just have been the torchlight, but no—there it was again, a flare of light. I took a deep breath and raised my sword.

We made our way slowly down the hall, on the lookout for any sudden movements. The light flickered again, and I crept toward an open door. I could make out the sound of voices, but not quite what they were saying.

Through the door was a garden very like the one we'd come from filled with plants and fountains and . . . hundreds of towering glass sculptures. The first being I saw was the dragon lying on the ground, and then the emperor, leaning back against its flank. The dragon was breathing fire erratically, its flames coming dangerously close to the greenery. And there, lying near a wall of mirrors, was Sev.

I barely resisted the urge to run to him. He was *alive* and seemed to be in one piece. I hadn't been able to count on that, after the fall he had taken. He looked so pale—and so angry.

Movement at the corner of my eye caught my attention, and I saw the Aurat we had previously encountered in the other garden was standing against the wall. So I had lost the element of surprise. But the emperor had always known I was coming. He had counted on me chasing him back to the palace. He had used Sev to lure me here, and here I was.

I took a deep breath and let it out deliberately. I stepped into the light.

CHAPTER THIRTY-EIGHT

Sev

I opened my eyes. It was dark around me—was it night? No—I was somewhere inside, lying sprawled on the ground. My entire body ached.

This was all wrong—I had been flying; I had seen *Maren* fly. What had happened?

Someone spoke near me, and I froze, straining to hear.

"My lord." That was Faris—where had *she* come from? "The girl has arrived at the palace."

Maren! My heart leaped, but I held still. How had she gotten to the palace? Come to think of it, how had *I*?

"What about the dragon?" the emperor replied.

"None of the large ones. She only has the baby."

"And where is she now?"

"Coming toward the gardens."

"Then it won't be long."

I turned my head minutely, trying to keep as quiet as possible. We were in the Garden of Glass, named for the glass trees hung with shards so sharp, they could cut a throat if they fell—but the lanterns had gone out. Why had no one relit them? I shifted, trying to suss out the space around me. I was still shackled, and weaponless. But this was the Garden of *Glass*. If I could find a loose piece . . .

A flare of fire in the sky illuminated the garden for a brief moment, and I saw Vix the Ruiner splayed on the ground, its breathing labored. Two people stood next to the dragon—Faris and Rafael.

The light faded as quickly as it had come, but I knew what I had seen. The emperor's clothes were torn and dirty, his hair askew and an ugly slash across his face. But he still held his sword at his side, ever at the ready.

Scattered images were coming back to me—the sky battle, the Seratese force, the massive dragon that had appeared from the south. Maren's face, white lipped when she'd seen me. And then we'd ... fallen?

I didn't know how much time had passed, or how we had gotten back to the palace, but it was eerily quiet. Where had everyone gone?

Rafael looked my way. "I see you've rejoined us, Prince Vesper," he said. He pointed his sword at me, sneering. "Don't even think about moving. I wouldn't want to have to punish you before our guest arrives."

Once such a threat would have made me quake with terror. And I was—afraid, and exhausted, and alone. But so was he. Once the Flame of the West had seemed all-knowing, all-powerful. Now, abandoned by his followers and stripped of his dragons, he was still dangerous, still deadly. But he was just a man.

One of us would die today, I was certain. But it might not be me.

I tried to catch Faris's eye. She had said she would help me—did that only extend to looking the other way during my escape attempt? Hadn't we become some sort of friends?

There was a footstep in the silence. I turned my head in time to see Maren come through the doorway, a sword raised in her hands, as if she had walked out of my dreams and into reality. The dragon kit walked beside her, so much larger than I remembered. She'd tripled in size at least—now her head came up to Maren's knee.

And Maren! She looked tired but resolute, and she walked into the garden like a queen. Her gaze skimmed over Vix, Faris, and the emperor before landing on me. For one split second, her face crumpled with emotion.

Then Rafael laughed. "So you are the so-called dragon mistress? You're scarcely more than a girl."

But his laughter was hollow. He was nervous, no *frightened*. Watching, I saw Maren's hands tighten on the hilt of the sword. She raised her chin, staring him down. She stepped forward, and her gaze flicked to me for one more moment. Then she looked back at the emperor. At once I realized—Faris and Rafael were looking at Maren. She had their complete attention, and as long as they were focused on her, I had an opening.

I looked around. There were glass shards hanging from a decorative tree to my right. Could I get to them without being noticed?

The emperor's jaw tightened. He motioned with his hand, and Vix struggled to its feet.

"Your dragon is wounded," Maren said. "It will injure itself further at your command."

"I am the Flame of the West, emperor of Zefed," Rafael rasped harshly. "I am the flame eternal and I will not be commanded by a traitorous peasant. You will die for your insolence."

He gestured once more, and the dragon trudged forward, laboriously, planting itself between Maren and the emperor. I couldn't see Maren now, could only hear her—I assumed that was her, though I could not make sense of the sound I heard. It was a song, I thought, but the notes were discordant and jarring to my ear. All the same, the dragon seemed to be affected—it had opened its mouth to spew fire, but now it wavered.

The emperor shouted, unscrewing another vial of oil, and I seized my chance. I pushed myself to my feet and hopped awkwardly toward the tree—but something hit me from behind, sending me sprawling. I rolled over, raising my arms to block a blow that didn't come.

Faris knelt at my side, shoving something into my hands—a key. "Hurry up!" she whispered. "He won't be distracted forever!"

She stood up and aimed a kick at my ribs so soft that I barely felt it. I faked a yelp of pain and curled into a ball, fumbling to unlock the shackles. Success! I lowered the shackles quietly to the ground and rose to my feet. My limbs ached from being bound for so long, but I had no time to tend to them. I ran to the tree and yanked down a glass shard, then tucked it into my pocket. On the other side of the garden Vix was spitting fire, engulfing the garden in brightness and flame. Then there was an enormous crash, and the air turned smoky and even darker.

It seemed that Maren had succeeded in distracting Vix from attacking her directly, but now the dragon was crashing through the garden, bellowing out indiscriminate plumes of fire. Both Maren and the emperor were running from its attacks. Sweat beaded on my brow as the garden burned. We had to get out of here before we were trapped.

I looked at Faris. "Let's go!"

We picked our way toward the door, dodging glass as it fell and shattered on the ground. I ran for Maren and grabbed her by the hand. "Come on!" I cried, dragging her out of the garden and back into the hallway. The dragon kit scrambled after us. For a moment I felt relief as we sprinted down the hall . . . and then I heard a crash behind us.

"*Severin!*" shouted Rafael, his voice echoing down the hall.

"Give me the sword," I said urgently. Freeing a dragon was not the same thing as dueling a desperate tyrant, and I could tell from the way that Maren held the sword that she did not stand a chance in a straight fight. She handed it over without hesitation.

"Deal with the dragon, if you can. Don't worry about the Aurat—she's a friend."

She nodded and beckoned to the dragon kit. The two of them backed away as I turned to face the emperor, holding my sword at the ready.

Rafael stood alone in the middle of the hall. He was backlit by the torches on the wall, and I could barely make out his features. This far away, he looked like a statue cut from my nightmares. In an instant I was a child again, listening to the report of my brother's death. Watching my mother cut down for no reason other than her existence.

Every night that I had dreamed of revenge was a night that he had spent in excess, feeding his court while the people of Zefed went hungry. Every moment I had spent in preparation had led me here, now. Every day I had promised myself that I would finish this.

We sized each other up. Though he was without his dragon,

the odds were not in my favor. He was still stronger than me, and hadn't recently been imprisoned with little to eat. I had fury on my side, but that wasn't enough to lift a sword for longer than a few minutes.

I hefted the sword in my hand and readied myself. I could not rush in—I had to save my energy for when it would count. I had to wait for the emperor to come to me.

But I still was not prepared when he charged. I parried the first cut well enough, though the shock of it jarred my arms all the way up to my shoulders, and thrust back. Rafael blocked so hard that I lost my grip—the sword flew out of my hands and across the hall. I scrambled back, ducking as he slashed forward with so much force that the sword caught in the wall molding, buying me precious seconds. I ran and scooped up my sword, just in time to block another ferocious attack. Our swords locked—the emperor punched me in the face with his free hand, sending me reeling backward. I tripped and fell hard, and he was on me in an instant.

I threw up the sword in defense—he struck the blade from my hands and I had nothing.

Someone screamed, and the emperor looked up. Maren stood behind him, a torch clutched in both hands—as I watched, she wielded it like a club, catching Rafael in the head. He shouted in pain, swinging his sword wildly at her, but that moment was enough for me to scramble to my feet. Sword—where was the sword?

There! I sprinted across the hall—but Rafael barreled into me and sent us both to the floor. I grabbed his sword arm and wrenched it back, trying desperately to keep myself safe from his blade. Something cracked as we rolled, and I remembered—the glass in my pocket. Could I reach it? I held my breath as I grabbed the emperor's collar, pulling him even closer to me. With my free hand I snatched the glass shard from my pocket—and stabbed him through the eye.

Blood spurted into my face. Rafael screamed incoherently, writhing on the floor. I rolled to my feet shaking, and brought my foot down hard on his hand. The sword fell from his grip and clattered away across the floor. Slowly, I picked it up.

A myriad of agonies flashed through me as I watched Rafael struggle to rise—every terror he had inflicted, every loved one he had stolen, every lie he had told to clutch power ever closer. I thought I would feel fury. Instead there was only icy resolve.

I took a deep breath, carefully adjusting my grip on the sword. I walked to the emperor, raising it high. And I brought the blade down, plunging it through the tyrant's chest.

There was a bloody gurgling sound as his chest expanded, collapsed, then fell still. His remaining eye went vacant.

Rafael, emperor of Zefed, Flame of the West, was dead.

CHAPTER THIRTY-NINE

Maren

S ev let go of the sword The tyrant's body lay still, and I could not look away. Strange, how terrible that man had been in life—how much he had laid waste to. How terrified I had been of him. And in death he was just like any other human. Empty.

We had done it. We had killed the emperor of Zefed. We had toppled the tyrant and freed the dragons. I should have felt utterly elated, but instead I couldn't catch my breath. My body was trembling, on the verge of collapse.

Sev walked toward me, his hair catching the light as he passed underneath a torch. Should I have gone to him? I could do nothing other than stand with my hands at my sides, watching him come to me, his eyes intense and fixed on my face. And then he was standing in front of me.

"Maren," he said hoarsely, and then his arms were around me, and I was hugging him so tightly, it was as though I was afraid the world might come apart if I let go. He pressed his forehead against mine, and we breathed together until my heartbeat evened and slowed.

"I was so afraid," I whispered.

"You never showed it. You *saved* me." He drew back abruptly. "What happened to Vix?"

The emperor's dragon. "He's dying," I said, a lump forming in my throat. I had failed him—though I'd been able to sense his consciousness, it was clear that the emperor had ruined him through long years of cruelty. When I'd returned to the garden, he'd collapsed again, too injured to get to his feet. I'd watched his labored breathing as the fires burned out around us, helpless to ease his suffering.

"Perhaps your mother dragon can help?" Sev suggested.

"Naava?" I shrugged. "I don't know."

Tasia danced around our feet, impatient to greet Sev. He laughed a little and bent down to offer her a hand to sniff before he gently scratched the scales along her spine.

"She's gotten so big," he said, marveling.

I tried to smile, but I could not do so in this hall anymore. "Let's go," I said, taking his hand. "There's nothing left here."

It seemed wrong to walk away from this place as though nothing had happened. But there were no witnesses, no speeches to be made. That would come later. For now we walked slowly together, hand in hand, and it wasn't until we were halfway down the hallway that I looked down at my feet and remembered.

"I dreamed of this place," I said.

"I know—we saw each other," he replied.

"No. Before." I closed my eyes, remembering. "When we went to Deletev, the first time. I dreamed of standing in this hallway with you. I dreamed of—"

I cut myself off. At the time, my dream had felt transgressive and wrong. But I had done what I'd set out to do. I had rescued Kaia, and she had chosen to leave me. I was indebted to no one, promised to no one.

"What did you dream?" Sev prompted.

"I dreamed that I kissed you here."

He nodded solemnly, but a hint of a smile touched the corner of his mouth. "A prophecy, do you think?"

He looked at me as though he truly saw me—as though he could drink me in for days and never tire of it. So I stepped forward, closing the distance between us, and kissed him.

It was impossible not to think of Kaia, but I let the flash of her surface in my mind and then disappear. Then it was all Sev's hands framing my face, my arms around his waist, our chests against each other, and the beat of his heart against mine. Kissing Sev felt completely new, like stepping into the unknown—and at the same time like a strangely familiar culmination to a journey I had been on for longer than I knew.

Tasia chirped near us, jogging my memory, and I broke off the kiss.

Sev's eyebrows knit together. "Are you all right? Is it Kaia?"

"No," I said. "I told you, she—we parted ways." I could not bring myself to say that she had left me. "I remembered, there's something I need to do. Come with me."

I wasn't prepared for the sight of Neve's lifeless body on the floor near the oubliette. By the choked sound he made, neither was Sev. "She was a friend to me here," Sev said. "What happened?"

"Milek attacked Tasia. Neve saved us from him."

"And Milek?"

"I . . . pushed him into the oubliette."

Sev leaned over the edge, looking down at what remained at the bottom of the pit. "Good," he said. Suddenly he looked around. "What happened to Faris? Did you see her?"

"The Aurat?"

Sev nodded.

"No. There was so much happening," I said. "She helped you?"

Sev touched his wrist. "She gave me the key to the shackles." There was more to the story, I could tell. But there would be time for all of that later.

"I don't know if I can free them from the oils," I said. These dragons were not like the others. The Talons had kept their dragons in servitude, but they had treated them like valuable tools. These dragons had been broken time and time again. I didn't know if there was anything left underneath their pain. "But I have to try."

"I know." Sev walked around the oubliette. "Naava would want to know of this, surely?" he said after a while.

Of course, Naava. In the midst of our struggle in the palace, the larger fight had flown from my head. I listened. There were no more dragon screams in the sky.

"Come outside," I said, taking his hand.

The palace grounds were still deserted. And though there were sounds of small skirmishes in the distance, the battle in the sky was over. Now a full flight of dragons soared through the air, led by Naava . . . and they were *singing*.

Abruptly I was so homesick, a lump formed in my throat. No Verran in my lifetime had seen such a sight. And now this would be *normal*.

Sev put his arm around my shoulder, and I leaned into him.

"We should go out into the city—we should be helping," I said.

Sev looked up at the sky. "Do you really think that any of us could keep fighting under a sight like that? All the fighting will soon be over, I'm sure of it. But there will be wounded fighters and civilians. And what better place to treat them than the emperor's own well-stocked palace?"

So we opened the palace doors, and soon enough, the citizens of Irrad began to trickle in. We told everyone we spoke with what had happened within these walls—though most did not believe it until they had seen the emperor's body for themselves. After that the word spread like wildfire, and as the day wore on, the palace was crowded with people eating and talking and resting. Sev walked among them all, offering words of comfort and encouragement. Soon it seemed he knew every single one.

The dragons flew for hours, but eventually I could not ignore the cries of the imprisoned dragons any longer.

Naava, I need you, I called. Then I returned to the oubliette and sank to the floor, my legs wobbly. I reached within myself and sent down not the strident song that had freed the other dragons but a Verran lullaby that calmed those that were trapped in the pit below, soothing them into slumber. Naava would be here soon. She would help them better than I could.

There was a voice calling my name. I opened my eyes to find a blurry figure standing over me—I blinked, and the figure resolved into Sev, standing next to Tovin. I turned my head and found a small force of Seratese fighters behind them, Davina among them.

"You made it," I said.

Tovin smiled, though it was clear he was exhausted. "You

promised me that you would be on the back of a dragon, not—"
He waved a hand, indicating the wreckage that surrounded us.

"Couldn't be helped," I said.

"And are you the person to thank for turning the emperor's palace into the town square?"

"That was Sev's idea," I said.

"And the emperor?" Davina asked.

"Dead," Sev said flatly. I looked over at him. He must have been feeling more than he was letting on, but his face was expressionless.

A flurry of emotions crossed Tovin's face. "The battle is over. We are at peace, but the Seda Serat require a formal treaty to avoid future . . . unpleasantness. Who can they negotiate with?"

"We can negotiate," a familiar voice interrupted smoothly. "We have a ruling council already in place."

I looked past Tovin to find that somehow, impossibly, Rowena ben Garret was standing in the doorway.

"You received my message?" I said, at a loss for what else to say.

Rowena looked at me. "Yes. Although I have to say it was poor form, reneging on an agreement only a few days old."

"There were circumstances that couldn't be helped," I said defensively.

"Rowena," Sev cut in. "Thank you for offering your council, but we cannot accept."

"No?" Rowena arched an eyebrow. "You were begging for my help just a few days ago. Here we are, having fought against the emperor's army at your behest. Don't forget that I know very well that you led our operative into a trap. I don't know what games you've been playing here in the emperor's palace, but we have *earned* the right to take part in planning the future of this empire."

"You'll have a part," Sev said. "All the small kingdoms will participate, Oskiath included. But *I* will negotiate with the Seratese on behalf of Zefed. Maren will advise on behalf of the dragons." He spoke confidently, and I was suddenly reminded of the act he'd pulled on our way out of Deletev, fooling the Aurati at the gates. Despite his time on the run, he still wore the mantle of royalty with ease.

"Strong words for someone with no army to speak of," Rowena said.

"I am the rightful king of Ruzi, and the person who killed the tyrant," Sev said hotly.

A rumbling voice swept through my mind. *I have come,* Naava said.

I smiled sweetly at Rowena. "And have you looked to the sky? Because you will find that Sev has the support of the dragons."

Rowena looked incensed. She took a step toward me, but Davina barred her way. Tasia planted herself in front of me and hissed, baring her fangs. It was clear she remembered Rowena.

"This is ridiculous. You're a peasant with no understanding—"

Wind swept through the room, and Rowena turned. Naava stood in the doorway, her body barely fitting in the hall. The humans around her fell back as she entered the room. She came to my side and inhaled deeply, then snorted in anger at the sight of the oubliette. *What is this travesty?*

I nodded. *I know. I was able to help them sleep, but I hoped that you would be able to free them. I couldn't do it.*

Her wings rippled in anger, but she nodded. *And what else is happening here?* She looked around at the humans that surrounded her.

The tyrant of Zefed is dead. The humans must decide who will take command of the empire. I hesitated before I spoke again. *Will you lend your support to my friend? We want to remake this land.*

Naava sniffed. *The heartmate you came to save? We will support him. But tell them to find somewhere else to plot. I must see to these—* The sound she made was mournful.

The emperor's dragon, Vix, is also injured. He is in the garden.

The great dragon shook her head. *That one has already passed from this world.* She approached the oubliette and folded her wings, settling down on the far side of the pit. *Now tell the humans to leave.*

I relayed the message to the group. Rowena had the good sense not to argue with Naava, who bared her fangs for emphasis. The humans filed out of the room, leaving only Naava, Tasia, and me standing over the oubliette.

Softly, Naava began to sing.

It was a quieter sound than the song she had thrown across the skies today, and it cast chills over my skin. I should have been happy that Naava was here, but I was suddenly afraid. What if she couldn't help them? When Naava looked up at me, I knew my fears had come true.

It is as I feared. They are too far gone, Naava said. *You have done the best you could. Take the kit with you now—this is not for you to see.*

A sob lodged in my throat. These dragons had done nothing

wrong. They'd been mistreated their entire lives, and there was nothing I could do to help ease their passing. All I could do was stroke Tasia on the nose and retreat from the courtyard, leaving Naava to her task.

Her words followed me into the hall. *You have done well, daughter of dragons. Be proud.*

I wasn't so sure, if this was what had come of it.

"Maren."

I knew that voice—I had feared I would never hear it again. I turned around. *Kaia.*

CHAPTER FORTY

Maren

Y ou left without saying a word," I blurted, and immediately cursed myself for doing so.

"Maren—"

"You ran off with a stranger," I cut her off. "You could have been anywhere. *Anything* could have happened to you. How could you do that to me?"

Kaia inhaled sharply. "I left because I felt I had to. King Idai gave me a horse, and I rode for Ruzi. I was able to convince some of the Aurati to return with me. We used the Talons' oils to start bonfires in the city—to confuse the dragons during the battle."

The Talons' oils . . . ? It came to me suddenly—she was talking about the oils we had confiscated from the Talons and brought with us to Irrad. She had taken them with her when she left our camp, and I hadn't even noticed. That was what I had smelled, flying high above the city.

It *had* been a good plan. Maybe even an important one, though I didn't know if I would ever be able to trust an Aurat the way she seemed to. But it still didn't excuse her actions.

"But you still *left* me," I said. "I didn't know you intended to come back. How could I have known?"

"I only left because you didn't *listen* to me," Kaia said. "But

I'm back now. And I've been told that the emperor is dead. So you've done it—you've freed the dragons; you've done what you set out to do. We can be together now, turn to the future."

She reached for me, and almost without realizing what I was doing, I shook my head. "No."

Kaia recoiled in surprise. "What?"

My heart was beating so, so fast. I knew that what I was about to say was right, but that didn't make it any easier. "I know we fought. Maybe it was mostly my fault. But you broke my heart when you left me. And . . . I don't think I can move past that."

"What are you saying?" she whispered, looking stricken.

Now that I had started, I couldn't stop. "Kaia, I care about you. I'll *always* care for you. But we are different people than we were before we left Ilvera. We want different things. You want to reform the Aurati—and I know not all of them are evil, but I can't go along with that. What they did to you is too painful for me to forgive, even if you can. And you want recognition—you want people to know your greatness. *I* know your greatness. But that's not enough for you. I don't—" I paused and took a deep breath. "You told me to make a choice. Kaia . . . it's not you."

Anger flared in her eyes. "Is it *him?* The prince?" she asked, her voice deadly calm.

I shook my head. "It's not because of him. It's because of *me.* We've grown apart—you must feel it too. Kaia, I'm so sorry."

As the apology left my lips, Kaia's face crumpled with tears. She turned and ran from me without another word, and my heart shattered into pieces.

The broken pieces of my heart splintered even further as I watched her go.

"There you are," Sev said, leaning out of a nearby doorway.

I started. I wasn't sure how long I'd been standing here with Tasia, watching the empty hallway down which Kaia had fled. My sorrow had turned time slippery and evasive. I swallowed, blinking away tears.

"Are you all right?" he asked.

"Kaia was here," I said miserably.

Indecision crossed his face. "Do you want to be alone?"

I thought for a moment, then shook my head. "Maybe away from surprises for a little while. Not away from you."

He smiled, and that smile was like sunshine. "Come with me," he said, almost shyly.

He led us away from the great hall and the gardens to a little-trafficked corridor and a nondescript door, which he shouldered open.

"Welcome to my chambers," he said. "This is where they put me when the emperor . . . when I was pretending to be loyal. It's where I dreamed about you."

He drew aside a curtain to reveal a bed pushed against the wall. Then he sat down and patted the space next to him. "Come, sit. Tell me—what's happened since I saw you last? We've scarcely had a chance to exchange one word alone."

I sat, and Tasia jumped up beside us. Gods, it was good to see his face. I still couldn't believe that this was real. I shook my head, looking up at the ceiling. "So much. It would take forever to tell you everything."

He gestured around the room. "I don't see anything else that needs attending to."

And he was right. The world had shrunk to this room, to Sev sitting at my side, to our hands clasped, to Tasia snuggled between our bodies.

So I told him everything I had done and everything I had seen, and he did the same, our conversation ebbing and flowing like a gentle stream. And when we were done, we lay back on the bed, holding hands, and waited for the world to start turning once more.

CHAPTER FORTY-ONE

Sev

Piera Sil'Danne was caught three days after the Battle of Irrad trying to cross the border into Old Zefed with her son. It was the first real test of our temporary governing body, for we debated fiercely over what to do with her and the crown prince.

It took days of deliberations, but we finally came to a unanimous ruling. The prince was blameless and young enough to be brought up in a world that was different from the one into which he had been born. He would be adopted into a family that would raise him as their own. But Piera had stood by the tyrant, and for that she was sentenced to die.

She faced the sword on the last day of summer, and it took everything I had to see it through. Vicious though she was, I could not look at her without seeing the ghosts of my brother and the girl she used to be. There were only a few people who could bear witness to my childhood—when Piera died, there was one fewer.

I thought of Faris, too, that day. She had fled the palace the day I killed the emperor, and I wondered often what had become of her. If I'd had the chance, I would have pardoned her. But perhaps she thought her crimes were so great, the council would never accept such a ruling. And she would likely have been right.

Sometimes I woke up, my heart pounding, and thought I was still dreaming—that Rafael was standing over me, sword in hand, ready to strike. It was nights like those that I was especially grateful to have Maren—exceptional, brave, dauntless Maren—to listen without judgment and to offer her love.

She was adamant that I could not offer her a troth ring while I sat at the head of the ruling council of Zefed—and perhaps not even after that.

I smiled and acquiesced, and did not mention the ring I had already made. It would keep.

Every day the emperor's palace belonged less to him and more to the people of Zefed, and every day it was easier to walk those halls.

Sometimes I went to sit in the garden that Idai had taken me to. We had started a tentative correspondence, and I liked taking their letters through the secret passageway to read.

And sometimes I thought about my parents, and my brother, and considered the question of whether they would have been happy with what I was doing. If they would have been proud of who I had become.

And for the first time in my life, I knew the answer would be yes.

CHAPTER FORTY-TWO

Maren

The mood in Irrad was somber at first. Naava's first order of business was organizing the newly freed dragons to carry the bodies of those that had been imprisoned in the oubliette back to Ilvera, to be laid to rest in the dragon way.

A council consisting of representatives from each of the kingdoms—both from the ruling families and democratically chosen people who were not courtiers—as well as representatives from the Seda Serat and the Aurati, was neck deep in negotiations. Sev and I sat on the council as well, though my input was mostly limited to constantly reminding everyone that the dragons would not agree to participate in the governing and security of Zefed on an official basis. Given how integral Talons had been to the creation and perpetuation of the empire, I found myself saying "no" quite a lot.

When I wasn't in council, I spent time in Irrad, walking with Tasia by my side. The fires from the dragon battles had torn through the city, but rebuilding efforts had already begun. The vitriol that the tyrant had stoked against the Seratese lingered, in pointed glances and malicious whispers—but such cruelty was punished swiftly and without lenience. I had hope that Zefed would be able to correct this failing, but I supported

Zefedi-born Seratese who chose to return to the islands. It was not their duty to improve those who wished them ill.

Efren and Jase returned to Ruzi, escorted by Alora and Braith. And on the sixth day after the battle, my parents arrived in Irrad.

After many songs and many more tears, the story poured out of them. They'd wanted to leave the mountain to find me immediately after Naava had arrived, but they hadn't had any idea of where I might be. And as more dragons came to the mountain, Ilvera was overwhelmed by the prospect of learning how to live alongside them once again. So instead of rushing off in search of me, they'd sent a letter to Tovin and hoped we would somehow reunite.

They spoke in awe of the sight of dragons flying over the lake—the first in generations—and the ways that Verrans had begun to interact with them. Now that the Zefedi empire had fractured and the dragons had returned, there was hope once again for an independent Ilvera—something my mother had never thought she would live to see. They were alternately furious about the risks I had taken and overjoyed that I was alive, impressed with what I had accomplished—and more than anything else, they wanted to know when I was coming home.

I didn't know. For all that I longed for the mountains and the lake, there was still so much work to be done. Besides that, I had begun to realize that there was so much more of the world that I yearned to see.

And Sev—we were each other's touchstone. What relationship we had was tentative and almost unspoken. Some days the only time we spent together was when we fell, exhausted, into bed and immediately into sleep. But occasionally we stole away for a few hours, talking freely about our past lives. Sev told me about his parents and his brother Callum, and I painted pictures of the beautiful mountains of Ilvera. I didn't leave Kaia out of my stories, and though Sev was quiet when I shared them, he never asked me to stop. He understood that she was a part of who I had been, and that to erase her from memory would be to erase a part of myself. He told me about Piera, too—who she'd been to him as a boy and how sharply her betrayal had cut him. Any jealousy I might have felt was swept away when he confessed how he'd felt nothing when they'd finally kissed—and how his heart now belonged to me.

And eventually, there was more. Slowly, sweetly, gently, more. I'd forgotten that the beginning of a relationship could be simultaneously so exciting and terrifying—like standing at the edge of a cliff and yearning to jump into the water below—and I cherished it. Every touch, every kiss, everything that passed between us felt new and precious. I wasn't certain what I wanted from him yet. I'd barely had the chance to think about what I wanted for myself. But we still shared dragon dreams.

Everywhere I went, I was known. It was a strange feeling. What power I had was dragon granted, and even when I spoke on the council, my weighty decisions were run through Naava before I took a stand. But most humans regarded me with a certain amount of awe—they saw me as the person who had singlehandedly wrested control of the dragons from the emperor, and that made me an intimidating foe.

It was a power I embraced uneasily, the deferential way people looked at me. But negotiations would come to a close, and I could not commit to staying in Irrad to see every thread tied off. There would always be problems with governance, and I could not pretend I knew how to solve them all. If I took that as my reason, I would stay here forever. And every time a dragon left for Ilvera, I missed the mountain more.

My parents stayed in Irrad for almost a month—the longest they'd been away from Ilvera that I could remember. They refused to set foot in the palace, despite the ways it had been torn down and rebuilt. I didn't blame them. I couldn't set foot in the hall that housed the oubliette—never mind that the pit had been filled in, leaving only a smooth stone floor. The scent of those dragons would never be washed away.

Instead they stayed in a Verran-run tavern by the docks and helped with the recovery efforts. When I had the opportunity to steal away from the meetings, I did. Together with Tovin, we walked a lot, and ate, and sang, and wept.

"You've changed," my father said to me one night. Tasia was several months old now, and she had been flying for longer distances. Every time she left me, I felt a stab of unreasonable fear that she wouldn't return, alleviated only when she landed by my side once more.

I raised an eyebrow at him. "Isn't this exactly what you wanted when you sent me downmountain?"

He let out a bark of laughter. "I'm not going to respond to that," he said, but he still pressed a kiss to my forehead and whispered that he was so, so proud of me.

The negotiations had wrapped up successfully on all sides, I thought, except for perhaps the Dragons. Sev would remain in place as the de facto ruler, but only because there was no one else who could garner the same amount of support. He had announced that he would only remain until the transition from the empire of Zefed into the cooperative kingdoms of Zefed could be completed. As each kingdom would be ruled independently, the representatives from the Seda Serat—including Tovin—left satisfied with the dissolution of the empire, so long as it meant that Zefed would never threaten the islands again.

Which was no longer a problem, after all, since the emperor's warmongering was due to the scarcity of the mirth wood oil. And because the dragons were now free, Zefed had no need of it. Most of the dragons had chosen to return to Ilvera, to relearn how to live independently with Naava. But a few of them had remained in Zefed, at least for a little while, volunteering to help administer the transition of power and ensure that the border between Ruzi and Old Zefed remained peaceful.

Slowly, the people of Zefed were learning how to interact with the dragons while respecting their autonomy, and without fear. It was going better than I had ever imagined it might. There were kinks in the system to be worked out—the fact that the dragons were not animals of service, for example, and that anything they did on behalf of the empire was a favor, not a duty. Every kingdom would have to maintain their own armies—they would not be able to rely on the dragons to keep the empire safe any longer. But still, I ended each day awed at what I'd had a hand in bringing about.

I had accomplished everything I had set out to achieve when I left Ilvera. Sev and I . . . I didn't know what we were. I didn't want to admit out loud that I was in love with him, though sometimes I whispered it to myself. But he had taken command of the empire. It didn't matter that it was a temporary arrangement. I had seen firsthand what happened to those who grasped at power, and I didn't think I could rest easily until he had passed that power on.

I hoped it wouldn't be too long until he could. He talked about returning to Ruzi almost as often as I thought of Ilvera. When he left Irrad, perhaps Tasia and I would visit him. But first, home.

I was strangely nervous about the prospect, but Tovin had volunteered to come with me. It was a crisp day in almost-winter as we readied our horses for the journey. Tasia was looking forward to the trip—never having been to Ilvera, or even to the mountain, she was excited to see the place that Naava spoke to her about.

We were just about ready to leave when a runner came up to me, panting. "Mistress," he said. "There's a visitor for you."

I looked at Tovin, who shrugged. We weren't on any particular timetable, and it would be some time before I was back in Irrad. So Tasia and I turned and followed the runner out to the gate, where a young woman stood facing the city, hands clasped behind her back.

"Kaia." She turned, and I realized I'd spoken her name aloud. My heart thumped painfully in my chest. I'd thought of her often over the last few weeks. I'd known she was still in Irrad, but she'd been careful to avoid me, busying herself with the new Aurati administration. And here she was, and she looked . . . well.

"How are you?" I said.

"'How are you?' That's all you have to say to me?" she said wryly.

"Well, it's been busy, what with . . ." I waved my hands, indicating the bustle of activity behind us.

She smiled, just briefly. "I suppose you're right. Walk with me?"

We climbed to the top of the palace walls and looked out at the city. Most of the debris had been cleared, but it would still be some time before the reconstruction efforts would begin to show. For lack of more suitable quarters, the new government was occupying the palace, though there was an ongoing debate over whether to demolish it and build something new in its place. If pressed, I would have confessed I had very little opinion on the matter—it was something I preferred to leave to the citizens of Gedarin, especially those who lived in Irrad.

"You were right," she said quietly. "And I was wrong."

I was surprised. The Kaia I knew would never have admitted to making any kind of a mistake. "About what?" I asked.

"Not *everything*," she said. "But it was cruel to leave you like that. And . . . I think you were right about us. Growing apart." She turned away from the city, hugging her arms against her body. It was windy up on the wall, and her coat was thin. "I pushed you to make a choice, but I wasn't prepared for the possibility that I might lose you. You changed so quickly, and I wasn't ready."

Once, I'd never thought I would see the day when Kaia truly apologized to me. And now she was—trying, at least. But her words weren't hopeful. They were tinged with sadness.

"It's all right," I said. "I don't think I was really ready for it either."

She smiled at me.

That smile. Once, that smile would have made me swoon. Now it just made me feel the loss of a different time, a different life.

"Tovin and I are going to visit Ilvera," I said. "Would you like to come with us?"

She shuddered theatrically. "Not now. Everyone there knows me as I was. Not as I am."

"Then what will you do?"

She looked out toward the ocean. "I'm staying here for now. There is a place for me with the Aurati. I know your feelings about them, so I won't say any more."

I nodded. Kaia was right—I still harbored a deep well of fury over what the Aurati had done to her. But this was her choice, and it was no longer my place to speak so stridently about it. Instead I took her hand and held it tightly in mine, stroking her thumb. "It's going to be all right," I said.

"Maren—" She choked on my name, her eyes shining with unshed tears. I pulled her into a hug, pressing a kiss to her hair.

"We're always going to be family," I whispered.

Her voice came out muffled and low. "Promise?"

"I promise."

And I found that I meant it.

It was still difficult to watch her descend the wall and melt back into the city, but this time it was a dull ache in my chest—not a debilitating pain. I knew that someday, thoughts of Kaia wouldn't hurt me at all anymore.

I found Sev playing cards in a courtyard with one of Davina's cousins, a young Seratese man who had decided to stay in Irrad for a time. But when Sev saw me, he excused himself and came over.

"Is it time?" he said.

I nodded.

"And there isn't anything I can do to persuade you to stay?" He was mostly joking, but I could still hear the yearning in his voice.

I rolled my eyes. "I won't be that far away," I said.

"Ah, but you know I'm a terrible correspondent."

He leaned into me, pressing his forehead against mine and closing his eyes. "You know none of this would have been possible without you. You changed the world, Maren. My heart."

Tera's bones, when he talked like that, I wanted to stay.

But there were so many places I wanted to see, so many things I wanted to do. I wasn't ready to make a home with Sev—not as an empress, nor a queen. So I simply kissed him, letting him sweep me off my feet once more.

"Write me when you leave for Ruzi," I said finally. "Or come up the mountain."

"I'm sure your parents would love a Zefedi prince coming to woo their daughter," Sev joked.

I grinned at him. "You're welcome to try," I said. "When the time is right."

His eyes glowed with determination. "Then I will."

Our journey took four days by horseback and was completely, wonderfully uneventful. Only the changes in the landscape bore witness to everything that had come to pass since I had left, all those months ago. Tasia flew above the horses for hours at a time, though she still took breaks to ride with me.

"Everything's changed," Tovin said. The dragon fortress had been completely dismantled and burned out—as I understood it, Naava offered to accompany any dragon that wished down to the ruins so that they too could let loose their fury. Even now I could smell the smoke and ashes in the air.

But the inn that had long stood at the base of the mountain was transformed even more surprisingly. Now that the dragons had returned to Ilvera, there was a certain contingent of Zefedi people who wanted to visit them, and the inn was bustling with friendly energy when we stopped in for the night. It was an unexpected and welcome change, and I hoped it would mean the revitalization of our Verran nation.

The next morning Tovin and I stood at the base of the mountains, ready to climb. I wasn't back in Ilvera for good—too much of the world had been opened up to me. But the mountain would always have my heart. And when I looked up and saw the sky full of dragons, their song ringing through the air, I knew I was home.

Acknowledgments

I've been very lucky to return to Maren's story with many of the same people who helped shepherd *Shatter the Sky* into the world. Particular thanks are owed to Catherine Laudone, who put up with a whole lot of deadline-related anguish and helped turn *Storm the Earth* from a very messy Word document into an actual book, with an actual plot. Thank you again to the team at Simon & Schuster BFYR, including Justin Chanda, Milena Giunco, Katrina Groover, Emily Hutton, Brian Luster, Bara MacNeill, Martha Hanson, Charlton Villavelez, Chloë Foglia and cover artist Olivier Ponsonnet. And thank you to Catherine Ho, the wonderful audiobook narrator of *Shatter the Sky*.

Thank you to Rebecca Podos, who always fields my existential writing crises with patience and encouragement. And to my dear writing group friends, who have not yet gotten sick of me: Greg Batcheler, Heather Goss, Clarissa Hadge, and Kate Mikell.

Thank you to the following authors who took the time to read and blurb *Shatter the Sky*: Dahlia Adler, Melissa Bashardoust, Rin Chupeco, Audrey Coulthurst, Kate Elliott, Tessa Gratton, Mackenzi Lee, Saundra Mitchell, and Nancy Werlin. Now that I'm constantly on deadline, I appreciate your generosity at least five times as much. Special thanks to Dahlia Adler and LGBTQ Reads, for being such an invaluable pillar of support for queer literature, children's and otherwise. Thank you as well to the authors who took the time to join me at book events: Heidi Heilig, Rory Power, Gabe Cole, Sara Farizan, Elizabeth Fama, Megan Whalen Turner, and Ryan La Sala.

Books, particularly debuts, do not succeed without the enthusiasm and support of the bookselling community. I have been overwhelmed by the way you have embraced *Shatter the Sky*. A million thanks to the committee that selected *Shatter the Sky* as an Indies Introduce pick, especially Sami Thomasen and Casey Leidig (an extra special thanks to Casey for naming Piera, empress of Zefed!). Thank you so, so much to the indie bookstore community that chose *Shatter the Sky* as an Indies Next pick, especially Nichole Cousins for her wonderful blurb. My love and gratitude to the following booksellers and bookstores: Nicole Brinkley, Abby Rauscher, Stephanie Heinz, Abby Rice, Avery Peregrine, Michael Lasagna, Candice Huber, Tildy Banker-Johnson, Chris Abouzeid, Paul Swydan, Shana Hausman, Porter Square Books, Belmont Books, Print: A Bookstore, Oblong Books & Music, Books of Wonder, Kepler's Books, R. J. Julia Booksellers, The Silver Unicorn Bookstore, Books are Magic, Tubby & Coo's, and Hicklebee's. Thank you to every bookseller or reader who has picked up *Shatter the Sky* and recommended it to someone else. I appreciate every single one of you.

Finally, I could not do what I do without the support and love of my family. And Martin—thank you for always believing in me.

Turn the page for a sneak peek at
Briar Girls.

Cold wind bit at my cheeks, bearing the scent of fallen leaves in decay. I ducked my head and hunched my shoulders as I trudged along a path overgrown with wild grass, my feet aching with each step. My skin was chafing where my pack rested against the small of my back, and my boots pinched. We'd been walking for weeks—long enough for my resolve to wear thin, for my stomach to clench into an angry pit of hunger. Though we'd rationed the little food we'd brought with us, our provisions had run out yesterday morning.

Father looked over his shoulder, as if he sensed my dour mood. "We're almost there," he said.

I didn't bother to reply. Instead, I pulled my scarf up over my chin as he turned and strode ahead of me through an empty field, his walking stick striking a steady beat upon the ground. He had been promising *almost there* for days now, as though our destination were something to look forward to. As though we hadn't been forced to flee our last home because of what I'd done.

I supposed that an end to our journey *was* something to celebrate. We'd managed to outrun any rumors chasing us and avoid the notice of keepers of the peace. And most importantly, there were no signs that the witch had caught our scent. Still, part of me had welcomed the discomfort I'd endured during this flight. I deserved this pain. And at least my aching feet and empty stomach kept my thoughts from other, darker things. I didn't know what I would do when the distraction went away.

In front of me, Father stopped walking. "Look, Lena."

I lifted my gaze from the ground. We'd crested a small hill, and a valley lush with greenery lay before us, a huddle of houses at its base. There was a lake to the north that fed a stream running south through the village. And to the east, on the other side of the houses, was the Silence—a forest of trees so dense and dark they looked almost blue.

A prickling sensation skittered down my spine as I stared out at the trees. Even from a distance there was something unsettling about them. I couldn't shake the feeling that somehow they were watching me, too.

"What do you think is in there?" I asked.

Father shook his head. "We're to keep people from going into the Silence. It's not our duty to speculate on what might reside within."

"But shouldn't someone investigate—"

"No," he said sharply. "The Onwey council sent very clear instructions. The Silence is deadly. No one who walks into those trees ever comes out again. You're not to go near it, Lena."

He started down the hill without waiting for my reply, leaving me no choice but to fall in line. It didn't matter that I thought there had to be more to the Silence than what we'd been told. My father wouldn't listen to me, and I had long ago learned it wasn't worth challenging him—not on things like this.

The wind picked up, and I shivered, stuffing my gloved hands into my pockets. Maybe Father was right—maybe it didn't matter what was in the Silence. He would have taken the job no matter what risks it entailed. Anything to get us away from—*screams, the stench of blackened, burning skin—*

Don't think about that. I shook my head, as if I could shake the memory away. It was over. I was safe. I took a deep breath and followed my father down the hill.

The village houses were arranged in rough curves that gathered around a central square. It would have seemed quaint, were it not for the gloom that permeated the air. The streets were silent and empty, despite it being only midafternoon. Doors and windows were shuttered. The only sign of life was a thin plume of smoke rising from the chimney of a large building on the south side of the square, so we headed in that direction. The faded sign hanging above one window told us it was a tavern—the Midnight Song.

"Gloves?" Father asked, pausing on the stoop.

I held up my hands in answer. We were lucky to be traveling in autumn—no one would look askance at someone wearing gloves, even indoors.

He nodded curtly and pushed open the door.

My shoulders tensed as I stepped over the threshold, and I tucked my elbows in, trying to make myself as small as possible. But there were no drunken patrons veering clumsily in our direction, nor jovial groups brushing past us on their way out. In fact, it seemed unusually quiet. Only a few people bothered to look up from their glasses to take note of Father and me. I tried to force myself to relax.

As we moved farther into the tavern, my gaze fell on a small cluster of people on the other side of the room. At the center of the cluster was a single chair, which held a man with flushed cheeks and disheveled hair. His limbs were restrained by leather straps even though he was perfectly motionless, his head lolling to one side as though unsupported by his spine.

A charred corpse on the ground, unmoving—

Suddenly the man thrashed against his restraints, dragging me back to the present.

I drew a great, shuddering breath. *That's all in the past. This man is different. He's alive.* As if he could hear my thoughts, the man opened his mouth and began to sing in an eerie cadence that raised the hairs on the back of my neck and clawed against my skin.

"Down below the briars and the vines, let me down, until roses come to claim me, set me free, let me down . . ."

What was wrong with him? I glanced over at Father. His face was grim as he watched the man sing.

"Can I help you?" a woman's voice called out, cutting through the song like a knife.

Father and I turned to see an older woman with neat gray hair standing behind the bar, eyeing us suspiciously.

Father cleared his throat. "Yes. I'm Joren, the new watcher. This is my daughter, Lena." He nudged me with an elbow. I raised my hand in greeting, trying to avoid meeting the woman's eyes. "But it seems we've arrived at an inopportune moment."

She sighed, her expression turning resigned. "We were expecting you tomorrow, but you may as well stay. I'm Olinta, one of the council members."

The man in the chair thrashed harder, catching my attention once more. His song had dissolved into incoherent mutters, and as I watched, he began to weep.

"What's wrong with him?" The words burst out of me, unbidden and louder than I'd intended.

All eyes turned toward me. I felt my cheeks grow warm and saw Father's jaw tighten before I looked down at my feet. I shouldn't have said anything—Father would have the answers soon enough. There was no need to call attention to myself.

"Melor has been infected by the Silence, child. There's no hope for him now," Olinta replied.

I dared another glance at the man—Melor. A slight woman approached him now, a bowl of water in her hand. She dabbed at his brow with a cloth, then looked up at the others in the room. "It's time," she said.

The men standing next to her moved woodenly as they loosened the straps that held Melor down, then grabbed his arms and pulled him upright. He struggled and began to scream, and I stepped quickly aside as the men wrestled him toward the tavern door.

The unnerving cries cut through the air even after the door closed behind them. But those who remained in the tavern made no move to follow Melor and his escorts. Instead, a quiet hum of conversation picked up as they returned to their tables and plates of food. I looked around the room, surprised. Was it so easy for the residents of Onwey to ignore the sounds of such suffering?

"I'm sorry you had to see that, but it is the reason you are here," Olinta said, addressing Father as she came out from behind the bar. "Would you mind stepping outside with me?"

Father moved to follow her but put out a hand to stop me as I started after him. He leaned in, whispering in my ear. "Go talk to someone."

"What?" All my life he'd taught me to avoid close contact with others—why was he reversing course now?

"You're new here. It's only natural that you would be curious. That's what they expect. Be careful and you'll be fine."

And then he followed Olinta outside, leaving me standing by myself.

I wanted to press my back against the wall and will myself into invisibility. My palms were sweating inside my gloves. But Father was right—it was imperative that I appear as normal as possible. The illusion of normalcy might be the only thing that would save me if anyone ever came searching for us here.

Most of the people in the tavern looked at least as old as my father, but there was a group of three around my age sitting at a table in the corner. I took a deep breath, steeling myself. Then I walked over to them, stopping a safe distance away.

It was a few moments before they noticed me. "Come closer," said a girl with kind brown eyes and long dark hair. "We don't bite."

Ah, but I did.

I took a tiny step forward. "Hello," I said, trying not to let my voice quiver.

The dark-haired girl smiled at me. "That's quite a cloak you have."

I couldn't tell whether she was teasing or sincere. Years ago the cloak had belonged to my mother, and as such it was too long on me, falling almost to the ground. It had been mended over so many times that it was difficult to tell it had once been brown; now it was a patchwork of colors snatched from whatever scraps of cloth were handy.

"Thank you," I said uncertainly.

"You must be with the new watcher," said one of the others, a boy with a contemplative air about him.

They must have seen us arrive. "He's my father," I said. "I'm Lena."

"I'm Wren," said the first girl. She nodded to her companions in turn. "That's Jasper, and this is my sibling Corina."

Corina had the same dark hair as Wren, though it was cut shorter. They looked a little younger than their sister—or maybe that was because of the way they were nervously interlacing their fingers again and again.

"So, Lena," Jasper said, "where are you from?"

I shrugged. "Lots of places. Minos, for a few years." It wasn't quite a lie. We had lived in Minos, though not recently. But I couldn't risk naming a city tainted by my curse.

"*Minos*," Wren said, her eyes gleaming with interest. "What's it like, living in a city like that? You must know so many people!"

"Fewer than you'd think," I replied. I'd spent most of my time indoors or in our garden, hidden away. But there had still been things to love about the cities I'd seen only from a safe distance— the different foods Father had brought home, the books from the city libraries, the people from so many places I'd made a habit of watching from my window . . .

Now all that was gone, traded away for this beleaguered village and its wan and weary inhabitants.

I blinked and realized they were watching me—waiting for me to say something more. "It was fine," I said. "Crowded. Too noisy sometimes."

Wren sighed. "Sounds wonderful."

"I . . . suppose you don't get many visitors here?"

Jasper snorted with contemptuous laughter. "Do you think anyone's yearning to visit Onwey when we have *that* hanging over our heads every day?" He tipped his head in the direction of the door.

I smoothed the edges of my gloves, making sure my skin was completely covered. "I thought the Silence took people. But he's . . ."

"Still here?" Wren said.

I nodded.

"People don't just walk into the forest by accident. Something calls to them if they get too close. *Bewitches* them."

"And they just go?"

Wren and Jasper nodded in unison.

"You saw Melor. They caught him before he crossed the border into the forest, but he's not *there* anymore," Jasper said, tapping a finger to his temple for emphasis.

I glanced back at the chair that Melor had been strapped to. "Will he recover?"

Corina shook their head. "He's gone," they said, their voice cracking. They stood up from the table without another word. I shied away as they ran past me and out of the tavern.

I looked at Wren, who bit her lip. "Corina was sweet on him," she said.

"Well, there's no cure for what ails him now," Jasper said. "Once a person's bewitched, they rave about the Silence until they can't speak anymore. They stop eating and drinking—eventually they die. That, or find their way into the forest, never to be seen again."

Jasper's flat tone took me aback almost as much as his words. Dead? And these would be his last days, strapped down and delirious as his loved ones watched him waste away?

"So where did the men take him?" I said.

Jasper and Wren glanced at each other. "Sometimes the families elect to let them go into the Silence," Wren offered. "But Melor's family has chosen to . . ."

"Put him out of his misery," Jasper finished.

"You mean *kill* him?" My voice cracked. If this was what happened to *victims* of ensorcellment, what might they do to me, if they found out what I was capable of?

"He's already as good as dead," Jasper said. "It's better this way."

Wren grimaced but didn't argue.

A shiver ran down my spine. It was a horrific choice. Now that I was beginning to understand the extent to which the Silence preyed upon this village, it was shocking to me that anyone still lived here. "Has it always been like this?"

Wren shook her head. "The Silence has always been unearthly, but my grandmother said people used to go inside safely. She doesn't remember exactly when it changed, but I think something happened—turned it vicious."

"The *forest* itself does this?" What could a forest possibly want with befuddled humans? How could a forest possibly want *anything*?

Jasper shrugged. "No one who goes in ever comes out, so who knows?"

I took a breath to ask another question but was stopped by an inconsolable wail that rattled me to the core. That sound—*his piercing scream*—

"I—I have to go," I stammered, backing away from the table.

"Don't," Wren said. "It's better not to see."

But the roaring in my ears told me I had to flee—for anything was better than letting my legs fold beneath me here, where they might jump up to help. Might reach out and—

I turned and ran.

I yanked the tavern door open and stumbled outside. The sudden light was blinding, and I threw up a hand to block it as I crossed the square and saw the men from the tavern, solemn and still; my father, his hands clasped behind his back; a wailing woman, on her knees beside—the body.

From this vantage point I couldn't tell how they had killed him, only that it had been bloody. It was everywhere: on the stones, on their shirts, their hands. And I could smell it now, the warm, metallic tang causing my throat to seize. They'd killed him; they'd truly killed him; it had been a *slaughter*, and they would do the same to me—

The roaring in my ears returned, and I sank to the ground. I was sweating despite the cold, and my heart raced—there was the stench of burning skin again, the stench I'd tried so hard to wash off—

"Lena!" Father's voice came from far away as my vision blurred.

Flames crawling up the boy's skin but I cannot help him. The falling rain does nothing; he is already dead—

Hands under my arms lifted me up. I leaned against Father as he put an arm around my waist, taking my weight and leading me away from the grisly scene.

"You're all right," he murmured under his breath. "You're all right; it's going to be all right."

But I didn't see how it could. Not here and not anywhere, not after what I had done. And there was nothing he could say that would make it so.

RIVETED

BY *simon* teen ♥

BELIEVE IN YOUR SHELF

Visit RivetedLit.com & connect with us on social to:

DISCOVER NEW YA READS

READ BOOKS FOR FREE

DISCUSS YOUR FAVORITES

SHARE YOUR IDEAS

ENTER SWEEPSTAKES FOR THE CHANCE TO WIN BOOKS

Follow @SimonTeen on

to stay up to date with all things Riveted!